A CASE FOR
LOVE

A CASE FOR LOVE

All's Fair in Love and Lawsuits

KAYE DACUS

BARBOUR
PUBLISHING

Published by Barbour Publishing, Inc., P.O. Box 719, Uhrichsville, OH 44683, www.barbourbooks.com

Our mission is to publish and distribute inspirational products offering exceptional value and biblical encouragement to the masses.

Member of the
Evangelical Christian
Publishers Association

Printed in the United States of America.

DEDICATION:

For Ruth Anderson, because she "gets" me.

ACKNOWLEDGMENTS:

Great thanks to Meryll Rose and the *Talk of the Town* team at
Nashville's News Channel 5 (WTVF) for letting me shadow you for
a day. Thanks for giving Alaine her voice. Also, much gratitude to
Cara Putman for answering a few legal questions for me.

CHAPTER 1

*Y*ou did what?"

Forbes Guidry sank into the tall-backed leather chair, extremities numb, and stared at the couple sitting across the desk from him. As a partner in the largest law firm in Bonneterre, Louisiana, he'd heard a lot of shocking things over the fourteen years he'd been practicing. But nothing had hit him quite like this.

"We eloped." His sister held up her left hand where a diamond wedding band had been added below the antique engagement ring she'd sported for the past three months. "I know you were looking forward to being Major's best man, which is why we're telling you before breaking it to the rest of the family."

He hardly spared a glance at his best friend—now his brother-in-law—before pinning his gaze on his sister. "Meredith, this is a joke, right? What about the meeting Monday with Anne—the plans we discussed?" Sure, Meredith had been a little too quiet during that meeting, had voiced concerns about how big the wedding seemed to be growing, but she'd been coming off working a huge event that weekend and had been tired. . .hadn't she?

"Things were getting out of hand—had already gone too far."

"Stop." Forbes fought the urge to press his hands over his ears. "Way too much information."

Major chuckled; Meredith frowned at both of them. "Oh, for

mercy's sake. I'm talking about the wedding plans. Neither of us wanted a big wedding, but every time we met with Anne—or you, or anyone in the family—it grew exponentially. Especially once Mom and Dad stuck their oars in and started making lists of all of their business acquaintances that needed to be invited."

Forbes stared at his sister, dumbfounded. He prided himself on knowing exactly what each member of his family was thinking before they ever thought it. How had this blindsided him so completely?

He finally turned his attention on Major. "When you came in Tuesday to talk about the restaurant, did you already have this planned?"

"No. Not planned. We'd discussed it, but it wasn't until that night when we made the decision." Major had the good grace to look abashed.

And you didn't call me? Forbes reined in the childish words with a tight fist of control. He faced his sister again. "When and where did you get married?"

"Yesterday, when Mom and Dad met us at Beausoleil Pointe Center for lunch with Major's mom. We'd asked the chaplain to perform the ceremony, and we got married in the pavilion where Major proposed to me."

Forbes turned away from the dewy-eyed look Meredith gave her new husband, feeling ill. That would explain why Meredith hadn't shown up for dinner with the siblings and cousins last night. He'd just assumed she was working overtime preparing for an event this weekend.

When the silence stretched, Forbes looked at them again.

Meredith's eyes narrowed speculatively at Forbes. "Major, would you mind if I had a private word with my brother?"

"Sure. No problem." Major stood, smoothing the front of his chinos. "I–I'll wait for you out in the car."

"Thanks." Meredith never pulled her gaze away from Forbes—giving him the look that had always been able to make him squirm.

Forbes watched his friend leave the office, then pressed his lips together and faced his sister again.

"What is it that bothers you most? That you aren't going to be best man, that you don't get to be involved and have a say in the wedding plans, or that you didn't see this coming?" Meredith crossed her legs and clasped her hands around her knee, her expression betraying smugness and amusement.

What bothered him most was that over the past six or eight months, Meredith had slowly been pulling away from the family. Ever since she'd bought that house against his—and their parents'—advice, she'd started keeping secrets, spending less time with them. As the oldest, it was his responsibility to keep his six brothers and sisters in line, to watch out for and protect them, and to guide them in making their decisions. Mom and Dad had laid that burden on him early in life, and he'd gladly carried it. But how could he express that to Meredith without coming across sounding like a little boy who hadn't gotten his way?

"I'm not bothered, just surprised. You're the last person in the family I'd expect to do something without planning it out well in advance." He gave her his most charming grin. "It is what you do for a living, after all."

She responded with a half smile. "And thus the reason for eloping. Between the busiest event-load we've ever had, the Warehouse Row project, and Major getting ready for the groundbreaking on the restaurant, we were just tired of schedules and checklists and menus and seating charts. Now Marci won't feel like her wedding is being overshadowed by her oldest sister's, since she decided to plan a Christmas wedding and we didn't want to wait that long."

He could see her point, but. . . "Don't you feel like you've cheated yourself out of the wedding you always wanted? Growing up, you and Anne used to talk about your dream weddings."

Meredith shrugged. "Anne always had the ideas. I guess that's why she's been such a great success as a wedding planner—every week she had bigger and grander ideas. Whenever I really thought about it, I couldn't imagine myself in the big dress, my hair all done up, standing there in front of that many people. I guess I never dreamed about a wedding—I just dreamed about falling in love and being married."

Come to think about it, Forbes couldn't picture his jeans–and–T-shirt sister in a fluffy white gown, either. He ran his finger along the edge of the desk blotter.

"And look at the bright side: Now you don't have to find a date for the wedding."

He released a derisive sound in the back of his throat. "Yes, since that worked out so well at Anne's wedding—for my date, anyway."

"How do you always manage to find these women who're just trying to make their boyfriends jealous?"

He shrugged.

"You know, I know someone I think would be perfect for you, if you'd like me to see if she'd be agreeable to being set up on a blind date with you."

His insides quivered at the idea. "Thank you kindly, but I'll have to pass and just leave it up to chance. As I told George Laurence a long time ago; When God's ready for me to fall in love, He'll throw the right woman into my path."

"Uh, did you think that maybe your sisters' and cousins' attempts to set you up on dates might be God's way of throwing the right woman in your path?"

"Not unless He's shared something with you He hasn't told me." Forbes rounded the desk and held out his hand to his sister. She rose, and he pulled her into a hug. "Congratulations, Sis. I'm confident that you and Major will be happier together than you can even imagine."

"I know we will be."

"I'll walk you out."

Halfway down the stairs, he paused. "What about a honeymoon? Don't tell me you're going to just drop everything and take a two-week vacation that hasn't been on the schedule for the past six months."

"No. Since the events next week can be handled by our assistants, we're leaving next Wednesday for a long weekend in Colorado.

Amazing how this managed to coincide with the Aspen Food and Wine Classic that Major's always wanted to go to, huh?" But from the smile on her face, he could tell she didn't begrudge indulging Major's wishes in the least.

Heading back to his office after seeing his sister and *brother-in-law* off—would he ever get used to that?—Forbes feigned harriedness to keep anyone from trying to stop him for a chat.

"Samantha, no calls for the next half hour, please," he told his secretary on his way past her desk.

"Yes, Mr. Guidry."

He leaned against his door after closing it. His office, with its walls of built-in, dark wood cabinets and bookcases, seemed to press in around him.

What he'd told Meredith was true; he was absolutely certain that she and Major would have a happy marriage. Both of them were easygoing, almost too eager to give up what they wanted to make someone else happy. Forbes had learned a long time ago that he didn't have the right personality to get married. Every girl he'd dated in high school or college had wanted to go out with him because of his looks. And every one of them had eventually broken up with him for one of two reasons: Either she thought he was selfish and didn't pay enough attention to her, or she thought he was too controlling and tried to smother her.

He'd completely given up on dating after his ten-year high school class reunion, at which he'd overheard two of his ex-girlfriends having a laugh about how it was no surprise to them that he wasn't married yet.

He crossed to the window behind his desk and leaned against the frame, staring down at the visitor parking lot. His twenty-year reunion was coming up in the fall. And while he'd love to find some ravishing beauty to take to it to shut up all those exes, he didn't want the hassle of expectations that came from taking someone out on a date.

When the thirty minutes he'd given himself to brood expired, he opened the office door and asked Samantha to come in to review his schedule for the remainder of the day.

He made several notes in his PDA while she reviewed the afternoon's appointments and meetings. When she finished and closed her planner, she hesitated, biting her lips.

"What is it?" He leaned back in his chair, curious. She'd never acted in the least intimidated or scared of him before. She'd worked for him a little less than a year, but she was the first secretary he'd had who didn't seem to mind a boss others had called a micromanager—had even stood up to him a time or two.

"Someone from *Bonneterre Lifestyles* called a little while ago. It seems you didn't RSVP for the dinner tonight."

Forbes groaned. Ever since he'd assisted in partner Tess Folse's run for city council five years ago—during which he'd given many speeches, appeared on all the local channels' news broadcasts, and had his photo in the paper multiple times—he'd been a fixture on the magazine's beefcake list, having garnered enough votes to win and get his face on the front cover twice.

"I suppose it's black tie?"

Samantha nodded. "That's what the gal said."

"Seven o'clock?"

"They offered a car—a limo—for you, if you want."

He pressed his thumb and forefinger to the bridge of his nose. The three other partners—all women—were thrilled every year when he told them of his inclusion on the list. The articles enumerating his accomplishments were good exposure for the firm, they'd say. Up until now, he'd found some excuse or another to avoid the dinner. This year, Tess, Sandra, and Esther had strongly suggested he make an appearance at the magazine's big publicity event at which the magazine's cover would be revealed and the top five bachelors named and recognized with awards.

He glanced over Samantha's head at the three plaques and two glass trophies on a display shelf. Maybe they needed to give him a new award—Bonneterre's Most *Perpetual* Bachelor. He hoped this year he wasn't again the oldest man on the list.

"Call them back and tell them I'd be delighted to attend, but I'll drive myself."

"Will do, boss." Samantha scooped up her planner and the folders Forbes had given her to refile and crossed to the door. "And Mr. Guidry?"

"Yes, Samantha?"

"Do try to have fun tonight, okay?"

"Uh-huh. As fun as jumping into a pool full of thumbtacks."

Samantha's laughter followed her out of the room.

His gaze flickered back to the emblems of his perpetual singleness. He'd heard the magazine always invited the year's Most Eligible Bachelorettes to the dinner—possibly hoping to set up a relationship and eventual wedding they could report in their pages. Maybe he could find someone there to take to the reunion—so long as she understood there were no strings attached.

❧

Alaine Delacroix scrubbed off her on-air makeup. "Matt, have you seen Pricilla since I went off air? I need to talk to her about the event tonight."

The intern frowned. "I thought you were a guest at the thing, not covering it."

"Who else is going to cover something like that other than me? I'm the only reporter at this station who covers the social scene." Not that she wanted to anymore. But until the news director actually looked at the hard-news pieces she'd been doing on her own time, she'd be stuck covering the fluff stories as she had for the past decade of her life.

"If I see her, I'll tell her you need to talk to her." The college student waved and left the small prep room.

Alaine turned to check her appearance in the large mirror to make sure she didn't have mascara smeared down her cheeks. She made the inspection as quick as possible, hating to see her own reflection with no makeup. Even with her shoulder-length black hair still styled from her noon broadcast, with no makeup on, all she saw in the mirror were flaws—dark circles under her eyes, freckles scattered across her nose and cheeks, and the bumps on her forehead that never seemed to go away.

She applied concealer under her eyes, powder all over her face, and a touch of eye makeup, blush, and lip gloss before returning to her desk in the newsroom. Once upon a time, Alaine Delacroix would have thought nothing of walking around with no makeup on. But that had been a very long time ago; she'd been a different person then.

An envelope with the station's logo and return address in the top left corner sat on her chair when she got back to her cubicle, bearing her name in handwriting she didn't recognize. She opened it—and smiled. She'd hoped the marketing director would be able to come through for her.

She picked up her phone and dialed a number from memory.

"Boudreaux-Guidry Enterprises, Events and Facilities, this is Meredith."

"Hey, girl. It's Alaine."

"Oh—hi." Meredith sounded funny. "What's up?"

Alaine laughed. "I can't believe you're going to pretend you don't know why I'm calling you."

"You—how did you find out?"

All traces of amusement evaporated, her reporter's instincts kicking in. Meredith sounded like someone who had a secret. "You know a journalist can't reveal her sources. So? Spill it. I want details."

"I haven't told most of my family yet. If I give you details, you have to promise you won't say anything to anyone until after Sunday. We're telling the family at dinner after church."

"Strictly off the record." Alaine picked up a pen and steno pad, but forced herself to put them down again and rotate in her chair so that her back was to the desk.

"We had the chaplain at Beausoleil Pointe Center marry us yesterday afternoon. We surprised our parents."

All the air in Alaine's lungs froze solid. Meredith Guidry and Major O'Hara had eloped? "But I thought you were having your cousin Anne plan a big wedding for you. I was hoping to cover it, since Major has become quite the celebrity, what with his cooking segments on my show."

"We decided we were just too busy to try to plan a big wedding. And we've already wasted eight years. Why put it off any longer?"

A flash-fire of jealousy forced the air out of Alaine's lungs. Meredith had been one of her few friends who was still unmarried—and the only true friend Alaine had had in years. She hated being single; even more than becoming a serious journalist, getting married was the one thing she wanted most in life. Yet at thirty-two years old, she was starting to worry that the chances of either dream coming true were not just slipping, but sprinting, away.

Alaine had to swallow past the huge lump in her throat to make her voice work. "Congratulations, Mere. I'm really happy for you." She glanced down at the envelope crumpled in her fist. "Oh, I got the passes for the Art without Limits exhibit preview and fund-raiser at the Beausoleil Fine Arts Center, if you're still interested in going."

"Of course I am. And since Major's catering it, I won't have to feel guilty about going off and leaving him home alone. Thanks again for thinking of me."

"I don't know anyone else who likes art, and I hate going to those things by myself." She twisted the spiral cord around her finger tightly, trying to see if the slight pain would help squeeze out her envy.

"Same here—oh, my other line just lit up. I'll talk to you later."

"Okay. Bye." Alaine turned around to hang up the receiver, then put her head down on her folded arms atop the desk. *God, why is everyone I know married or engaged? Am I the last old maid left in Bonneterre?*

She knew the answer to that, of course. Twenty-four other "eligible bachelorettes" would be at the *Bonneterre Lifestyles* dinner along with her, if they all showed up. And who wouldn't, when they'd have VIP access to the handsomest, wealthiest, highest-profile single men in town for the evening?

Mother's constant harping on her to get married—and soon—was starting to make Alaine feel like something was wrong with her for still being single at her age. The facts that Joe and his wife couldn't have kids and that Tony, at age twenty-six, wasn't anywhere near ready to settle down put all the pressure of producing grandchildren anytime soon on Alaine. And she wasn't even sure she wanted kids.

She sat up and tried to run her fingers through her hair—before remembering it was still shellacked with hair spray.

Maybe tonight she'd give those bachelors more than just a professional glance. Maybe it was time to get a little arm candy to show her parents—and anyone else who might be looking—that she was at least trying. And she never knew: Mr. Right could be Bachelor Number One, Two, or Twenty-Five.

CHAPTER 2

*A*laine stared into the camera lens as if she were talking directly to a person instead of a machine. "The publicist for *Bonneterre Lifestyles* reported that participation in voting for this year's Most Eligible Bachelors was up more than 200 percent over last year. And they expect the July issue, which hits newsstands Monday, will be the top-selling edition in the magazine's thirty-five-year history."

Much more so than the June issue, on which Alaine's photo appeared as the number one old maid in town.

"Tonight at ten o'clock, I'll reveal the winner and give you a preview of the magazine's cover, which will be announced after the dinner feting the twenty-five nominees. Live from the Plantation House restaurant, this is Alaine Delacroix for Channel Six News." She stood still, smiling, until receiving an all clear.

Instead of mingling and making small talk with everyone gathered in the exclusive second-floor dining room of the most expensive restaurant in town, Alaine walked around followed by her cameraman and stuck her microphone in people's faces, asking them silly questions so she could file a story that no one would remember three days from now.

A frisson of excited whispers in the group near the entrance caught her attention. She turned to find the source, and her jaw almost unhinged. In walked one of the most gorgeous men she'd ever seen—and he looked vaguely familiar. His hair was a cross between brown and auburn, and he looked better in a tuxedo than Fred Astaire ever had. But could he dance like the silver-screen legend?

"That's Forbes Guidry."

"I can't believe he actually came."

"He's been on the list for five years in a row."

"I heard he drives a Jaguar and lives in one of those fancy town houses in Old Towne."

Alaine focused on the last whispered comment from the women behind her. One of those town houses in Old Towne? Of course! That's where she recognized him from. They lived in the same community, and she'd seen him out running almost every morning on her way to work.

While she'd toyed with the idea of trying to meet him, she'd never followed through, assuming someone that good-looking must be married. She couldn't believe she hadn't connected her eye-candy jogger with the infamous Forbes Guidry. He was what her mother would call a confirmed bachelor—or in other words, a hopeless case other women had long since given up on trying to make settle down.

Which meant he was definitely not the man for her. But to tide her mother over until Mr. Right came along? It was worth a shot.

Alaine turned to motion Nelson over—but he wasn't behind her. She scanned the room and saw him chatting up the woman who'd been second behind Alaine on the old-maid list. She started toward him, but before she got there, the microphone on the dais at the far end of the room squawked, drawing everyone's attention.

"Ladies and gentlemen, bachelors and bachelorettes, if you would find your seats, dinner service will begin in just a few minutes."

Alaine had arranged a seat and meal for Nelson ahead of time, so she sent him to go eat and went to find her name on one of the tables.

Paying more attention to the place cards than anything else, she gasped and jumped when she stepped on someone's foot.

18

"I beg your..." Though her four-inch heels brought her up to five foot six, the close proximity to the man forced her to crane her neck to see his face—his gorgeous face—and grayish-blue eyes looking into hers with such intensity, her whole head grew hot.

"No apology necessary, Ms. Delacroix. I believe this is your seat." Forbes Guidry pulled out the chair he stood behind.

"Thank you." She sat, hoping he would walk away with no further conversation so she could compose herself before she had to speak with him again.

He pulled out the chair to her left and sat in it. "I'm Forbes Guidry."

"Yes, I know. I mean. . . ." She ripped her gaze away from his, and her eyes fell on the place card. She nodded toward it. One thing she'd learned over the past ten or twelve years: Men as good-looking as this guy had big egos and loved it when women knew who they were before they were introduced. Even if he was wearing the faintest trace of her favorite cologne—which nearly made her eyes cross with giddiness every time she took a breath—she wasn't about to give him the satisfaction.

Once everyone else settled around the large, round table, they each introduced themselves, coming to Alaine last.

After her turn, one of the bachelors across from her said, "Congratulations on being named Bachelorette of the Year, Alaine." He followed the statement with a wink.

Forbes Guidry's brows formed a straight line that hooded his eyes. "How long have you been at Channel Six, Ms. Delacroix?" Though he addressed her, his intimidating expression stayed focused on the other side of the table; and it worked, as the winking bachelor turned to engage the woman on his right in conversation.

Alaine hid her amusement. "I've been with WCAN twelve years—two as a college intern and ten full-time. And please, call me Alaine." She wracked her brain to find a way to bring up the fact they lived in the same complex without coming across like either a stalker or a fangirl.

"You live in one of the older row houses on the south side of the complex, don't you?" Forbes asked.

"I, uh, yes." Her surprise must have shown, because Forbes smiled apologetically.

"I usually see you in the mornings when I'm out running. Black Mazda RX-8, right?"

He'd noticed her? She nodded. "Right."

"Is yours in the row that overlooks the old Moreaux Paper warehouses?"

"Don't remind me. My house probably declined 10 percent in value as soon as I closed on it a few years ago." She sighed. "Can you imagine that description in a real-estate ad? 'Great view of the highway and a bunch of decrepit, abandoned warehouses.'" She leaned to the side to allow the server access to put her salad on the charger in front of her.

"But once that area's developed, it should increase your property value." Forbes pushed the lettuce leaves around on his plate, looking under them as if checking to make sure no surprises lurked, waiting to jump out at him.

Alaine took a bite. Not the best raspberry vinaigrette dressing she'd ever had, but it would do. "I was told when I bought it a few years ago that some investment company or another was going to go in and revitalize that area, but nothing's ever come of it."

Forbes picked out the three cherry tomato halves and ate them, then put his fork down. "I've heard that it's pretty close to being a done deal."

"It would be nice to have some retail stores closer than having to drive all the way across town to the mall area. Don't get me wrong, I love the boutiques and shops on Town Square, but sometimes a girl just needs to shop at a big chain store."

The handsome lawyer assiduously avoided her gaze. She could almost smell the scoop. "Any word on how soon this deal might be closed?"

The corner of his mouth quirked, and he turned those piercing eyes on her again. "Digging for a story, Ms. Delacroix?"

"Avoiding the question, Mr. Guidry?"

A smile slowly overtook his lips. Alaine almost forgot what they'd been talking about.

"Hey, Guidry, don't monopolize her attention all night."

Forbes held her gaze a moment longer before looking away. Alaine blinked and turned toward the man who'd interrupted them.

❧

Forbes slowed his breathing to try to get his heart rate back down to normal. He'd been around his fair share of beautiful women in his life, but never before had one so discombobulated him that he'd almost revealed confidential information without a second thought.

If he'd blabbed to a journalist about his parents' involvement in the development of the Moreaux Mills area and she'd gone public with it, he would be in all kinds of trouble. If the deal fell through, as it had for the other five or six national and international developers who'd tried to do the same thing over the years, they didn't want the Boudreaux-Guidry Enterprises name held up for derision and judgment in the media.

They also wanted to keep it quiet to try to eliminate any competitors from coming in and buying adjacent land out from under them.

For the remainder of the meal, he participated in conversations around the table, but observed Alaine Delacroix closely. She seemed unflappable, deflecting with aplomb the puppyish attempts at flirting she received from several of the younger men at the table.

The publicist from the magazine came around shortly after the main course was served—Forbes had ordered the chateaubriand the restaurant was famous for and enjoyed every bite.

"I can see y'all have taken the time to get to know each other." She gave a salesperson's fake smile, which faded when she took a second look around the table. Her gaze fell on Forbes and Alaine.

He raised his brows, daring her to comment on the fact that he'd done a little rearranging of the place cards.

She shrugged, but a sly look entered her expression. "Well, if y'all need anything, I'm more than happy to be of assistance." She moved on to the next table.

Forbes allowed the server to take his empty plate. Alaine had eaten only half her meal but insisted she was finished. Well, she was a little thing, so maybe she didn't have much room for more food than that.

"Alaine, I believe you know my sister Meredith." He rested his hands in his lap, trying to set an example for some of their uncouth dinner companions who now leaned their elbows on the table.

"Yes. In fact, I spoke with her earlier today and was shocked to hear she and Major eloped yesterday."

Forbes tore his attention away from the way a few ringlets of Alaine's black hair had either escaped or been left loose from the halo of curls atop her head and caressed her long neck. "Meredith told you about her elopement? I thought she was keeping mum about it until she told the family Sunday."

"I pried it out of her." Instead of looking guilty, though, her expression was more disgruntled than anything else. "I think it's wonderful—very romantic. I don't blame them for not wanting to wait."

Forbes opened his mouth to speak, but the server interrupted them to deliver their desserts—chocolate-cherry bread pudding. Never having been a fan of bread pudding, as it was one of his mother's least successful attempts at baking eons ago, Forbes waved his off.

"Is there something else I can bring you, sir?" the server asked.

"Is it possible to get a fruit plate?"

"Yes, sir. We have a berry salad that has strawberries, blueberries, raspberries, and pomegranate seeds with a citrus-mint dressing."

The idea of combining citrus and mint didn't appeal. "If I could get it without the dressing, that would be great—maybe with a drizzle of chocolate instead?"

The server nodded. "I'll let the chef know immediately and should have that to you shortly."

Forbes nodded his thanks, and as he did so, caught sight of Alaine quickly turning away an amused smile. He leaned toward her. "Yes, I know," he said in a low voice. "I'm high maintenance."

She laughed. "Tell me, Forbes, are you accustomed to getting your way like that everywhere you go?"

"Not everywhere, no. But you have to figure that an establishment like this doesn't garner rave reviews and a James Beard award unless they're willing to accommodate their customers' wishes." He shrugged. "And it never hurts to ask. The worst they can say is no."

Alaine shook her head, looking at him as if he were some strange science experiment. "I have a feeling that there are very few people in this world who have ever said no to you, Forbes Guidry."

He could get lost in the dark brown pools of her eyes. "Want to put that to the test?"

"How?"

"By seeing if someone says no to me when I ask them to do something." He masked his amusement with a serious expression.

Her perfectly arched brows raised. "Okay."

"Go out with me tomorrow night."

She blinked a couple of times; then a smile parted her full lips. "That sounded more like a command than a question to me."

He inclined his head—she had him there. "Alaine Delacroix, will you go to dinner with me tomorrow night?"

"No." She pressed her lips together; he tried not to stare at her mouth but was having a hard time.

"Now you're toying with me. You want to say yes, but you said no just to prove a point." He looked up and leaned away from Alaine when the server arrived with his plate of chocolate-dressed berries.

"No. I actually mean no. No dinner with you tomorrow night."

He scooted his chair a little closer to hers so he didn't have to lean so far to hear her hushed voice. "No because you can't, or no because you don't want to?"

Alaine's olive complexion darkened. "No. . .because I can't." Her shoulders drooped slightly, and she turned narrowed—but amused—eyes on him. "I so want to be able to say no to you. That's not a fair test."

"Because you do want to go out with me?" What was he doing? This was headed for disaster. But he just couldn't help himself. It'd been a long time since he'd fallen so completely under a beautiful woman's spell.

Before Alaine could answer, the publicist returned and knelt beside her chair. "We're getting ready to start the program, Ms. Delacroix."

"Oh—thanks." Alaine dabbed her mouth with her napkin and placed it on the table beside her half-finished dessert. She turned back to Forbes. "I've got to get back to work. If you're serious about dinner, your sister has my phone number."

He watched her walk across the room, her burgundy gown hugging her curves in a way that made him wonder how she could possibly still be unmarried.

Ignoring the glares of the other men at the table, he turned his attention to his dessert, tuning out most of what the people at the microphone said as bachelors number twenty-five through six were named. Every so often, he glanced Alaine's direction, fascinated to watch the intensity with which she applied herself to her job.

"And now, the moment we've all been waiting for." The publicist had taken over at the microphone. "Will our top five bachelors please rise?"

Since his name hadn't already been called, Forbes wiped his mouth, tossed the napkin on the table, and stood—along with the other four men at his table. He smirked, having assumed that's why they'd had assigned seats.

"This year's Most Eligible Bachelor is someone who's no stranger to the title. Born and raised right here in Bonneterre, he graduated valedictorian from Acadiana High School and summa cum laude from the University of Louisiana–Bonneterre."

Forbes sighed. Looking around at the other four men, he was pretty sure he was the only one with those honors.

"He graduated top of his class from Loyola Law in New Orleans, where he practiced for three years before returning to Bonneterre to join one of the most prestigious law firms in the state, and he became the youngest partner in the firm's history."

Once again, the other men at the table turned to glare at him. Once again, he ignored them.

"In addition to his work, this bachelor sings in a quartet and works tirelessly with his family to raise funds for the Warner Foundation, the organization that supports research and helps cover the cost of care for patients at the cardiac care unit at University Hospital. Ladies and gentlemen, for the third time, Bonneterre's Most Eligible Bachelor, Forbes Guidry."

Forbes acknowledged the applause with a wave as he made his way to the dais. He suddenly had a vision of himself ten or fifteen years from now, coming to this dinner and being named the nine- or twelve- or even fifteen-time winner of the top spot on the list. A cold chill washed over him.

He accepted the glass trophy from the publicist and waited for her to adjust the microphone stand's height before speaking.

"I don't know if I should be flattered or take this as a hint that I need to get on the ball and try to find a wife. I guess this'll help." He motioned toward the poster-sized front cover with his photo on it. The laughter his remark garnered was about as tepid as the joke itself. "What else can I say but thank you to *Bonneterre Lifestyles* and everyone who took the time to vote. I'm truly humbled that so many people in my beloved hometown think so highly of me to bestow any kind of award on me."

He raised the trophy. "Thank you."

If he'd been on the Academy Awards, they would have had to scramble to start playing his exit music, so short was his speech.

Apparently the announcement and his speech were the signal that the event was over because, before he could get back to his table, bachelors and bachelorettes were standing, shrugging into discarded tux jackets or grabbing purses, and heading for the door. Though from the sounds of it, many of them were leaving here to go down to one of the clubs on Riverwalk. No one bothered to invite him, though, and that was fine. He got his fill of those places whenever he had to entertain the firm's out-of-town clients.

He glanced around for Alaine—well, for the cameraman, since the petite reporter would be hard to spot—and just caught sight of the two of them exiting the dining room.

A few women stopped him on his way out. He applied the polite evasion he'd learned over the years and escaped as quickly as he could. At his car, he divested himself of his jacket and tie and climbed in.

Alaine Delacroix. She was something else. He'd had his DVR set to record her noontime show for the last two years—and not because he had any interest in Bonneterre's social scene. Ever since his next-door neighbor had pointed her out over at the mailboxes one afternoon as they'd jogged by, Forbes had been knocked back to his teen years when he could plaster posters of the female celebrities he found attractive on his locker door and pretend that, someday, he would meet one of them and she would fall madly in love with him.

He pulled out of the parking lot and headed the short distance home.

"Okay, God. It's time You let me in on whatever plan it is You have for my dating life. I have a feeling I made a big mistake tonight asking Alaine out, but I also feel like there's a reason why You chose tonight, of all nights, to throw her in my path. If she's the one, I guess You're about to prove that it's never too late to teach an old dog new tricks."

CHAPTER 3

"That was the lamest acceptance speech I've ever heard."

Forbes grabbed Jonathan in a headlock. "Yeah? When you win next year, you can show me up."

"Right. Like I'd ever do anything to become that high profile."

"Anyone can be nominated. Get the girls to write you a killer nomination essay, be sure to have them mention you're my little brother, and I'm sure whoever puts together the final list of fifty will include you—and Kevin and Rafe, too. I think they might just love the idea of featuring the four devastatingly handsome Guidry brothers on their front cover. Imagine how many magazines they'd sell." He released his brother.

"Well, don't count on us all still being eligible for the contest next year." Jonathan swept his fingers through his reddish-brown hair and looked around the emptying church parking lot, probably checking that no one had seen his big brother overpower him so easily.

"What do you mean?" Forbes strained to see if the minivan parked beside his car at the back end of the lot was really as close to his baby as it appeared.

"Rafe. He's getting pretty serious about that Tonya girl."

"It'll never happen. Rafe may not realize it right now, but he wants a girl with aspirations, with drive. He won't be happy with someone who's just biding her time working as a receptionist until she

27

can hook some wealthy man who'll support her shopping habit."

"Dude, that's cold. Even for you." Jonathan shook his head. "And how do you know? Have you ever met her?"

"I've seen her when I go down to B-G for Dad's prayer breakfast. When I found out Rafe was dating her, I started observing her. She's a very nice young lady. But she's not for Rafe."

The minivan had parked close enough that Forbes had to edge in sideways between the two vehicles. In all places, he'd assumed his beloved Jaguar would be safe from encroachment in the church lot. He inspected the paint as best he could for door dings.

"Hey, you going to unlock the door or are we going to stand out in the heat all afternoon?" Jonathan slapped the top of the car.

"You damage it, you pay to have it repaired." Forbes continued his inspection, but used the remote to unlock the doors. He didn't see any scratches or dings from this angle; he'd have to remember to check again when he got home. He'd worked too hard to keep the three-year-old sedan in just-off-the-showroom-floor condition to just let a door-ding slip by unnoticed.

As soon as Forbes squeezed in and turned on the ignition, Jonathan began fiddling with the satellite radio. Forbes had figured out a long time ago the reason why Jonathan usually rode to church with one of his roommates and then bummed a ride with him over to Uncle Errol and Aunt Maggie's for Sunday dinner instead of with anyone else in the family: Forbes let him play with the high-tech radio.

"Did you get everything straightened out with the registrar's office to graduate in December?" Forbes slid the sleek sedan into the light traffic on University Avenue.

"Yeah. My advisor hadn't signed off on my internship from last summer, so they hadn't counted the hours." Jonathan settled on a station that labeled itself as "Christian Alternative."

Forbes, who usually kept it set on talk or news radio—or greatest hits of the '80s when assured no one else would hear it—adjusted the volume down from the controls on the steering wheel. "So they're letting you count your work with Anne last summer as an internship?"

28

"No, the job I had working with Meredith in the Facilities Management Department at B-G—I helped her out with a lot of the OSHA stuff: made sure that safety rules were being enforced, that appropriate signage was posted, and stuff like that."

"I forgot you'd done that. If you're serious about going into business law, that's a good foundation to have." He'd only recently convinced Jonathan that law school was the next logical step after attaining a degree in human resources—and to insure he had more options than just going to work at Boudreaux-Guidry Enterprises.

"Yeah. You know, in talking with my advisor, I'm actually thinking that I might pursue a master's degree in HR, instead. The university has a program where I can work full-time and take classes on weekends and in the evenings." Jonathan flipped down the sun visor and looked at himself in the mirror. "And Dad and I have been talking about a position in B-G's Human Resources Department, if one comes open. If not, I think Meredith might could use me."

"Could. Not *might could*; it's redundant." Forbes couldn't help but vent his frustration by correcting his brother's grammar. "Are you sure you're not just looking at doing that because it's the easiest option?"

The sun visor flipped back up with a pop that made Forbes look to make sure it hadn't broken. Jonathan's lips formed a straight, thin line, and he stared through the windshield. "Nothing says I have to go to graduate school immediately after I finish my bachelor's. I've been in school for a long time now, and I'd like to take some time off, just work for a while, make some money, enjoy not having to study and write papers every night."

"But if you want to be successful in your field—"

"I'll be working in my field, which is more than I can say for a lot of people who've gone to law school or graduate school immediately after college. I'd rather work for a couple of years and figure out what direction I want to go, instead of locking myself into a path right now, investing a couple of years in it, and *then* figuring out I wanted the other thing."

Though he didn't say it in so many words, Jonathan's tone clearly said, *lay off*. For now, Forbes would have to concede the point. "You're right. You have to do what you feel is best. I just don't want you to miss out on any opportunities because you didn't think of them."

He pulled up and parked on the street behind a white Volvo SUV, out of which Meredith and Major exited.

Jonathan hopped out as soon as the Jag's wheels stopped turning. "Hey, y'all! Didn't see you at church this morning."

Forbes caught Meredith's eye and smiled at her as he climbed out of the car. His *married* sister. The first of the seven siblings to get married. The thought twinged. Up until their younger sister Marci had gotten engaged on New Year's Day, Forbes had always been the first at everything among the seven of them. The first to get his driver's license; the first to graduate—high school, college, law school; the first to have a job; the first to not work for Mom and Dad's company. The first to not get married.

Did he really want that distinction? The outlook on spending the rest of his life alone was bleak, especially once all his peer-group siblings and cousins got married and had children and started pulling away from their closely bonded group.

"What's wrong?" Meredith asked when he drew up beside her.

He shook himself from his dismal thoughts. "Nothing." He started to give her a hug in greeting, but she'd been so touchy about that the last six months that he backed off a step. He walked around the vehicle with her to join Major and Jonathan, who'd already devolved into talking about sports.

"I ran into an acquaintance of yours Friday night, Mere." Forbes fell into step with his sister across Maggie and Errol's front yard.

"Oh, yeah? Who?" Meredith, whose high heels sank into the grass, slipped her hand through Forbes's arm for support.

He crooked his arm and slowed his pace. "Alaine Delacroix. She said you told her." He inclined his head toward Major.

Meredith shook her head, a wry smile on her face. "I'd be a horrible secret agent. She called me to tell me she had tickets to an art exhibit we'd been talking about, but the way she opened the conversation, I was sure she'd found out about the—about what happened." She glanced at Jonathan, who paid no attention to her. "So I told her because I didn't want to lie about it. It was only after I got off the phone that I realized I was ten times a fool—that it was my own guilty conscience that made me assume she knew."

Forbes chuckled and squeezed Meredith's hand. "That was how Mom could always get you to confess when we were kids: pretend she already knew, and you spilled the whole thing. Of course, you weren't usually the one who'd done anything wrong, so you never really had a reason to learn how to keep secrets."

"Yeah, well, don't forget that I'm the one who spilled the beans about the surprise party on her fiftieth birthday. She's always known how to push all my buttons."

"But things do seem better between the two of you since you had that talk with them a few months ago."

"After *someone* told them I was feeling taken for granted." She swerved into him, causing him to momentarily lose his balance.

"Only because I knew if I didn't tell them, you never would. You're the least assertive person in this family when it comes to them, and I've never been able to understand why."

"It's just the way I am, I guess." As soon as they reached the wide, wraparound front porch, Meredith squeezed his arm, then let go of him. She laughed when she looked up at him. "Forbes, I know you'll never understand why anyone would have a hard time trying to control every single situation she's involved in. Just accept that we have polar-opposite personalities and let it go at that."

He caught the edge of the storm door as it started to close behind Jonathan and Major.

"So, what did you think of Alaine?" Meredith asked over her shoulder, passing him into the entry hall.

"She's more beautiful in person than on TV. She's little, though. I always assumed she was your height."

Meredith's smile morphed into an exasperated expression. "Other than her looks, what did you think?"

Forbes made sure the glass door latched, schooling his expression before he turned to walk toward the back of the house with his sister. "She's nice."

"Just nice?"

"Yeah. She's a nice person."

Disappointment filled Meredith's light brown eyes. "So you wouldn't be interested in going out with her?"

"Why?" Realization dawned. "Is she the one you wanted to set me up with?"

"Yeah—"

He grabbed her shoulders and kissed her forehead. "Remind me in the future to take you up on your blind-date offers."

"What?"

"Alaine and I sat together at dinner Friday night. By the time dessert came, I asked her out."

Meredith beamed at him. "You did?"

Heat climbed his throat toward his face. "I did. We haven't set it up yet." Because he had to figure out how to get her number from his sister without telling her Alaine hadn't been forthcoming with that information.

"Hey, are you two coming?" Major reappeared in the hall that connected to the kitchen.

Meredith joined her husband. "Guess what. Forbes asked Alaine out."

Major's eyes widened in surprise. "Alaine Delacroix?"

Forbes nodded, wishing they wouldn't make this a big deal.

"Congrats, man." Major grinned shamelessly. "She's a great gal." He looked down at Meredith. "Speaking of great gals, you ready to face your family?"

A hollow feeling that had nothing to do with the fact he'd skipped breakfast this morning filled Forbes at the look that passed between Meredith and Major.

He didn't want to be Bonneterre's Most Eligible Bachelor anymore.

❧

Alaine kept her sunglasses on after entering the restaurant, despite the dim interior. One of the many things she'd learned from her sorority sisters when they'd made her over was to emit an aura of mystery. If people couldn't see her eyes, it created mystery, right?

Well, even if it didn't, it kept her from having to make eye contact with the burgeoning, Sunday-lunch crowd at Market Street Grill, Daddy's favorite restaurant. Even though she would usually feel comfortable in her black capris and black-and-white, graphic-print halter top in the casual bistro, the fact almost everyone surrounding her had just come from church made her feel underdressed. And if they recognized her, they'd judge her: *Alaine Delacroix doesn't go to church!*

Holding her head higher, Alaine crossed the main dining room, her low-heeled sandals clipping with authority as she headed toward the glassed-in porch in the rear. She went to church—to the Saturday night service that most of the other young professionals attended. Which left her free to sleep in on Sunday mornings. And to dress casually to meet the family for lunch—though usually at her parents' home.

Her brother Joe waved from the round table in the far corner when Alaine stepped down through the doorway. She slid her glasses on top of her head, pushing her bushy hair back from her face. Curly hair and humidity. *Thanks, God.*

When she got to the table, she leaned over to give Joe a squeeze around the shoulders. "Hey, Joe." She edged behind his wheelchair to hug her sister-in-law. "Hey, Nikki."

"Hey, Alaine." Even though the creamy-skinned redhead had been around since Alaine's early teens, Alaine never failed to have a momentary feeling of being a child when next to the woman with the Amazonian stature. "Did you have fun with all those bachelors Friday night?" Nikki's blue eyes twinkled.

Alaine groaned and slid into the chair beside her.

33

"I see that blush, Al." Joe waved a roll dripping butter at her. "Tell."

"Only if you promise not to call me *Al* any more."

"What? You don't-a like-a being part of the three Italians—Joe, Al, and Tony?" Joe did a horrible Italian accent.

"Considering that we're half Cajun and half Portuguese? No, I don't particularly want people to think I'm a mafioso from Jersey." She melted into a smile when Joe ducked his chin and raised his brows at her. When they were kids, she could yell and scream at him and hold a grudge forever. But since he'd come home from Iraq six years ago with a severed spine, she'd made it her purpose in life to indulge him. Even if it did drive Nikki crazy. "Okay, fine. Whatever. Call me Al."

"You'd better tell us before Mother and Daddy and Tony get here, if you want to save yourself the full-family embarrassment." His triumphant look did still grate on her after all these years.

"Yes, I had a good time Friday night at the dinner. I met several very handsome, very eligible bachelors. With most of them, it's quite easy to understand why they're still bachelors. I got hit on quite a bit. And Forbes Guidry asked me out." She grabbed her water glass and took a huge gulp.

Nikki grabbed her left wrist. "What did you just say? Forbes Guidry—*the* Forbes Guidry? The Bachelor of the Year? Asked you out?"

Flames ignited in Alaine's face. "Why? Is it such a shock I should get asked out?" She forced herself to look at her sister-in-law—who'd known her since before her extreme makeover in college.

"No—just that you'd get asked out by Forbes Guidry and wouldn't be crowing it to the world. He's hot."

"Excuse me?" Joe gaped at his wife.

"I'm married, not dead, Joe." Nikki turned her back on her husband. "So, when are you going out with him?"

"I said no." She cocked her head and tried to recreate Joe's triumphant expression.

"You did *what*? Even if he was a complete jerk, just being seen out on a date with him would rate you a photo on the front of the 'Style' section of the paper."

"And maybe even a mention on my show, huh? Or even take a camera crew along with us." Her viewers would love that, actually. She could see the caption under the newspaper photo now: "Most Eligible Bachelor Has Pity on Number-One Old Maid and Takes Her Out for Dinner."

She wasn't too gentle putting her glass down.

"Why did you say no, Alaine?" Joe started slathering butter on a second roll.

"Because he wanted to go out last night."

"And you couldn't get up and go to church on a Sunday morning to accommodate going out on a date Saturday night with someone like him?" Nikki pressed her hand to her chest as if her heart were failing.

How desperate for a date did everyone think she was, anyway? "I'm not going to rearrange my life just because some guy I've only met once asks me out with less than twenty-four hours' notice."

"Who asked you out?" Tony flopped into the chair on Alaine's right.

She glared at her younger brother—and resisted the urge to push his tousled hair back from his face. He'd had it highlighted again this week, but with blond this time instead of red or purple or green.

"Forbes Guidry," Joe muttered around a mouthful of bread.

"Oh. Who's that?" Tony followed his brother's example and grabbed one of the two remaining rolls and an unused ramekin of butter. He tore off a chunk of the bread and dipped it into the butter before stuffing it into his mouth.

"He's a successful lawyer—who happens to be the most eligible bachelor of the year, according to *Bonneterre Lifestyles*." Nikki turned her head and closed her eyes at the display of macho bread eating surrounding them.

"Oh." Tony shrugged. "Good catch if you can reel him in, Al."

Alaine sighed. God would never have to teach her humility. Her brothers took care of that just fine.

"Wait ... Guidry—is he part of that family that owns everything in town?" Tony flicked crumbs from his navy polo shirt.

To keep from adjusting Tony's askew collar, which he hated, Alaine picked up her utensil set, unrolled the napkin, and draped it across her lap. "He is."

Joe and Nikki exchanged a look that made the hairs stand up on Alaine's neck. Neither of them ever looked that serious about anything these days. When Nikki turned back toward Alaine, her smile seemed forced.

"You're certain he's part of *that* Guidry family? There are a lot of Guidrys in Bonneterre."

Alaine looked from Nikki to Joe and back. "Yes, I'm sure. I worked with his sister Meredith when I covered the charity event for the hospital back in the spring. Why? What's wrong with his being part of that family?"

Nikki and Joe exchanged another look.

"Nothing." Joe stabbed at the remaining half of his roll with his butter knife.

"Hey, kids, sorry we're late!"

Alaine tore her gaze away from her brother and sister-in-law to greet her parents. "Daddy, you shaved your beard."

Already divested of the coat and tie she knew he'd worn to church, he rubbed his jaw. "A full face of fur is just too hot during the summer. Besides, don't I look younger without it?"

With a full head of silver hair and wrinkles to mark his age? "Of course you do."

Mother, whose dark Mediterranean features Alaine had inherited in abundance, muttered something under her breath—which sounded like Portuguese—as she lowered herself into her seat with the grace only a former beauty queen could possess.

Both of them looked tired. Maybe it was time to talk to Joe and Tony again and see if this was the year to try to convince them to retire. Working the nursery and flower shop in this kind of heat and humidity couldn't be good for two people their ages.

After ordering lunch, each of them gave a short recap of the week and what each had coming up. Alaine couldn't help noticing the looks that passed between Joe, Nikki, and their parents.

Finally, halfway through her quiche lorraine, Alaine shoved the plate back and slapped her fork down on the table. "What is going on?"

Five pairs of startled eyes turned toward her.

"Alaine Desideria Delacroix." Mother rolled the names off her tongue the way only she could. "I raised you to have better table manners than this."

She refused to be cowed. "I'm sorry, Mother, but I know something is going on. I can tell by the way the four of you are acting."

Daddy's shoulders drooped in a defeated way. "I suppose there's no sense in keeping it from you two any longer." He looked at Tony, then back at Alaine. "There's a possibility we could lose the business."

"What?" Tony sputtered around a mouthful.

"How?" Cold clamminess slithered over Alaine's skin.

"Well, you know that a lot of the people who bought up properties in our area to try to flip them have gone into foreclosure. And a bunch of home businesses, like ours, are really struggling and wanting to get out if they can." Daddy took a deep breath, and Mother laid her hand atop his. "At the Moreaux Mills Business Owners' Association meeting Thursday evening, we were informed that a local corporation has been quietly buying up all of those foreclosed properties, and now they're offering a buyout package to about two dozen homeowners and businesses in our section of the Mills so they can tear down all of the old houses and businesses and build luxury condos and apartment buildings and bring in national, retail chain stores to replace us. It's all part of the Warehouse Row development project we've been hearing rumors about." Daddy's whole face drooped.

"Without our knowledge," Joe added, "the president—well,

former president now—of the association met with the city council and agreed on what they call 'fair market value' for all of our properties. If the figures weren't so insulting, they'd be laughable. But so many people want to take the money and run it's going to be hard for the rest of us to stand our ground."

"We did not say anything to you, Alaine, because we believed you might try to do something with the information that might jeopardize your job." Mother suddenly looked much older than her sixty-five years.

"Wait—you said a *local* corporation. You don't mean—" She looked at Nikki and Joe. "It's not Boudreaux-Guidry Enterprises, is it?"

The four exchanged another look.

Nikki pushed a long lock of fiery hair behind her ear. "It is."

The weight of the revelation pressed against Alaine's chest until she could hardly breathe. She couldn't let this happen. If Mother and Daddy lost the business, they lost everything—because it wasn't just a nursery and florist shop, it was their home. . .her home. And Joe's business—and house—just a block away would be gone, too.

With a shaking hand, she raised her iced tea to take a sip, then returned the glass to the table with cool deliberation. "Well, I guess it is a good thing I told Forbes Guidry I wouldn't go out on a date with him, after all."

CHAPTER 4

*A*laine trudged up the steps from the garage, the heaviness of her parents' and brother's situation dragging at her feet. She dropped her purse and keys on the dryer in the combination laundry room and pantry, then entered the kitchen to stow her box of leftover quiche in the fridge.

She grabbed a bottle of sparkling water before the door swung shut and took a swig as she turned around. A package wrapped in brown paper on the dining table caught her eye. She swallowed hard and walked over to open it.

While the frame she'd chosen wasn't overly expensive, it was attractive. What it contained, though, brought instant tears to Alaine's eyes. It had taken her weeks to track down the artist whose art deco–inspired work she'd heard Meredith exclaim over. Alaine had been pleasantly surprised that the man hadn't charged her more than she wanted to pay for the commissioned piece—a piece that looked like it was original to Meredith's favorite art era, a chef superimposed over a structure that resembled the Chrysler Building in New York, with era-appropriate lettering across the top and bottom announcing CAFÉ O'HARA. Her wedding present for Meredith and Major.

When it had arrived last week, she couldn't wait to get it framed and figure out a time to present it to her friend. Now she wasn't sure if she could face the daughter of the people trying to force her own parents out of their home and business.

Turning the frame facedown and heading for the stairs, she tried not to think about losing her friend. She was halfway up to her bedroom when her phone started playing the Portuguese national anthem. She ran back to the pantry and dug it out of her purse.

"Mother?"

"Are you about ready?"

Alaine frowned. "Ready for what?"

"The grocery shopping. I told you last week I'd have to do it today because it's going to be a busy week at the shop."

"Right. I forgot. I'll be ready to go when you get here."

"Good. Because I'm turning onto Spring Street now."

Alaine stifled a groan. "Okay. See you in a few minutes." She tossed the cell phone back into her bag, pulled off her sandals, and sprinted upstairs, where she peeled herself out of her capris and slipped into walking shorts and canvas sneakers. Since her hair had decided to completely bush out, she sprayed it with some antifrizz stuff and tried to get it into some semblance of curls with her fingers.

When her mother let herself in through the garage entrance a few minutes later, Alaine was in the pantry pretending she knew what she was doing in making a grocery list.

Mother looked over her shoulder and sighed. "How did I raise such a daughter? Give that to me." She snatched the steno pad and pen from Alaine's hands. "You should get that handsome cook from your program to come over and give you cooking lessons, since you won't learn from me."

"It wouldn't help. Besides, he got married a couple of days ago, so you can quit hinting." *And he works for the enemy.*

The good thing about Major O'Hara's segments for her program: She didn't have to deal with them. They were handled by a production assistant. So she didn't have to worry about what to say or do around him in the foreseeable future.

"Too bad. You need to marry a man who can cook."

The image of Forbes Guidry clattering around her kitchen

bloomed unbidden. She forced it aside. As long as this thing with his parents hung over them, she couldn't allow herself to entertain any kind of daydreams about the gorgeous lawyer.

"Maybe you should try some of those Internet dating sites." The end of her mother's statement was muffled as her head disappeared behind the refrigerator door.

"What? You can't be serious!" Try an online dating service? Only dorks, dweebs, geeks, and losers who couldn't meet people to date in real life used those.

Wait. *She* couldn't meet anyone to date in real life. Guess that made her a dork, dweeb, geek, and loser all rolled into one.

"Or a matchmaker service." Mother continued rummaging in the fridge and writing things on the list. "I had been married ten years by the time I was your age."

How many times a month would Alaine have to hear that? "Yes. And you and Daddy only knew each other a week before you got married. If I followed your example there, you'd disown me."

Her mother straightened and closed the fridge. "Not so long as he's as wonderful as your father."

Alaine leaned against one of the chairs across the large island from her. "I'll make you a deal. I'll make more of an effort to meet someone—and I won't take twenty years to get around to marrying him, like Joe and Nikki—if you promise to ease up on the pressure. Deal?"

Mother smiled. "Deal."

❧

Forbes tried to think of an excuse to run past Alaine's town house one more time. He'd made the circuit of the neighborhood five times already—almost three miles—and the heat and humidity were getting unbearable. He wasn't sure if he'd be able to make it all the way around again.

Half an hour ago when he'd rounded the corner onto the street he knew she lived on, her black Mazda coupe had pulled into the garage of the town house in the middle with the sand-colored brick facade and the bay window. He'd never taken the time to notice just how much smaller and less-expensive looking the structures in this part of the neighborhood were until now, even though he knew they went for less than half the price of the all-brick duplex-style town houses in his section.

The next two times he passed her place, an older model, burgundy Lincoln Town Car had been parked in her driveway; but the fourth time he made it around, the visitor was gone. It was the kind of car a parent would drive—maybe her mother?—not a boyfriend. He hoped so, anyway. But she *had* turned him down for a date.

He was pretty sure one of the requirements of eligibility for the magazine's lists was that the person nominated wasn't involved in a committed relationship. That thought helped to quicken his step back home.

When he reached the entrance to the cul-de-sac, he slowed to a walk to start cooling down. He mustered the energy to wave when a blue Porsche Cayman rolled past him and pulled into the garage of the house attached to his. His chest twinged with envy, the way it did every time he saw the luxury sports car. If only he didn't have to occasionally drive clients around, he could have gotten the two-door Jaguar instead of the more stodgy sedan.

A tall, slender African American man came out of the garage, shading his eyes against the glaring sun even though he wore designer sunglasses. "Man, do you have a death wish? What are you thinking, running in this heat?"

Forbes powered off his iPod and used the hem of his soaked T-shirt to swipe at the sweat streaming down his face. "I know. I just had some excess energy I needed to burn off since we didn't run this morning."

"You found out where that chick lives, didn't you?" Shon loosened his tie and unbuttoned his collar.

"What 'chick'?" Forbes started stretching before his muscles froze up—and to have an excuse not to look his neighbor—and client—in the eye.

"The girl from that talk show on Channel Six."

"It's not a talk show—no studio audience. It's a news magazine." At least that's how the on-screen digital cable guide classified it, which he'd seen when he set his DVR to record it every day.

Shon snorted. "Whatever. Look, I've been telling you for years that I can set you up with some of the most attractive women in this city. You'd be amazed at the quality of our clientele."

Even though Forbes had represented LeShon Murphy's business for almost five years, the idea of personally making use of Let's Do Coffee's matchmaking services never entered his mind. "Thanks, but I think I'll stick with the old-fashioned way of doing things."

"That's right—she was at the dinner Friday night, wasn't she? So did you ask her out?"

Sometimes, living next door to someone who'd made his first million by age twenty-five from setting people up on blind dates wasn't ideal. "Not that it's any of your business, but yes, I did ask her out."

Forbes stopped midstretch when Shon didn't respond immediately. A huge grin broke over Shon's dark face. "She said no."

Since the man was an important client and someone he considered a friend, Forbes bit back a sharp retort. "She already had plans for the night I wanted to go out. She didn't close the door for good, though."

"Right." Shon unknotted his tie and pulled it off. "Do me a favor and just remember what the Bible says: 'It is not good for man to be alone.'"

First his mother, sisters, aunts, and cousins, now his client. "Will do. We back on schedule tomorrow?"

"I'll be out here at 5:00 a.m., ready to go, old man."

"We'll see about that." He raised his hand in a dismissive wave as his friend disappeared into his garage.

Forbes dragged himself up the front steps and was met with a blast of chilled air when he opened the door. He stood in the entry hall, leaning over a floor vent for a few minutes until the drying perspiration on his face, neck, and chest began to itch.

After a quick shower and change of clothes, he sat down to check his e-mail at the desk in the bedroom he'd converted to an office. He replied to a couple of notes from high school friends about their upcoming twenty-year reunion, then turned off the computer.

He wandered downstairs, looking for something to do. In the study, he ran his fingers across the spines of the leather-bound editions of the complete works of Charles Dickens. He stopped at *Bleak House*. He'd read the massive tome at least once a year since he'd been assigned to read it in college. It had been only six months since he'd last cracked the covers. But beginning it would be a good way to fill a long, empty evening.

From a drawer in the cabinet below the bookshelves, he pulled out a small bottle of leather conditioner and the cloth he kept with it. Having paid quite a bit for his collection, he wanted to keep them as pristine as the day he received each one.

Settling into the Queen Anne–style wing chair, he opened the cover, breathing deeply to take in the aroma of the leather, the paper and ink, and the faint scent of dust that accompanied reading his favorite author's books. But today, instead of being transported to the foggy, muddy, raw November day in early Victorian England, Forbes's mind wandered.

A year ago when he'd met the man who would become his cousin Anne's husband, Forbes had known a thrill of excitement at the possibility of discussing Dickens's work with an actual Englishman. . . until he found out that George had never been able to make it all the way through *A Christmas Carol* and had never attempted any of the longer works.

He shook his head and tried once again to focus on the words: the beautiful, magical prose that never failed to carry him away to cold, dreary London.

Had Alaine ever read any of Dickens's work?

An image of her curled up in the chair beside him with one of the other leather-bound books in her lap, twirling an ebony curl around one finger while she read was so palpable, he almost reached over to touch her hand.

Okay. He was losing it. He shifted position and once again turned his attention to the first page of his favorite book. The "ten-thousand stages of endless causes." The "slippery precedents." The Chancery Court of 1840s England. The case of Jarndyce and Jarndyce. The legal system and the fictional court case on which he'd written his senior thesis as an undergraduate student.

As points from his thesis emerged from the mists of memory, Forbes finally cleared his mind of all distractions and lost himself in the familiar imagery and language.

Only when his stomach started growling did he emerge again. He needed to eat dinner. He leaned his head back against the chair's high back and stared at the ceiling. This was the first Sunday evening in a long time he didn't have anything to do: no evening church activities during the summer, no out-of-town clients to entertain, no family get-together, no homeowners' association events. . .nothing.

He picked up his Blackberry from the end table. Scrolling through his contacts, he dismissed Meredith—no way only three-days married she'd be interested in getting together; Jenn would be busy down at her restaurant; Rafe was piloting a late charter back from New York; and the four remaining younger siblings most likely all had plans tonight as well, none of which included hanging out with their decrepit oldest brother.

He tossed the phone on the table and rubbed his eyes. He could always go down to Riverwalk, get dinner, and listen to music over at the new jazz club. He almost always ran into someone he knew when he was out.

Anything would be better than sitting here alone all night.

Shoving himself out of the chair, he started upstairs to change into something more appropriate than shorts and a T-shirt.

Halfway up, his cell phone trilled. He jogged back to the study. Meredith's picture flashed on the PDA's touch screen. "Hey, Sis. What's up?"

"Hey. Major's cooking, which means there's about to be a lot more food here than either of us can eat. I thought if you don't already have plans you might like to come over."

"Yeah—that sounds great. Casual, I assume?"

"Did you hear me say this is at *my* house?"

He laughed. "Right. Fancy food. Ultracasual dress."

"So you're coming?"

"I'll be there in about twenty minutes. Can I bring anything?"

"Just a hearty appetite. Oh, wait—bring that classic-movie trivia game you have. I'm calling Anne and George, too."

"Will do. See you in a few minutes."

"Bye."

He tucked the phone in his pocket, then ran upstairs to put some shoes on. He could wear the new leather loafers—but this was Meredith. He grabbed his oldest, most comfortable pair of Top-Siders and slipped them on.

It was nice to know that some things would never change.

CHAPTER 5

"Are you going to talk to her?" Meredith sidled up beside Forbes at the kitchen island.

He continued layering the thinly sliced prime rib onto the sourdough roll. "I'm waiting until tomorrow to call her."

Meredith frowned. "Who are you talking about?"

He paused. "Who are *you* talking about?"

"Evelyn," Meredith whispered, leaning around him to look through the kitchen door. "You've done a pretty good job of ignoring her since you walked in the door."

"Oh, right." The annoyance he'd felt when he walked in and saw a stranger seated in Meredith's living room resurfaced. "Sorry. I didn't mean to ignore her. Tell me what she's doing at B-G again."

"She's an executive with the development company Mom and Dad are working with on the Warehouse Row project. She doesn't know anyone here, and when we had lunch earlier this week, she mentioned how lonely she gets when she has these temporary assignments she has to relocate for. . . ." Meredith's voice drifted off. Forbes glanced at her, then followed her smiling gaze to the door to see Major walking into the kitchen.

Forbes sighed. By no means unhappy that his sister had married one of his closest friends, he simply had not accustomed himself to how the dynamics of his own relationship with Meredith would change.

Quickly putting his sandwich together, he carried his plate into the living room, leaving Meredith and Major alone in the kitchen. He crossed to the Stickley club chair near the fireplace—and closest to where Evelyn Mackenzie sat on the sofa.

He gave her a few examining glances as he settled into the chair—shoulder-length dark hair, dark eyes, and legs that went on for miles, modestly displayed by the knee-length shorts she wore. She graced him with a smile, then returned her attention to George's story of how he and Anne had met and fallen in love.

Evelyn set her plate on the coffee table. "Wait. Let me get this straight. Anne, you didn't know that George was filling in for his boss? And George, you didn't know that Anne had once been engaged to your boss?"

"Precisely. But there was one person, who happens to be in this very room, who knew the truth about everyone—and chose not to reveal it to us." George's clipped accent poked at Forbes's conscience.

He smiled at his cousin's husband. "Just as you were bound by the contract you signed, George, I was bound by attorney-client privilege." He really hoped they wouldn't decide to air family laundry in front of a total stranger.

Anne *humphed*, but left it alone and continued the story. Forbes ate his sandwich in peace. Though used to being blamed by his younger siblings—and Anne—of trying to control their lives, they all eventually realized it was for their own good. After all, things had turned out more than all right for Anne and George.

Major and Meredith rejoined them, sitting a respectable distance from each other on the love seat across from Forbes.

"You know so much about all of us now"—Anne shifted her still-full plate on her lap—"why don't you tell us a little about yourself, Evelyn?"

Forbes's eyes snapped to Evelyn's legs as she shifted position. He quickly glanced away, berating himself for such a juvenile reaction.

"Well, I'm originally from Boston, but we lived all over as my father built his business. I went to Columbia for my undergraduate work, then to Harvard Law." She tilted her head and slew her coppery brown gaze at Forbes.

He nodded in acknowledgment at the prestigious pedigree.

"Since then, I've been working for my father's company."

"And what do you do?" Forbes set his empty plate on the table and relaxed into the buttery leather chair.

"I'm the retail development director. Whenever Mackenzie and Son partners with a local company to develop an area, as we have with Boudreaux-Guidry Enterprises, I come in to handle all the details—from the broad legal questions to finalizing the acquisition of the real estate to the day-to-day tasks, such as working with contractors, surveyors, materials wholesalers, and all those sort that the investors don't need to be bothered with."

Frowning, Forbes leaned forward, propping his elbows on his knees. "Mackenzie and *Son*? You're not a named partner in the firm?"

Though Evelyn laughed, a slight tenseness showed around her eyes. "It's not like a law firm where it's named after the partners. When my father incorporated the company, my brother and I were just kids. He assumed that my brother would enter the family business and I would pursue something else—like marriage and a family, or teaching, like my mother did before she got married. I guess he just didn't realize that things would be a lot different for women in the new millennium."

Forbes opened his mouth to remind her that her father could easily file an amendment to his business license to change the name—but a wide-eyed look of warning from Meredith stopped him. He resumed his former, relaxed posture in the chair. He'd taken up for Meredith with their parents a few months ago when she'd admitted to him that she felt like their parents didn't respect her position as an executive director in charge of two of B-G's largest departments—facilities and events—but her unspoken reminder that it wasn't his business to get involved in how Evelyn's father ran his company was correct.

"Evelyn, how do you feel about old movies?" Meredith asked.

Major took that as a cue to clear everyone's empty plates from the coffee table.

"Are we talking stuff from the '80s or what?"

"Oh, no. We're talking old. Black-and-white." Meredith skirted the table and grabbed the game box off the top of the built-in cabinet behind Forbes.

George rubbed his hands together. "Brilliant. I love this game."

"That's because you've seen every old movie known to man," Forbes groused. Over the last year, he'd become more familiar with Anne's and Meredith's—and their husbands'—favorite kinds of movies, mostly because either that's what they watched whenever they all got together or because they now loved to play this game, which he'd bought in self-defense to keep from having to actually *watch* the old movies.

"Uh. . .I think I have a classic movie channel in my digital cable package, but I'm never home long enough to watch any of them."

"Oh, it'll be fun. I think you'll be surprised at how many you probably know and just don't realize it. Isn't that right, Forbes?" Meredith dug her knuckle into his shoulder.

"Sure."

"Tell you what. Evelyn, why don't you team up with Anne. Forbes, you can partner with George. And Major and I'll be a team."

Like there would be any thought of splitting up the newlyweds. "Sounds fair." He moved onto the sofa beside George while Anne went around to sit with Evelyn.

As the game progressed, Forbes heard many of his own sardonic remarks about some of the questions and the corresponding film clips on the DVD-based game coming out of Evelyn's mouth at the same time. For the first time, he started to enjoy playing this game because, for once, he finally had someone else in the room who felt the same way he did about old movies—better off forgotten.

He did get a couple of answers no one else did. Though they came as no shock to his relatives, Evelyn gave him a quizzical look.

He shrugged. "I've tried to see every film version ever made of my favorite author's work."

"Your favorite author?"

"Charles Dickens."

She scrunched up her face. "Dickens? Dickens is your favorite author? How did that happen? You don't strike me as the dusty-books-in-library type."

No. He kept his complete Dickens collection well dusted. "I minored in English in college. Rhetoric, but I had to take several literature classes. We read excerpts of *Bleak House* in one of them, and I was hooked. Had to read the whole book—which was not an easy task the first time, I'll tell you. But he had so much to say about the legal system in England in the mid-nineteenth century. I ended up writing my senior thesis on it."

Anne, Meredith, and Major stared at him.

"You never told me that." Meredith looked hurt. "I knew he was your favorite, but I just figured it was for the same reason that John Wayne movies are my favorite. Just because."

He clapped his hands to his knees. "Well, now you know. Shall we continue with the game? I believe George and I just moved into the lead."

❧

"Alaine, come on. You've got promos to do." Pricilla stood in the doorway of Alaine's cubicle Monday morning, tapping her foot.

"Hold on just a second." Alaine bookmarked the Web page on class-action lawsuits in real-estate and eminent-domain cases. "Okay. I'm coming." She shrugged into the cropped red blazer the sponsoring clothing shop had dropped off last week. It pulled a bit in the shoulders, but she only had to wear it for ninety minutes.

As soon as she hit the studio, she got wired up with her lapel microphone, then hooked her interruptible feedback box onto the back of her waistband, turned it on, and plugged in her earpiece just in case someone from the control room needed her. The printout of the show rundown was on her chair on the set.

"Hey, Lainey!" Brent Douglas, the daytime meteorologist, gave her his standard, cocky grin when he entered the studio a few seconds later.

Not only did she hate that nickname, but now every time she looked at him, she couldn't help but remember Meredith Guidry's confession that she'd been in love with him in college, he knew it, and he'd dated and then married her roommate. "Hey, Brent."

"Alaine, fifteen second promo in six. . .five. . .four. . ."

She pasted on a smile and looked into the glass in front of the camera lens that reflected the teleprompter feed. "Tomorrow on Inside Bonneterre, go green with energy saving ideas for the home from a local contractor. Veterinarian Andrew Blakeley will be here to take your calls and answer questions about keeping your pets healthy in this heat. Plus, LeShon Murphy, founder of Let's Do Coffee, will be here to talk about relationships and dating. See you at noon."

After recording a five-second spot and a "Today on Inside Bonneterre" spot that would run the next morning, Alaine went around behind the backdrop and gave her hair, makeup, and wardrobe one final check in the full-length mirror.

Pricilla entered the studio with two interns on her heels. "Guests are all here, and the remote that Jeff did for us this morning just came out of editing and is ready to roll after the third break."

"I think we need to start doing a regular legal-advice segment. We already have a pediatrician and a veterinarian coming in regularly."

"Because they're married to people who work here."

"That's beside the point." Alaine applied a little more lipstick, then checked her teeth to make sure none had transferred. "I would imagine someone here is related or married to a lawyer who could come in and take calls." Forbes Guidry would send her viewers into a frenzy. But she couldn't allow herself to think about him; she had a show to do and couldn't afford the distraction.

An hour later, Alaine fought frustration at the near-flubs and minor mistakes she'd made all through the program because her concentration kept lapsing. A virus named Forbes Guidry had infected her brain.

When she tossed to the news anchor for a quick update at five minutes till one o'clock, Alaine took several deep breaths to try to compose herself before giving the tease for the next day's show and the bye-bye.

As soon as she was clear, she closed her eyes and shook her head. "I'm sorry, everyone. I don't know where my brain is today." She looked around at the three cameramen, Rebekka Blakeley, and Brent, knowing everyone in the control room could hear her as well. "I promise I'll be back on form tomorrow."

Bekka shrugged and gave her an understanding smile. "It's a Monday. We all have those kinds of days." She crossed the small studio, carefully avoiding tripping over the thick cables snaking all over the floor, and perched on the edge of the chair beside Alaine's. "Is everything okay? Anything I can do?"

Alaine could have hugged the newscaster. Bekka Blakeley had been one of the sports reporters when Alaine first started at the station. In fact, watching Bekka rise from reporter to weekend sports anchor to morning news anchor to her current position as the sole anchor of the noon news updates and the five o'clock news hour encouraged Alaine's dreams to move into real news reporting, too.

And Bekka was the only person at the station who was shorter than Alaine. . .by a whole inch. That thought brought her a genuine smile for the first time in twenty-four hours. "Like you said—it's just one of those days." She stood and removed her microphone and IFB box and earpiece. "Bekka, since you were kind enough to let us use your husband for the veterinarian Q&A segment, you don't happen to have a relative who's a lawyer, do you?"

"I do—a cousin—but she lives in Tennessee. I'll ask around for you, if you want me to."

"No, I need to work out the idea for the segment before I start looking for someone, I guess."

"Okay, just let me know if—" Her eyes went vague for a second, a sure indication someone was talking to her from the control room. "Oops, they're calling me to do my teasers." She scurried back over to the main news desk.

Alaine sat and watched the woman only five or six years older than herself record her first promo spot. Bekka—petite with looks that could still pass for a teenager when she didn't have her makeup on and hair done—had managed to climb the ladder due, in part, to her connections but also in large part because she was good at her job. Alaine still struggled to figure out how to get the executives to realize that she, too, had the potential to become an anchor.

She let the whine reverberate in her head as a prayer, begging God to make them give her a chance to prove herself.

Back at her desk, though tempted to get online again and do more research on legal recourse for her parents, Alaine applied herself to her work. First order of business: calling tomorrow's guests, confirming their arrival time, and answering any last-minute questions.

The call to Bekka's husband was quick. He'd done his segment once a month for the past two years. The contractor wanted to know what kinds of things he could bring in for demos, so she invited him to come half an hour early to see what would work and what wouldn't. She saved the call to LeShon Murphy until last.

When she'd booked the twenty-nine-year-old entrepreneur a month ago, she'd done so grudgingly. She'd read his interview in *Bonneterre Lifestyles* and seen the response it had generated from readers from their comments online.

Her conversation with Mother yesterday came back and made Alaine more than a little curious about his service. She pulled up the contact entry for him on the computer and dialed his number.

"This is Shon." The few times she'd talked to him, he'd always sounded breezy and casual. No difference today.

"Mr. Murphy, it's Alaine Delacroix from Channel Six. I hope I've caught you at a good time." She leaned her elbows on her desk and supported her forehead on her free palm, her back starting to ache between her shoulders.

"Yes, Alaine. Please, call me Shon. Are we still on for tomorrow?"

"We are. Do you need directions to the studio?"

"No, no. Our offices are just a few buildings down from y'all." Amusement laced his deep voice.

She could have kicked herself. Right there on the computer screen was the address. Now that she thought about it, the last time she'd talked to him, they'd discussed his proximity to the studio and the fact that he could just walk over.

"Right. Do you have any other questions?"

"Nope. Think I'm good."

"Great. I'll see you tomorrow around eleven thirty, then." They exchanged farewells, and Alaine hung up, feeling like a complete idiot.

Before she made a total fool of herself tomorrow, she opened her Internet browser and went to Let's Do Coffee's Web site to find out how the program worked. She took notes and wrote questions to ask Shon tomorrow on air. The more she read about how his system operated, the more intrigued she became.

"Alaine, are you ready to meet about the remotes for next week—what are you doing?"

Alaine quickly minimized the screen to hide the personality profile she'd been filling out as part of the membership application process. "Just research for tomorrow's guest. I'm ready for the meeting."

She hid her grin until Pricilla turned to precede her to the small conference room. Yes, Alaine Delacroix was ready for a meeting: meeting the man of her dreams.

CHAPTER 6

*I'*m sorry, sir, she's in a meeting right now. May I take a message or put you through to her voice mail?"

He'd left her a voice mail message yesterday, after trying for more than an hour to get past the dragon guarding the switchboard. But now that Forbes had actually reached a real, live person in the newsroom, he wasn't going to let this opportunity slip by. "Before you transfer me to voice mail, please give me her direct phone number in case we get disconnected."

"Hold on a sec, and let me look it up. I'm just an intern and don't have everyone's numbers memorized. Oh, here it is. Three-six-nine-four. Hold on, and I'll transfer you."

Well, her extension number was better than nothing. Not wanting to leave another message in less than twenty-four hours, he hung up and programmed Alaine's extension into her information in his Blackberry. Now when he called, he could get to her straight from the automated answering system on the main line.

He took some files he was finished with out to Samantha's desk.

The secretary looked up from her computer when he dropped the heavy folders into her in-box. "I suspected your chipper mood yesterday wouldn't last all week." She leaned over and looked at the files. "Ah. I see why. The case that just won't go away."

"My own personal Jarndyce and Jarndyce."

Samantha frowned and thumbed through the folders. "I don't see that one in here—and I haven't run across that name. Is it new?"

Forbes smiled for the first time today. "No. It's a fictional case in my favorite book. It went on for many, many years and financially ruined at least three generations of the Jarndyce family."

Samantha returned to her computer. "Sounds boring."

"There's a romance story in it, too." He picked up the stack of unopened mail and flipped through it. He never saw it at this stage—and never this much of it.

"Whatever. You're supposed to be over at the courthouse in thirty minutes. The Pichon injunction."

"Right. Thanks. Oh, file—" He looked up from the mail to see Samantha holding the thick folder toward him.

"Here you go, Mr. Bonneterre."

"Thanks, Ms. Impertinence." He took the folder.

"You're welcome, Dudley Do-Right."

Forbes laughed, glad to have a secretary with a sense of humor who could give as good as she got. In his office, he jammed the file into his attaché case, shrugged into his jacket, and headed out for the parish courthouse.

After going through the metal detector, he checked his courtroom assignment and went to the bank of elevators. One opened immediately and disgorged a bunch of people before he could step in. Some of the judges must be getting their earliest cases on the docket cleared quickly. He hoped his case didn't get called early.

The elevator doors were nearly closed when a hand jutted between them and they reopened. "Sorry. Didn't want to miss this one—oh hey, Forbes."

The doors slid shut behind Russell LeBlanc, a high-school classmate who had turned his back on a fast-track position at a law firm to start a community legal aid office, where most of his cases were pro bono.

"Hey, Russ. So, we're squaring off again today."

"Yep." The other lawyer grinned. "Don't you ever get tired of defending all these businesses that are only out to protect their bottom lines?"

"Not when the cases brought against them are trivial nonsense."

"We'll see what Judge Duplessis has to say about that, won't we?"

"Yes, we will." Forbes tried to keep a stern expression but had never been able to resist Russell's constant good humor. "How's Carrie?"

"Home on bed rest."

"So she's okay?"

"Fine. We've gotten to twenty-eight weeks. We're shooting for thirty-four. But with quads, you just never know."

The doors slid open on the fifth floor. Forbes motioned Russell to exit ahead of him. "Quadruplets. I still can't get my head around it. You with four kids all in law school at the same time."

"Eh. You never know. One might go over to the dark side and decide to become a doctor or a teacher—or even worse, a social worker like their mom." Russ cocked his head and laughed. "See you in court."

Forbes waved and headed the opposite direction. He filled his small water bottle at the drinking fountain, then looked for his client.

Mr. Pichon paced the hallway near the main doors to the assigned courtroom. Forbes straightened his tie, adjusted his jacket, and approached.

"There you are." Mr. Pichon plucked at the knot of his tie as if it was too tight. "I was starting to wonder. . .no matter. Let's get this done today. I'm tired of this property hanging around my neck like an abalone."

"Albatross," Forbes corrected under his breath.

"What?"

"Never mind. Mr. Pichon, again, my recommendation is that you not contest the injunction and that you look at the proposal from the community group."

58

"I've looked at their numbers. I have six bidders coming in at twice what that group of yahoos wants to pay for my land."

Forbes kept his expression neutral, his voice level. "Yes, but they have e-mails proving that three years ago you promised them that if they developed the lot into a park, you wouldn't sell it without giving the community association the opportunity to purchase it for fair market value. That's going to be a big sticking point for Duplessis."

"But why should I sell it to them when I can make twice the money? Look, Guidry, you're my lawyer, and you're going to do this the way I want. I don't care what's done with the property so long as I get what's coming to me."

Sometimes Forbes did wish he'd taken Russell's path in the legal field. "You know I'll work to get you the outcome you want, Mr. Pichon. That's what I'm here for."

An hour and a half later, walking out of the courtroom, Forbes sent up a silent prayer of thanks that Judge Duplessis had been assigned this case. Duplessis, like Russ, had worked most of his career in legal aid centers and tended to rule in favor of the underdog, so long as there was any legal justification for it. Still, Forbes had made his arguments dance and twirl and spin—like that guy, Fred or Frank or whoever, in the old movies—until he'd had Duplessis in the palm of his hand. Then Russ had reminded the judge of the e-mails with the promises given by Pichon to the community group.

"Mediation. Mediation!" Pichon pulled at his thinning, steel gray hair and let out a string of curses. "I want to sell that blasted lot now, while the buyers are hot for it, not sit down across a table from these idiots and pretend like I'm the least interested in anything they have to say. It's not my fault those people spent too much money building paths and gazebos and other idiotic things that they had no right to build on my property."

Forbes didn't want to reiterate what Russ had brought up in argument: that if the community had not pooled their resources together to rehabilitate the lot which Mr. Pichon had allowed to become a weed-choked dumping ground for trash and old appliances, no one in his right mind would be interested in buying it now.

"Mr. Pichon, I know you want to move on this, but we have to do whatever the judge orders." From the corner of his eye, he saw Russ parting company with his clients. "If you'll excuse me, I need to speak with opposing counsel."

"Yeah. You do that, Guidry." Mr. Pichon stormed off, still muttering obscenities under his breath.

Forbes waited for Russ to get off the phone.

"That was Carrie. She says hi."

"Everything okay?"

"Oh, yeah. She just gets bored and so calls me every hour or so." Russ smirked. "I guess I should be thankful, since I know we'll have little enough time together after the babies come, but it's really starting to. . ." He shrugged. "What's up, old man?"

Forbes cocked a brow at the man only a few months his junior. "I wanted to volunteer for some pro bono work. I'm well short of where I need to be to get my fifty hours this year, and I know y'all are probably overwhelmed with cases. Just keep in mind—"

"I know—nothing going up against any of your firm's clients. That severely restricts what I could be able to send you." His friend grinned. "But I'll keep you in mind. With Carrie likely to pop any day now, I'll be needing the extra help. See you in mediation."

"Right. Later." Forbes reached for his Blackberry when it started vibrating against his belt. After clearing up the notes he'd written in a file for Samantha, he headed back to the parking garage.

The overwhelming workload that Russ carried must be inordinately stressful, yet every time Forbes saw him, Russ looked like he was having the time of his life. Though Forbes enjoyed most of his cases, certain clients gave him cases that made him feel like the Big, Bad Wolf in court. He hated looking across at the plaintiffs and seeing regular people—people who couldn't afford a lawyer's fee many times—and knowing that because of the legal dance he was about to do, they would lose their case. Meaning they would lose the time they'd taken off work to be there, lose money, lose their homes, lose the court costs they'd be required to pay. And when they won, he hated the fact that his clients blamed it on him instead of their own, usually unethical or at least unfair, business practices.

There was a certain glory in the job Russ did. He went to bat for the little guys. He made sure they got their date in court if their case warranted it. He helped them make their voices heard against corporate bigwigs with teams of lawyers on retainer and money to burn.

Forbes took the stack of files Samantha held out toward him without even speaking as he walked back into his office. He paused just inside the door and took in his surroundings.

Of course, there was nothing glorious about the dingy little office where Russ worked, with the secondhand, mismatched furniture and the strong smell of cat urine from the Siamese rescue center that used to be located in the converted house before Russ bought it for an office.

Though his work was sometimes unpalatable, Forbes would take partnership in a prestigious firm over legal aid any day.

⋘✦⋙

Alaine tapped her thumbnail against her front teeth—but stopped when she realized what she was doing. She tried to turn her attention back to the staff meeting, but changes to the content on the Web site didn't interest her much.

How could she have been so stupid? The least she could have done was wait until after the interview. But no. She'd had to jump the gun and activate her Let's Do Coffee account last night. What if LeShon Murphy knew she'd signed up for an active matchmaking account? After all, he only had twenty employees. Surely whichever one of the data entry people saw her name pop up on a new account this morning would have told Shon. In their preliminary phone chat, he'd told her that he personally handled their high-profile clients. She qualified as that, didn't she?

She'd just tell him it was for research purposes—that she hadn't meant to activate the account. . .or input her credit card info for the membership fee. . .or click on the boxes to say she agreed to the morality clause and the terms of service and that she was seriously interested in meeting a variety of men they would choose for her based on the extensive personal profile and personality-type quiz she'd filled out.

He'd never believe her. Besides, the truth was that she did, in fact, want to make use of his company's service.

She should have asked him to bring his wife—or girlfriend, whichever one he had. Getting the story on how they met would make a nice addition to the piece. She grabbed her pen from behind her ear and made herself a note to follow up with him about that. After all, if she was going to trust him with her love life, it would be nice to be sure he was happy and successful in his own relationship.

"Alaine. Alaine!"

Alaine looked up when Bekka Blakeley elbowed her and nodded toward the head of the table, where the news director glowered at her.

"Yes?"

"I'm sorry, are we boring you?"

She could do without the sarcasm. "Just making notes for the interview I'm doing in less than two hours. Was there another question you wanted to ask me?" From the corner of her eye, she could see Bekka shaking her head in exasperation. Antagonizing the very person who could help her move to the news desk—probably not a great idea.

"The Web site. Any special requests from your viewers you'd like to pass along?"

"Just to get the recipes up sooner than Sunday or Monday. Since Chef O'Hara provides those for us when he films on Tuesdays, I don't see why they're not going up as soon as his segment airs on Fridays."

"We'll pass that along." The head honcho of the newsroom smirked at her and moved on to Bekka. He always did that to her—

made her feel like a high-school intern who'd accidentally walked into a place she shouldn't be and wasn't welcome. Well, her program had higher ratings than the ten o'clock news, so he could take his condescension and shove it where—

"Hey, are you okay?"

At Bekka's whispered question, Alaine looked around. Everyone was getting up from the conference table.

"Yeah, just thinking. . .about the interview I'm doing with LeShon Murphy today."

"Just checking. You really zoned out there for a while."

Alaine stood and tucked her steno pad under her arm, pen behind her ear. "These staff meetings are a waste of my time. No one ever says something that effects my show, and they're not interested in anything I have to say anyway, so what's the point?"

"The point is"—Bekka followed her out of the room—"if you want to move into main news, you're going to have to start acting like you're interested in what's going on in the rest of the newsroom. And you have to make yourself heard—but not by alienating the one person with the most sway around here."

Alaine shook her head, shoulders drooping. "I know. I knew as soon as I heard the words coming out of my mouth it was a stupid thing to say. I just get so tired of his constantly sniping at me. It's like he doesn't want me to be there."

"Well, my suggestion—and it's just my opinion—is that you do whatever it takes to impress him. To show him you not only deserve to be at that table, but that you also deserve to be moved up the ranks."

Bekka stopped Alaine with a hand on her arm. "Alaine, you've been here for ten years. Granted, when you took over the noon show six years ago, that was a pretty big coup for someone so young. But for someone who's been saying you wanted to be at the big desk for as long as you've been saying it to not have made it one step closer, you really need to stop and take stock of what might be holding you back."

Alaine snorted. "What's holding me back is all the upper-ups who take one look at me and can't get past my exterior to see that I could handle breaking news stories or an evening news anchor position. You didn't have to worry about it the way I did. Your dad was the news director here for twenty-some-odd years, not to mention a silent partner in the ownership of this station and Cannon Broadcasting. Of course you were going to get promoted." Alaine pressed her lips together to stop herself from saying anything else. What was wrong with her, just letting stuff slip out with no apparent ability to censor herself today?

A hurt, resigned expression entered Bekka's brown eyes. "As I said, it's only my opinion. You can take the suggestion or not, as you choose."

"Bekka, I'm sorry. I didn't mean. . .I'm just frustrated. I know you had to work hard to get a job here and to get the promotions you've gotten. The truth of the matter is that I'm jealous that you managed to find a path to do it that I haven't seemed to figure out yet."

Bekka cocked her head. "Did I ever tell you that I didn't want to be in main news?"

Alaine jerked her head in surprise. "What?"

"That's right. I was perfectly content being a sports reporter. It's all I ever wanted to do since I was six years old. Once I became the weekend sports anchor, I was very happy to stay there until John decided to move on to Cannon Sports News so I could take over the sports director position. But John, of course, isn't going anywhere. And once I got married to someone whose career is here in Bonneterre, I didn't want to leave, either. Then, because the marketing department had created so much of an image for me, they started having me cover non-sports stories. When the morning show co-anchor position opened up, I gave it a lot of prayer—just ask my husband; I kept him up plenty of nights because I couldn't sleep. Finally, I decided to take that step. And I've never regretted it."

"But do you miss reporting sports?"

"Every day. But I'm content doing what I'm doing because I

know it's where God wants me. So you have to ask yourself this: Do you want to move into main news because you feel like it's where *God* wants you, or do you want it because *Alaine* wants it?" Bekka shrugged. "Until you figure that out, you probably aren't going to be happy no matter what happens." Her cell phone buzzed. "Gotta go. See you in the studio."

"Thanks, Bekka."

Alaine trudged back to her cubicle and tossed the steno pad on top of the papers scattered across her desk. She sank into her chair, slumped over the desk, and dropped her head into her hands, rubbing her temples.

Pray about it? She'd done nothing *but* pray about moving into main news for years. But for some reason Bekka's words continued to niggle at her. Was becoming a news anchor what God wanted for her, or something she desired on her own? Wait. Wasn't there a verse in the Bible somewhere that said something about how if she loved God, He would give her the desires of her heart?

The phone rang, and she picked it up without looking at the caller ID window. "Alaine Delacroix."

"Alaine? This is Forbes Guidry. Are you okay? You sound upset."

How could someone she'd met only once be able to sense her turmoil through just the way she said her name when she answered the phone? "I think I just hurt a very good friend of mine here at the office—one of my few good friends, in fact."

"What happened?"

"Oh, I seem to have lost my internal editor and spouted off at the mouth about something I had no business saying to her that was coming from a need to vent my personal frustrations on someone else." Hey, wait a minute. Speaking of personal frustrations, what was she doing talking to Forbes Guidry—the *enemy*! "Look, now isn't a good time to talk."

"Okay. When would be a good time?"

She sighed. "Forbes, listen, I have a lot going on in my life right now, and. . ."

"And you're just not that into me. I get it. But you can't blame a guy for trying, right?"

Something inside of her broke in half—one side of it crying for her to recant and go out with the handsome lawyer, the other half screaming to get off the phone immediately and have no more contact with the man whose parents were trying to put hers out of home and business.

"Right." Her voice croaked; she cleared her throat. "I really have to finish up some stuff for my program."

"I'm not going to give up. But I'll let you go for now. Bye."

"Bye." She held the receiver to her ear until the dial tone sounded, then slowly lowered it to the cradle.

She wanted to burst into tears. Wanted to bury her head in her arms and just sob like she hadn't done since she was eighteen and Bobby Ponnier broke her heart when he laughed at her invitation to be her date to the Chi Omega Sadie Hawkins dance.

Why was everything in her life falling apart all at the same time?

CHAPTER 7

$\mathcal{M}$r. Murphy. It's nice to finally meet you face-to-face." Alaine walked forward, right hand extended toward the young, African American man.

Even as he clasped her hand in his, LeShon Murphy cocked his head and gave her a remonstrative look.

"Sorry. . ." She grinned at him. "Shon."

"Alaine. I'm thrilled to be here." He flashed a neon-white smile at her. He was much better looking in person than in his press photos— and he was plenty good-looking enough in those.

"Did they get you wired up with a microphone?" She motioned him toward stage three—the dais to the right of the news desk featuring two dark-brown Naugahyde armchairs.

"I'm all wired up and ready to go." Shon sat in the chair adjacent to hers, eyes darting around at the hulking cameras, the flat-panel TV monitors on thick metal poles in strategic locations around the room, the cords snaking across the floor, and probably the giant green-screen in the weather center on the opposite side of the studio from them.

"It's a lot smaller than I pictured it." Shon settled into his chair, his dark eyes fixed on Alaine. "And I by no means intend to be out of line here, but the camera doesn't do you justice."

It wasn't the words that created instant heat in Alaine's cheeks—

she'd heard them often enough before. No, it was the way he looked at her, as if appreciating a painting by one of the masters.

"Thank you." She glanced down at her steno pad. Right. Focus. "Once you come out, I'll introduce you and then ask you to tell the viewers about your business. From there, we'll just have a conversation. I won't even have this"—she touched the notebook—"with me."

"You said something about me giving some tips and advice about dating?"

"Yes. I'll eventually lead the conversation in that direction. But don't worry—my job is to make you feel comfortable and look good." Not that he needed any help with the latter.

One of the interns came in with the rundown pages.

"Is that your script?" Shon leaned forward.

"Just for the few parts that are scripted, in case the teleprompter goes out. Most of the segments are extemporaneous. I want the viewers to feel like I'm sitting in their living room—or lunchroom or restaurant—with them, just having a chat about what's going on around town in culture and entertainment." How many times had she given that spiel at speaking events? Yet she managed to conjure a real smile to go along with the serving of dreck.

She waved one of the interns over. "I'm going to have Matt show you around while I record some promotional spots for tomorrow's show. I'll see you in a little while."

Well, at least he hadn't said anything about her account. Alaine blew out a deep breath and reviewed the script for the fifteen-second promo.

Most men flirted with her—but something about Shon made her think he might be interested in her. Strange. She was pretty sure she remembered reading in the article that he was involved in a long-term, serious relationship. Whoever the girl was, she must not have a jealous bone in her body if he was like this with every pretty girl he met.

"Alaine, promo."

"Right." She sat up straight and arranged her face into her on-air smile—the one that looked real but didn't squinch up the skin around her eyes to make it look like she had wrinkles.

❧

At the 12:32 p.m. commercial break, Matt brought Shon to the stage and departed for the control room again.

Alaine smiled at the camera as Nelson counted down "six…five… four…three…" then the hand signals.

"Welcome back to *Inside Bonneterre*. With me right now is LeShon Murphy, founder and president of Let's Do Coffee, a matchmaking service he started here in Bonneterre that has proven so successful, he's expanded into six major cities." She turned to face him. "Welcome, Shon."

"Thanks for having me, Alaine." He flashed that high-wattage smile at her again.

"You know. Shon, it's impressive that someone as young as you were started a business like this that not only survived, but became a runaway success. What is it about Let's Do Coffee that makes it stand out in the market of online dating sites and forums and chat rooms?"

"You've actually nailed it on the head, Alaine. Our clients' first communication with each other is when they meet face-to-face the first time."

"For coffee." Alaine tried to control her expression but couldn't help showing true pleasure over talking with Shon.

He'd probably been voted Biggest Flirt his senior year of high school. "For coffee. Or lunch. Or a jog in the park. Something casual and nonthreatening. Not a big, fancy dinner date."

Alaine asked him a few more questions about how his system worked. Shon was accommodating, vague where necessary. Alaine kept a quarter of her attention on feedback from the control room coming through her earpiece, but the rest of it focused on the wire of electricity that seemed to be growing stronger between her and Shon

KAYE DACUS

with each passing moment.

Finally, at the two-minute warning, she turned the conversation. "In this day and age, when people are so busy they don't have time to search for that special someone, what are some tips you could give to help make it a little easier?"

Shon rested his elbows on the arms of the chair and templed his fingers. All he needed was a pair of glasses, a pipe, and a cravat to look like some Harvard professor relaxing in his library. "Well, naturally my first suggestion is to sign up for Let's Do Coffee and let us do the looking for you." He cocked a grin at her. "But other than that, it's all a matter of priorities. We make time for what's important in our lives. But don't waste it hanging out at bars or in clubs. Get involved in the community or your church. Volunteer to work at the food bank a couple of weekends a month. If you're politically active, call the office of a local politician you like and see if they need volunteers. Work with the youth group at your church or a teen crisis center. No matter where your interests lie, you can find some way to turn it into an opportunity to do some good for others—and also meet other singles who share the same interests."

Alaine got the bye-bye signal in her earpiece. "Those are wonderful suggestions, Shon. Thank you so much for coming in to talk to us today."

"Thanks for having me."

Alaine turned to face the camera. "When we come back, veterinarian Andrew Blakeley will be taking your calls."

Once clear, Alaine shook hands with Shon, even as Bekka's husband came up to take his place. Then she observed while every female in the studio—with the exception of Bekka—watched Shon walk out of the room.

As soon as the program wrapped, Alaine got unwired and left the studio—only to find Shon standing just beyond the door, waiting.

"Hey." He beamed. "I hoped you might have a few minutes to chat."

"Uh...sure."

He asked her about what went into planning each day's show as she led him upstairs. The small conference room near her cubicle was unoccupied at the moment, so she waved him in. He waited to sit until she'd settled into one of the old office chairs at the beat-up table.

"What can I do for you?" Alaine clasped her hands atop the table.

"It's more of what I can do for you. Your file landed on my desk this morning." He raised his brows. "I wouldn't have thought you'd need a service like ours, but I'm thrilled you signed up."

Mortification blazed across her face. Was that why he'd been flirting with her downstairs? Because he knew she was single and desperate?

"Don't worry. Lots of folks get embarrassed when they realize that someone personally handles their information. But everything remains confidential until you agree to meet another client. No names exchanged until the meeting—and definitely no photos exchanged. Neither party knows more than a general description of the other until you meet. That way, there's no prejudgment based on what someone looks like in a picture."

"O–o–okay. So what's the next step?"

Shon grinned. "The next step is that I take some of these ideas running around in my head about who I want to set you up with, and we start getting you out on some coffee dates."

"What if I don't like coffee?" Alaine kept a straight face.

"You can have tea or cola." Shon leaned his elbows on the table. "You see? There's always a choice out there that's the right one for you."

She hoped so. She really did.

❧

"Mr. Guidry, Ms. Landreneau's assistant just called. She'd like to see you in her office pronto." Samantha leaned through the door, hanging onto the frame like a kid hanging on a garden gate.

KAYE DACUS

Forbes held his groan in. Getting called into the managing partner's office meant one of two things: either a high-profile client with a new case none of the other partners wanted to deal with, or a top client visiting from out of town who needed to be entertained—neither of which he was particularly interested in today.

"Thanks, Samantha. Let her know I'll be there momentarily."

"I'll let her know you're thrilled." Samantha winked and disappeared.

He rolled his sleeves down, straightened his tie, and shrugged into his suit coat before leaving his office. Must keep up the image of a partner—even if he was relegated to an office one floor down from the executive suites, down where all the senior associates slaved away, hoping to be in his position someday.

He paused a moment outside the door to Sandra Landreneau's suite to collect himself. Squaring his shoulders and trying his best to affect indifference—a lawyer's best choice of facial expression—he entered the antechamber.

The secretary, an older woman whose attitude was as frosty as her hair, cocked her left brow at him as if he were an unwelcome intruder.

"Good afternoon, Mary. She asked to see me." He kept his tone light and friendly—not going to let the old battleax join in the ruining of the rest of his day.

Mary's icy expression melted into a smile that almost reached her eyes. She nodded her head toward the door to the inner sanctum. "Go on in. She's expecting you."

He rewarded her with his most winning smile, then entered Sandra Landreneau's office.

A tall woman with shoulder-length dark hair sat in one of the guest chairs across from the still-beautiful sixtyish lawyer at the enormous desk.

"Oh, good, Forbes. Come in. I want you to meet Evelyn Mackenzie of Mackenzie and Son."

Forbes smiled as Evelyn stood and turned to face him.

"I've already had the pleasure of meeting Ms. Mackenzie." He crossed the room and shook her extended hand. He hadn't realized just how tall she was. In heels, she was only a couple of inches shorter than his six foot three. "But it is wonderful to see you again so soon."

"Likewise. I knew you were a lawyer, but not that you were on the legal team for Boudreaux-Guidry Enterprises." Evelyn resumed her seat, crossing her mile-long legs.

Forbes pinned his eyes assiduously to her face, chastising himself for remembering what those limbs had looked like in a pair of shorts instead of black trousers.

"I have recused myself from handling any of B-G's legal affairs," Forbes took the chair beside her. "Ms. Landreneau handles it, as she has since long before I joined the firm."

"Oh, I see." The way Evelyn's eyes crinkled up at the corners when she smiled led Forbes to consider that she might be older than the midthirties he'd originally guessed.

"Forbes, I know this is short notice," Sandra said, drawing his and Evelyn's attention, "because it totally slipped my mind that she was coming in today. But I know how much our other clients rave about their evenings when you entertain them. So would you be available this evening to show Evelyn around town?"

He inclined his head toward his boss. "It would be my honor."

"Wonderful. Oh, and I volunteered your secretary to help Evelyn find a more permanent place to stay than the Bonneterre Oaks Executive Suites, since she'll be with us for a few months."

Samantha would be so pleased to know that. "I have a few ideas that I can get Samantha to look into." Like the town house a couple of streets over from his that the owners were trying to lease out while they traveled around Europe for the next six months.

"Very good then."

He took that as his cue to leave. Standing, he fished out one of his business cards from his inside coat pocket. Evelyn leaned down to pull one out of her briefcase. They exchanged the cards and shook hands again.

"Shall I pick you up at Bonneterre Oaks around six thirty?"

Evelyn's half-hooded eyes sent a bolt of warmth through Forbes. "I look forward to it."

"Ladies." He half bowed and measured his pace out of the office. He stopped in the hallway to catch his breath and let his heart rate return to normal. He hadn't had a reaction like that to a woman in ages—well, actually since he'd met Alaine Delacroix face-to-face a few days ago. But before that, it had been a very long time.

Between thoughts of Evelyn—and the inevitable comparisons to Alaine—interrupting his concentration, the rest of the day proved a test of his perseverance. He eventually managed to lose himself in dictating some motions for Samantha to type. When he surfaced, he glanced at the clock—six twenty! Why hadn't Samantha come in before she left? He threw random files into his attaché, flung his coat over his shoulder, and ran out to the car. He pushed the speed limit and squeezed through a couple of yellow lights to arrive at Bonneterre Oaks right at six thirty.

Evelyn waved and rose from the lounge chair on the wide front porch of the extended-stay hotel. He got out and opened the passenger door just as she reached the car.

"You know, you really didn't need to do this, Forbes. I'm used to finding my way around new cities."

"I wasn't lying when I told Sandra it would be my pleasure to show you around town. Believe me, this is the first time I'm actually looking forward to spending my evening entertaining an important client." He motioned toward the door he still held open.

She sparkled—eyes, teeth—when she smiled at him before getting in. She'd changed from her pantsuit into a sundress. . .that showed quite a bit of those magnificent legs, and more than hinted at the rest of her assets.

Forbes closed his eyes and shut the door. Aside from the fact he'd given up on dating, he had to keep this professional. Not only did he represent Folse, Landreneau, Maier & Guidry, he also represented his parents and, by extension, their company.

He got in and started the engine. "What part of Bonneterre would you like to see first?"

"Warehouse Row. Since that's what I'm here to change, let's start there."

Forbes pointed the Jag toward the southeast side of town. He asked her about her travels, and she spent the next ten minutes telling stories about her last few business trips.

He pointed out Town Square as they drove behind the western side of it, along with several of the more prominent shops and businesses in the restored Victorian buildings lining Spring Street.

"I can see why they call this area Old Towne." Evelyn bobbed her head side to side, taking in the sights. "I'll bet those town houses back there are pretty exclusive."

"The newer section that borders Old Towne is. The older section that's adjacent to the highway is more economical, though still high-end." Especially if they all had kitchens like Alaine's. Forbes had seen it only the one time on TV when Major had shot his first cooking segment there, but it had been a far cry from what he'd expected. "And what you're here to do will only increase their value."

"Is that. . .?" Evelyn stared straight across the intersection where they now sat at a red light.

"That's Warehouse Row."

"It's right across the highway from Old Towne."

"Now you see why my parents have been trying to develop it for years." He drove carefully through the potholed parking lots running throughout the complex of warehouses, empty since the second-largest paper mill in the state went out of business.

"How long ago did your parents acquire the property?"

"The warehouse complex, about five years ago. It's only been in the last six or seven months that they've started buying up all of the foreclosed or high-risk properties in Moreaux Mills—the mixed-use area adjacent."

Calculation entered Evelyn's brown eyes as they raked over the buildings. "This is a wonderful structure. The whole industrial-loft look is quite the cutting edge in retail space design." She folded her hands in her lap, and the motion once more drew Forbes's attention to her legs.

He cleared his throat and averted his gaze again. She either knew the effect she had on him, or she was just one of those creatures out of whom sensuality oozed with no conscious effort. Kind of like Alaine Delacroix.

"So, let's see the rest of the area. I want to know just how run-down it is or if there's any hope in saving any of it."

"Your wish is my command." Forbes drove out into the subdivision. "Before the paper mill closed, a large majority of these houses were owned by the mill workers—and those who worked in the warehouses. That's why the subdivision is called Moreaux Mills. Twenty-five years ago when it shut down and the workers left—either selling or being foreclosed on—the area became mixed-use, with people conducting business out of their homes or buying the vacant home next door to convert into a business."

He'd only driven through this part of town once or twice—and then back in high school to attend youth group activities at someone's home. He slowed when he approached Azalea Lane and decided to turn left, just to see what was there.

The houses were a far cry from the minimansions in his parents' neighborhood, but they weren't the run-down shacks the local news had been making them out to be in recent months. Most of them—the ones that appeared occupied, anyway—were well-kept Cape Cod or ranch-style houses with good curb appeal. While they didn't have the visual impact of the Craftsman bungalows or Victorians in Plantation Grove where Meredith and Anne lived, the mid-twentieth-century neighborhood had its charm.

Many of them also had signs out front for their businesses. He slowed again when he recognized one. "That's the company that cleans the carpets at the law firm. I had no idea they were based down here."

The road curved, then straightened out and opened into a broad cul-de-sac. But instead of a continuous line of houses, the half-circle at the top of the street featured one house in the midst of what looked like the Garden of Eden. He pulled up to the curb to read the sign in the deepening twilight: DELACROIX GARDENS, NURSERY & FLORIST.

"What an eyesore." Evelyn's sneer reminded him of her presence. "Overgrown and unkempt."

Forbes loved it. It reminded him dually of Jamaica and Spain—his two favorite vacation spots.

"*Dee-la-croy.* Looking like this, they can't possibly be doing great business."

Forbes looked at the sign again. "*Del-ah-qua,*" he corrected without thinking. Delacroix. Could Alaine be connected with this business?

"Well, it doesn't matter how it's pronounced, because they'll be gone soon enough. Out with the old and dilapidated, in with the new and luxurious." Evelyn sighed. "I've seen enough. Shall we go to dinner?"

Forbes turned the car around, his mouth tightening. He hadn't allowed himself to think about what would happen to the people who lived and worked down here when his parents took it all over and razed the existing structures to build luxury town houses and condos and create a completely new retail district with major national retailers they hoped would lease the spaces in the old warehouses.

He glanced at Evelyn from the corner of his eye as she rambled on about her ideas for the development. Suddenly, the sight of her long legs had only the effect on him of imagining her grinding these people into the ground with her expensive, spike-heeled sandals. He didn't like that image at all.

"They drove off. Guess they didn't realize we close at six." Alaine's father returned to the table. When most people looked at the

Delacroix Gardens building from the street, they had no idea that it housed its owners on the second floor addition, nor that the home had a commanding view of the cul-de-sac and street from their dining room and living room.

"Hopefully they will come back tomorrow." Mother passed the dish of paella to Alaine. "Eat. You are wasting away."

Alaine took another small serving of the rice and seafood dish grudgingly. She couldn't afford to put on weight. The cameras already did a good job of that.

"Whoever it was, I hope they do come back. Fancy Jaguar like that—bound to have lots of money to spend." Daddy shoveled a heaping scoop of paella into his mouth.

Jaguar. . .Forbes Guidry supposedly drove one of those. Probably not the only person in town who did. But still, what were the chances. . . ?

"Alaine, what is the matter with you? Didn't you hear your mother?"

"What?" She shook her head to clear the unproductive thoughts. "No. Sorry. What did you say?"

"I asked if there was a reason you dropped in for supper. Not that we aren't always happy to see you."

"Yes, actually. I wanted to talk to you about this whole thing with the buyout."

Her parents exchanged a look that lit a fire of dread in Alaine's stomach. "What?"

Daddy cleared his throat and put his fork down. "We received notice today that a private investor has bought our mortgage from the bank. They're calling in the loan."

Alaine lost all muscle control in her jaw. She tried to form words, but all that came out was loud sputtering.

"Alaine, please, modulate your voice," Mother reprimanded.

Alaine softened her tone. "How can they do that?"

"Apparently it's the acquiring institution's prerogative to acquire loans and then call them in."

"How long do you have?"

"Ninety days."

Alaine wanted to cry. . .scream. . .yell. . .kick the table. . .something to break her parents' all-fired calm. How could they just sit there like that?

"You have to get a lawyer. You have to stop this. It can't be right."

"Oh, Alaine, you know we can't afford a lawyer." Her father picked up his fork and pushed his rice around on his plate. "We're operating in the black, but just barely. We're still trying to get caught up with the loan payments we missed last winter. According to the letter we got, that's why they're calling in the loan. Because it's more than five months in arrears."

"I'll pay for a lawyer. I'll report what's happening on my show. Surely when a lawyer of conscience hears about what's happening, they'll—"

"No." Mother brought her palms down hard on the table. "You cannot talk about this on your show. You cannot be involved."

"But I have to do something! I can't just sit by and watch y'all lose what you've worked all your lives to build. If I find a lawyer—quietly—who'll take the case without charging you too much, would you agree to meet them?"

Daddy mulled over her question for a while. "You know we're not the only ones in this situation. Joe and Nikki are, too. A dozen others that we know well, and who knows how many that we haven't met. The lawyer would have to be able to help all of us."

"Of course. I wouldn't imagine leaving out anyone who wants to try to stand up for what's right."

Daddy pushed his plate back. "But you have to promise us one thing, Alley Cat."

She actually smiled over the endearment from her childhood. "What's that?"

"You cannot be seen to be publicly involved in this. If this becomes more public than it already is, you have to step back from it. We don't want to endanger your career. You've worked too long and hard to get where you are to ruin it by marching out in front of everyone, carrying the flag of protest."

Alaine pictured herself as a majorette high-stepping in front of a marching band. She laughed, then instantly sobered. "But what if my position as someone with the ear of the public can have some influence on getting this settled quickly and quietly?"

"No. Unless you agree, there's no deal with the lawyer or trying to pursue this any further."

To see her always-happy father so stern, so serious, broke Alaine's heart. "All right. I agree. But I'm going to do whatever I can behind the scenes to make sure you don't lose this place."

CHAPTER 8

"*C*ongratulations. You have now successfully licensed a Chicago branch of Let's Do Coffee." Forbes reached across the corner of the table and shook Shon's hand.

"Thanks, man. I wasn't sure this one was ever going to go through. As always, couldn't have done it without you."

"Now," Forbes shuffled the folders in front of him, looking for one in particular, "there's just one more thing we need to talk about."

Shon gestured with his hand, open and palm facing Forbes, in a circular motion. "I don't like this facial expression. This can't be good."

Forbes forced a frown. "It has come to my attention"—he opened the red file folder and rifled through a few pieces of paper before finding the one he wanted—"that you appeared on Alaine Delacroix's show on Tuesday."

Shon looked down at the printout of the newspaper article Forbes slid across the shiny wood surface toward him. "Dude, don't do that to me. I thought you were talking about something serious." Shon flipped the page back toward Forbes. "She's a lot better looking in person than on TV—and I didn't think that was possible. Why're you passing up this prime opportunity to hook such a *fine* specimen?"

"What makes you think I'm passing her up?" Forbes feigned

interest in the news clippings still in the red folder.

Shon shrugged. "You haven't gotten her to agree to go on a date yet, have you? Have you even talked to her?"

"Yes, I talked to her Tuesday morning as a matter of fact." Forbes leaned against the back of his chair and crossed his arms.

"And. . .?"

"And. . .she's too busy right now to commit to making plans."

Shon narrowed his eyes speculatively. "Right. Too busy." He shook his head. "Classic evade."

Forbes thought back to their brief conversation. She'd been upset over something she'd said to a co-worker, which, he was certain, tinged their whole interchange. "No, I really believe she meant what she said. She sounded stressed out and like she was being pulled in five directions at once."

"Okay. If that's what you want to believe."

"It's what I know to be true."

Shon held his hands up in surrender. "Fine. But look. . .if you're reentering the dating scene, let me handle everything for you. No, listen," he said forcefully when Forbes tried to interrupt. "I know you don't like giving up control of things, but this is actually a way for you to gain control over the whole thing—meet only a select group of women already prescreened, by me, to make sure that their interests and lifestyles mesh with yours. I'd like to give you a three-month VIP membership for you as a thank-you for all of the extra hours you put in on the Chicago deal that I know you didn't bill me for. I'll handle everything. No one else in the company will ever see your file."

"Let you set me up on blind dates?" A week ago, Forbes would have laughed and said no immediately. Now, however, with his twenty-year reunion coming up, along with the rekindled ember of wanting to share his life with someone—someone like Alaine—the offer didn't sound quite so ludicrous.

What did he have to lose? "All right. Ninety days. I'll meet whoever you feel would be a good match for me."

Shon grinned. "You won't regret this. I promise."

"Yeah, and you won't regret being able to claim Bonneterre's Bachelor of the Year as a client, either."

"You said it, not me."

After Shon left, Forbes slumped in his chair and turned to stare out the window at the tops of the trees lining the opposite bank of the river. The wild tangle of greenery reminded him of Delacroix Gardens. There must be other people in town with that name—he'd gone to school with several Delacroixes both here at the local branch of the University of Louisiana as well as at Loyola Law School in New Orleans. But could Alaine be related to the owners?

He sat up. She'd sounded stressed on the phone. She'd said she couldn't go out with him. Could it be because relatives of hers faced losing their business to his parents' redevelopment plans?

He jumped when the intercom on the phone beeped.

"Mr. Guidry, opposing counsel in the Pichon case is in the first-floor conference room to discuss the schedule for mediation."

He turned and pressed the intercom button. "Thank you, Samantha."

Mediation. If his parents ran someone Alaine cared for out of business, Forbes would need mediation with her if she was ever going to agree to go out with him.

❧

"All right. Thank you, anyway. If you know of anyone. . ."

The line went dead. Alaine crossed the second-to-last name off her list and flipped the phone closed. Finding local lawyers who specialized in real estate law on Google probably hadn't been the best way to find the right person, but so far, her fears over getting hoodwinked by some smooth-talking ambulance-chaser hadn't materialized.

She headed back inside, having already taken five minutes longer than the fifteen she'd allowed herself for this personal break.

One thing was certain: If she wanted to get one of them to meet with her to find out more about the case, she needed to leave out the fact that the potential law suit was against Boudreaux-Guidry Enterprises; because as soon as that name came up, each lawyer hastily made some excuse or another to get off the phone.

She left a message for the last one on her way back to her desk and then tried to put the matter out of her head by finishing tomorrow's post for the Bonneterre Insider blog. Fortunately, her series on local artists to promote the upcoming Artisan Festival—of which the station was a major sponsor—interested her, making it easy to switch her train of thought.

She saved the post, and her cell phone rang. She grabbed it and flipped it open, not recognizing the number that flashed on her screen. "Alaine Delacroix."

"Yes, hello. This is Hank Biddle. You left a message that you wanted to talk to me about a case."

"Yes, Mr. Biddle, thank you for returning my call." Alaine stood up, looked around over the top of her cubicle walls, and, seeing no one at any of the nearby desks, she stayed at her desk instead of going back out into the intolerable heat and humidity. "I'm looking for someone familiar with real-estate cases—specifically with taking on the cause of a group of homeowners who are being forced out when a. . .large company wants to come in and force them out."

"And you're probably looking for someone who could take it on pro bono?"

"Well, we wouldn't have much money to spend, no."

"With as much as I'd like to take on a worthy cause, my current caseload is too full."

Alaine wanted something hard to bang her head against. "I understand. And I appreciate your calling me back."

"You might want to call the LeBlanc Legal Aid Center. This is the kind of case they specialize in."

She sat up straighter and grabbed for a pen, which she had to chase across the desk with her fingers. "LeBlanc Legal Aid, you said?"

"Yeah. Hang on, I have the number here somewhere. . . ."

Alaine scribbled the number in the top margin of her steno

pad. "Thank you so much. You have no idea how much I appreciate this."

"No problem. Good luck."

Alaine closed the phone and squeezed it tightly in her hand. Looking down the notepad page, she reviewed her day's to-do list. The few remaining things she needed to do, she could do at home tonight.

She left a note for Pricilla, out filming a story for tomorrow, to let her know she'd scheduled the blog entry for tomorrow. Packing up everything she'd need to work from home, Alaine hustled out to her car. She dumped everything in the passenger seat, climbed in, then dialed the number for the legal aid center and pulled out of the parking lot.

Someone who identified herself as a volunteer answered the phone and asked Alaine a battery of questions about her case. She assiduously avoided mentioning Boudreaux-Guidry Enterprises but did mention her parents' business and several others in the area by name.

"I will pass your information along to Mr. LeBlanc, and he will give you a call back soon."

"How soon?"

"I'm not sure, ma'am. But he always returns every call he receives, so you can be certain to hear from him."

Her surge of excitement faded. "Okay. Thank you."

Once home, she dropped her bag and purse on the coffee table and collapsed facedown on the sofa, kicking her shoes off. She'd thought finding a lawyer who'd relish the chance to take down a big company like this—to argue a high-profile case—would be a lot easier. The Guidrys had more clout in this town than she'd originally imagined.

After moping on the sofa for a while, Alaine forced herself up and went into the kitchen to see what she had to eat. She opened the fridge and read the tape labels on the stacks of plastic containers lining the shelves. The seafood paella from last night that Mother had made her bring home. *Cozido* stew—too heavy. *Bife*—no, she didn't need the calories in the pan-fried beef in sauce with seasoned rice. *Iscas com elas*—she hadn't had liver in a while, and she loved the flavor it lent to the potatoes Mother sautéed with it. *Feijoada*—no, it was too hot for the bean stew. *Alheira*—Mother's homemade duck sausage also with pan-fried potatoes. Was everything in her fridge meant to make her gain five pounds?

She pulled the half-gallon of skim milk out of the door and set it on the counter, then stepped into the pantry and grabbed a box of frosted flakes. She'd just poured the cereal into a large bowl when her cell phone started chirping. She nearly tripped on the edge of the living-room rug in her haste to get to her purse.

"This is Alaine."

"Alaine—girl, where are you? We were supposed to all meet up at six for supper."

"We—?" Alaine slapped her forehead and returned the milk to the fridge. "I completely forgot that was tonight. Give me"—she looked down at her crumpled blouse and pants—"half an hour, and I'll be there."

"Want us to order you a drink? The bartender seems kinda slow tonight."

Alaine shook her head and dashed up the stairs. "You know I don't drink anymore." Not that she had ever done much drinking in college. But there had been those couple of times. . . "Tell everyone I'm sorry I'm late, but that I'll be there as soon as I can get there."

"Okay. See ya in a little while."

"Bye." Alaine tossed the phone onto the bathroom cabinet and ducked into her closet to change clothes. The enormous walk-in held more clothes than some small boutiques. Yet she still couldn't find anything she wanted to wear for dinner with her sorority sisters.

Finally, she settled for a sleeveless, silky, royal purple blouse, a pair of close-fitting, dark-wash jeans, and strappy, wedge-heel sandals.

She touched up her makeup, trying extra hard to conceal the dark circles under her eyes. Oh well. If they noticed, she'd just tell them she was putting in long hours these days. With all of them being "corporate babes" themselves, they'd completely understand. Besides, there wasn't time to take off all her makeup, put some hemorrhoid ointment on the dark circles, wait for it to reduce the puffiness, and then reapply her makeup.

Halfway out of the complex, she remembered she'd left her phone on the bathroom counter. She rounded a block and, leaving the car running in the driveway, ran back into the town house, wishing she had some legitimate excuse to call them back and cancel. But she couldn't. They only did this once a month, and a couple of the girls had to take off half a day from work to drive in from Shreveport or Baton Rouge to attend.

The drive to the restaurant in midtown took about ten minutes, but the parking lot was packed, and she had to circle it twice before someone vacated a parking space. She zipped her purse closed before getting out of the car—with the way her day was going, if she didn't, she'd drop it and everything would go skittering under all the cars nearby—then climbed out, rolling her neck and trying to rid herself of the black cloud of annoyance and frustration that had dogged her all day.

She had no trouble locating the Chi Omega table as soon as she entered the restaurant. Her five sorority sisters laughed and talked loudly enough to be heard over the din of the full restaurant.

Alaine sighed. So much for a relaxing evening. Not that the girls from Chi-O had ever been accused of being shy and retiring—at least not in their suite, and not once they'd broken Alaine out of her nerdy, quiet, art-major-wannabe shell.

Shrill greetings went up around the table, and Alaine had to make the circuit to greet each one with an air kiss before she could take her seat.

Bethenny, her former roommate, pulled Alaine into a side-hug as soon as she sat down. "It's so good to see you. In person, I mean.

I see you on TV all the time."

"Yeah, every time I see you on that screen, all I can think is *I created that!*" Dover grinned at her across the table and passed the plate of fried mushrooms Alaine's direction.

"No you didn't!" Bethenny glared at the tall redhead. "*I'm* the one who had the idea to give 'Laine a makeover."

Alaine bit the sides of her tongue in an effort to keep from frowning and wrinkled her nose in an effort to look amused. Did they have to go through this every time they got together—reminding Alaine of what a dork she'd been up until her sophomore year of college?

" 'Laine, you look stressed. You need a drink." Crystal waved a jewel-encrusted hand to flag down their server. She had always been the heaviest drinker of the suitemates and the one who still tended to lead the rest of them into temptation.

"No—Crystal. I don't drink anymore."

"Yeah, don't forget she went all religious on us after college." Mallory gave Crystal a look dripping with condescension.

"Right." Crystal rolled blue eyes framed by lashes much longer and thicker than they'd been at their last get-together. Obviously she had followed through and gotten the lash extensions.

When the waitress arrived at the table, Crystal ordered herself another mixed drink, and Alaine ordered sweet tea and the biggest platter of fried seafood the place had. If the first ten minutes was any indication of how the evening would go, she would at least soothe herself by eating really bad-for-her food. That was their one and only rule for these get-togethers: No one was allowed to be on a diet or talk about calories or fat grams or going to the gym.

Jessica leaned her elbows on the edge of the table, cradling her super-sized frozen margarita in both hands. "So, 'Laine, tell us all about the Most Eligible Bachelors' dinner. Did you get to meet him?"

"Him?" Alaine smiled at the waitress and reached for the glass of iced tea.

"Forbes Guidry! Who did you think I meant?"

Alaine sprinkled salt on her cocktail napkin to keep it from sticking to the sweating tea glass. "Yes. I sat next to him at dinner, in fact." She looked around the table. Five pairs of eyes ogled her, expressions dripping with envy. She shrugged and allowed only one side of her mouth to curve up. "He asked me out."

The shrill shrieks that went up from her suitemates nearly deafened her and drew remonstrative glances from the diners around them.

Alaine told the story about meeting Forbes, lingering over describing what he looked like in his tuxedo, the reddish tint to his dark hair, the almost periwinkle color of his eyes, the fact that he wore her favorite cologne.

Smugness settled into her chest over the fact that she finally had something to make these girls jealous of her. She hadn't had that since she'd gotten to interview Cliff Ballantine last year after his engagement party. And since someone from each of the local stations had gotten to meet with the megastar actor for a five minute one-on-one, even that hadn't drawn the kind of looks she was getting from the girls now.

Of course, she couldn't tell them that Forbes's family's company was trying to steal her parents' home and business. Nor that she would never stoop to going out with him.

As soon as the girls had drawn all the details about Forbes out of her—the ones she was willing to tell them, anyway—talk turned to the latest celebrity scandals. Alaine drowned herself in greasy fried shrimp and clams and calamari and fish, savoring the french fries dipped in the spicy tartar sauce. She washed it all down with a huge chocolate dessert.

Yet no matter how satisfying the junk food was, she still couldn't get past the pain that came from realizing she had the shallowest friends in the world. While the focus of their monthly dinners was to get together and have fun, if she got to a point where she needed someone to talk to about something serious, she would never consider calling a single one of them. She would never confide anything to any of them—knowing it would not only get around to all of the others, but that they might use it as a source of amusement at a future get-together.

Regret formed a tight ball in the back of her throat. For years, these had been her only friends. When she'd met Meredith Guidry a few months ago, she'd thought she'd finally found a true friend—someone she could turn to, trust with anything. But now she had no one to turn to. No one to talk to about Mother and Daddy's situation. No one to trust.

Why did Forbes have to be a Guidry?

CHAPTER 9

*P*lease, Forbes? Go with me. I can't do this by myself."

Forbes stared at Jenn. His sister had asked a lot of him over the years—not the least of which was providing most of the start-up capital for the restaurant in which they now sat. "Ballroom dancing lessons?"

"Yeah. It'll be fun. I've always wanted to learn. Anne and George are going to do it." She inclined her head at them across the noisy table. "Meredith and Major wanted to, but some of the dates interfere with their work events. So will you sign up with me so that I don't have to worry about whether or not there'll be someone there for me to dance with?"

"What about one of the guys you're seeing? Why not ask one of them?"

Jenn shrugged, setting her strawberry blond ponytail to swinging. "Because I don't want to give Clay or Danny or Ward the wrong idea."

"And what would that be?" He probably didn't really want to know the answer to that question.

"That I'm serious enough about any of them to want to spend that kind of one-on-one time with them."

"Why not just split the time evenly between them?"

"Because you have to purchase a package. Plus, according to the

Web site, it's very important to be there for the entire series, because many of the steps build off of each other."

Forbes leaned back and crossed his arms. "What about the restaurant?" Even though she'd bought him out fully more than two years ago, he still liked to keep up with the goings-on around here.

"I hired a restaurant manager—didn't I tell you?" Jenn's expression was a little *too* innocent.

"No, you didn't, oddly enough. I trust this person has good credentials?" Maybe, if he got her talking about the restaurant, she'd drop the dancing thing.

"Yeah—well, Major was one of his references."

Interesting. Too bad Major and Meredith were currently in Colorado on their mini-honeymoon. "Well, if Major vouched for him. . ."

"So anyway"—Jenn sounded annoyed—"the lessons are on Monday evenings, which is my new day off. And I'd like for you to go with me."

Should he remind her now that his "Most Likely to Succeed" title his senior year of high school had come with an asterisk: *except in dancing*? His lack of physical coordination had kept him from success in sports and led to girls thinking he was arrogant for refusing to go out on the dance floor at homecoming or prom except for a couple of obligatory numbers. Even then, he picked slow songs so he could do his Fonz-style dance: hold the girl close and turn slowly in a circle.

"Please, Forbes?"

The word *yes* tripped out to the end of his tongue, but he caught it before it escaped. "Let me think about it."

"Don't think too long. The next session starts Monday."

"As in four-days-away Monday?"

"That would be the one." Jenn bounced up from her chair, kissed the top of his head, and flittered off to visit with other patrons in the nearly full restaurant.

Jenn wanted him to go dancing; Shon wanted him to reenter the dating scene. Forbes glanced up at the ceiling, half expecting God to peek around the pirogue hanging there and laugh at him. Just when he had everything under control...

"Come on." George nudged his shoulder. "Jennifer is playing our song."

Singing "Me and My Shadow" with George to kick off the Thursday night family friendly karaoke at Jenn's restaurant had become something of a tradition over the past few months. When Major was here, all three of them got up and sang it together.

Forbes could just make out Jenn's lithe figure darting around, working the room beyond the halo of the stage lights. Maybe he should push her a little more toward Clay Huntoon, the bass in their quartet. With Major and George officially members of the family now, adding Clay seemed like the next logical step.

Forbes and George surrendered the stage to a ten-year-old who started belting out "My Favorite Things" before they got back to the table. As usual, everyone had changed seats; Forbes took the empty chair beside his brother Rafe, who sat slumped over the table, cheek and eye distorted by the pressure of leaning his face against his fist.

"What's wrong?" Forbes stood to lean over and retrieve his tea from his original spot. He sat again and stretched his legs out under the table, crossing his ankles.

"Remember Tonya, the girl at B-G I was seeing?"

Forbes liked the sound of the past tense verb. "Yeah."

"Well, I found out she's been dating someone else all along. Apparently, he works for another company there in the building." Rafe stared morosely at the basket of now-cold hush puppies in the middle of the table.

"And. . . ?"

"And it turns out she was just playing me. She thought that since I'm a Guidry, I had some kind of huge trust fund or something. She flat out asked me how much money I have. I told her I'm saving to buy a plane, that I'd paid cash for the 'Vette, and I have equity in my condo because I did a big down payment. That's when she told me about this real-estate investment guy who apparently makes seven figures a year. It's like she was saying, 'Beat that—I dare you.'"

Forbes tightened his jaw to keep his joy from showing, happy that he hadn't had to figure out how to start convincing Rafe this girl wasn't worth his time and attention. "Sounds to me like it's a good thing you found this out now instead of when things got more serious."

Rafe groaned. "That's the problem. I thought things already were serious. I asked her to marry me. That's when she asked me about the money."

Forbes took in a deep breath, held it a few seconds, then released it slowly. "Had you already bought a ring?"

"No, thank goodness. I was going to take her shopping and let her pick it out herself." He blinked a few times, then sat up straight and turned to face Forbes. "Hey—the guy who lives next door to you. He owns that dating service, doesn't he?"

"Let's Do Coffee. Yes, that's my next-door neighbor."

"What do you know about it? Think it might work for me?"

Only if Forbes got a part-time job there so he could screen the candidates. Well, he'd agreed to trust Shon to find someone for him; maybe he could trust him to find someone for his brother. "It might be worth looking into a three- or six-month membership."

❦

Alaine groaned when the phone on her desk trilled yet again. Didn't people know it was rude to call at four o'clock on a Friday afternoon? If they didn't let her alone soon, she'd never get everything wrapped up before she had to be out in the field covering the concert tonight. She grabbed the receiver on the third ring. "Alaine Delacroix."

"Alaine, Russell LeBlanc here. I looked over the information you gave our volunteer, and I'm calling to set up a time for us to meet so we can discus the case in more detail."

She pumped her fist in the air, then glanced over her shoulder to make sure no one had walked past the opening into her cubicle and seen the gesture. "When would you like to meet?"

"Would you be available for lunch. . .next Wednesday?"

Impatience momentarily overrode her excitement at finally finding a lawyer who might be willing to work with them. She pulled up her calendar on the computer. Wednesday afternoon looked open. "It would have to be after two o'clock. I can't get away from the studio any earlier than that."

"That's great. I usually take a late lunch. Would it be better if I meet you somewhere near your office?"

Even though Alaine didn't have any set office hours—she could come and go as needed—she tried to stick to regular hours; so a nearby restaurant would allow her more time to talk to Russell LeBlanc. But what if someone else from the studio ended up at the same restaurant and realized she was meeting with a lawyer? "Where are you located?"

"In the Moreaux Mills area."

"Perfect! How about. . .Pappas's on Hyacinth Place?" Alaine clicked her pen with nervous repetition.

"The Greek place? Great choice. I didn't know anyone outside this neighborhood knew about it. Want to say two fifteen, since you'll have to drive all the way out here?"

"Two fifteen it is. See you then." Alaine closed her cell phone and typed a cryptic note into her calendar program and set a reminder to pop up that morning. She didn't think she'd forget, but with the way things got around here sometimes. . .

"Hot lunch date next week?"

Alaine whipped around. Pricilla, the production assistant, entered the large cubicle and perched on the edge of Alaine's desktop.

"Sometimes you forget just how thin these partitions are." The plain but hardworking younger woman tapped one of the walls. It wobbled to prove her point.

Alaine hadn't said anything that would clue anyone in to what she was doing. But still. . .she had to be careful. "A potential story. Won't really know until after I meet with him." That should work. Alaine, Pricilla, and Garnet, their show's producer, were forever chasing down stories that didn't pan out; and none of them wasted the others' time with details of a no-go piece.

Plus, there was the idea that even if he decided not to take on her case, Russell LeBlanc might be interested in doing a Q&A segment once a month like Andrew Blakely and the make-your-life-more-green guy did. So in essence, she'd told the truth.

"Big plans for the weekend?" Pricilla twirled a lock of dishwater-blond hair around her finger.

Alaine looked away to try to hide her annoyance at Pricilla's unconscious habit. "Live remote from the big gospel music concert tonight, and tomorrow I'll be taking Noah down to Riverfront to cover the christening of the *Bonneterre Beauty* paddleboat."

"Oh, I forgot that was Saturday afternoon. Are you doing the dinner cruise that night?"

"Noah's wife is going to meet him down there. Noah's going to cover it as a photo essay. I figured it was only fair. Since he's covering for Nelson, he should at least get to treat his wife to a free evening out, even if he is technically working." Alaine surreptitiously glanced around her desk to make sure that she hadn't left anything lying about that might indicate what her appointment next week was really about. She'd promised Mother and Daddy that she wouldn't turn this into a big news story; and if she wasn't going to break and cover the biggest business scandal in Bonneterre history, she wouldn't let anyone else here get a whiff of it from her.

"I thought I might go out to the dog agility competition at the park tomorrow afternoon, if it isn't raining. I'll take a camera if I do." Pricilla stopped twirling her hair and picked at the already chipped dark brown polish on her thumbnail.

Alaine cringed and looked away again. She kept her nails buffed because she couldn't stomach the idea that each time a piece of polish flaked off, it took a layer of nail with it. "Well, you know if Brent's the one forecasting rain tomorrow, it'll probably be bright and sunny."

"Why do you give him such a hard time?"

"Because I can. Because he hurt a really good friend of mine when they were in college." Alaine swallowed hard. Despite everything going on, she still longed to claim Meredith as a really good friend.

Pricilla shrugged. "To each his own. Oh, hey, you've always said you wanted to learn ballroom dancing, right?"

"I've thought about lessons. Why?" She picked up her pen and twirled it in her fingers. Hardly anyone knew she'd minored in dance her first year of college, and ever since dropping it when she switched her major to journalism, she'd longed to go back to it.

"One of the interns took a call today from someone at that new dance studio that just opened down in Comeaux. Apparently, they're going to be having a six-week ballroom dancing class, starting this Monday. They were hoping we might be interested in covering it for *Inside Bonneterre*. I thought since you already have an interest in the subject, you might want to take it on."

She'd rather be *in* the class than covering it for the show; however, she took the slip of paper from the assistant producer with a trickle of excitement. Maybe now was the time to start dancing again if the package wasn't too expensive. "Thanks, Priss. I'll look into it."

"Well, I'm done with everything. I fixed those links on the blog post and put it up." Pricilla stood and brushed the flakes of nail polish off her shirt and slacks. "Oh, and someone from Systems called. They wanted to know why we can't just post the recipes on the blog instead of on a static page on the Web site."

Alaine should have known that one would come back to bite her. "I'll talk to them about it next week. Have a good weekend."

"You staying much longer?"

"I'll just return this call to the dance studio and then call it a day." She waved the little piece of paper.

"Okay. See you Monday, then."

Alaine waited until all of the rustling from the adjacent cubicle stopped and the sound of Pricilla's footsteps faded away before picking up the phone.

"Arcenault Dance Studio. How may I help you?"

"Hi, this is Alaine Delacroix from *Inside Bonneterre*. I received a message from. . .Ruth about your ballroom dancing class. I'd like to speak with her to see about covering your opening night on the program."

A high-pitched squeak came through the line. Alaine smiled.

"That's so awesome. Ruth is going to spaz out. This has been her lifelong dream, to open a dance studio, and it all just kind of fell into her lap, so she hasn't had a lot of time for promotion or to contact the media. But your show was the one she definitely wanted to get on."

"Wonderful. May I speak with her?"

"Oh—well, she's rehearsing right now for an exhibition at the Savoy tonight. Should I. . . ?" The girl hesitated.

"No. Tell you what, I'll give you my cell phone number. Have her call me whenever she's free this weekend to talk about Monday." Alaine recited her number twice and made the girl repeat it back to her to make sure she hadn't transposed any of the numbers, which she had.

"I'll be sure to get this message to her as soon as she finishes up."

"Thanks." Alaine hung up, threw what she'd need at the remotes tonight and tomorrow into her bag, and left. She still had two hours before she was scheduled to meet Nelson at the football stadium at ULB, where the concert was to be held—so long as the rain held off—so she took a detour leaving downtown and, after a few minutes, pulled into the parking lot of her favorite shoe store—a warehouselike place that carried expensive brands at discount prices.

The clerk straightening the display of handbags near the front door greeted her by name. She waved in greeting but wasn't going to let herself be distracted by purses today. She wended her way through the aisles of hundreds of shoes. In a small alcove in the back of the store lay the siren that had lured her in. . .dance shoes of all makes, models, and sizes. Ballet slippers; tap shoes in a variety of colors, designs, and heel heights; jazz shoes; and on the end, the shoes she sought: the T-strap and X-strap pumps worn by ballroom dancers. Open toed for Latin dances. Closed toed for standard dances.

Lovingly, she picked up a silver shoe. Flexible at the ball of the foot, but, according to the shoe box, with a steel shank for stability. Suede sole. Slightly flared, two-inch heel—much lower than what she usually wore.

The mark of someone who danced.

"Finding everything okay?"

"Yes, thanks." She didn't even bother to tear her eyes away from the shoes she'd wanted since seeing her first Fred Astaire–Ginger Rogers movie at age six. Why she'd ever chosen art lessons over dance lessons, she couldn't remember right now.

When she'd taken her first two dance classes in college, the first had focused on popular ballroom steps, like the waltz and foxtrot and tango. Much of the second semester had been dedicated to the instructor's favorite areas of jazz and modern dance—and much of the routine they'd had to do for their final exam looked a lot like the routine the school's dance squad performed in the pregame show at every home football game. If every class had been ballroom, she might not have dropped the minor.

Gingerly, she replaced the shoe on top of its box and pulled her hand away with great reluctance. Even if she did end up taking lessons, she couldn't justify the expense of shoes she'd never wear anywhere else. Especially since she had two utility bills at home she was waiting to put in the mail until her next paycheck hit the bank.

She was almost back to her car when her cell phone rang. "Alaine Delacroix."

"Ms. Delacroix, this is Ruth Arcenault of Arcenault Dance Studio!"

Alaine pulled the phone away from her ear to keep her eardrum from bursting at the woman's excitement. "Thank you for calling me back." She climbed into her car and pulled her day planner out of her bag. "I wanted to see if you would have time to meet with me for an interview before your ballroom dance class starts Monday evening. Maybe about thirty or forty-five minutes beforehand?"

"Yeah, of course. Whenever you want to come is fine with me. The class starts at six thirty."

"Will people who don't come on Monday still be able to sign up for the class?"

"Definitely. This first session will be just a basic overview of what the six-week program will include to give people a better idea of whether or not they really want to commit to it. That was why I've been doing a major promotional push this week, trying to get the word out to all the major media outlets in town, so that just in case people don't hear about it till next week, they still have time to sign up."

Alaine made a few notes in her planner. "Okay, that'll help me in determining the direction of the piece."

"I'm super excited that you're coming. You know how to find us?"

"All I have here is that you're located in Comeaux."

"We're three buildings down—south, I think—from The Fishin' Shack restaurant. In the old karate studio."

Alaine's mouth instantly started watering at the thought of the crawfish bisque she'd had the one and only time she'd visited The Fishin' Shack—when she featured it on her show right after it first opened. Maybe it was time to go back and do a feature on them again, since it had been at least five or six years. Something about the owner of the restaurant niggled the back of her mind, but she couldn't put her finger on it.

"Okay. I'll be there between five thirty and six on Monday evening. If you have any information you'd like to send me to review between now and then, you can e-mail it to my address on the TV station's Web site."

After exchanging good-byes, Alaine started the car and headed toward the university campus. A huge raindrop spattered her windshield. Great. Now everything would be in an uproar as they moved the concert into the basketball arena. Hopefully the featured groups would still have time for the preconcert interviews she'd been promised.

The one benefit of being the social-scene reporter: backstage access to every big-name concert that came to town. Not that she listened to much but Christian indie-rock. But it got her face on the evening news broadcasts.

Weariness blanketed her as traffic slowed to a crawl in the now-pouring rain. Sometimes, all the time and energy she put into dreaming and desiring a move to main news didn't seem worth the effort.

She blinked a couple of times. Effort. What had Bekka had said about making an effort to prove herself to the uppity-ups at the station?

Her mind whirled. She had a good video camera at home, and the bookcases in her third bedroom–turned office would make a great backdrop. She'd promised her parents she wouldn't *broadcast* anything about the case. She'd never said anything about not recording an audition tape to show the news director that she could not only report hard news but could do the investigative work behind it as well. And if it happened to create a stir and help stop the Guidry family from ruining Moreaux Mills, all the better.

CHAPTER 10

*A*s soon as Alaine saw the Fishin' Shack restaurant Monday evening, her memory kicked in. The owner was a Guidry. One of Meredith's younger sisters, if she remembered correctly. She made a mental note to add a sidebar investigation into just how many properties and businesses that family owned in Beausoleil Parish for her reel.

Nelson slowed the van, and Alaine shook herself out of her thoughts. "There it is, on the corner." She pointed to a stand-alone building a few doors down from the restaurant. A hastily printed vinyl sign draping the existing one announced: ARCENAULT DANCE STUDIO NOW OPEN.

"Pull up on the side of the building—that way the van can still be seen from the street, but we're not blocking the main strip of parking spaces." As soon as the van stopped, Alaine climbed out and opened the side door to get her large, overstuffed canvas briefcase as well as the tripod for the camera so Nelson didn't have to hold it while she interviewed Ruth Arcenault.

What Alaine had learned of the woman's story in her initial research fascinated her—good thing, as it would make a good story for the program instead of coming across as Alaine giving in to a local business's desire for self-promotion.

A young woman so rail thin she couldn't possibly have eaten

anything in the last three years jogged out from behind the reception desk to hold open the door for Alaine and Nelson. "We're so glad y'all're here. Come in. Come in."

Music faintly wafted out into the lobby—a jazzy, instrumental recording of what sounded like "Cheek to Cheek." Alaine's heart quickened. Finally, after so many years of regret, she was going to be the closest she'd ever been to actually stepping back out on the dance floor.

"Ruth and Ian are warming up right now, but she said for y'all to come on in once you arrive and she'll give you a tour before the interview."

Alaine nodded and extended her hand. "I'm sorry, I didn't catch your name."

The girl turned redder than her cayenne-colored hair. "Sorry. Talia."

Alaine cocked her head and pulled out her steno pad and pen. "You're gonna have to spell that one for me."

Talia complied, while Nelson shouldered his camera and began shooting footage of the decor of the reception area.

"I'm going to go get some exteriors." The string of bells hanging from the door clanked against the camera as he went outside.

Alaine asked Talia a few questions—the girl had been a ballet dancer trying to make it in New York when she met Ruth and Ian and they offered her room and board and to train her in ballroom, modern, and jazz dance as part of her salary if she moved down here to work as their receptionist.

As soon as she could break away from her, Alaine moved down the long, narrow reception room that overlooked the parking lot to the archway at the far end that led into the studio itself.

The music switched to another jazzy trumpet interpretation of "I've Grown Accustomed to Her Face." Alaine stopped in the arched doorway and let herself be transported. On the other side of the large room, a tall, dark-haired couple glided across the shiny hardwood as effortlessly as clouds through the sky.

Before the song ended, Nelson had joined her, shooting film of the reigning International Dance Grand Prix champions. As soon as the music stopped, the couple seemed to transform from unbelievably elegant to so tall and gangly they looked like they'd been stretched lengthwise.

Dressed in a formfitting, one-shoulder, asymmetrical-hem dress that showed off just how toned she was, the owner of Arcenault Dance Studio approached. "I'm Ruth Arcenault." She held out her hand. "Thank you so much for coming."

"It's nice to meet you." Alaine had never felt as short as she did right now. She shook hands with Ruth, who towered over her by almost a foot. In what looked like almost two-inch heels, Ruth was even a little taller than her dance partner. "How tall are you?"

What idiot would let that just blurt out?

Ruth laughed. "I get that all the time. Without shoes, I'm six-foot-two. Ian is six-three. He usually wears shoes with a little lift in them for competitions so that we're at least the same height. Oh, sorry, this is my husband and dance partner, Ian Birtwistle."

Alaine greeted him as well. She always made an effort to not notice when a married man was extremely good-looking, but in this case, she couldn't help but be affected by his dark good looks. He'd been created to ooze sex appeal without even trying. The British accent didn't help matters much, either.

"Is there a place where we can sit to do the interview?" Alaine bent to hoist the tripod from where she'd set it on the floor.

"Yes, of course. Our office." Ruth motioned for them to return the way they'd come. Over her shoulder, she said to Ian, "Can you run over to the restaurant to see about the refreshments?"

"Yes, love." He kissed her cheek and returned to the studio.

"I don't know what I would do without him." Ruth smiled. Alaine returned it, trying to push jealousy aside, and followed her through the door on the other side of the reception desk.

After getting set up, she began the interview...and got so involved in learning everything she could about the world of competitive ballroom dancing that Ian had to interrupt them to let Ruth know clients were arriving.

Alaine quickly conferred with Nelson about getting some on the spot interviews with the customers before the lesson started, and moments later, he followed her out of the office, camera on shoulder, floodlight beaming.

"Neither of you have dark soles on your shoes, do you?" Ruth asked when they reached the studio.

Alaine lifted her foot to look at the bottom of her black pumps. "No. Tan."

Nelson's athletic shoes had white soles. Ruth waved them in.

Across the dance floor, Alaine immediately spotted the person she wanted to talk to first. Tall—but not quite as tall as Ruth Arcenault—and full-figured, Anne Hawthorne Laurence stood in a small group, conversing animatedly while her husband stood off to the side, speaking with Ian Birtwistle, no doubt talking about their home country of England.

Nelson hung back while Alaine approached the group. "Excuse me, Mrs. Laurence?"

Anne's smile glowed when she turned around. "Yes? Oh, you're Alaine Delacroix." She extended her right hand. "It's so nice to finally meet you in person. I've heard a lot about you."

Alaine couldn't stop a genuine smile, Anne's warmth proving contagious. "I hoped I could ask you a few questions for a piece I'll be doing on the studio."

"Of course." Anne turned back to the others. "If you'll excuse me."

Alaine motioned her over to where Nelson stood. She positioned Anne, then took her place beside the cameraman. She started out with a few general questions about what kind of dancing most people did at wedding receptions these days and let Anne talk about the subject from the point of view of someone who actually had experience helping couples choose places to learn classic dance steps.

"A few of my clients are here, if you'd like to speak with them as well." Anne motioned to the two couples she'd been talking with.

"Yes, that would be great." Alaine motioned Nelson to follow her over to get some more sound bites. Anne stood by, looking like a proud parent ready to offer any assistance necessary to the twenty-somethings.

As the two young women answered Alaine's final question, she glanced around to find her next interview—and her breath caught in her chest. In an open-collared, cobalt blue dress shirt and dark gray pants, Forbes Guidry strode across the floor toward them.

Nelson cleared his throat. Alaine snapped her attention back to the people in front of her. "Thank you all, very much, for your input. Nelson, I think we're done here."

"Didn't you want to get some footage of everyone dancing?" he asked.

Why'd he have to remember that? "Yeah. I did." And they couldn't start soon enough.

❧

Forbes waited until Alaine lowered her microphone and turned to her cameraman before approaching. Her being here, at the very last place in the world he wanted to be tonight, must be a sign. The cameraman walked away, apparently getting shots of the studio's interior.

Forbes had to detour slightly to put himself in Alaine's path to stop her from walking away. "Ms. Delacroix, I do believe you've been avoiding me."

Alaine's dark eyes narrowed coolly. "Mr. Guidry. I thought I'd explained sufficiently over the phone. Things in my life are complicated right now and I can't. . ." She shrugged and shook her head, dropping her gaze from his.

Not the reaction he'd hoped for—it seemed to confirm his suspicion that she was connected with Delacroix Gardens and knew his parents were trying to buy up all the property in Moreaux Mills. Surely she couldn't blame *him* for that.

"Alaine, I—"

Forbes broke off when Anne joined them. "Where's Jenn?"

He looked around the studio for the first time. "She's not here yet?"

"Do you think something came up at the restaurant to keep her from leaving?"

"She wasn't supposed to be working today."

Alaine backed away from them. "If y'all will excuse me, I need to get back to work."

"Of course," Anne said graciously.

Forbes wanted to argue, but right now he had a bigger concern. "I'll call her and find out where she is. She's probably just running late as usual."

He stepped out into the front room that ran the length of the dance studio and overlooked the parking lot and street and hit the speed dial button for Jenn's cell phone number.

It rang four times before he heard a click.

"What do you want, Forbes?"

He frowned at her harassed tone of voice. "Jenn, where are you?"

She groaned. "Oh, don't ask. But I'm not going to be able to make it tonight."

Warning bells sounded in his mind. "What's going on?"

"You'll just get mad if I tell you."

He was already getting mad because he could tell from the background noise that she was, indeed, at the restaurant. "Tell me anyway."

"Okay, fine. Wait, hang on. . ." She hollered a couple of commands to her staff over the din of the kitchen. "He lied about his credentials."

"Who?"

"The restaurant manager I hired. *Don't* say, 'I told you so.'"

"I thought you checked him out with Major." Forbes paced the length of the lobby. He had a mind to march out the door and down the block and have this conversation face-to-face.

"Well. . .he listed Major as a reference. I never actually called. I mean, why would he list my brother-in-law as a reference if it weren't true? Come to find out, though, he did work as a *commis* a few

107

times at large B-G events a long time ago, but Major didn't even remember him."

"Two questions. . .what's a *commis*, and I thought you said you
hadn't checked with Major."

"A *commis* is an apprentice—basically someone who comes in and
does prep work to learn the ropes in a kitchen from more experienced
chefs. And I talked to Major today after. . .after it happened."

He sank into one of the molded plastic chairs. "After what
happened?"

"He seemed to be fine when I worked with him Saturday and
Sunday. Nice guy. Seemed to know what he was doing in the kitchen
and in front of house, which is a rare find these days." Jenn paused
to yell something else at one of her staff. "Anyway, I figured he'd be
okay handling things by himself today. But then my head waitress
called me during lunch service to tell me she'd seen him making
photocopies of people's credit cards."

Now it was Forbes's turn to groan. "And?"

"And so I came in and confronted him. Things got a little
hairy—"

"Jennifer!" Forbes sprang from the chair and jogged toward the
door.

"Cool off! The sheriff and three of his deputies were here for
lunch so they sorted everything out. Ended up arresting him for
disorderly conduct. But now, until I find another restaurant manager,
I'll be here every day for the foreseeable future. Sorry about the dance
lessons."

"I'm coming over. I'll be there in a minute."

"No!"

While he'd heard her use that tone with her employees
occasionally, he'd never heard it directed toward himself. He stopped
just outside the dance studio doors. "What do you mean, no?"

"I mean, I'm at the beginning of what looks like it's going to be
a very busy dinner service, and I don't need you underfoot, getting all
up in my business when I don't have time to deal with you right now.

It's handled; there's nothing you can do here except get in my way. Now, I have to get back to work, and if I'm not mistaken, that dance lesson should be starting any minute now."

Consternated by Jenn's sudden show of self-reliance, Forbes couldn't decide what to do. She needed him. He knew she did. But as Meredith had been continually saying for the past several months, Jenn was thirty-two years old. It was time for her to stand on her own two feet.

He turned and went back into the lobby. "Okay. I won't come over. I won't even ask you any more questions about it. But if you decide you want me for any reason, you know I'm just a phone call away."

"Thanks. I appreciate that."

He bade her good night, closed the phone, and set the alert to vibrate-only. Inside the studio, everyone was just taking seats in the chairs lining the mirrored walls of the large room. While the owners gave a brief introduction of themselves and talked about all their international dancing awards, Forbes quickly gave Anne the rundown on what Jenn had told him.

Then there was nothing for him to do but watch as the championship dancers took the floor and exhibited a grace of movement Forbes would never be able to achieve. Dancing with his sisters and cousins at wedding receptions was one thing; gliding across the floor with arms at weird angles and faces angled away from each other was just strange.

His gaze drifted over the others in the studio. Half were silver-haired; he, Anne and George, and the two young couples Anne had brought with her. . .and Alaine Delacroix, whose feet moved in rhythm with the music and whose eyes never left the dancers, made up the other half.

Forbes flexed his jaw to hide his grin. Jenn might not be able to do this with him, but it looked like he might not be partnerless after all.

The music ended, and a smattering of applause forced Forbes to look away from the gorgeous newscaster.

"Now, though we're not officially beginning the lessons in the package until next week, we thought this week we could begin teaching you one of the most simple dances, the waltz." Ruth Arcenault turned slowly as she spoke to make sure she looked at everyone scattered around the room. "So if everyone would line up—men over here, your partners facing you over here—we'll get started."

"Forbes, what are you going to do with no partner?" Anne asked.

"Don't worry about me." He winked at his cousin and passed her in the opposite direction from where all the men were lining up.

Alaine was looking down, writing something on a steno pad, when he stopped in front of her. Her cameraman noticed him and looked away from his eyepiece before Alaine looked up. Surprise, pleasure, and an attempt at aloofness rushed through her expressive chocolate eyes.

Forbes half bowed and extended his hand. "May I have this dance?"

"No—I—" Alaine looked at her cameraman and then back at Forbes. "I can't. I haven't paid for a lesson. I'm working."

"My sister isn't going to be able to make it, and I need a partner." Forbes removed the notepad and pen from her and took her hands in his. "And as you can see, you are the only other person here to dance with." He glanced at her cameraman. "No offense."

The guy grunted what might have been a chuckle. "None taken."

Forbes started backing away. After a moment's initial resistance, Alaine rolled her eyes and followed him, the hint of a smile playing about her enticing mouth.

They had to practice the steps for a good ten minutes standing three feet apart, not touching. Finally, though, Ruth and Ian demonstrated what they called a *standard hold* and told everyone to try it.

Forbes's arms tingled, and as soon as he had his right hand on her back—just below her shoulder blade—he had to grit his teeth to keep from sighing with pleasure. Her hand was so small in his, and he hadn't realized just how short she was until he looked down at her from such close proximity.

She, on the other hand, stared straight ahead, at his chest. Color had risen in her cheeks, and she pressed her lips together as if trying to suppress an unwanted emotion.

A touch on his shoulder brought him out of his admiration for her. He looked around and found Ruth Arcenault standing beside them—throwing Alaine's petite stature into even starker relief, since Ruth was slightly taller than Forbes in her high-heeled dance shoes.

"Find the rhythm in the music and start whenever you feel comfortable. Remember, gentlemen, lead off with the right foot forward and just make a box. You won't be traveling around the room for at least a week." She wandered over to Anne and George, who, of course, performed the steps perfectly.

"Ready?"

Alaine looked up at him. He could lose himself in those endless dark eyes. "Ready."

He tuned in to the classical music playing through the speakers in the ceiling and, under his breath, began counting the rhythm. "One, two, three. One, two, three. One, two, three. . ."

Alaine giggled. "You go on the one," she whispered.

"I know." Heat tweaked his cheeks, and he suddenly remembered just how bad a dancer he was. Now Alaine was about to find out, too. What had he been thinking? *One, two, three. One, two, three. Now, two, three. Go, two, three. Fool, two, three.*

He lifted his foot to start. Alaine anticipated and began to step back, but Forbes hesitated—and threw both of them off balance. Alaine's momentum pulled her backward, and he stumbled forward, stomping on her tiny foot.

She winced. "Ow."

"Sorry. I'm so sorry." He dropped the dance hold and grabbed her shoulders. "Are you okay?"

"I'm fine." She pushed his hands away from her shoulders and put her arms back into the standard-hold positions. When he hesitated, she grinned at him. "Why, Forbes Guidry. I do believe we've finally found something at which you aren't 100 percent confident. In fact, I think you're completely and utterly out of your element."

He narrowed his eyes at her, mortified at having been called out. He had to regain control of this situation. "But that's why I needed you as a partner. Because I am confident that I won't learn this nearly as well with anyone else."

"Will it help if I lead?"

He'd never live it down. "No. I've got this." He started counting again, under his breath. He closed his eyes and visualized his feet moving to the rhythm of the music. "Ready?"

"As I'll ever be."

He didn't have to open his eyes to know her eyes sparkled with silent laughter. He took a deep breath and stepped. *One, two, three. One, two, three. One, two, three. One, two, three. I'm doing it. I'm actually dancing.*

Taking a risk, he opened his eyes. Alaine's eyes bored into his with barely suppressed amusement. "Yes, you are doing it. You are actually dancing."

Ruth came over and observed them for a few moments. "Very good, Ms. Delacroix. I like the way you're staying on the balls of your feet. Mr. Guidry, too stiff—and don't hold your breath. Try bringing your heels up off the floor—and bend your knees a little more on each step. No Frankenstein's monsters allowed here."

He probably could have lived his entire life without learning to dance—and given the choice between that and being called *Frankenstein's monster* in front of Alaine Delacroix, he would have found it preferable. He had to hand it to Alaine, though. She didn't laugh at him. At least, not out loud.

Ruth and Ian stopped the class and demonstrated what they saw most of the students doing and then how they wanted it done. Forbes watched Ian carefully, determined not to draw any criticism this time. Heels up. On the tiptoes for the *two* and *three* counts. Sliding the ball of the foot to the next position instead of lifting the foot and putting it down. He could master this.

He would master this, even if he had to take private lessons. Because when he married the woman standing beside him, he wanted to dance like that Fred-guy from the movies at their wedding reception.

CHAPTER 11

*A*laine slid her sunglasses to the top of her head and pulled open the door of Delacroix Rentals.

"Hey, Sis. What're you doing here?" Joe wheeled out from behind a display of candelabra.

"Do I need a reason to stop by and see my big brother?" She leaned her hip against the front counter.

"No. It's just that you don't usually drop by on a random Tuesday night unless something's up. So what's up?" He parked himself directly in front of her.

"Well, I was hoping to talk to you."

"Just me or me and Nikki?"

She shrugged. "Either way."

"Tell you what. Let's you and me go for a walk." He turned to look over his shoulder. "Hey, Nik!"

Her sister-in-law appeared from the back room. "Yeah? Oh hey, Alaine."

Alaine raised her hand in greeting "Hey, yourself."

"Al and I are going for a walk if you don't mind keeping an eye on things here."

Nikki glanced around the otherwise vacant showroom. "I'll try to keep the crowd under control."

"Thanks, dollface." Joe whipped his wheelchair around and

headed for the door. "We'll be back in a bit."

Alaine rushed ahead of him to hold the door, then took her place behind him, not pushing, but touching the bar across the top of the seat back, just in case.

Joe cleared his throat. "Alaine, it's been seven years. I'd hope by now you'd remember that I don't need or want to be pushed, and I'd much prefer it if you'd walk beside me so I can see you when I'm talking to you."

Alaine released her hold and moved up beside him. "Sorry. I just can't help it."

He stopped where the walkway joined with the small, paved parking area in front of the store. "I may have lost the use of my legs, but I'm not helpless. I know you feel like you have to protect me from the world, but you don't. I was an Army Ranger, remember? Even now, you could drop me anywhere in the world, and I'd not only survive, I'd be able to find my way home."

"That's not because you were a Ranger. That's because ever since you were fifteen years old, you've had this weird homing signal that can take you wherever Nikki is."

He grinned. "Too right. Come on. Let's walk up and see what Mother's making for supper." Joe set a quick pace toward the only other house on the cove that had survived the Great Moreaux Mills Fire twenty-five years ago. "Are you going to tell me what's up?"

"I'm meeting with a lawyer tomorrow."

"Having a will drawn up? I can't wait to find out if I get the shoe collection or the treadmill." He made a face.

She punched him in the arm. "No. I talked at length with Mother and Daddy. . .about the business situation. I'm meeting with a lawyer who might be interested in taking on the case."

Joe slowed. "What do you mean 'the case'?"

"If the guy thinks we have a chance, he'll put together a lawsuit of some kind to stop the Guidrys from forcing everyone out of the Mills."

"You're serious?" He stopped, bracing the wheels to keep from rolling backward down the slight incline.

"Yeah. But of even more concern is. . .did Mother and Daddy tell you that their mortgage was bought by an investment firm that's going to foreclose in ninety days if they don't pay what's left on their mortgage in full?"

Joe's normally deep complexion paled. "Them, too?"

Her stomach roiled. "What—you mean you and Nikki are in the same situation?"

"Business has really slacked off in the last few months—especially business from B-G Enterprises. No surprise there, since they're wanting to run us out of business. But I'd never have suspected it of Meredith."

Alaine didn't want to think ill of her new friend, either, but facts were facts.

"Anyway, we've fallen behind in our payments the last couple of months. With our loan coming through a locally owned bank, they were working with us on a plan to get caught up. Three weeks ago, we go in to talk to them about signing the paperwork for the final arrangements, and there's all new people at the bank and they tell us that it was bought out by this investment firm that is in the process of reviewing all accounts and loans. Then last week, we get served with the foreclosure paperwork. More than ninety days in arrears."

Alaine nearly crumpled. "You got that far behind? I wish you'd said something to me. I could have helped."

"How? Mother and Daddy are in the same situation, and we all know that you tend to live paycheck to paycheck because you have a huge mortgage and car payment of your own."

Not to mention the money she spent on clothes and shoes every month. Guilt wrung at her heart. If she'd been a better steward of her finances, if she hadn't had to have the *right* address and the *right* clothes and the *right* shoes, she could have been in a position to keep her family out of this situation.

"Anyway, it wasn't your responsibility to bail us out. We have to face it. The economy tanked. Frankly, with more than half of the business in the Mills closing over the past six months, it's a miracle we're still here." Joe's dark eyes clouded further; he closed them and dropped his head.

"What? There's something else you aren't telling me."

"Nikki and I were finally at the top of the list for a baby, and when the adoption agency found out we'd been served foreclosure papers, they dropped us. All that money and all the time we spent waiting—hoping, praying we'd finally have a child of our own—and we get kicked to the curb just like that."

Moisture welled in Alaine's eyes, followed by bitterness in the back of her throat. How could the Guidrys do this to her family? "Just one more thing I'll be telling the lawyer tomorrow."

⌘

Thick, black clouds boiled on the horizon. Forbes stepped on the gas, determined to make it to Comeaux before the thunderstorm did. Twenty-four hours should be all Jenn needed to realize that she wanted him there to help her get through this fiasco and back on track.

Huge raindrops splatted against the windshield as he pulled into the parking lot. Grabbing his umbrella—for the deluge that would surely be happening when he left—Forbes dashed into his sister's restaurant. For six o'clock on a Tuesday evening, she had a pretty good-sized crowd. Of course, given that he'd found her a piece of prime real estate—right on the main highway between Comeaux and Bonneterre—she would have had to try really hard to fail in this venture.

Several of the servers greeted him, including the head waitress, the one who'd discovered the short-term manager's criminal activity. He stopped, returning her greeting.

"You here to talk to her about what happened yesterday?" Lynne asked.

He nodded. "Where is she?"

"Where else?"

117

"In the kitchen. Thanks." He headed toward the rear of the building and let himself into the kitchen through the EMPLOYEES ONLY door. He cringed as soon as he entered. He'd been more than happy to go into the restaurant business with Jenn when she'd decided this was what she wanted to do with her life—because it had been under the express agreement that he'd never have to set foot in the kitchen.

Chaos surrounded him—cooks, servers, porters, dishwashers all hollering at each other over the din of equipment, fans, machines, and the clanking of pots and pans.

"Chef, someone here to see you!" The white-clad yeller hardly even looked up from his task of shucking oysters.

Forbes's mouth watered at the sight of the succulent, juicy mollusks just waiting for a splash of lemon juice and hot sauce and ready to slide across his tongue with a velvety sweet saltiness like nothing else in the world. Maybe he'd have a plate of them before leaving.

Jenn came around the end of the stainless steel island where the shucker worked. As soon as she spotted him, her eyes narrowed and one hand went to her hip. "What do you want, Forbes?"

He worked hard to keep his surprise from showing. "I figured you'd want to talk about what happened yesterday."

She cocked her head to the side, ponytail swinging. "I don't remember calling you and begging you to come down here to take care of me. Don't Marci or Tiffani need you to come rescue them from some crisis?"

Meredith's recent bid for independence from the family was having a bad effect on the rest of their siblings. "I'm not here to try to rescue you from a crisis. I'm here as your legal counsel to talk to you about the consequences and ramifications of what happened yesterday—because I need to hear it firsthand from you and see all of the paperwork."

Jenn blinked a couple of times, then her expression cleared. "Oh. Okay. Have you had supper yet?"

Fortunately, the kitchen was loud enough that she couldn't hear his stomach growling. "Not yet." He nodded his head toward the oysters. "Those any good today?"

Jenn walked over and leaned down to smell those already on a platter. "Yep. Fresh as can be. Delivery just came in an hour ago. Decker, plate of twelve for my brother."

The prep cook nodded. "Yes, Chef. Plate of twelve."

"Forbes, go on and get a table. I'll get the paperwork and then bring the food out to you."

Even though the dining room would have its own set of distractions, Forbes was grateful that his sister didn't want to do this in her office—a cramped little room that, while well organized, still reminded him of the chaos just beyond the doorway. He waited for two servers and a busboy to exit ahead of him, then went out into the restaurant.

He fixed himself a glass of iced tea at the waitress station, then chose a booth in the corner farthest from the kitchen where there would be fewer interruptions, as members of the staff wouldn't be walking past them every few seconds.

Just when he was about to return to the kitchen to find out if Jenn had gotten distracted by something, she came around the corner, followed by a waiter balancing a tray on his hand and shoulder. She directed the placement of the platter of oysters, the basket of hush puppies, and the bowls of side dishes before taking a seat opposite him.

The first oyster went down like nectar of the gods—the perfect hint of clean salty seawater followed by the sweetness of the meat and the sting of the lemon juice and hot sauce. Forbes barely suppressed a shiver of pleasure.

When six empty shells lined his side of the plate, and three on Jenn's, he finally leaned back, ready to talk.

Jenn grinned at him and bit into a hush puppy. "I'm starting to wonder if you really came to talk to me or if you really wanted an excuse to come down for the oysters."

"Ones that size are hard to come by this time of year. But I did really come to talk to you. Tell me what happened yesterday."

Forbes guided his sister through the story with a series of questions while he sated himself on the greens, macaroni and cheese, and beet salad. . .and the remaining three oysters for dessert.

"So do you really think there are going to be legal ramifications for me—like the people whose information he was trying to copy, could they sue me or something?" Jenn swirled a straw in her tea.

"No, because nothing actually happened to their information."

"I dunno. The sheriff's department confiscated all the photocopies as evidence when they arrested him. While I'd like to have faith that everyone who works at the sheriff's department is trustworthy and ethical, you never know."

"If anything happens now, it'll fall on them, not on you. But if it'll make you feel better, I'll pay them a visit tomorrow just to make sure those copies will be destroyed once they're finished with them."

"Thanks."

"Now, are all of your employees' files up-to-date? Has everyone signed the ethics policy?"

"Do you realize I'm probably the only restaurant that requires everyone to sign one of those things?"

"Do you realize that it gives you the legal recourse to fire someone like that manager when they break it? You're just covering all your bases by doing it. Speaking of ethics policies. . ." He caught himself just before a big, stupid grin broke out on his face as he reached for his wallet. He pulled out a twenty and handed it to his sister.

"What's this for?" She eyed the bill but didn't reach for it.

"It's from Alaine Delacroix. She took your place as my partner last night, but since she was there covering the studio's opening for her TV show, she couldn't accept anything for free. So she asked me to reimburse you for her participation in the lesson."

Jenn's gray blue eyes twinkled. She took the money and pocketed it. "Alaine Delacroix, huh? She's kinda cute."

He shrugged and hoped his face didn't reveal more than he

wanted it to. "I guess so." If one liked short, gorgeous women with a Mediterranean look about them. Which he'd recently discovered he did. "She's a great dancer already. Looked like she's already taken some ballroom dancing lessons."

"Sounds like she's the perfect person for you to partner with, then, because she can help you out when the instructors are paying attention to the other students. Goodness knows you'll need all the help you can get." She dodged the straw paper he threw at her. "Hey now, don't go trashing my restaurant!"

Forbes looked up and thanked the server who refilled their tea glasses, then returned his attention to Jenn. "Have you talked to Meredith today?"

"Got an e-mail from her about catering some event in a couple of months. I didn't even know they were back yet."

"They flew back yesterday. I had lunch with Major today to finalize the paperwork for his restaurant."

"That's finally going through, huh? I thought there was some problem with the building permits or something." Jenn's eyes wandered around her own restaurant, taking in everything her staff and customers were doing.

"Well, Mom and Dad—and the consultant they've brought in— are working to get everything squared away with the city and the few property owners who haven't decided to sell yet."

"There're a lot of good restaurants over in Moreaux Mills—at least, there used to be. I've heard a bunch of them have closed down over the past few months. It's a rough time to be a business owner." She heaved a dramatic sigh.

"Yeah, especially for you." He made a face at her.

"No, seriously. It hasn't been easy here, either. My revenues have been down almost 10 percent. I had a waitress quit a few weeks ago, and I decided not to replace her because the workload just wasn't there."

"What kind of marketing are you doing right now?"

She shrugged. "Same kind of stuff as usual: newspaper ads high-lighting family-friendly karaoke four nights a week, radio spots on the top tier of stations, TV commercials during the news hours and primetime on local channels, and scattered day parts on cable. Sponsorships—I'm a sponsor, and the caterer, for the fishing tournament down on the lake in October. Trade-out agreements with other businesses in Comeaux—like supplying the beverages and finger foods for the grand opening of the dance studio last night. You saw my banner, didn't you?"

"Looked good. The food was good, too. And Alaine interviewed someone standing in front of it, so that will give you free promotion on her show, too."

"You know, she interviewed me when we opened. I ought to see if I can get her back out here for something. Free coverage by the news—for something positive anyway—is always a good thing." She waved a server over. "Tell Ruiz to bus six, twelve, and fifteen. Cara has customers waiting to be seated."

Forbes leaned around to survey the restaurant. How Jenn had noticed those tables and customers—when they were all almost directly behind her—was beyond him. Of course, that's what had made her such a success.

"So did Meredith and Major have a good time in Colorado?"

"Apparently. Major said he filled a couple of notebooks at the festival with ideas and recipes for the restaurant. Said Meredith came back with almost as much information she wanted to put into use in the events division. He was talking about it like it's going to become an annual trip for them. Maybe next year they'll let you tag along."

"If I can ever get away from this place." Jenn grimaced, then quickly replaced it with a smile. "Not that I don't love doing this. But it would be nice to take a vacation every now and again."

Aha. The perfect opening. "That reminds me." Forbes picked up his suit coat and pulled something from the inside pocket. "Major sent this for you."

"Ooh, what is it?" Jenn's whole face lit up.

He handed her the slip of paper.

As soon as she unfolded it, her expression darkened. She looked up at him with narrowed eyes. "What is this?" She waved the slip of paper at him.

"A list of people Major suggested as potential restaurant managers for you. He already has someone in line to interview for his place—if it ever comes into being—and these are some of the other people he considered or talked to. Most of them he's known for years and trusts implicitly."

A color to rival Jenn's famous beet salad rose in her face. "You told Major?"

Only years of practice kept him from reacting to the venom in his sister's voice. "Yes, I told Major. If anyone would understand, he would; and he's the best person we know to suggest someone who won't do to you what this last guy did."

Jenn slammed the paper down on the table and shot out of the booth. Then, gripping the edge of the table and the back of his seat, she leaned in close. "Forbes, when are you going to stop interfering in my business? I told you I didn't need any help."

He raised his chin—and his left brow—blindsided but unwilling to relinquish his position. "I was only trying to do you a favor by getting a list of names for you instead of having to watch you kill yourself to try to run the restaurant, review résumés, check references, and conduct interviews."

"I don't need you to do me any favors. It's my business. Mine. While I will be forever grateful that you loaned me the capital to get it started, I bought you out more than two years ago. I don't need my big brother swooping in and trying to bail me out every time you think I'm in over my head. I know what I'm doing."

She wadded up the list and tossed it at him.

"I think you're making a mistake if you don't give them serious consideration."

Her fingers contracted into claws. "When I am ready to start thinking about hiring another restaurant manager, I will go and talk to Major myself. But until that time, I'll appreciate it if you'll keep your nose out of my business."

He opened his mouth to speak, but she held up a hand to stop him.

"I know. You're my lawyer. So be my lawyer. You wouldn't have talked to me about another client's problems with her business, so why are you going around behind my back talking to Major about my problems? Where was your high-and-mighty attorney-client privilege?"

Her words took him aback. He hadn't thought about it in that light. "I'm sorry, Jenn. It won't happen again."

His apology seemed as blindsiding to her as her anger had been to him. "You're. . .sorry? Well, I. . .I. . .fine. Thank you. Apology accepted." She straightened and dropped her hands to her sides—after picking up the wadded list and sticking it in her pocket. "Look. I know it's a hard concept for you to grasp, but you can't go around controlling the lives of everyone you love. You have to let us make our own decisions—and our own mistakes. 'Kay?"

"Okay."

One of the servers approached. "Jennifer, I have a customer who'd like to speak with the manager."

"I'll be there in a second." She nodded at the waitress and waited until the girl walked away before turning back to Forbes. "Are we squared away?"

"Yes, Chef. We're squared away as long as you make me a deal."

Curious trepidation entered her eyes. "What's that?"

"If you'll agree to keeping your meddling old brother informed as to what's going on here, I'll agree to stop trying to control it." He stood and extended his right hand. "Deal?"

She narrowed her eyes as if contemplating it, then shook his hand. "Deal. I'll inform; you won't control. Now if you're finished, sir, we need to bus this table so we can seat *paying* customers."

He dropped twice as much cash on the table as the meal cost, then kissed Jenn's cheek in farewell. "Thanks for dinner."

"Get outta here, you control freak, you." She laughed and waved him away, then went to speak to her customers.

Even with his umbrella, Forbes was nearly soaked when he got back to his car. He put the key in the ignition—but didn't turn it. He wrapped his arms around the steering wheel and rested his forehead on his wrist. Jenn was right. He didn't know why he thought he could—or should—control what his siblings were doing in their lives. After all, how could he when he could barely control his own?

CHAPTER 12

*A*laine held her wrist to her ear to make sure her watch hadn't died. Staff meeting had never dragged like this before. She reached for her pen—then remembered Bekka had confiscated it a few minutes ago to stop her from tapping it on the arm of her chair. Instead, she pulled a lock of hair over her shoulder and twirled it around her finger. Only four more hours until her meeting with Russell LeBlanc.

"What have we heard about the Warehouse District and Moreaux Mills development project?" Rodney Milton looked at the chief investigative reporter.

Alaine stilled, interested in the meeting for the first time since she'd been employed by WCAN.

"It's no secret that Boudreaux-Guidry Enterprises bought the paper-mill warehouses and that they've run into a couple of zoning problems that delayed ground breaking on the project about six or eight months. I'm currently tracking down rumors that they're quietly buying up foreclosed properties in the Moreaux Mills subdivision, but so far, all I'm finding is that all trails lead to a development firm called Mackenzie and Son out of Boston."

"So nothing we can run with?"

"Not yet."

Alaine elbowed Bekka and pantomimed writing. Bekka gave the pen back—along with a warning look. Alaine pulled her steno pad onto her lap and started making a list of everything she already knew about the situation that the chief investigative reporter obviously didn't. She also wrote *Mackenzie & Son* down, planning to research it after the show. . .after the meeting with Russell LeBlanc.

And tonight, she'd start piecing the story together. The sooner she got it on tape—her face, her voice—the sooner she could show it to the producers and the sooner she'd be promoted to main news.

She was still scribbling notes as quickly as she could when the meeting broke up.

"Delacroix—a word, please."

Her stomach twisted at the news director's voice. Surely he couldn't be on to her. No way could he know she knew anything about the Moreaux Mills situation. She flipped a few pages in the notebook so he couldn't see her notes, and set the pad and pen on the table.

As soon as the room cleared, Rodney closed the door and sat in the chair opposite her. "I'm glad to see you're finally starting to take these meetings more seriously." He nodded toward the pad and pen. "It's been hard for us to nip in the bud the cocky attitudes of some of the younger up-and-coming reporters when they see someone with her own show flouting authority openly."

Alaine pressed her lips together, all of Bekka's warnings ringing in her head. Besides, she hadn't meant to cop an attitude with him. He just always seemed to go out of his way to point out she was the person in charge of the *fluff* pieces. . .in front of everyone else. . .in such a way as it seemed calculated to embarrass her. But she didn't want to be known as a diva. That was definitely one way to ensure she never made it into main news.

Rodney cleared his throat and leaned forward. "I understand that you're related to the people who own Delacroix Gardens and Delacroix Rentals over in the Mills area."

Aha. "That's right." She leaned back and crossed her arms.

He cleared his throat again. She enjoyed watching him squirm. "Do you think. . .I would imagine that they're being affected by this apparent scheme to buy up all the properties in that neighborhood and redevelop it. Do you think they might be willing to give an interview?"

"I don't know. If there is something like that going on, they might not be able to talk about it." And she was going to make sure to ask the lawyer if they could tell everyone who got involved in the lawsuit not to talk to any reporters—except her.

"So you don't know of anything already pending?"

She shrugged. "What am I supposed to know?"

He gave her a tight smile in return. "Well, if you do hear of anything, you'll be sure to say something, right?"

"I'll do what I can." Oh, yeah. She'd share what she knew—just as soon as the Gulf of Mexico froze over.

"Hey, you busy?"

Forbes looked up from the stack of paperwork on his desk to see Evelyn Mackenzie's lithe figure framed in his doorway. He stood, embarrassed to be caught sans jacket, tie loosened, and sleeves rolled up.

He stood. "Always. But do, please, come in."

Evelyn sauntered into his office, none too subtle in her visual appraisal of the space. He motioned to one of the chairs opposite his desk and waited until she sank into the chair before regaining his seat. Somehow those mile-long legs didn't have the same effect on him today as they'd had in their previous encounters.

"I was just upstairs going over some paperwork with Sandra and your parents, and they suggested I come down and invite you to go to lunch with us." When she leaned forward, the lapels of her suit jacket gapped a bit and revealed a V-neck blouse that showed an extraordinary amount of cleavage.

Somehow, Forbes couldn't imagine Alaine Delacroix doing something quite so inappropriate. No, the top she'd worn under her suit Monday had featured a modest crewneck. And none of the skirts he'd seen her wear on TV had ever ridden up to midthigh when she sat down, the way Evelyn's did now.

"Forbes?"

He pushed the image of Alaine aside and returned to the present. "Sorry." He turned to his computer and pulled up his schedule. "Looks like. . .looks like I'll have to take a pass on lunch. I have a deposition at one o'clock."

Evelyn's expression of disappointment seemed calculated. Or maybe Forbes read too much into it since he found himself not trusting her as much as he was sure he should.

"Well, then, you'll just have to make it up by meeting me for drinks after work. The group playing the Savoy tonight is supposed to be excellent."

He should feel much worse about turning down a gorgeous woman's invitation. "Alas, tonight is out as well. I have a couple of meetings at church tonight I can't miss." One of which was quartet practice. If he canceled again, George, Major, and Clay would hunt him down and personally see to tarring and feathering him.

"Church in the middle of the week?" She cocked her head. "I knew you attended regularly on Sundays, but I hadn't pegged you for the middle-of-the-week type."

He wasn't sure he wanted to know what *type* she'd had him pegged as. Her type, possibly, though he could be flattering himself; her interest might be born solely out of boredom and not knowing anyone else in town. "Oh, yes, I've been called to lead in many different areas of ministry—from music to serving on several committees to chairing the board of trustees."

Though she was a pro at showing only what others wanted to see, Forbes detected a moderate amount of surprise and skepticism in Evelyn's eyes. "That's wonderful. It's always great to hear of people in the community who are successful giving back in such tangible ways."

Or in such visible ways, maybe. Okay, he had to stop second-guessing everything this woman said simply because she'd shown no mercy toward the people who could possibly be losing their homes and businesses. "I do what I can."

His phone rang. He looked down at the console and recognized the number. "If you'll excuse me, I really need to take this call."

"Of course." Her smile seemed much more forced than when she'd come in. "I'll talk to you later."

The phone only rang twice, as he knew it would. No sooner had the door closed behind Evelyn Mackenzie than his intercom buzzed.

"Russell LeBlanc on line one for you, Mr. Guidry."

He pressed the intercom button. "Thanks, Samantha." He pressed the button for the correct line as he raised the receiver to his ear. "Russ, what can I do for you today?"

"It's happening—I'm heading to the hospital—emergency C-section—"

Forbes sprang out of his chair. "Whoa, hold on there. Take a deep breath. What's happening?"

On the other end of the connection, Russ gulped air. "Carrie started having contractions half an hour ago, and her water broke. They just called me from the emergency room. She's in labor, but they're going to have to do an emergency C-section or else might none of them survive."

Forbes paced behind his desk. "That's unbelievable. I'll be praying for all of you. But what else can I do?"

"I'm supposed to be meeting with a potential client—can't remember her name. Left the office without my planner. But I was supposed to meet her at Pappas's Greek Restaurant on Hyacinth in Moreaux Mills at two fifteen this afternoon. You said you were wanting a pro bono case, and this looks like it'll probably be one. Could you take it for me?"

"Of course." He dropped into his chair and wrote down the meeting location and time. "You just get to the hospital safely and don't worry about anything but naming those babies when they finally make their appearance in this world."

"Thanks."

"No problem." Forbes repeated Russ's farewell and hung up, then pressed the intercom again. "Samantha, come in for a moment please."

"Coming." A moment later, she sat across the desk from him.

"Russ LeBlanc's wife just went into labor, so he's asked me to meet with a client in a potential pro bono case at two fifteen this afternoon. I'm supervising that deposition at one, but the associates can handle it if I step out early." He turned his computer monitor so they could both see it. "What's this meeting here?" He pointed to a block of *busy* time that started at two thirty.

"That was the time you asked me to block off for you to work on the Pichon case."

"Right. Great. That means you won't have to reschedule anything for me. I'll need to leave here by about one forty-five if I'm going to get down to Moreaux Mills by a quarter after two. If you don't see me coming out of the conference room by then, stick your head in and remind me."

"Will do, boss."

"Thanks. That's all, then." He nodded his dismissal.

"I'll go ahead and take my lunch now so I'm back by then, if that's okay with you."

"Go ahead." He returned the computer monitor to its original angle.

"Want me to pick up something for you?" She paused in the door.

"No. I'm meeting the new client at a restaurant, so I'll just eat there."

"Okay. I'll see you in a bit." She turned and headed for the door.

"Oh, Samantha?"

"Yes, boss?"

"That woman who was here earlier—Evelyn Mackenzie?"

Samantha raised her brows. "Yes?"

"Next time you see her coming, could you give me a little

forewarning? I'm not real fond of surprises, you know."

"Sorry about that. I won't let it happen again." Samantha had the good grace to look sheepish. "She was past my desk and standing in your doorway before I knew what was happening."

He could see Evelyn being stealthy like that. "Don't worry about it. Enjoy your lunch." He waved her out of the room.

❧

Alaine bolted from the office as soon as the meeting about tomorrow's show wrapped. It would put her at the restaurant far too early, but she wouldn't be able to concentrate on work anyway.

The last of the lunch rush was just finishing up when Alaine walked into Pappas's.

"Alaine!" Voula Pappas bustled forward and hugged her. "We haven't seen you around in forever. Why don't you come by more often?"

"Oh, you know how it goes, Mrs. Voula—busy, busy, busy."

"But you are here for lunch?" Voula grabbed a menu.

"I am. But I'm meeting someone else—he won't be here for another fifteen or twenty minutes. His name is Russell LeBlanc."

The middle-aged woman grinned. "Oh, yes, we know Russ quite well." She grabbed two laminated menus.

"I wonder if we could have the table in the back corner overlooking the park. I have. . .a sensitive matter I need to talk to him about and don't want to be overheard."

Voula nodded. "I understand. This way."

Alaine took the chair with her back to the window, eliminating the distraction of watching the squirrels and birds outside in the old, drooping oak tree.

"I'll bring you an iced tea."

"Thanks, Mrs. Voula." Alaine pulled out her steno pad and pen. The dark pink gerbera daisy in a bud vase in the center of the table caught her eye. Every morning, her mother stopped by to get a box of pastries for the flower shop's customers in trade for the flowers for the tables. Yet another argument for why this area and these businesses needed to survive: to remind people how businesses should be run.

Voula brought the tea, and Alaine doctored it with sugar until sweet enough. She flipped open her notepad to a clean page and started an outline for the Moreaux Mills story. She would start it with a soft feature on the businesses in the Mills—the Gardens, the rental center, this restaurant. . .and she could use her small video camera at the Fourth of July street fair to get footage to include in the soft open.

Oh—and she could probably find some archive footage of the Guidrys and possibly some questionable sound bites to use. Not to mention contrasting the footage of the lavish Valentine's Day charity dinner she herself had covered with the current conditions in the Mills. And then she could—

A clearing throat broke into her flow of ideas. Though annoyed by the interruption, Alaine affixed a smile and looked up to greet Russell LeBlanc.

"Uh. . .hi."

Her insides froze at the sight of none other than Forbes Guidry towering over her. She shoved back from the table and shot to her feet. "What are you doing here?" She wanted to cover herself with her hands, so exposed and naked did she feel in his presence.

"My friend Russ LeBlanc called me a couple of hours ago and asked me to come in his place."

"Why? So you can exert your charm over me and convince me to give this up?" Fury shrouded her like smoke, hot and suffocating. She should have known better than to trust any lawyer in this city.

An upside-down Y formed between Forbes's well-groomed brows. "What are you talking about? Russ called me because his wife went into early labor and he knew I was looking for a pro bono case to take on. So he asked me to come."

"I don't believe you." She planted her fists on her hips and fought boiling hot tears pressing the corners of her eyes. She would *not* give him the satisfaction of breaking down in front of him.

Forbes glanced around, then returned his steel blue gaze to her. "Obviously there's some miscommunication going on here. Why don't we sit down, have lunch, and talk about your case?"

"Why would I want to talk to you about it?" She wished she'd sounded more authoritative and less like a howler monkey.

Forbes puffed up slightly. "Because I'm one of the top lawyers in this state, and I rarely lose. So no matter what your case is about, I can probably get you a desirable outcome."

Cold suspicion doused the heat of her anger. "You're going to stand there and act like you don't even know what this is about?"

He held both hands up, palms out. "All I know is that my friend called and asked a favor of me."

Could he be serious? Could he really not know why he was here? The chances were astronomical that of all substitute lawyers Russell LeBlanc could call, it would be the son of the people she wanted to sue. She dropped into her chair and frowned at Forbes as he lowered himself into the seat opposite her. She'd worry about giving herself frown lines later. Right now, she wanted to be sure he understood just how displeased his presence made her.

Forbes took a deep breath and gave her a look she could only describe as lawyerly. "Since we're both here, why don't you tell me what your case is regarding, and we'll see what we can do about it."

"You think you're always going to get what you want, don't you?" Alaine crossed her arms and continued to glare at him.

"When it comes to you? No." He high-beamed a smile at her.

She had to look away, perturbed at the way his smile got to her every single time. Only now it reminded her of the way her skin had tingled at the touch of his hand to her back, of her hand clasped in his, of the light tang of his cologne when they'd danced Monday evening.

She steeled her will and looked at him again. The flirtatious expression faded from his eyes.

"Look, I can tell something is wrong, and apparently you need legal help with it. I promise you: Anything you tell me is strictly confidential, and there will be no personal bias in any advice or legal aid I render to you."

She tapped her front teeth together. No personal bias, huh? She'd just see about that.

CHAPTER 13

*O*kay. But I'm holding you to your promise: No personal bias on your part."

Curiosity bubbled in Forbes's chest, but he kept his posture relaxed, his face neutral. "I wouldn't have said it if I hadn't meant it." What kind of trouble could she possibly be in that would elicit this kind of anger—toward him? "So what can I help you with?"

"Let's order first." She nodded over his shoulder, and he turned to see the middle-aged woman who'd pointed him to Alaine's table.

He grabbed up the cheap, plastic-covered menu. "I've never had Greek food before." He flashed a smile at the hostess. "What do you recommend?"

"For a white boy like you, I'd start you off with *spanakopita* or *pastitsio*."

"I'll take the first one you said." He handed her the menu.

"I'll have *horiatiki salata* and *tiropeta*, and I'll finish with baklava."

For someone who'd eaten like a bird at the bachelors' banquet, that sounded like an awful lot of food.

"I'll be back with more iced tea." The woman bustled off.

"So, do you come here often?"

Alaine quirked her head to the side, as if confused by his subject-changing tactic. "All the time. Ms. Voula and my mother are good friends." Her expression closed again at the words *my mother*.

Forbes cringed inwardly. So. . .his suspicions had been on the right track. This did have something to do with Delacroix Gardens. "Your parents are here in Bonneterre?"

"They're *here* in the Mills. Didn't you know that? I know you've seen their business—Delacroix Gardens Florist and Nursery."

Yep. He was right. No wonder she'd been rebuffing him since they'd met.

"Or you've at least heard of Delacroix Rentals—your cousin Anne does a lot of business with my brother Joe. Your sister used to, but for some reason that's petered off in recent months. No need to wonder why." The acidity in her tone could burn through steel.

He rocked back, shocked. "Wait—I thought you and Meredith were friends."

"*Were* being the operative word. How can I be friends with someone when her parents—whom she works for—are trying to run my family out of their businesses and homes?"

And by extension, how could she go out on a date with the son of said parents? Her complete one-eighty attitude change since the night of the dinner now made sense. "You think my parents' company is trying to put your parents out of business?"

She pressed her lips together, raised her eyebrows, and nodded. "And you only needed one guess."

Once realization began to dawn, it burst immediately into fullness. "You mean this—you were going to be meeting with Russ to talk to him about. . .what? Suing my parents?"

She shrugged as if going around suing people's parents was something she did every day. "Their company, anyway."

"For buying up foreclosed properties and revitalizing the area?" He couldn't keep the shock out of his voice.

She snorted. "If that's all they were doing—on properties that were *legally* foreclosed upon—then there wouldn't be a problem. But there's more than that going on. A lot more. As in, they've gotten another company that calls itself an 'investment firm' to come in, buy up loans from local banks, and call them in—and then when the mortgage holders can't pay ten or twenty years' worth of their mortgage in one lump sum, they receive foreclosure notices. Or even when the original bank had worked something out with the mortgage holder so they could get caught up with their payments when business picked up, those loans have been bought out and are now being foreclosed on. It's not right, and I'm going to see that it's stopped before a lot of good people end up losing everything they've worked their whole lives for."

Forbes tried to process what she was saying. He was pretty sure he got it, but emotion had sped her words to the point where they nearly ran together. "So you're saying that what you've seen is something you consider to be unfair or unethical business practices on the part of an investment firm that has come in and bought up the mortgages of property owners in Moreaux Mills." He pulled his Waterford pen out of his inside jacket pocket, flipped open his leather portfolio, and started taking notes.

"Not just any investment firm. A company called Mackenzie and Son. I just discovered the name today so I haven't had time to do any research; however, I think I'll find that once I start digging into their past business dealings, I'm going to learn that they do this all over the country."

A cold dread settled in Forbes's stomach. "Do what?"

Alaine flapped her hands in an irritated manner. "Swoop in when a developer is trying to force a few people out of an area the developer wants to tear down and rebuild as something else. Force them out by shady business deals and questionable accounting and making them feel like there's nothing else they can do but accept a price for their property that's not only much lower than the property's really worth, but definitely not enough for those people to be able to start over somewhere else."

The way her eyes flashed with passion for her topic mesmerized Forbes to the point where he almost forgot what she was talking about. He looked down at the legal pad. The last line he'd written

A CASE FOR LOVE

was a scrawl of gibberish. He angled it toward him against the edge of the table so she couldn't see it.

"It's my understanding that the city council decided on fair market value for the homes and businesses in the Mills. Are you saying that they're now being offered a buyout package that's lower than the official assessments?"

She cocked her head again and looked at him as if a rosebush had just sprouted from his nose. "The city council. The *city council?* The city council voted on the property values. The city council that is chaired by Tess Folse—partner emeritus of Folse, Maier, Landreneau, and Guidry, Attorneys at Law. The law firm that—oh, let me think— boasts as its most lucrative client Boudreaux-Guidry Enterprises, the same company that wants to buy up all of the property in Moreaux Mills dirt cheap, plow it under, and then build a planned condo community that they can turn around and sell for fifty times what they originally paid for the property. That city council? No conflict of interest there."

Forbes shifted in his seat and couldn't look up from the legal pad. That was the way development companies worked. Buy low; tear down; rebuild; sell high. But the way Alaine described it shed a new, somewhat seedy light on the whole process. And it tainted Forbes by association—with not just his parents' corporation but the law firm as well.

No wonder she hated him. But Mom and Dad wouldn't be involved in something so underhanded. They loved Bonneterre and all its diverse and unique neighborhoods. And they were huge supporters of local enterprise.

This had to be coming from Mackenzie and Son. Evelyn's voice rang in his head. *Out with the old and dilapidated, in with the new and luxurious.*

He took a deep breath and looked up, letting the air out in a controlled stream. "Alaine, I promise you that if there is something like this going on, my parents don't know anything about it. They're the most ethical people I know."

KAYE DACUS

A slight raise of her brows and flattening of her mouth indicated her disbelief.

Before he could say more, the restaurant owner returned with their food. She set a Greek salad and something that looked like cheese melted between layers of pastry before Alaine, and something similar to her second dish in front of Forbes—except it also had green stuff between the layers of pastry.

"What is this?" He tried to keep his voice light.

"Spanakopita—phyllo layered with feta, spinach, and herbs."

Should have asked before he ordered. He hated spinach. On principle. Anything that got slimy and stringy when exposed to hot water wasn't worth eating. But he couldn't very well send it back now. "Oh. Okay. Thanks."

Across the table, Alaine ate the olives from her salad first, not raising her gaze from her food. Forbes cut off a small corner of one of the three triangular pieces of spanikopita and lifted it to his mouth, trying not to breathe in through his nose as he did so.

The flaky, buttery phyllo pastry melted on his tongue. The creamy saltiness of the cheese coated his mouth, and the spinach. . . what spinach? Mixed with whatever herbs were in it, the spinach was unobtrusive. He'd have to get Major to come out here and tell him exactly what was in it—and see if he could re-create it.

He followed Alaine's lead and didn't speak while they ate. He tried to pace himself so he didn't finish before she did—and just as he scraped up the last few crumbs and drippings of green-flecked cheese, the woman Alaine had referred to as Ms. Voula reappeared with a plate of baklava—with two forks. Alaine pushed her half-finished salad and cheese pastry aside and picked up one of the forks from the dessert plate. She used it to wave at the other.

"Have one." She cut into one of the sticky-looking pastries.

He'd always heard of this dish but had never tried it. "What's in it?"

"Um. . ." Alaine lifted the top layer of phyllo. "Walnuts, cinnamon, sugar, probably other spices. Oh, and honey over the top."

That, he could do. He cut into the small square on his side of the plate. The warm, spicy, sweet smell of it made his mouth water. And when he bit into it. . .

Baklava was his new favorite dessert—even if it did make his teeth hurt from the combination of honey on the outside and sugar on the inside. Even though the piece was small, he couldn't finish the whole thing, already feeling like he'd need to add a few hours' running tomorrow just to work off his entrée.

He waited until Alaine put her fork down and ordered coffee before broaching the subject of this meeting again—and prayed her anger had abated. "I know it's going to be hard for you to believe me, because in your mind I'm part of the problem, but I want to help you find a solution. I'm certain that with a little digging and possibly bringing together the information from all parties involved, we can discover where the breakdown in communication has happened and get it straightened out." He rested his hands flat on the table. "I'd like to take your case."

She shook her head. "I don't want you as our lawyer. No one would ever trust that you're truly working for us and not to get the best outcome for your parents' company."

⋘⋙

Alaine wished she could recall the words as soon as they left her mouth. She couldn't remember everything she'd said to him in the past forty-five minutes, but that last one had been uncalled for—and intentionally hurtful.

And he'd obviously never had someone tell him to his face that he was untrustworthy. Though he'd worn an emotionless mask since she'd started berating him for something he might not have any part in, his too-handsome-for-her-peace-of-mind face now expressed betrayal, disbelief, and a profound pain.

"I'm sorry. What I mean to say is that we need to find a lawyer who doesn't have a personal vested interest in the opposing side of the issue. Who isn't going to be torn or influenced by emotional—and

141

familial—involvement with the defendants. From my preliminary conversations with a few business owners, we're ready to take this all the way—a big, public court case, which, even if we lose, could cause irreparable damage to Boudreaux-Guidry Enterprises' reputation in Bonneterre."

Forbes nodded, stared at the flower in the center of the table for a few seconds, then raised guarded, gray blue eyes to hers once more. "You keep saying *we*, but I know for a fact you don't live in the district. And you don't work here, either. So other than being related to people who are affected by this, what's your involvement in it?"

"My involvement?" She tried not to let him see how his question flustered her.

"Yes. Plaintiffs in a case like this need to be those who are directly affected by the wrongs they're accusing the defendant of. I understand that as a reporter, you have an interest in the public side of it—in arguing the case in the court of public opinion. But do you truly have a stake in the case, or are you just the public face of it to bring more attention and quicker action?"

Her conversation with her parents replayed in her head. She'd made a promise. "No, I'm not the 'public face,' as you put it. I'm the... liaison. Think of me as the agent for the actual plaintiffs. I'll get all the pertinent information, and then I'll gather everyone together and share it with them." She nodded for emphasis.

His right brow quirked slightly. "You realize that if this does go to court, I—your lawyer will take over that role? Are you going to be okay with turning everything over to me—him?"

"Or her. Yes, if I feel that person is trustworthy and isn't out to appease his parents." She clamped her lips shut. She was behaving just like Meg Ryan in *You've Got Mail*—unable to stop herself from piling up the hurtful remarks.

Of course, Meg Ryan and Tom Hanks ended up together at the end of that movie.

No. She couldn't think that way—not about Forbes Guidry, no matter how handsome he was and how her insides melted like a chocolate bar left in the car in August whenever she was around him.

"Have you spoken with any other lawyers about this case?" Forbes reached for his leather portfolio and pen.

She thought about the list in her steno pad of all the crossed-out lawyer names. "I tried."

"What did they have to say about it?"

She might as well give him the truth. "As soon as I mentioned Boudreaux-Guidry Enterprises, they pretty much hung up on me."

"So Russ LeBlanc was your last hope?"

Chewing the inside of her bottom lip, she nodded. "Yes, but I hadn't told him whom the case was against." She regarded Forbes for a long moment. Not a single dark hair out of place. Thick, perfectly groomed eyebrows. Long, dark lashes framing eyes that sometimes looked blue and sometimes dark gray. And no reason to distrust him other than the fact he was one of the best-looking men she'd ever encountered. "Do you really think you'd be able to be objective about this?"

Forbes pushed his plate aside and folded his hands atop his pad on the table. "I have to be honest and say that I don't believe my parents are involved in any wrongdoing. But you've definitely raised some questions about the legalities of things that are going on in the Mills. If you can trust me enough to act on your—well, the plaintiffs'—behalf, then I can promise you that any legal advice I give will be as objective as I possibly can be. Though you may have a hard time believing it, I hold personal and professional integrity at the highest level—not just for me, but for everyone I work with as well as every member of my family. If I discover anything that isn't completely aboveboard, I'll do whatever it takes to make it right."

She wanted to believe him—whether it was because she was attracted to him or not was something she'd deal with at another time. This was just one of those step-out-on-faith moments the pastor always talked about, she supposed.

"Okay. Fine. If you can do this for us, I'll set up a time for you to come meet with everyone who's interested in participating in the case." She bit her bottom lip and swallowed hard. Of course, now she had to rely on her family and their neighbors taking Forbes *and* her at their word that he was on their side.

His forehead relaxed and his perfect teeth showed, even though he wasn't actually smiling. "Great. That's all I ask for—to be given a chance."

"The others might not be as understanding as I am about your involvement."

The booming laugh he emitted wasn't the reaction she expected. "If this is an example of your being understanding, I definitely have my work cut out for me, don't I?"

A sharp retort tripped out to the end of her tongue but stopped when his laughter made her realize the idiocy of her statement. She let out a chuckle and rolled her eyes. "Okay, so I haven't been all that understanding. And I apologize for saying anything that might have been out of line. But just know you'll be facing that from a lot of folks once they find out who you are."

"I'll be prepared; don't worry." He cocked his head to the side and gazed at her with hooded eyes. "I convinced you, didn't I?"

She ran her tongue over her teeth to try to hide the fact that she wanted to devolve into a thirteen-year-old schoolgirl when he looked at her like that. "Only because I know how difficult it will be to find another lawyer who'll take our case."

Her phone beeped with an incoming text message, interrupting Forbes, who'd taken a breath to make a reply. She looked down at it—shocked to see that nearly an hour and a half had passed. "It's the studio."

"I've got to get back to work as well." He picked up his portfolio and slid his pen into his inside coat pocket. "I'll call you later to discuss the meeting with the clients—and we need to set up a time to review all the preliminary research you've done. I'll need your notes to see what you've discovered so far and what avenues you haven't yet explored."

"Okay. . .but I should tell you, I did promise my parents that

I would keep this out of the public eye as much as I can. It'll get suspicious if I start coming to your office." She stuffed her steno pad and pen into her briefcase, then stood and slung the strap over her shoulder.

Forbes rose and motioned her to exit ahead of him. "We already have the perfect cover for getting together at least once a week."

She stopped and turned, and found herself tilting her head far back to look up into those mesmerizing eyes. "We do?"

"We do. That is, if you'll agree to be my partner for ballroom dancing lessons for the next six weeks."

She wasn't sure if he leaned closer to her or if she leaned closer to him. . .but she jerked herself out of the trance and took a step back.

"Dance lessons? You want me to be your partner for dance lessons?" The soles of her feet tingled with the memory of sliding across the parquet floor at Arcenault's. Not to mention the heady feeling from breathing in Forbes's spicy cologne from such a close proximity—like now.

He shrugged. "My sister Jennifer talked me into doing it with her, but now she's had to back out because of. . .personnel issues at her restaurant. I had a good time dancing with you Monday night. And if I'm not mistaken, you were having a pretty good time yourself. You're a good dancer already—I need someone who's better than me to help me figure it out."

Alaine crossed her arms to protect herself from the barrage of charm Forbes lobbed her way. "I insist on paying for my portion of the package."

"Okay."

"And I'm only agreeing to this because, as you said, it gives us a good excuse to see each other regularly to discuss the case."

"Right."

She turned and started for the door again, then stopped and turned so fast, Forbes nearly ran into her. She poked her finger into his chest—his solid, muscular chest. She tingled. "And if anyone asks, we are *not* dating."

"If you insist."

She did insist. Why, she wasn't certain. But for her own sanity, that was the way it had to be.

CHAPTER 14

$\mathcal{F}$orbes slammed on the brakes to keep from running a red light. He wanted to believe Alaine, but all his instincts screamed she was wrong—or at least misled.

The one thing he knew beyond a doubt: His parents would never do something like that. When they'd taken over Grandfather Boudreaux's commercial real-estate venture thirty-odd years ago, they'd not only championed small businesses, they'd started the Bonneterre Small Business Owners' Association. Eventually, they'd had to leave it based on the guidelines they themselves had written. But they still supported it by donating the office space in Boudreaux Tower as well as conference-room space in the building for the association's monthly meetings. The president of the BSBOA came to Dad's prayer breakfast every week, for crying out loud.

Except. . .Forbes wracked his brain. Come to think of it, the guy hadn't been there for the past few months. But people came and went, turning up some weeks and then not being seen for a few months, then showing up again as if they'd never been gone.

At the next light, he pulled out his phone and called his sister.

"Facilities and Events, this is Meredith." She sounded harried.

"Mere, it's Forbes. You got a minute?"

"Just. What's up?"

"I'm wondering—why did you stop using Delacroix Rentals as a supplier?"

She paused a long time. "Where'd you hear that?"

"Oh. . .I had lunch today with an acquaintance who knows the owners and mentioned they hadn't gotten a lot of business from you recently."

"Really? I hadn't noticed. These things go in cycles, you know. Sometimes a supplier will have what we need, and sometimes we'll have a spate of events that we use other suppliers for. Why the sudden interest in the running of B-G? Doesn't that give you hives or something?"

"Just curious, I guess."

"Well, Mr. Suddenly Curious, I just had eight people walk into my office for a meeting I'm supposed to be leading, so I hope I sufficiently answered your question."

"Yeah. Thanks." He bade her farewell and hung up.

He'd deal with his family members after he looked into whether or not there was any breach of ethics or actual lawbreaking going on—by Boudreaux-Guidry or by Mackenzie and Son.

He groaned when he walked into his office and saw the stack of files in his in-box. Samantha followed him in, reciting a list of things she needed from him before she had to leave—"And I can only stay until five thirty tonight. I have class at six, and we're having a test tonight, so I can't skip. And you can't stay much later than that, because you asked me to remind you that you have a committee meeting at church tonight at six thirty."

He rubbed his neck, trying to stop the tightness from forming into a knot at the base of his skull. "I'll do my best."

He dived into the work, forcing himself to keep on task, not allowing himself to turn to the computer to search though B-G's files to see what they'd been up to, legally speaking, in the last six or eight months. He was down to the last file when Samantha reentered his office at 5:25.

"Well?" She leaned against the doorframe and crossed her arms.

"I still need about twenty minutes on this one."

She closed her eyes and appeared to wilt before his eyes.

"You go on to class. I'll make the necessary copies and put everything on your desk before I leave. Where's your logbook?"

She giggled. "It's all on the computer now, boss. But don't worry about it. I still have to number them, so I'll input them into the log tomorrow morning before I hand the copies over to the courier service for delivery."

"Thanks. Now go on, get out of here. Don't want you to miss your test."

She gave him a jaunty wave and disappeared.

Though most of the associates, interns, clerks, and assistants were still hard at work, the silence in Forbes's office grew oppressive soon after Samantha's departure. Not even the '80s music playing softly through his computer from the Internet radio station helped.

At 6:15, he laid the copies of the last file on Samantha's desk and returned to his office. He glared at the clock. He wanted to stay here and delve into his parents' company's files to start answering some of his questions. But he'd already asked the nominating committee to reschedule twice. He couldn't ask them to do it again—especially not at the last minute.

Frustrated, he turned off the lights and locked the office door behind him. Peeking into files that he hadn't had any part in by choice would have to wait until tomorrow.

An accident left traffic snarled getting out of downtown on North Street, turning a ten-minute drive into twenty-five and making Forbes late for his meeting. The other six members of the committee showed a mixture of relief and annoyance when he sailed into the room.

"Sorry I'm late. Traffic." He flung his suit coat over the back of the only empty chair at the table and rolled up his shirt sleeves before digging the legal pad out of the expanding folder marked *Personnel Committee*.

He closed his eyes and sent up a quick prayer for calmness.

"Why don't y'all go ahead and get started on…workers for Extended Session. I've got to run back out to the car and get the correct file."

The committee secretary launched into the list of names she'd compiled before he got to the door. Of course, she'd never seemed to understand why everyone else on the committee had elected him chairperson over her. Today, he could clearly see it from her point of view. He had to pull himself together and regain control over his thoughts and actions.

He swapped the personnel committee file for the thicker nominating committee file from the brown file box in the trunk of the car and returned to the small Sunday school classroom—just in time to see Jean rise from her seat and lean over the table.

"Just because people aren't married doesn't mean that they're disposable."

"That isn't what I said, Jean, and you know it. You're too sensitive about it. What I said is that we shouldn't require parents to work in the nursery just because they're parents. It's discrimination."

"Discrimination? To ask people who're creating the work to do the work? Why should single people be required to work in the nursery when they don't have kids?"

"But parents come and put their kids in the nursery so they can attend services. The least those without kids can do is to work in the nursery to afford them that opportunity."

"So people without kids don't come so *they* can attend services?"

"Whoa, hold on a minute." Forbes placed his hand on Jean's shoulder and, with firm but gentle pressure, guided her back into her chair. He set his folder on the table, then settled one hand on his waist, using the other to rub his forehead. "We've discussed this before. We can't require *anyone* to work in the nursery. They have to volunteer, and they have to be approved by the Children's Department director. Now, if we can talk about this calmly?" He looked pointedly at Jean and her adversary. Both nodded. "Good."

Forbes sat and led the discussion into safer paths. He finally ended up assigning Jean and another committee member to approach

A CASE FOR LOVE

the people on their newly formulated list to ask them about working in the nursery.

Sunday school teacher appointments were easier to agree upon—usually because there was only one volunteer for each slot, and almost always it was the person who already taught that class. When they got through the list, he looked at his watch and, to his profound relief, discovered they'd only run a few minutes over their hour. "That'll be all for this week. I'll present these names"—he tapped his legal pad—"at next week's business meeting. Frank, will you close us in prayer?"

Jean's adversary nodded, and said a quick, perfunctory prayer. Forbes's mind whirled. Alaine. His parents. Meredith. Nominating committee. Evelyn Mackenzie. Work. Personnel committee. His younger siblings who still needed their big brother. Board of trustees...

The knot at the base of his skull grew worse. Great. Now all this stress was going to add getting back in to see the chiropractor to his growing to-do list.

After chatting with a few of the committee members, he stepped out of the classroom into the flow of people coming out of the choir room down the hall. He could go back to the office and spend a few hours looking through B-G's case files—

"Hey, Forbes!"

He turned and searched the crowd for the owner of the booming voice.

Almost head and shoulders above everyone else, the Polynesian man raised his hand to motion Forbes toward him. Forbes excused his way past the dozen or so people still lingering in the foyer.

"Hey, Clay. What's up?"

Clay Huntoon gave him a quizzical look. "Uh. . .rehearsal. Did you forget?"

Quartet rehearsal. They were singing Sunday and hadn't practiced in more than a month. "I just need to go put this out in the car and get my music."

"Oh. Okay. I'll tell the guys."

The heat of the day hadn't dissipated at all, and the humidity

151

seemed to condense on Forbes's skin as soon as he stepped out of the over-air-conditioned building. He returned the committee file to the box in the trunk and pulled his music folder out.

As he slammed the trunk, his phone beeped a new text message. He pulled out the PDA and turned it sideways to read the new message:

> 3 GRLS 1 BOY
> CARRIE DOING GR8
> RUSS

Forbes tapped back a congratulatory message, though he didn't necessarily feel the happiness for his friend he would have if this had happened twenty-four hours later. Forbes glanced up at the still-bright evening sky.

"God, you have a sick sense of timing."

If Carrie LeBlanc had waited one more day to go into labor, Russ would have been the one to meet with Alaine, and Forbes would still be blissfully unaware she had any grievance against his parents' company. And he wouldn't be stressing over it.

Before walking into the choir room, he took a deep breath and composed himself very much the same way he did before walking into a courtroom. He needed to get through the next hour or so, and then he could go home and start putting things into perspective by making a list of actionable items to follow up on.

He strode through the door, trying to give the best appearance of someone with no concerns in the world. Major stood beside the piano, warming up the top of his range while George played scales. Clay paced the opposite end of the large chamber talking on the phone—a sports reporter's work was never finished.

And Anne and Meredith sat in the front row, talking. They looked up when he approached.

"Hey, Forbes. . .you look tired." Meredith's forehead crinkled with her expression of concern. "Are you feeling okay?"

He waved his hand in a dismissive gesture. "Just have a lot on my mind."

His sister's eyes narrowed slightly; then she shrugged. "If there's anything I can do. . ."

A list of questions scrolled through his mind. But now wasn't the right time. "I'll let you know." He walked over to the piano. "So what are we singing Sunday?"

"We were thinking about the a cappella version of 'God of Our Fathers.'" George flipped through several pieces of music on the music rack in front of him. "We know it best."

"And Sunday is Father's Day," Major added.

"Sounds good to me." Forbes flipped through his folder and pulled out the sheet music George and Clay had arranged and written down for them. The main thing he loved about singing second tenor, even though it strained his voice, was that he usually had the melody—as he did in this piece.

George wasn't the best pianist in the world—he admitted it himself—but he could at least play the four parts along with them as they practiced, which none of the rest of them could do. Forbes observed the other three men as they sang, each concentrating hard on learning his part so they could sing it without accompaniment.

He needed someone to talk to, someone he could vent his frustrations to, someone who wasn't involved in family business. With George and Major both married into the family, that excused them from the role of confidante. And while he liked Clay and considered him a friend, Clay was one of the guys Jenn dated regularly—that and Forbes didn't feel comfortable bringing someone he knew as casually as Clay into such extreme confidence.

Anne and Meredith—and everyone else in the family—he excluded for obvious reasons. He needed an outsider, someone who could be objective but also keep everything he said in confidence.

His voice broke on a high note when the reality hit him. He didn't have friends outside of his family circle. He steadied his voice and resisted taking a look at Meredith over his shoulder. Was this

153

the realization she'd come to that had led her to start distancing herself from the family over the past few months?

After they practiced enough so that they could sing the piece all the way through a few times without accompaniment and stay on key, they called it a night.

"We're going to grab dinner," Meredith said to Forbes, joining her husband at the piano. "Want to go with us?"

His stomach had been rumbling the past half hour. "No. I think I'll pick something up on my way home. I've still got some work to do before I can turn in tonight." He edged toward the door and his escape.

"Okay. We'll see you tomorrow night, then."

"I'll try to make it, but I'll let you know if I won't be there." In the few years he and Anne and Meredith and the rest of their siblings and cousins around their ages had been meeting for dinner on Thursday nights at Jenn's restaurant, he'd only missed attending a couple of times.

He slipped out the door as they started to discuss where they were going to eat. In the car, he turned off the radio and let the silence enfold him. He wanted to pray. . .yet he couldn't find the energy or focus to do so.

At the town house, while waiting for the garage door to open, movement next door caught his eye. Shon stepped out of his front door and acknowledged Forbes with a lifting of his chin.

Shon. The weight that had pressed down on Forbes's shoulders all afternoon suddenly lightened. If anyone could keep his confidence, it would be his next-door neighbor.

He stepped out of the garage and met Shon at the bottom of his neighbor's front steps.

"'Sup, man? We running in the morning?" Shon returned Forbes's handshake.

"Yes. Definitely."

"Good. I've got a couple of prospects for you."

"Prospects?"

"For dates. Remember? Your ninety-day membership."

"Right. I'll make you a deal."

"Huh-uh." Shon shook his head. "You already made me one deal on this."

"But I really need this favor."

Shon crossed his arms and leaned against the banister. "Let's have it."

"I'll go out with anyone you want to set me up with, sight unseen, if you'll let me use you as a sounding board for some stuff I have going on in my life right now."

"Dude, you know you can tell me anything." His grin flashed in the gathering twilight.

"This is big stuff, Shon. Stuff I can't talk to anyone else about because if it ever went public, it could create a lot of chaos for people I care a lot about."

Shon sobered. "You're serious. Whatever you need, man, I'm here for you. And you know me: Everything you tell me will be held in strictest confidence, no matter what. You know, that whole lawyer-client confidentiality thing."

Forbes laughed for the first time all day. "That only applies to me as your lawyer."

"Whatever. I promise to listen to what you have to say and not repeat it to anyone."

"Thanks. I appreciate it."

"No problem." Shon's grin reappeared.

"What?"

"I'm just thinking about all those ladies I'd like to introduce you to."

Forbes groaned.

CHAPTER 15

$\mathcal{A}$laine refilled the two glasses of iced tea and handed the second glass to her co-worker. "I'm really glad you could come over for dinner tonight."

Bekka Blakeley accepted the glass and followed Alaine from the dining table into the living room. "I'm glad you asked. One of my grandfather's horses is foaling tonight, so Andrew's probably going to be out there all night."

"After working all day?"

"He loves it. He worked full-time for my grandfather for a few years—started just before we got married. But then when Grandpa decided to go into semiretirement, stop breeding, and sell off most of the stock, Andrew went back to the animal hospital. I don't know if he misses working with Grandpa every day or being a full-time equine vet more."

"Is that how you met? Because he worked for your grandfather?" Alaine curled up in the opposite corner of the sofa from the newscaster.

"No. He was still at the hospital when we met. I had an emergency with my horse, and he came out to take care of it for me."

"And it was love at first sight, I'll bet." Alaine teased.

A wry smile spread over Bekka's face. "No. Actually, we didn't start off well. He asked to speak to one of my parents."

Considering it had been more than ten years ago and Bekka could still pass for a teenager when she had on no makeup and was dressed in jeans and a T-shirt—like now—Alaine could understand Andrew's mistake.

"I was dating someone else at the time. You're a bit younger than me, so you may not remember when I was in the news instead of just reporting it. Tim, the man I'd been seeing, had been arrested, and some accusations were made regarding me and whether or not I'd bribed someone to get him out of jail. It was right after I'd gotten the weekend sports anchor position."

"Oh, yeah—he went on Channel Three, on Teri Jones's show, and tried to discredit you, and then she brought out a surprise guest who ended up discrediting him. We watched all of that as it happened in one of my J-school classes. I'd forgotten it was you."

"I haven't."

"So it was after all that when you and Andrew started dating?" Alaine swirled her glass to mix the melting ice into the tea.

"We never really dated. We were always just together. I went to Iowa with him at New Year's to see his parents, whom he hadn't spoken to in years. We were really close after that, but it wasn't until he proposed to me Memorial Day weekend that I knew exactly how he felt about me." Bekka sipped her tea. "Why the questions about how I met my husband?"

Alaine shrugged.

"Have you met someone?"

She shrugged again. "I thought so. Then I found out who he is, and it'll never work."

"I can see this is eating you up. Spill it, girl."

Alaine didn't need a second invitation. It took nearly an hour for her to explain everything; and several times, she questioned the wisdom of telling another reporter all of the details of what could become a huge story, if not one of the biggest scandals in Bonneterre's history. But she trusted Bekka implicitly, especially after having just been reminded of the integrity with which Bekka'd handled her own public scandal years ago.

When Alaine finished speaking, Bekka just stared at her for a moment.

"Do you realize if Rodney knew you were involved in this, he'd flip his toupee?"

"He's already tried to pump me for information because he knows I have family connections in the Mills. Which is why you can't say anything to anyone about it. I promised my parents I'd keep quiet about it—that I wouldn't make a stink about it on my show, as I'd really like to." Though it felt good to have spoken everything aloud, anxiety started chewing at Alaine's insides over bringing an outsider into the situation.

"Don't worry. I'll keep it to myself. But what are you going to do if this does become a lawsuit? Once that happens, it's public knowledge, and Rodney is bound to find out you knew about it." Bekka slipped off her sneakers and tucked her feet up under herself.

"I'll just have to deal with that if and when it happens." Alaine couldn't meet her friend's eye. If Bekka didn't know Alaine was planning to film her own story and turn it in just before anything went public, Bekka wouldn't have to lie to protect her.

"What about this Forbes Guidry? Didn't he ask you out a couple of weeks ago?"

Heat flooded Alaine's cheeks. "He did. But that was right about the time I learned what was going on. Of course I said no. At that time, it was a major conflict of interest."

"At that time? But not now?"

"It doesn't matter. It would be a conflict of interest."

"But you like him?"

Alaine sighed and put her dripping glass of now watered-down tea on the table. "I do. But—"

"I know. 'It doesn't matter.' What are you going to do?"

"About?"

"About trying to make the fact you're attracted to him not matter?"

"I signed up for a membership to Let's Do Coffee. Shon Murphy is even now supposed to be finding matches to set me up on dates with."

"You know, I have a cousin your age who isn't married." Bekka's brown eyes twinkled.

Alaine made a cross with her forefingers as if warding off a vampire. "If I had a dollar for every time someone told me they have an unmarried relative." She giggled. "Is he cute?"

"I think so. I'm sure you've heard of him: Clark d'Arcement."

Alaine sat up straighter. "Clark. . .one of the twins who made a couple million dollars when they were in college because of that Web site they started and then sold?"

Bekka nodded. "Yep. They're partners in a Web site designing company now. I could give him your number. I know he knows who you are."

Alaine chewed the inside of her bottom lip. Was cuteness and wealth a good enough reason to go out with someone? Oh, heck yeah. "Okay. But you can't tell him it's my idea."

"Of course not. Because no man's ego needs the boost it gets from knowing a beautiful woman is interested in him."

Very true. Alaine led the conversation into more casual, less personal topics, but Bekka's statement kept whirring in her mind, bringing the vision of Forbes at the bachelors' banquet to mind. No, his ego hadn't needed the boost it had gotten from the interest she'd unwillingly shown. And no matter how much she protested that her attraction to him didn't matter, she couldn't help but tingle with the anticipation of dancing with him again Monday night.

❧

"Um, boss?"

Forbes looked up from the paperwork in front of him. "Yes, Samantha?"

"That e-mail you sent with the list of files you want copied. . .you know those are in the partners-only file room?" His secretary twisted

159

her long necklace around her fingers.

"Oh, right." He opened his top drawer and pulled out a key, which he held toward her. "Here. That should get you in."

She crossed the office but hesitated before taking the key. "If someone else asks me why I'm pulling the files, what case should I tell them it's for?"

Forbes's insides squirmed. "It's background research for a real-estate development case I'm looking at taking. I need to see if there's any precedent in any of those files that can help me decide if the case if viable or not."

Samantha's anxious posture eased. "Oh. Okay. I just wasn't sure what to say if Mary—I mean, if someone decides I'm not supposed to be up there."

He tried to give her a reassuring smile. "If she—someone happens to ask you what you're doing in the partners-only file room, you can simply remind her that I'm a partner and tell her I asked you to copy some files for me. She doesn't need to know anything beyond that."

His voice oozed confidence but guilt burned through his stomach. While he had every right to access the room containing files of clients handled by the partners—because he *was* a partner, as he'd just reminded his secretary—pulling B-G's files to see what kind of information he could find about their legal dealings with acquiring the property in the Warehouse District and Moreaux Mills wasn't necessarily on the up-and-up. He could go through proper channels and request them through the court system, but that could take weeks, if not months.

He had to know now. And he couldn't tell much from the briefs he found in the electronic files on the server. He needed to read the transcripts, to see the paperwork, to find out exactly what kinds of legal action they'd been pursuing to gain those properties.

He rubbed the bridge of his nose and tried to concentrate on the Pichon file. . .but it was no use. He reached for the large ceramic mug with the Delta Chi fraternity logo on it. Empty.

He moaned and made his way down the hall to the break room.

The extra-large coffee carafe was more than half-full, meaning it had only been made a few minutes ago, as it never lasted very long. He poured the mug three-quarters full, topped it off with skim milk, and sweetened it with two packs of artificial sweetener.

"Oh, good morning, Mr. Guidry." One of the paralegals came in bearing a pink mug with PRINCESS in purple scripty letters across the front.

"Good morning, Geoff. Nice cup."

"Thanks. My daughter's. Only clean one in the house this morning. And if I forget to take it home by tomorrow, I'll never hear the end of it—this is my weekend to have the kids."

Forbes clamped his teeth together to keep from asking when Geoff had gotten a divorce. He needed to get out of his office more often and mingle with his co-workers. He didn't want to be one of those kinds of partners who knew nothing about the people in the ranks who worked longer and harder hours trying to gain what Forbes had already accomplished.

"How old are they now?" He leaned against the counter and unbuttoned his coat.

"Twelve, nine, and five. What about you? You got kids?" Geoff poured his coffee to the rim of his mug and took a slurp before turning to the granite-topped cabinet to doctor it with powdered creamer.

"No. I'm not married."

Geoff chuckled. "Yeah, knew that from the whole Bachelor of the Year thing. But marriage isn't required for someone to have kids."

"For me, it is."

"Nice to hear someone still has some old-fashioned values these days. I mean, my wife comes to me a year ago and tells me she wants us to have an 'open' marriage—because she's met someone else but doesn't want to go through the trouble of a divorce. And she gets majority custody of the kids because I was the one who asked for the divorce, so it looks like I'm in the wrong. Does that seem right to you?"

Okay. Maybe he really didn't need to spend more time with the staff.

"Just because I'd mentioned wanting to go back to school to work on my law degree and asked if she'd be able to make sure she had the kids the nights I had class. And when I had to work late. . ."

Forbes edged toward the door, trying to figure out a tactful way to extricate himself from the conversation.

The administrative coordinator's appearance gave him just the out he needed. "Good morning, Mr. Guidry. Geoff."

"Good morning, Cheryl. Well, I've got to get back to it." Forbes raised his hand in a farewell wave and made a hasty exit. Geoff resumed complaining about his ex-wife before Cheryl got two words out.

Forbes sank into his chair, grateful to have escaped without having to pass judgment on the outcome of the paralegal's divorce and custody. The guy was a few years younger than Forbes, and his life was already a mess.

He turned and stared out the window, across the parking lot to the slice of river he could see through the trees lining it. He'd abandoned the idea of dating years ago because no woman he'd dated had ever been satisfied with him. Had he chosen the wrong ones, or was he really not marriage material? While he'd never been as attracted to anyone he'd dated as he was to Alaine Delacroix, would it turn out the same way with her? Would she end up walking away from him either because she felt like he was too controlling or that he didn't take enough of an interest in her, as he'd been accused in the past?

He'd rather never marry than to go through the pain of a divorce, especially if there were children involved.

Is that what You're trying to teach me, Lord? That I'm not cut out to be married? That if I did, I'd end up like Geoff with my wife wanting out to be with someone else?

Shaking his head, he turned back to his desk and ran the dictating machine back to listen to where he'd left off. This motion had to be filed today, which meant he needed to be finished dictating it so

Samantha could type it before he went down to the courthouse after lunch.

He was almost finished when the phone rang. With Samantha still upstairs making the copies for him, he couldn't let it go unanswered.

"Forbes Guidry."

"Hey, it's Anne."

"Why are you calling me on my office phone?"

"Wasn't sure if you'd be in court or a meeting or something—you usually are. I figured I'd just leave you a message to call me when you had a minute."

"What's up?" He marked his place in his notes and leaned back, propping his right foot on the corner of his partially open bottom desk drawer.

"I just wanted to know if you're going to make it for supper tonight."

The knot started forming at the base of his skull again. "I hadn't gotten that far yet." Really, what he wanted to do was to take the copies of the files home and start reading through them. And maybe order a pizza or something. Or maybe even see if Shon wanted to grab dinner so they could talk—since their run had been rained out this morning. "Why? Is there something going on tonight I'm unaware of?"

"Well, I couldn't say anything in front of them last night, but George and I got to talking and figured that since Meredith and Major are going to put off having any kind of formal reception indefinitely—as in, Meredith has decided she doesn't want one but doesn't know how to break it to the family—we thought it would be fun to have a little informal reception for them tonight. Jenn is decorating the Shack's back room in a wedding theme, Aunt Maggie made a little wedding cake, and George and I are handling everything else."

Why hadn't he thought of that? Oh, yeah. Because he wasn't the professional wedding planner. "Who all's going to be there?"

"Just us—the regulars. If anyone else in the family wants to do something more formal for them, they can. We wanted to celebrate with them before it gets too far down the road and they start to feel like none of us cared enough to recognize their momentous occasion."

When she put it like that, how could he not go? "I'll be there. Are y'all going to be giving them your gifts tonight?"

"I think Jenn said something about a gift table, yeah."

"Okay. I'll have to run home and get mine on the way then."

"But we can count on your being there?"

"I'll be there. Just make sure there's plenty of room on that gift table. I have two boxes and they're somewhat large." For the first time in days, an emotion other than anxiety started stealing over him. Meredith would love the gifts he'd gotten her. At least she'd better, with all the trouble he'd gone through to find them.

"Going to show us all up, huh?"

"That's my goal in life." He grinned. If he couldn't be best man in their wedding, at least he could give them a gift that would make them feel guilty that he never got the chance.

"Okay. We'll see you tonight, then."

As soon as he got off the phone, Forbes finished his dictation and wrapped up a few other small projects he needed to clear off his desk before his meeting in judge's chambers with opposing counsel on his longest-running case. He was tempted to ask the clients if he could request to fast-track the case, just so they could get a court date set and end the barrage of motions and continuances from the other side. But with what his clients paid for Forbes's retainer, in addition to billable hours, the other partners wouldn't be happy if he tried to push for a hasty conclusion to the case just because he was tired of dealing with it.

Samantha returned just before he needed to leave, pushing a rolling cart stacked with hundreds of photocopies. His heart sank. He'd known he'd asked for a lot of information; he just hadn't realized how much it would be.

"Stack those on my conference table." He moved out of the way so she could push the cart in through his office door. "The Pichon motion is ready to be typed. Have a courier bring it to me at Judge Aucoin's office when it's ready, and I'll file it while I'm down there."

"Yes, boss."

"How'd your test go last night?"

"I think I aced it."

"What class is it?"

"Pharmacology."

Forbes shuddered and crossed to help her unload the copies from the cart. While he'd done well in the required math and science classes he'd had to take in college, the idea of purposely majoring in a science-based field gave him the heebie-jeebies. "Are you sure you want to leave all this and become a nurse?"

"Nurse practitioner. Big difference. Once I finish all of my schooling, I'll be able to see patients on my own and write prescriptions." She grunted as she heaved a stack of papers onto the table.

"But people throw up on nurses."

Samantha mumbled something under her breath.

"I didn't quite catch that." He covered the two remaining stacks of copies on the cart when she would have just kept moving them.

"I said, I'd rather have people throw up on me occasionally than to be making copies and taking dictation the rest of my life. No offense, Forbes, but this isn't the most intellectually challenging job in the world."

He leaned over the cart, rested his elbows on the papers, and propped his chin on his fist. "No offense taken. But why nursing? Why not become a lawyer or a literature professor or an artist? If you think working for a lawyer is a thankless job, wait until you work for a doctor." He waggled his eyebrows at her.

She laughed, as he'd hoped, and waved him off the cart. He stood and picked up the few remaining copies and stacked them on the table. His fingers itched to start flipping through them and see what lay in their murky depths, but it would have to wait. Again.

He followed her out of the office. "I won't be coming back

tonight, so go ahead and lock up my office when you leave. And once you finish the Pichon motion—and type up those couple of other things I put in your box, go ahead and leave. You can use the extra time to study all that nasty science stuff."

"Gee, thanks." She pushed the cart to the side of her desk and went back into his office for the dictating machine. "Aren't you supposed to be on your way to Judge Aucoin's right now?"

"Yeah. I am. If you need me—"

"I've got your number."

He had to return to his office twice—once for a secondary file he'd left behind, and the next time for his large, red and black University of Louisiana–Bonneterre umbrella. He made it to the courthouse with bare minutes to spare—but ran into opposing counsel in the line waiting to get through the metal detectors, so let his anxiety ease. They weren't sitting up there, waiting on him.

Two hours later, his expanding files stretched well beyond their original capacity with multiple new motions he would have to write responses to in the next week, Forbes left the judge's chambers. The secretary handed him a courier envelope. He thanked the woman and took the paperwork out of the envelope to look over while walking toward the court clerks' office. For as much as Samantha didn't want to be a lawyer's secretary the rest of her life, she was very good at it.

He filed the motion, stopped and chatted with a few colleagues on his way out, and finally left the courthouse with just enough time to go home and pick up the gifts. He pulled into the garage, leaving everything in the car, and jogged up the three flights of stairs to his bedroom. In the large, walk-in closet sat the boxes wrapped in silver paper and decorated with dark blue velvet ribbons—a rather impressive wrapping job, if he did say so himself.

He carried each one gingerly down the stairs. Not only were they heavy and somewhat bulky, if he broke anything, there were no returns.

Driving with them in the car made him nervous, and he drew nasty looks from fellow drivers in a hurry to get home from work as they whipped around him on Highway 77 when northbound traffic in the opposite lane eased enough that they could safely pass him.

Though he usually tried to park far away from the restaurant to keep anyone from parking too near his baby, tonight, he pulled into the closest space he could find. He leaned in to get the first box.

"Hey, there. Need a hand?"

He hit his head on the top of the doorframe in his surprise. Leaving the box, he stood and turned, rubbing the back of his head.

Evelyn Mackenzie would turn every head in the place tonight in her sleeveless black dress that accentuated every curve the woman had.

Wait. What was she doing here? "Hey, Evelyn. No, I've got it, thanks."

"Well, at least let me get the door for you, huh?"

"Sure." He carried the first box in. "Did Anne invite you?"

"No, Meredith did." Evelyn nodded at the box. "Someone's birthday?"

"We're celebrating Meredith and Major's wedding tonight."

"I wish I'd known. I'd have picked something up for them." Evelyn held open the glass-and-chrome door into the Fishin' Shack.

"Thanks. I just found out about it a couple of hours ago myself." He wound through the buzzing restaurant. He wasn't sure if heads were turning at the sight of the gift he carried or because of Evelyn, but both of them drew the attention of pretty much every customer.

"Hey, you made it early." Anne's eyes widened at the size of the gift in Forbes's arms. "Wow. You really are going to show us up."

He arched his brow at her. "There's another one just like this out in the car."

"Put it here." Anne pointed to a place on the long table covered with a dark blue tablecloth broken up by a silver runner down the middle.

"Anne, you remember Evelyn Mackenzie."

"Yes, of course. Meredith mentioned she'd invited you to come. I'm sorry I didn't know how to get in touch with you to forewarn you we're having a little wedding reception for them tonight."

"Oh, that's quite all right. I just hope I'm not intruding on family time."

"Not at all. We're thrilled to have you and glad we can include you in some of our family activities since you're so far from your own."

After a second trip—with Evelyn insisting she hold the door for him, which, for some reason, included walking back out to his car with him—Forbes collapsed into a chair at the large, round table in the semiprivate room, relieved he'd gotten the gifts here without incident. Transporting them safely back to Bonneterre was now up to Meredith and Major.

"Wow. Looks like the owner went all out for you guys."

He chuckled. "Given that the owner was supposed to be Meredith's maid of honor and just happens to be our sister, yes, she went all out."

Pink, blue, and brown streamers draped over everything stationary enough to hold it—from the fishing paraphernalia tacked to the walls to the pirogue hanging from the ceiling. The pink was Jenn's contribution to the color scheme—back when planning the wedding-that-wasn't, Meredith had insisted she only wanted to use her favorite color, brown, and Major's favorite color, blue, in the wedding decor.

"Is that lace on the cake?" Evelyn leaned over to look closer at what looked like airy, florally brown lace around the base of the three tiers of the white cake dripping with blue and white frosting flowers. "My word. I never knew someone could pipe icing that fine."

"Our aunt, my mother's sister, is a professional pastry chef. She's famous in Bonneterre for her cakes."

Forbes saw to introducing Evelyn to his younger siblings and cousins as they arrived, each expressing his or her displeasure over the size of Forbes's gifts in comparison to his or her own.

"Just remember," Anne said, arranging the gifts in an artful presentation, "it's not the size of the gift that matters, but the intention with which it's given." No one agreed with her.

When Meredith and Major arrived—having been purposely delayed by Mom, according to Anne—both exhibited genuine surprise. . .tempered by the claim that they'd suspected Anne would have planned something like this tonight.

Hearing all about their trip to Colorado took up most of the conversation over dinner. Anne made a production of having them cut the cake, just as if it were a real wedding reception—with George taking plenty of pictures.

"Gifts!" Jenn squeaked like a schoolgirl as soon as the cake was sliced and served. "Mine first."

Anne sat beside them and wrote down each gift and who'd given it. While his family members had given them nice things—mostly items for their house that they'd listed on their registry wish list, Forbes grew more and more confident that nothing anyone else gave them would compare with his gift. He leaned forward with eager anticipation when his two boxes were the only ones remaining to be opened.

"Wow, these are heavy."

Forbes stood to stop Jenn from picking the box up and potentially dropping it. "They'll probably need to open those over at the table instead of putting them on the floor."

Meredith and Major came over, as did Anne and George with the list and camera.

"Should we open them at the same time?" Meredith asked.

"You can."

She nodded at Major, and both started tearing away paper and ribbons. Forbes tried to keep the smug look from his face.

"Oh. . ." Meredith breathed. "Where did you find them? Oh, Forbes, they're beautiful!" She turned and threw her arms around his neck. It was the first hug she'd given him in a while. That reaction made all his trouble in finding the two arts-and-crafts era antique lamps worthwhile.

"You're welcome. I knew you wanted something like those for your living room but couldn't afford the real thing and didn't want to settle for cheap imitations."

She finally stepped away and wiped a couple of tears from her cheeks. "Are they really. . . ?" She returned to the box to examine them. "This one's a. . .Bradley and Hubbard."

"And this one's a Handel." Major carefully extracted the ivory, slag glass shade from the mounds of paper it had been packed in. "They're not identical, obviously, but they're as close as I could find. Both are supposed to be cast iron bases, and the scrollwork on the shades is brass."

"They're perfect, Forbes. You shouldn't have done something this extravagant, but I'm so glad you did." Meredith hugged him again. "I can't wait to get them home and plug them in."

He returned to the table to the good-natured jeers and ribbing of his relatives and indulged in a slice of Aunt Maggie's cake.

Evelyn pressed her shoulder into his and leaned her head close to his. "You're going to make some woman very happy some day, Forbes Guidry."

He hoped so. . .and that Alaine's tastes ran to lamps that were easier to find than these.

CHAPTER 16

$\mathcal{A}$laine stood at the rear of the sanctuary. Most of the people who came to this Saturday night service were young—and dressed to go out afterward. Would they leave here to go hit the bars and clubs in midtown, feeling as if they'd had their dose of church for the week so it was okay to go get plastered afterward?

Her sorority sisters had lived that way—and so had she, even for a few years after college. It was so much easier to maintain good church attendance when one could go *before* getting smashed instead of dealing with the hangover while trying to look properly worshipful on Sunday morning.

"Alaine? Alaine Delacroix, it is you."

She turned at the masculine voice. Her heart gave a little lurch at the sight of Shon Murphy. She could rack it up to his dark good looks, but in all honesty, running into him embarrassed her more than excited her. Seeing him reminded her of her current status as one of his company's clients. . .and the several e-mails from him she hadn't yet responded to.

"I didn't know you went to church here." *Wow. Great opener, girl.*

"This is my first time to come to the Saturday service. Tomorrow's my mama's birthday, and I promised to go to church with them over in Pineville." He looked around the sanctuary. "Looks like we'd better find seats. Mind if I join you?"

KAYE DACUS

"Please do." She took a few deep breaths when she turned to start down the central aisle, trying to keep the heat climbing her throat from progressing into her face. She stepped into a pew in the middle of the large room and edged her way down to the center of it.

Shon sat beside her and flipped open his order of service. Alaine did likewise but didn't take in anything on the page. While she hated attending church alone—and *alone* was how she'd always felt in the regular services on Sunday morning, looking around at all the couples and families—the idea of sitting with the guy she'd paid to set her up on blind dates was a bit weird and uncomfortable.

"Did you have a good week?" Shon's soft voice startled her.

"I did. But really busy. And you?"

"Same here. I saw your piece on the dance studio opening down in Comeaux. Looks like you had a really good time. Was that Forbes Guidry you were dancing with?"

Heat burst full force into her cheeks. "It was. I...I met him at the *Bonneterre Lifestyles* bachelors' dinner, and since there was an uneven number of people at the dance studio, he asked me if I'd partner him."

"You looked like a natural. That wasn't your first dance lesson, was it?"

"Thanks." She curled the corner of the bulletin, rolling it between her thumb and forefinger. "My mother thought that my brothers and I should at least know a couple of basic ballroom dance steps, so she taught us at home. It came in handy more for the boys than for me come prom time. I didn't have the advantage of being asked by a boy whose mother thought he should know how to waltz and foxtrot."

Shon cocked his head and gave her a quizzical look. "Did they actually play music conducive to dancing like that at your school?"

She laughed, then cringed when it carried, drawing the admonishing glances of several people sitting nearby. She thought about sticking her tongue out at them but knew that would only draw more glares. "No. But it has come in handy at wedding receptions when older men have asked me to dance. Or my brothers. I tried teaching my sorority sisters, but that wasn't the kind of dance moves they were interested in learning. By then, the lambada was all the rage."

"That. . .or just two people writhing with their bodies pressed indecently close to each other." Shon sighed. "That's when I stopped going to the interfraternity dances. I didn't want any woman getting that close to me but my wife, and since I hadn't met her then, there was no point in going."

"When did you get married?"

"Oh, I'm not—" Shon suddenly became interested in finding the scripture reference for the sermon in his burgundy leather Bible.

"You're not married?" She narrowed her eyes. "But surely you have a girlfriend."

His jaw tightened; his full lips pressed together.

"Let me get this straight." She lowered her voice and leaned closer. "You run a matchmaking agency that's so successful you've opened offices in six or seven major metropolitan areas. . .and you haven't found someone for yourself?"

He shrugged. "What can I say? I'm the pickiest client I have."

She chuckled and shook her head. "You are so lucky I forgot to ask that question when I had you on my show. My, my. What would people say if they knew Mr. Matchmaker himself couldn't get a date."

"Hey, now. I date. Occasionally. Okay, rarely, and usually with the niece or daughter of someone my mom teaches with at Louisiana College, just because I can't get out of it. But I'll have you know that we have a very high success rate of long-term relationships out of the matches we make at Let's Do Coffee."

She held her hands up and stifled her laughter better this time. "No need to sell me on it, I'm already a client, remember?"

"Are you? I was sure you were having second thoughts since you haven't responded to any of the e-mails I sent you this week. I've got at least three clients I'd like to set up meetings for you. . .with." He frowned and shook his head. "With who I'd like to set up for you. . . . You know what I mean. But I can't do it if you don't communicate with me. Remember, you are a paying client. What have you got to lose to give these guys thirty minutes to an hour of your time? If you don't like them, you don't have to see them ever again."

The praise band started playing a soft but fast-paced introduction. "Fine. I'll look at the e-mails as soon as I get home tonight, and I'll let you know Monday if I want to meet any of them. Okay?"

People around them got to their feet when the praise leader stepped to the microphone and started singing.

Shon stood. "Okay. Seems like I'm making a lot of deals outside the parameters of the service recently."

Alaine's forehead barely reached his shoulder, and she craned her neck to look up at his profile. "What's that?"

"Huh—oh, nothing. I just have another client who's giving me a little difficulty when it comes to agreeing to go out on dates, and he also offered me a deal just the other day."

"Isn't that part of the 'package customization' we VIPs get?" She winked at him.

"Careful now. I made you a VIP. I can very easily make you *not* a VIP." He held his index finger up to his lips. "Shush. It's time to sing now."

With a wry grin, she turned her attention to the giant screens at the front of the auditorium and started singing the familiar chorus. She'd never admit to Shon that she hadn't gotten back to him because of Forbes Guidry.

Forbes would never need to stoop to using a matchmaking service. No, he most likely had women throwing themselves at him all day long. But she wasn't going to be one of them.

⚜

Forbes rubbed his eyes and checked his watch again. If he was going to make it in time for the seven o'clock game, he needed to go. He changed into linen shorts and a dark red silk T-shirt and slipped into a pair of Top-Siders. Though sandals would be cooler, he hated walking across the dirt parking lot—littered with who knew what—

174

and ending up with filthy feet.

In the car, he let his mind wander back over everything he'd read today. Spending his Saturday reading case files on his parents' company's legal proceedings hadn't been the most fun way to start his weekend—nor the most productive. So far, none of the files revealed anything pertinent to Alaine's allegations of wrongdoing.

The one thread of information that led him to believe there might still be a case was the mention of Mackenzie and Son in the files dealing with the acquisition of the Moreaux Paper Company warehouses—Warehouse Row—which had been legally purchased from the bank that had acquired the property when the previous development company went belly-up before they could get around to developing the site. The information he needed a copy of, but couldn't get to because it was active and therefore still in Sandra's office, was the file containing the negotiations, formal agreements, and contracts between Boudreaux-Guidry Enterprises and Mackenzie and Son. He needed to know what his parents had authorized Evelyn—and her father's company—to do in their name and on their behalf.

As soon as he got out of the car, the heavy, humid air enveloped him with the sticky tang of cotton candy and perspiration. The clanks of bats hitting balls and the jeers and cheers of the spectators surrounded him—along with an immediate swarm of mosquitoes. He locked the Jag with his remote and crossed the dirt lot toward the rickety concession stand—the old wooden shack that had served junk food, sodas, and frozen slushes to players and fans of church league softball every summer since Forbes could remember—to check the schedule and find out on which field the men's team from Bonneterre Chapel would be playing.

He slapped at the sting of a bite on his neck and hurried over to diamond three, hoping Meredith's game was already over. A couple dozen members of University Chapel sat on the first-baseline side of the diamond, so he angled that direction. Most sat in their own lawn chairs instead of on the splintery, old wooden bleachers.

Stopping near a group of people from the singles Sunday school class, he greeted everyone and checked up on their weeks. The shout of "Two minutes!" from the field stirred Forbes to action.

"See y'all later." He jogged over to the bleachers to join the girl in a pink Bonneterre Chapel Women's Softball T-shirt and a ball cap with a ponytail of strawberry blond hair sticking out the hole in the back of it.

Meredith glanced up at him when he leaped up the bleachers and plopped down beside her. "You're late. I thought you were going to try to come for the first game."

"I was working."

"Figures. Here. I know you didn't bring any."

"Thanks." He took the can of bug repellent she held toward him and sprayed every exposed surface of his legs and arms—carefully avoiding getting any on his shirt and shorts lest he stain them. "Your shirt isn't all sweaty. What happened?"

"The other team almost had to forfeit because they were one player short." Meredith looked away from him to watch their team running in from the field.

"Almost had to?"

"Yeah. . .I volunteered to switch over and play for them." She kicked the duffel bag on the board beside her feet. "So the sweaty one's in there, since someone on that team brought an extra. I told her I'd take it home and wash it and bring it back to her next weekend."

"Oh. How'd that go?" A mixture of pride and incredulity filled him. Only Meredith would do something like that.

"Close game. But Chapel managed to pull it out in the end, by one run. I almost had her, too. Look." She held her arm out in front of her and twisted it so he could see the underside of her forearm. A large scrape was already starting to turn a magnificent shade of purple. "I wasn't sure either of us was getting up from that one. But her foot slid over the plate just as I dived for the ball to tag her. It was exciting. You should have been here."

Unable to resist, he wrapped his arm around her neck, pulled her close, and kissed her cheek. "Good job, Mere. Way to take one for the team. Even if it wasn't your team."

She dug her knuckles into his side, right into his most ticklish spot, and he released her and scooted away. But her laughter showed she was getting better on the whole being-touched issue. "I'll be wearing long sleeves to work for a few weeks until that bruise goes away. Mom'll have a cow if she sees it—but only because she wouldn't want any of our clients to see it. Sometimes I have a hard time believing she played basketball all four years in college. She's so anti anything physical or sweat-producing nowadays."

"Whereas you can't get enough of it."

"I'm not real hip on the sweat-producing part of it, but it does feel good to get out of the suits and formal dresses and makeup and get dirty—whether it's sawdust or ball-field dirt." She looked him up and down. "You, on the other hand, are more like Mom and Dad. You'll sweat when it's 'exercise,' but heaven forbid you do anything fun that would raise a bead of perspiration on your brow or get your clothes mussed."

He hoped he was like his parents in more than just that way. His high sense of morals and ethics came from them. . .he prayed that they still held them as dear. He opened his mouth to continue the subject of their parents when Meredith stood—along with everyone else around them. Both teams lined up along the first- and third-baselines, caps in hands.

Forbes stood and bowed his head for the prayer—which he couldn't hear—and asked God to help him find the right questions to ask Meredith to get some usable information.

"Play ball!"

Meredith pressed her fingers to the corners of her mouth and let out a shrill whistle. On the field, Major and their three brothers all waved before taking their positions: Major, Rafe, and Kevin in the outfield and Jonathan as pitcher.

"Here." Meredith reached into her small cooler and handed him a dripping can of diet cola once they were seated again. She held her can away from her when she opened it, then leaned over to slurp the

177

frothing foam that threatened to spill over the edge.

Forbes tapped the top of his can and pointed it well away from his silk and linen garments to open it. He licked the drippage off his thumb—and regretted it as soon as he tasted the bitterness of the bug spray. He took a big swig of the soda to wash the nasty flavor from his mouth, then set the can on the bleacher beside him.

"So what do you know about this Evelyn Mackenzie girl?" His voice had been suitably nonchalant, hadn't it?

"She's a hard nut to crack." Meredith cupped her hands to her mouth. "Straight in there, Jonathan. One more, and you've got him!"

"What do you mean?" He leaned back, propping his elbows on the edge of the bench behind them.

"She's perfectly nice. Seems to be a sweet person, yet she doesn't say much about herself. She's very closed off." A sharp clank from the field. "Foul ball," Meredith muttered under her breath—and sure enough, a millisecond later, the ball landed outside the third-base foul line. "That's okay, Jon, he just got a piece of it. Put him out on the next one."

Forbes didn't bother hiding his smile. While Meredith wasn't aggressively competitive when it came to playing, as a spectator, she was a lot of fun to watch.

"So you don't really feel like you've gotten to know her very well?" He persisted.

"Great strikeout, Jonathan. Two more to go." Meredith took a swig of her cola. "She doesn't talk about herself or her family much. She'll talk about all the different places she's been, about the restaurants she ate in, and her favorite sites, but there isn't really anything personal in any of it. I've seen her around the office for three or four weeks and had lunch with her a few times, but I still don't feel like I know her any better than I did that first night she came over to the house."

"So she's working out of the corporate offices?" Forbes kept his gaze trained on the ball field. Jonathan pitched low and outside to the batter.

"Yeah. Out of the office Rafe used when he was the company

pilot." When Jonathan threw another ball, Meredith turned her golden brown eyes on Forbes. "Why? Are you. . .you're not interested in her are you?"

"No."

Maybe he shouldn't have been so quick with his denial. Feigning a romantic interest in Evelyn might have been a good way to get Meredith to try to garner some information on the woman. "What I mean is, I'm not sure. I've only seen her a couple of times and she was. . .well, you said it: closed off. I couldn't get a good read on her, which is unusual for me."

A clank from the field drew their attention. The ball sailed toward right field.

"Come on, baby, catch it!" Meredith stood and continued yelling at her husband as if that would help him catch the ball sailing in his direction.

Major must have misjudged exactly where the ball was, because he ended up having to dive for it, bounced it with the edge of his glove a couple of times, and finally got it to fall in for a catch.

Meredith pounded Forbes's shoulder. "That's my man." She grinned and dropped back onto the bench. The entire set of bleachers wobbled. "Of course, I've been badgering him for weeks to go get his eyes checked. He's having trouble with his depth perception, and I think it's because he needs glasses. He thinks I'm just saying it to tease him because he's almost forty."

"He's not almost forty! He's only two months older than me, and we both just turned thirty-eight."

Meredith stuck her tongue out at him. "In my book, that's almost forty."

"Yeah, well at thirty-five, you're not that far away from it yourself, missy." Forbes couldn't remember the last time he'd been able to just sit and joke around with his next-oldest sibling. They'd both been too busy—and she'd been spending all of her free time in the last six or so months working on her house or with Major, or both.

After Jonathan retired the batters from the other church—giving up only one hit—Meredith picked up their previous topic. "So you're definitely not interested in Evelyn Mackenzie?"

He thought about fudging, then looked into Meredith's eyes. He couldn't. "No. Definitely not."

"That's a relief."

He straightened. "Why?"

"Because I thought you were interested in. . .someone else." Her cheeks looked pinker than usual. But she had been out in the sun all afternoon.

"Someone else?"

She lolled her head to the side. "Alaine Delacroix. Major and I were talking the other day about how well we think the two of you would get along with each other."

"And what prompted that conversation?" He tried to regain his casual air by once again leaning back on the bleacher behind them and stretching his legs out on the one below, crossing his ankles.

"Seeing the two of you dancing together on her show. I was impressed. I've never seen you dance so well."

"That's because I was taking a *lesson*."

Alaine had aired the piece on Wednesday's show. He'd only watched it four. . .maybe six times since then.

"I thought Jenn was going to do that with you."

Without going into the detail of Jenn's trouble, he explained why he'd ended up dancing with Alaine instead. "Since Jenn had to back out, I convinced Alaine to be my partner for the remainder of the lessons."

Meredith jumped to her feet and cheered as Kevin's pop fly hit the grass between the center and left fielders, and he ran to first base. She sank back onto the seat, and the three people who'd been sitting down below them on the first bench got up and moved their blanket to the grass.

Forbes didn't blame them. If Meredith got any more enthusiastic about the game, the whole contraption might just collapse.

"Did you know she minored in dance for a year in college?"

"Alaine?"

"Yeah. Before she changed her major to journalism in her sophomore year, she was majoring in art history and minoring in dance."

A totally new image of Alaine Delacroix started to form in his mind—and a strange one, at that: Alaine, in a long, flowing gown—like the ones they always wore in the movies—swirling around with a paintbrush in one hand, a painter's palette in the other, her hair up in a cascade of curls the way it had been at the magazine dinner, a smudge of paint on her cheek. He chuckled to himself.

"What's so funny?"

"Huh? Oh, nothing. Just picturing Alaine as a dancing artist." He shook his head to clear it. "What do Mom and Dad think of Evelyn? Do they seem to like her?"

"Woo-hoo, good hit, Jon!" Meredith once again leaped to her feet as their brother's hit sent Kevin to third and landed Jonathan on second. Rafe stepped up to the plate next, and for the moment, Forbes gave up on trying to pump his sister for more information.

Forbes frowned, observing his brother. "Isn't Rafe on the wrong side of the plate?"

"How have you never noticed this?" Meredith shook her head. "His high school baseball coach trained him to be a switch-hitter because most pitchers are right-handed and tend to throw fewer strikes against lefty batters."

The depth of his sister's baseball knowledge never ceased to amaze him. Of course, the only times he watched anything close to resembling baseball were the several times a year he came here to watch his family members play fast-pitch softball.

Sure enough, the pitcher walked Rafe; and Major entered the batter's box with the bases loaded—with his own kinfolk, which did not go unnoticed by their entire fan base. A chant of "Guidry grand slam" went up all around them.

"When did Major change his last name to Guidry?" Forbes drawled, hoping to raise his sister's ire.

"Oh, shut up." She whistled again, nearly piercing his eardrum. "Come on, sweetheart! Bring the boys home."

Major swung and missed the first pitch, then the next two hit the dirt in front of the plate. The opposing pitcher looked unnerved by the constant chatter from the three Guidry brothers on base behind him and by the Chapel crowd and their rhythmic chanting and clapping.

Even Forbes could tell that the fourth pitch would be perfect. Major swung. . .and sent the ball over the fence behind left field. Meredith and the rest of the crowd yelled their approval. She jumped down off the end of the bleachers and ran around the end of the fence behind the players' bench, where she threw herself into her husband's arms as soon as he got back from running the bases. The kiss she gave him drew wolf whistles from the rest of the team.

If Alaine were as enthusiastic a softball fan as Meredith, Forbes might just consider taking up the sport.

CHAPTER 17

$\mathcal{F}$orbes checked his reflection in the visor mirror one last time. He smoothed his thumb over his eyebrows and checked his teeth—and the corners of his mouth to make sure he'd washed off all the toothpaste residue. He hadn't been this anxious since the first time he stood up to give an opening argument before a jury.

A black Buick LaCrosse pulled into a parking space, leaving an empty slot beside the Jag. Forbes climbed out as if he'd just arrived and greeted Anne with a hug—which kept two other cars from pulling into the empty space next to his baby.

"So, did we miss anything important at lunch yesterday?" Anne slipped her arm through Forbes's. They joined George on the sidewalk that ran the length of the dance studio building.

"Nothing at all. How'd the Father's Day wedding go?"

"Went off without a hitch—once everyone in the bridal party showed up." Anne twisted to exchange a look with George. They both laughed, and she turned her attention back to Forbes. "I didn't see your folks at church yesterday morning. Did I just miss them?"

"Meredith said they decided they needed a weekend getaway, so they flew up to Boston."

"Really? On Father's Day?"

"Apparently Dad thought the best Father's Day gift he could receive would be to get away from all of his kids. But it's not like they don't see us every week, anyway."

"I wish I'd known they were going."

"To Boston? Why?" Forbes opened the front door.

Anne dropped her arm from his and proceeded inside. Forbes motioned George to go in ahead of him, too.

"Because that's where my father was from originally, remember?"

George joined Anne and took hold of her hand. "As soon as we have a free weekend, we shall follow Lawson and Mairee's example and take a weekend trip up there. It's especially nice in the autumn." He lifted Anne's hand and kissed the backs of her fingers.

Anne's forehead knit in a worried frown. "I don't know. It's an awfully long flight."

"You did fine from here to London and back."

Her worry lines melted into a wry smile. "That's exactly what I wanted you to think." She gave him a quick kiss when he looked like he wanted to say more. "Besides, you know my rule. I won't agree to fly anywhere until we go for three weeks without hearing about a plane crash somewhere in the world on the news."

George looked to Forbes, who just shrugged. The fact that Anne had conquered her fear of flying enough to go to England for their honeymoon was a greater accomplishment than he'd ever hoped for his cousin.

Anne turned the subject. "Is Jenn coming after all? When she didn't show last week, I thought you might be off the hook."

"Jenn isn't going to be able to do the lessons. She lost her restaurant manager, so she has to be there until she hires another one." Which, since she had accepted Major's offer to co-interview applicants for his restaurant with him, would hopefully be soon.

"But you're supposed to have a partner for these lessons, so they could make sure everyone had someone to dance with at all times."

"I know. I'll have a partner, don't worry." He glanced around at the dozen or so people already in the lobby filling out paperwork—which they'd done last week. Alaine's story must have drawn in a bunch of new customers. The petite newscaster wasn't among them.

Maybe she was already in the studio. He trailed Anne and George halfway down the lobby, then left them when Anne stopped to speak to her clients who'd come last week.

Only one of the older couples who'd been here last week was in the studio—along with Ruth and Ian. No Alaine. He looked at his watch. She still had almost ten minutes to get here.

He turned when a commotion from the lobby caught his attention. He lost all muscle control in his jaw. In walked Alaine in a snug, black top that displayed her strong, tanned arms, and a black skirt that accentuated the curve—and sway—of her hips and ended in a swirl at midcalf. She wore high heels again, making him wish the skirt showed just a bit more leg.

Stopping that line of thinking, he clamped his teeth shut and considered cutting through the crowded lobby to greet her. But something held him back. Several women fluttered around her, acting as if she were a famous movie star descended among them. And she was coming to him. Maybe not at this very moment, but she was here to be his partner; and everyone would see her come to him, take his hand, and give him her undivided attention for the next two hours.

The chirps of "Miss Delacroix, Miss Delacroix!" quickly faded when Ruth Arcenault stepped into the foyer and announced time for class to start.

So he didn't block the doorway, Forbes stepped into the studio to wait for Alaine to come to him. He stepped forward when she entered. The flutter of young women—their sullen and bored-looking partners trailing behind—parted, eyes widening, whispering Forbes's name and coming to the apparently obvious and surprising conclusion that *Bonneterre Lifestyle*'s Bachelor and Bachelorette of the Year were dating. He turned his amusement into a smile of greeting for Alaine, extended his hand, and, once she'd taken it, led her away from the tittering crowd.

"Anne, George, you remember Alaine."

Anne's eyes widened slightly at Forbes's reintroduction. He kept his amusement in check. Unless he was sadly mistaken, the rumor

185

that he and Alaine were dating would be making the rounds in Bonneterre—and his family—by week's end. And other than serve as a boon to his ego, their fair city's love of gossip about its highest-profile citizens would give Forbes and Alaine exactly the right amount of cover he needed while he figured out if her parents and their neighbors had a case or not.

Alaine shook hands with Anne and George. Her movement brought a hint of her fragrance to his attention—something both flowery and spicy. Alaine's scent seemed to whisper, to beckon him to move closer to try to get another whiff. So different from the trumpet blast of Evelyn Mackenzie's perfume, which announced her arrival before she could be seen, created a distracting noise while she was near, and left a lasting echo reverberating around the room long after she left.

Forbes clasped his hands behind his back to keep from either taking hold of Alaine's hand again or putting his arm around her, a restraint he'd learned long ago from far too many female acquaintances who got the wrong idea of his feelings and intentions toward them because of his tactile nature.

Ruth Arcenault went through her spiel once again. Good thing Forbes had listened last time, as the occasional enticing whiff of Alaine's perfume drove him to distraction.

When Ruth called for the couples to take their positions in two parallel lines, Forbes grabbed Alaine's hand and led her out on the floor before anyone else could move. The sooner they got past this in-line stuff, the sooner he could hold Alaine in his arms again and surround himself with that magical scent—er, the sooner they could discuss any developments since their lunch last Wednesday.

The music started. Forbes counted in his head as Ruth counted aloud and demonstrated the steps.

"Now, you all try it."

Forbes immediately and confidently stepped forward with his right foot. One. Slid the left out to the side. Two. Brought his right foot over to join it. Three. Back, one. Out, two. Together, three. Front, out, together. He wasn't even frowning in concentration—okay, not much. He eased his expression with a slight smile. And instead of looking at his feet, he could actually look at his partner without losing the rhythm.

Alaine's brows arched. "You've been practicing."

He shrugged. . .two. . .three. "Not really." Only every morning and evening in front of the mirror. . .three. One. . .two. . . And whenever a three-quarter meter song played on whatever Internet or satellite station he happened to be listening to when in private. . .two. . .three. One. . .

"Well, I'm impressed, nonetheless."

He gave her his most charming smile. . .and lost the beat. Alaine's nose wrinkled when she smiled big enough to show all her teeth. Could she get any more adorable?

Though he'd hoped that the intimacy afforded by dancing together would allow them to talk, Forbes found himself having to concentrate more on his footwork—and keeping his arms up and stiff and in the right positions—which stopped him from being able to keep up a conversation with Alaine.

Finally, though, their taskmasters called for a break. "There are snacks and beverages in the lobby courtesy of the Fishin' Shack restaurant just up the road."

"Annie, can you bring us a couple bottles of water?" Forbes held Alaine back from following everyone else into the foyer.

"Sure." With her grin all lopsided like that, it meant she was thinking something that wasn't necessarily true, but Forbes didn't correct her impression.

❧

Alaine followed Forbes to a row of chairs against the end wall of the studio. She tried to write off her shortness of breath to the fact they'd been waltzing nonstop for the past forty-five minutes. Yet it hadn't really started until she found herself alone with Forbes.

He waited to sit until she lowered herself into one of the molded-plastic chairs. "Have you had a chance to set up a meeting with the

Mills residents and business owners yet?"

"My parents are still working on getting something scheduled. They're thinking it'll be toward the end of the week—I hope you don't mind its being last minute like this."

He shook his head. "No, that's fine."

"What have you found out since we last talked?"

"I looked over the last six months' worth of my parents legal files. There isn't anything in them that leads me to believe they've done anything wrong or unethical. However"—he held his hand up to keep Alaine from interrupting—"I didn't get a chance to speak to them this weekend as I'd hoped, because they decided to go out of town. My next step is to look into Mackenzie and Son a little further."

Alaine sat a little straighter. "I did a little digging on them."

"How?"

"Internet." Where else would she have started? "They keep a pretty low profile. Other than their own Web site, which didn't tell me anything, I found a few links to corporate reports where their names were mentioned—but most of them are password protected beyond just a brief, one-paragraph summary of what's contained in the report. There are scant few mentions of them in any news outlet, either. And I called a contact at the newspaper in Boston to see what he might know about them, and he only knew of the company because he's seen the name on a floor directory in the downtown office building that his wife works in." She sighed and slouched in her chair. "I hoped I'd find some message boards somewhere with people posting nasty messages about how horrible they are and how they made a habit of running people out of their homes."

Forbes leaned forward and braced his elbows on his knees. "I could have told you it wouldn't be that easy." He stared at the parquet floor for a long moment.

She'd never noticed before that his hair had a bit of curl to it. Her hand spasmed with her unwilling desire to touch it to see if it was soft or wiry.

"No company that does business on such a large scale could keep *that* low a profile. What about the companies whose corporate reports Mac and Son were mentioned in? Did you look up any of them?"

Why hadn't she thought of following through on those leads? "No. I didn't think. . . I didn't have time to think about looking at them to see if I could find anything showing that they do this with every company they act as consultants for."

He looked at her around his shoulder. "With your work schedule, when do you have time to do all this research?"

When she wasn't in the film archive trying to find footage on his parents that would put them in a bad light for her story. "In the evenings, mostly. I spent a lot of time on it this weekend—when I wasn't helping out in the flower shop, that is."

"What flower shop?" Forbes sat up and turned slightly toward her in his chair.

"My parents' flower shop. They had to let go of their last part-time employee, and since Mom had a couple of events she had to get flowers to, I helped out by working the shop while she made all her deliveries."

"Do you arrange flowers?" The corners of his eyes crinkled up in a very nice way when he grinned like that.

She took a deep breath and clenched her teeth to keep from shivering at the tingle that ran up her spine. "I do some arranging. I did grow up there, you know. I spent every summer since I was fourteen working in the shop or the greenhouses."

"What's your favorite flower?"

"Lavender. It's the national flower of Portugal."

"Portugal?" The little upside-down Y appeared between his brows.

"That's where my mom's from. And it's one of my favorite places to visit."

The sound of a throat clearing snapped Alaine out from under Forbes's enchantment. Anne Hawthorne Laurence stood over them, grinning, two bottles of water extended toward them.

"Thanks, Annie." Forbes took them and handed one to Alaine. She was rather surprised he didn't open it for her.

To cover her embarrassment at Anne's knowing gaze, Alaine took a huge swig of the icy water—and inhaled half of it. She wheezed and coughed, throat burning, eyes tearing, and cheeks flaming from complete mortification.

"Take it easy there, girl." Forbes patted her between the shoulder blades. It didn't help, but the gentleness with which he did it brought the tingles back. She took a few gulping breaths and finally started feeling normal again.

That was, until Forbes stopped patting and started rubbing his hand in a circular motion on her back. "You okay?"

She pushed out of her chair at Ruth Arcenault's entrance. "Looks like it's time to get started again." She tried to clear the raspiness from her throat with another drink of water. She went back to where she and Forbes had been stationed before, as the two lines formed again.

"To make sure both partners are really learning the steps and one isn't just relying on the other. . ." Ruth walked down to the end of the line and laid her hand on Alaine's shoulder. "Miss Delacroix, I'd like for you to go to the other end of the line, and the ladies will shift up to dance with the gentleman standing to her original partner's left—your right."

For the next thirty minutes, Alaine tried to occupy herself by thinking of all the possible avenues of research she might have missed in the Internet search she'd done yesterday. She should have spent more time working on that and less time in the film archives at the studio looking for sound bites from Lawson or Mairee Guidry about their company or about the community that could be construed as negative.

She'd found a couple that, taken completely out of context, could be seen as Lawson Guidry saying Moreaux Mills on the whole was an eyesore and should be demolished. But only after she edited off enough of the beginning of the sentence to take out the part that proved he was actually talking about the old paper mill being the eyesore that should go.

She glanced across the room at Forbes, looking at his feet again, and guilt pressed in. He was so sure his parents were innocent. Was she letting her own emotional involvement get in the way of being objective about the facts? Or was he?

"Sorry." Again.

Her toes were going to be black and blue after this. "That's okay." She stiffened her arms more to try to put more distance between herself and her stranger-partner. Even though Forbes occasionally lost count and got off rhythm, at least he didn't step on her toe almost every downbeat.

"And return to your original partners."

Thank goodness. She gave Mr. Stompy Toes a tight smile, then hustled back down the line to rejoin Forbes. She never thought she'd be so glad to see him.

They fit better. Even though Ruth had said something about dancing being easier for partners closer in height, the fact that even in her heels Forbes was almost a foot taller than Alaine didn't seem to matter.

"How'd your guy do?" Forbes cast a glare down the line.

"My toes hurt. How'd you do?"

"I've danced with Anne before—at her wedding a few months ago, as a matter of fact. She tries to lead. She can't help it."

Alaine giggled and turned her attention to the couple to her left. Anne and George glided together with almost as much poise and ease as Ruth and Ian.

"Now we're going to work on moving around the room in a circle."

"Oh, boy."

Alaine bit her bottom lip and wrinkled her nose in a grin at Forbes. His tongue stuck out slightly between his teeth and everything around his eyes and forehead had tightened. Could he be any cuter?

No, no. She wasn't supposed to be thinking that way about him.

191

Until he proved otherwise, his status of enemy hadn't changed.

In another half hour, when the lesson ended, Alaine's sides hurt—from holding in her laughter as much as she could at Forbes's formidable frown. For a man used to having things go his way, trying not only to remember the one-two-three but also the quarter-turns and extra steps that moving around the room in a circle required had been an exercise in frustration for him. And the more frustrated he got, the cuter he became.

"We'll work on that more next lesson—which will be in two weeks. Don't forget the studio is closed next Monday for the Fourth of July."

Alaine dropped into the chair she'd sat in earlier and downed what remained of her water. "Do you have plans for the Fourth, Forbes?"

"What? Oh, we do a family barbecue at Schuyler Park and watch the fireworks there."

"Is that an all day thing or just in the evening?"

"Just the evening. Why?"

"I thought maybe, if you didn't have plans already, you might want to come out to the Mills that afternoon for the street festival. It is the most culturally diverse area of town. There's tons of food and lots of different stuff going on. It would give you a good idea of what it's really like over there." And it would mean she wouldn't have to go a full two weeks without seeing him again if her father couldn't get the meeting set up for this week.

Forbes's exasperated expression vanished. "What time and where should I meet you?"

Her heart did a little twirl. "I'll e-mail you the details." Her phone beeped. She picked it up to read the new message. "It's from Daddy. They've gotten the meeting scheduled: Thursday evening at eight o'clock." She looked up at Forbes. "Does that work for you?"

He glanced at his cousin, talking with a few potential customers several feet away, before looking at Alaine. "Yeah. That should work. Come on, I'll walk you to your car."

Alaine oscillated between euphoria and consternation walking out to her car. She wanted to skip, wanted to tell all the young women who'd come because they'd seen the segment on her show and who were now whispering about her that yes, she was here *with* Forbes. But she wasn't here *with* Forbes. It was just a convenient cover for them. Right?

Then why had the thought that she might not see him for two weeks struck her like a bucket of ice? Unbidden, a Bible verse floated through her mind: *Love thy enemy.*

CHAPTER 18

$\mathcal{F}$orbes swiped at the sweat pouring down the sides of his face. "I can't go tonight."

"Dude, you made me a deal. I'd be your sounding board, and you'd go out with the women I set you up with." Shon bent over, hands braced on his knees.

"It's not that I'm backing out on the deal—it's that I already have plans tonight. A business meeting."

"Okay. Brunch Saturday morning. I won't take no for an answer."

"Fine. Send me the details."

Shon pulled his phone out of his pocket and tapped on the screen a couple of times. Forbes's phone vibrated in his pocket.

"Thanks. I'll let you know how it goes."

"I look forward to it."

Forbes raised his hand and waved off his client. "Later."

"Later." Still full of the youthful energy of twenty-nine, Shon jogged up the stairs to the front door. Forbes went in through the garage, preferring to climb to the main level in the air-conditioning.

In the shower, while getting dressed, and in the car on the way to work, Forbes rehearsed what he wanted to say to the Moreaux Mills Business Owners' Association tonight. Alaine had finally texted him the details on the meeting yesterday—he'd been in the middle of presenting the nominating committee's report during the business meeting and, fortunately, had remembered to silence his phone before getting up to speak.

He sent Meredith an e-mail as soon as he got into the office, telling her he'd had a meeting come up and wouldn't make it to the Fishin' Shack for dinner. He could have mentioned it to her or to Anne at church, but he preferred doing it by e-mail in such a way that it looked like this was an urgent, last-minute meeting so they wouldn't question him further. They usually didn't, when it came to his job, but he didn't want to risk it.

He groaned when Samantha went over the day's schedule with him. Meetings all day, with barely enough time between each to return to his office to get the files for the next one. Maybe it would help to stay busy—to keep his mind occupied with all of these other cases instead of having time to make himself overanxious about tonight.

Rubbing his eyes, he stifled a yawn.

"You look tired, boss."

"Haven't been sleeping well the last couple of nights." He waved his hand over the stack of files on his desk. "Lots on my mind."

She glanced at the paper cup with the Beignets S'il Vous Plait logo on the outside. "Need me to bring you more coffee?"

"I'll get it. You just work on those briefs we discussed."

"Will do."

He followed her out of his office and headed down the hall to the break room. Four people stood staring at the coffeepot, which dripped the black stuff about as fast as an icicle melted at the North Pole in January.

Though he didn't usually make use of the executive kitchen, today called for desperate measures. He left the employee break room without disrupting the other caffeine zombies and took the stairs up to the fourth floor, bypassing the large conference room and partners'-only file room to the walnut-paneled executive dining room and into the kitchen beyond.

Mary looked over her shoulder, then turned to stare at him in surprise. "What're you doing up here?"

"I am a partner, and I do have the privilege of making use of the executive areas—even if my office isn't up here." He waved his coffee cup. "Besides, there's a line for the java downstairs."

The executive secretary's expression said as clearly as words, *I hope you don't plan to make a habit of this*, but she shuffled out of his way, two mugs of coffee clutched in her claws. "Have at it. But if you empty it, you'll have to start a new pot. Or send that secretary up here to make one, if she knows how."

"Samantha is a very capable assistant. And she makes great coffee." He toasted Mary with his mug and turned his back on her to remedy its empty state.

He drank more than half of what he fixed standing there in the kitchen. Once he'd topped it off, he returned to his office to face the first meeting of the day.

By late afternoon, his record for being able to get most of his cases resolved without having to result to courtroom litigation had stayed intact. He passed the files and paperwork off to Samantha and prepared for his last meeting of the day, down at the courthouse.

"I won't be coming back afterward." He signed several documents Samantha handed him. "Just leave everything else in my box. You're off tomorrow?"

"Unless you think you're going to need me. A temp from the pool will be filling in for me. I've left notes on everything she'll need to do to keep you operating at peak efficiency."

"You make me sound like a robot."

"Well. . ." She grinned and shrugged.

"I know. Don't get you started. Your fiancé is coming in town this weekend?"

"Boyfriend, not fiancé."

Forbes steepled his fingers and rocked in his tall-back leather chair. "Mark my words, he'll be your fiancé before he heads back to Denver Sunday night."

Samantha's face contorted as if she was trying to look skeptical instead of giddy. "You've never even met him. You hardly know anything about him. As a matter of fact, you probably don't even know his name."

"Jared. He's a computer geek, and you met him at your best friend's wedding. He was one of the groomsmen, and you were the maid of honor." Pride—and a touch of indignity—struck him at Samantha's incredulous look. "You see, I do listen to you when you talk about your life outside the office. You just have a tendency to keep most of it to yourself."

"But still. . .it's just wild speculation on your part that he'll propose to me. I'm not sure we're to that point in our relationship, since it's only been six months and this'll be the first time we've seen each other since then."

Forbes arched his left brow. "If you insist. But I have a feeling. . . ." He looked at his watch. "I've got to go if I'm not going to be late. It's taking longer and longer to go through security every time I go down to the courthouse."

"Okay. Have a great weekend, Forbes."

"You, too." He packed up his files and left the building. On the way to the courthouse, he called his favorite florist to see if they could deliver an arrangement to Samantha before the end of the day. Even though she'd never know it, teasing her had been just the distraction he'd needed to clear his head from his previous meetings and allow him to refocus on his next two meetings—the official one and the unofficial one.

Maybe he should have called Delacroix Gardens—but if they were so short staffed that Alaine had to help out on the weekends, they probably couldn't do a one-hour turnaround on an order for him.

He arrived at Judge Duplessis's chambers with about five minutes to spare. Russ LeBlanc sat waiting in the secretary's outer office.

"Hey, Forbes." He stood and extended his hand.

Forbes grabbed it, then pulled Russ forward to clasp him around the shoulders in a back-pounding hybrid handshake-hug.

"You know," Forbes stepped back, "you could have asked for a continuance. I'm sure Plessy would have been more than happy to give you a few more weeks."

"Are you kidding me? My mom, Carrie's mom, and Carrie's sister are all at our house. I couldn't wait to get away. Besides, I have four more mouths to feed—not to mention a bunch of medical bills to pay."

Forbes nodded and infused his frown with as much sympathy as he could muster. Next week once all members had a chance to donate, the president of the Bonneterre Bar Association would be presenting Russ and Carrie with a check that would not only cover their medical expenses—Forbes had seen to that with the donations he'd drummed up—but also be substantial seed money for college funds for all four children.

"Well, it's good to see you, even if we are about to go head-to-head in there."

"Hey, that reminds me—did anything come of that case I sent your way?"

"I'm meeting with a group of potential clients tonight." In a way, it was a good thing Russ hadn't been able to meet with Alaine. This case had the potential to become something that could destroy a legal aid lawyer without the money to pour into it.

"Hope it works out well for you."

Judge Duplessis opened his office door. "LeBlanc—you better have brought pictures, young man, or I'm ruling in Guidry's favor on everything today."

Forbes and Russ exchanged smiles, even as Russ reached into his pocket. "Of course, your honor."

❦

Alaine paced the lobby of the community center, watching the parking lot through the windows as she passed them. She'd told Forbes to be here at six thirty so he could meet her family before everything got crazy.

She jumped at a loud squeal of feedback through the PA system in the auditorium, followed by a few choice expletives—at least, she assumed that's what they were, since they were in what sounded like Farsi.

"Joe, you shouldn't use language like that," she called and stopped in the door at the back of the auditorium. Nikki, up on stage, checked the wired microphone attached to the podium, while Joe wheeled around, checking the wireless mikes on stands in each of the three aisles.

"Y'all are sure people are actually going to show up for this?" Alaine leaned against the doorframe.

"Everyone's been chattering about it on the association's e-mail loop. Quite a few have confirmed they're coming."

The squeak of the front door caught Alaine's attention. Mother and Daddy entered, each carrying a pot containing a fully bloomed azalea bush.

"What're those for?" Alaine asked.

"This place is so old and worn down, I wanted something to look nice for your little friend."

Alaine tapped her back teeth together a couple of times. "He's not my friend, Mother; he's a lawyer."

"Eh." Mother swept past her into the auditorium. Daddy just shrugged and followed her.

"Mother, Voula Pappas told me to let you know she's in the kitchen and could use your help, because everyone else is still at the restaurant and won't be here until later."

"Okay." She set her azalea to the left of the podium and showed her husband where to put his, then exited stage right toward the kitchen and reception hall.

"Have I missed anything?"

Alaine shivered at the sound of Forbes's voice, at the tickle of his breath on the side of her neck.

"I didn't hear you come in."

"I can be sneaky like that—like a tiger in stealth mode."

Yes. Sneaky. She had to remember—she couldn't fall for him. She couldn't trust him. Not until he'd proven himself worthy of her trust and affection.

More feedback—more swearing from Joe, only this time it sounded like it might have been Russian or Polish or something.

"Joe!" Nikki snapped upright, her fists popping onto her hips so fast it looked like it hurt.

Alaine's brother muttered something under his breath in another language—which could have been Greek or Latin for all Alaine could tell—and turned his chair so he was facing away from his wife.

Seeing Forbes's gaze fall upon Joe, she hurried to explain. "Joe was a linguistics specialist for the Army for almost fifteen years—until his convoy in Iraq was hit by an IED. He prides himself on being able to swear in twenty languages."

"Twenty-eight, Al. If you're going to apologize for me, make sure you get your facts straight."

Forbes's gray blue eyes twinkled, and he mouthed, *Al?*

"You *so* do not have permission to call me that." She poked him in the middle of his expensive silk tie.

"You need a nickname. Everyone should have one."

She crossed her arms and cocked her head. "Oh yeah? What's yours?"

He had the good grace to look sheepish. "Does Control Freak count as a nickname?"

She'd have to remember to call him that to his face sometime. "In your case, yes." She tried to make her eyes twinkle like his. Not that she had the first clue how to make it happen.

The moment stretched, and Alaine leaned closer, then cleared her throat and broke eye contact. The enemy, remember?

Love thy enemy.

No. She had to stay objective because if he ended up betraying them to support his parents, she didn't want to be hurt. She'd managed to live almost thirty-two years without suffering a broken heart—sure, bruised a couple of times—and she didn't intend on letting Forbes Guidry be the one to break it.

"I'll be at the podium?" Forbes walked past her down the aisle toward the front.

"Yes. And Joe's setting up the mikes out here so everyone can hear during the question-and-answer part."

"You'll be on stage with me?"

She shook her head. "My father's going to introduce you. I'm supposed to be keeping a low profile, remember?"

"But you're staying, right?"

Was that a touch of vulnerability in Forbes's voice? "Of course. I may not be a claimant in the case, but I'm still concerned about what's going on in the Mills."

"Okay." He joined her midway up the center aisle—just in time for her to hear his stomach growl.

"Why don't I take you back to the kitchen so you can meet my parents before everyone else shows up?" Without waiting for a response, she led him out the same way Mother and Daddy had gone.

As soon as she stepped through the side stage door, a delicious aroma overwhelmed her.

Forbes inhaled deeply. "That smells like. . .like the Greek restaurant we ate at the other day."

"You have good scent memory. Mrs. Pappas is catering the refreshments for after the meeting." She stopped and leaned closer when he halted beside her, as if telling him a secret. "I'm hoping to go ahead and grab a snack. I'm starving." She wasn't really. She'd eaten supper less than two hours ago. Why she felt the need to spare his ego, she wasn't certain. But his smile made it worthwhile.

Mother's eyes widened when she looked up at Alaine and Forbes's entry into the kitchen. Alaine grabbed a Danish wedding cookie from a tray and popped it in her mouth—taking a brief moment to close her eyes and enjoy the sheer bliss of the way the confectioners' sugar and the crumbly cookie mingled together as they melted on her tongue.

When her mother's expression turned from surprised to questioning, Alaine quickly chewed the cookie and swallowed it. "Mother, this is Forbes. Forbes, my mom, Solange Delacroix."

201

Forbes took her mother's proffered hand in both of his. "Mrs. Delacroix, it's wonderful to meet you."

"And you, Mr. . . .Forbes." Mother cast a sidelong glance at her friend.

Alaine let out her breath, thankful Mother had remembered to not mention Forbes's last name. Having people figure out who he was when Daddy introduced him would be soon enough.

"And you remember Mrs. Voula Pappas from the restaurant."

"I'd shake your hand, but. . ." Mrs. Pappas held up sticky fingers.

"Quite all right." Forbes gave her the smile Alaine hadn't been able to resist at the bachelors' banquet. "It's nice to see you again."

"We're hungry." Alaine crossed to look over her mother's shoulder at what she was stirring in a large metal bowl. "Any chance of getting a sneak peek at the pickings tonight?"

"Sure—if you'll put all those trays out—those there, the ones covered with plastic wrap." Voula motioned toward several trays sitting in the serving window between the kitchen and the hall.

Alaine snagged another cookie on her way past. Forbes didn't. Several minutes later when all the prepared trays had been moved, she hadn't seen him touch a morsel of food for himself. The longer they stayed in the kitchen, the more certain she became that Forbes Guidry, Mr. Calm-Cool-and-Confident, was so nervous he'd made himself queasy.

"Where's Daddy?" She needed to get Forbes out of here before he ruined all their appetites.

"He went back out to help Joe and Nikki finish with the setup." Mother pulled a tray of spanakopita from the oven. Alaine really wanted a piece of the cheesy, spinachy goodness, but it would be too hot to eat right now. And besides, she'd gained five pounds in the past few weeks already. She didn't need any more.

And Forbes was definitely turning a pretty good shade of chartreuse. She hid her amusement and led him back down the hall to the auditorium. A dozen or so people milled about, greeting each other and finding seats. She prayed a lot more would show up. If they could get almost all of the two dozen or so people involved in the buyout here, that would be great.

"Excuse me, can I borrow my dad for a minute?" Alaine pulled her father away from the guys who owned the bicycle repair shop a few blocks over from her parents' place. "Daddy, I wanted to introduce you to Forbes."

Though not as green as just a minute ago, Forbes still looked pale when he shook her father's hand. "Mr. Delacroix, it's great to meet you, sir."

"Please, it's JD. We're happy to have you here."

Alaine scrutinized her father's face. Though he'd agreed to invite Forbes to come and to hear what Forbes had to say, the guarded expression in his eyes clearly indicated he still didn't consider this a good idea.

Around them, the noise level grew. Alaine estimated the crowd had at least doubled just in the past thirty seconds or so, with more people still flowing in from the lobby.

"Alaine, dear, if you'll excuse us, there are a couple of people I need to introduce Forbes to before we get started."

"Okay." She joined Nikki and Joe on the front row, where his soundboard was set up, but kept Daddy and Forbes in view.

By the time Daddy'd found the third person to introduce Forbes to, she understood. He didn't want the other members of the board to be blindsided by Forbes's identity.

Alaine twisted the hem of her blouse and chewed the inside corner of her bottom lip. Maybe Daddy was right. Maybe this wasn't such a good idea after all. More and more people entered the hall, far more than she'd hoped for. Just how many people did this thing involve?

Her father led Forbes up the two steps onto the stage and to the podium. Joe gave him a thumbs-up.

"We're going to get started, so please find your seats."

While the crowd—which had to number at least a hundred by now—jostled into the old, wooden, theater-style seats, Daddy pulled

Forbes a few steps away from the live microphone to talk to him. Alaine strained to try to hear, but too much noise filled the echoing room now.

As soon as JD Delacroix, recently elected president of the Moreaux Mills Business Owners' Association, stepped back to the podium, the room quieted.

"I'd like to thank everyone for making the effort to come out tonight on such short notice. I know a lot of you even closed your businesses early so you could be here. I pray you'll feel like your effort is rewarded. As you read in the e-mails that went out this week, this meeting is so you can hear what a lawyer has to say about the threat the Mills is under. Then we'll have a question-and-answer session. We'll get to as many people as we can. If we can't get to you tonight, we'll make sure you get an answer by e-mail soon." He looked over his shoulder. Forbes nodded and joined him at the podium.

Alaine's stomach lurched. Moment of truth.

"So, since you didn't come to listen to me yammer, I'll turn the meeting over to Forbes Guidry, the lawyer who's going to try to figure out how to help us."

A frisson of whispers jolted the stillness of the room. Her father left the stage and took the seat beside her, just as Mother and Voula Pappas entered through the side door.

Forbes cleared his throat and rested his hands on either side of the podium. Though he smiled, from this distance, the grimness in his eyes couldn't be plainer. "Thank you, Mr. Delacroix. Good evening, ladies and gentlemen. I'd like to begin by talking about the elephant in the room. You heard Mr. Delacroix correctly. My name is Forbes Guidry. Yes, I am the son of Lawson and Mairee Guidry, who own Boudreaux-Guidry Enterprises."

The trickle of whispers turned into a shower.

Alaine tried to beam encouragement and enthusiasm at him with her smile when he caught her eye.

"I am not here on behalf of my parents nor of their company. I have never worked for B-G Enterprises in any capacity and have acted as legal counsel for my parents only in personal business matters."

Her heart squeezed. He hadn't told her that before.

"But you're a partner in the law firm that represents them," a man called from somewhere in the middle of the small auditorium. "You're here to make us back down, to make us sell out."

"I know it might seem like I'm the most unlikely candidate for someone to help you oppose B-G Enterprises if it's found they've done anything illegal—"

"D'ya hear that?" A woman shouted from the back of the room. "*If!* He's already trying to whitewash Mommy and Daddy's dirty deeds."

"No, ma'am. I'm telling you what any reputable lawyer would tell you: No matter how injured you feel you've been, we'll have to prove the other side has actually done something wrong—broken laws or contracts or conducted business in ways that violate the charters of this city, parish, or state—before any formal legal action can be taken. That means"—Forbes had to raise his voice another notch to make himself heard over the tempest now—"that I'll need to meet with each of you individually to see if you have a claim that is actionable."

"Why should we trust you?"

"Don't listen to him. He's not here to help us!"

"This is a travesty. Delacroix, what are you doing to us?"

With a sigh, Alaine's father returned to the podium. Forbes stepped aside for him, his expression apologetic.

"Quiet please." As soon as a semblance of quiet had been reached, her father adjusted the microphone lower. "I asked Mr. Guidry to come here in good faith. He has promised that he will set aside any personal prejudices and look only at the facts. If he discovers that B-G Enterprises—or any company they're doing business with—has done anything illegal, he's sworn he'll act only on our behalf. Now please, listen to what he has to say."

"Listen to him?" a woman shrieked. "Listen to him? Can y'all believe this? They brought the enemy right into our community—practically into our homes."

"Look at him in his fancy suit, standing in our community center that probably isn't worth as much as that fancy car of his."

"How much money are you going to make when they tear down all our homes and businesses?"

"Yeah, how much of the Mills are you going to own once we're all kicked out?"

Why wouldn't he stand up for himself? The desire to use one of Joe's favorite foreign words or phrases propelled Alaine out of her seat. Her feet didn't even touch the two steps up to the stage. She bumped her father—who was trying to calm down the frenzy—out of the way and grabbed the microphone from its holder, since she could barely see over the tall podium.

"Everybody sit down and be quiet!" She didn't have to raise her voice much; too many years of live remotes from concerts, club openings, and festivals had taught her how to make herself heard over a lot of background noise. And Joe had probably dialed the volume all the way up on the microphone. She stared at the twenty or so hecklers still on their feet. Slowly they each sat down.

"Thank you." Recomposing her expression from stern to professional took only an instant. She tucked her hair behind her ear. "Most of you in this room know me—if you don't know me in person you've seen me on television. I grew up in the Mills. All of my family still live in the Mills."

Well, that wasn't exactly true. Tony lived in an apartment over in University Heights. "My parents—whom you all know—and my brother and sister-in-law work side by side with everyone here to make a living. So trust me when I say that securing the future of Moreaux Mills is my highest priority."

She scanned the room, keying in on faces she recognized, making eye contact. "*I* asked Forbes Guidry to come here to talk to you tonight. *I* am the one who talked to him about what Boudreaux-Guidry Enterprises is doing in the Mills. And you know why I talked about this with someone who's related to the owners of that company? Because there isn't another lawyer in this city who's willing

206

to take on a case against them. Not a single one would even agree to meet with me. But he did."

Of course, he hadn't known why or even whom he was meeting. "I know you've got your doubts. I did in the beginning, as well. All I can ask you to do is set them aside just for a little while and listen to what he has to say. Let's engage in some civilized discourse and see what we can do to save the Mills."

"But why should we trust him?" one of the original hecklers called.

She licked her lips, heart hammering. "I can't make you trust him. All I can do is tell you that I trust this man with my entire being."

And her entire being included her heart.

CHAPTER 19

All Forbes's nervousness vanished at Alaine's proclamation. Heretofore, the nearly paralyzing anxiety had been inexplicable. Now he knew: He'd been afraid of disappointing her.

The microphone trembled in her hand as she stood watching her parents' friends and neighbors discuss her words quietly among themselves. He moved closer and rested his hand on her shoulder, trying to express his gratitude wordlessly when she looked up at him, her eyes wide as if she'd just witnessed a horrible accident.

He reached for the microphone, which she seemed only too happy to relinquish. She backed away, then returned to her seat with surprising haste.

Forbes looked over the crowd as he would a group of people considered for jury duty. Very few wore suits. Even Alaine's father wore his button-down oxford with the collar open and no jacket. Appearances could go a long way in a situation like this. He laid the mike on the podium, took his coat off and hung it from the corner of the stand, loosened his tie, and rolled up his sleeves.

The hall quieted again. Rather than stand behind the podium, he picked up the microphone and moved to stand beside it.

"If, as Miss Delacroix suggested, you'll give me a chance, I promise I will do whatever I can to make sure justice is served for the residents and business owners of Moreaux Mills."

As no one seemed inclined to argue this time, he forged ahead, giving a bit of his professional background, then beginning to explain what he'd learned so far—couching everything in generalisms so that nothing he said could be deemed as firm statements of accusation, but so that they understood to what extent he would investigate and fight for them.

The longer he talked, the more the attitude of his listeners changed toward him. Alaine, however, looked as if she'd rather be anywhere than here. He purposely avoided looking at her often. And he could imagine how embarrassed she must be for having made a public spectacle of herself after she'd been determined to honor her promise to her parents not to be seen as the public face of the issue. His trepidation for what she might hear from her parents after this magnified his own over how his parents would react when he told them of his involvement in it.

During the question-and-answer time, though there were still a few folks obviously intent on giving him a hard time, he got the feeling that most of the people were willing to give him a chance, and that most of them were not under imminent threat of losing their property—they were concerned that if development moved forward, they would be run out in a second or third phase of building. Forbes had represented too many people like Mr. Pichon in his career to deny the legitimacy of their fears.

Finally, JD called an end to the meeting. "Thank you all again for coming out tonight. There are refreshments in the fellowship hall, thanks to Voula and Spiro Pappas. Mr. Guidry has graciously agreed to stay for about an hour to try to answer more questions. If you've already had a chance to ask a question in here, please allow those who did not get a chance to talk with Mr. Guidry first. And of course, let's show him the kind of hospitality we pride ourselves on in the Mills."

The sound of the old wooden seats flopping closed almost drowned out the immediate drone of voices.

Forbes needed to get to Alaine, to try to let her know how much he appreciated her standing up for him, but her father waylaid him before he could leave the stage to join her.

"I'd like to apologize to you, son, for the things that were said earlier. I—"

"No, don't." Forbes held up his hand. "You're not responsible for anything anyone said here tonight. When sentiment runs high, people will say things they'd never even think under normal circumstances."

JD's shoulders sagged, and he appeared much older, world-weary, than just seconds before. "No, I need to apologize. Because when you first stood up here, I felt the same way they did. I didn't want to trust you, didn't believe you had any interest other than to defend your—to defend the corporations on the other side."

"You *felt* that way then? But now?"

"I trust Alaine; she's a good judge of character. If she says you can be trusted, I'm willing to take that leap of faith."

The warmth in the older man's eyes succeeded in driving away the remainder of Forbes's anxiety. "Thank you. I will do my best not to squander nor betray that belief."

With a handshake accompanied by a shoulder-squeeze from Alaine's father, Forbes contemplated what he'd just done. Though no paperwork had been drawn up or signed, he was their lawyer, by conscience if not by contract, committed to the cause, to the community, to the case.

"We should join everyone else in the hall." JD motioned him toward a side door.

Forbes looked around at the mostly empty auditorium. Alaine hadn't waited for him. He'd just have to wait until after the reception to try to have a private word with her. He followed JD into the fellowship hall, the crowd parting for them. Some people still looked skeptical, a few downright hostile, but most smiled and nodded in greeting when he made eye contact with them.

JD motioned him through to the kitchen where Solange handed Forbes a plate of what looked like a full serving of each of the hors d'oeuvres Mrs. Pappas had prepared. He ate as much as he could, but even after not being able to eat anything since his early lunch, his riotous stomach wouldn't handle much.

"Where is Alaine?" Solange asked her husband, her accent making her daughter's name come out as *Ah-la-ee-na*.

"I figured she'd come in here with you." JD served a plate for himself and leaned against the counter beside Forbes to eat.

"I have not seen her since the meeting ended. She said she would assist in the kitchen."

The door swung open with a bump and a scrape, and the guy in the wheelchair and the tall redhead who'd set up the sound system entered the kitchen. Alaine had introduced them before, but Forbes's nerves had kept him from taking in their names.

"Ah." JD wiped his mouth with a paper napkin and set his half-full plate aside. "Forbes, this is our oldest, Joe, and his wife, Nikki."

Forbes met Joe halfway across the kitchen and greeted him and his wife with handshakes. "I've heard a lot about you. It's nice to put faces with the names."

The husband and wife exchanged a telling glance—the same kind Anne and George had been giving him and each other at the ballroom lessons the other night.

When Joe turned back around, Forbes got a flash of recognition. "Wait—you were in the Latin Club at Moreaux High School. You were a couple of grades behind me, but you competed on our level my senior year."

"I almost beat you at the All-State Competition, too." Joe grinned. "But they said my accent needed work. My accent, in a nonspoken language."

With a twinkle in her eyes, Nikki poured herself a soda. "So you were a language geek in high school, too, Forbes?"

"My parents wanted each of their children to be competitive in something, and since I wasn't cut out for sports and found Latin easy, it seemed like the best option to make them happy." Okay. Maybe not the best anecdote, given present company.

Nikki laughed. "Sounds like what I would have done."

KAYE DACUS

"Don't let her fool you. She came to almost all of the Latin fairs, exhibitions, and competitions. It's why she fell in love with me." Joe rolled over to her and took the cup out of her hands. She swiped it right back from him. He made a doleful face, and with a sigh, she poured him his own drink. "Thanks, babe." He rotated so he faced Forbes again. "Did you take any other languages?"

"No. Just Latin. I knew before I started high school that I wanted to be a lawyer, so really Latin was my first and only choice. And as I said, I found it easy, so what was the point in switching to something else?"

"I know what you mean. We all grew up speaking Portuguese as easily as English. So Spanish, Italian, and Latin were all simple. French is a pain—because of the pronunciation." Joe went on to talk about the ease or difficulty with which he'd learned his first six languages.

Forbes wanted to hear Alaine speak Portuguese. He already loved the way she spoke English, so he could only imagine hearing the Romance language rolling off her tongue would be symphonic.

When he returned his attention to the conversation, Nikki and Joe were bickering good-naturedly, and Solange and JD were across the kitchen speaking in tones too low to carry.

"I should probably go out and start answering some more questions." Forbes tossed his plate into a nearby trash can before anyone could see how little progress he'd made in the pile of food—food that was at least as good as Aunt Maggie's gourmet offerings and perhaps even better in their ethnic rusticity.

"I'll join you out there in a moment," JD called across the room.

Forbes waved but was glad he'd be on his own, even if just for a few minutes. People would speak more freely and honestly without someone else standing there waiting to censor or stop them if he felt like they were crossing a line.

And frankly, he hoped to be able to speak with Alaine sooner rather than later.

Though at least fifty people milled about the hall, it took only

212

seconds for Forbes to realize Alaine wasn't among them. Had she been so afraid of her parents' reaction that she couldn't face them in a public setting? Or perhaps she sought to minimize the damage by avoiding more attention with her presence at the reception.

Either way, no matter how harsh her parents were on her—though he couldn't imagine it could possibly be too bad, given what he'd observed in JD and Solange—he would do his best to make up for it by showing her just how much her defense of him meant.

※

Alaine dug through the pile of notebooks and printed research piled on her desk one more time. It had to be here.

She still couldn't believe that she'd practically come right out and said, "I love you" on stage. Had he seen it in her eyes? Had she betrayed her feelings without meaning to?

A stack of papers slid onto the floor.

"Oh, for heaven's sake!"

Instead of picking it up, she pulled the shredder and recycling bin over and started sorting through the avalanche. Most of it was trash—articles and blog entries she'd printed out from various Web sites, including her blog at the station, containing any mention of the Guidrys or Mackenzie and Son. Junk mail. Magazines she'd been meaning to get to for a few months. Notes she'd pulled from her interviews with Mairee and Meredith before the HEARTS to Hearts banquet back in February—those needed to be re-filed.

She shoved the pages back into the green folder and picked it up to set in the seat of her chair—and suddenly found herself being stared at by Forbes Guidry. She'd found it. She grabbed the July issue of *Bonneterre Lifestyles* and threw it into the recycle bin. The blue box slid across the wood floor, coming to a stop when it bumped the base of her credenza.

A heartbeat later, she jumped up and ran to the crate to rescue the magazine. She flipped the magazine open—it automatically parted on the first two pages of Forbes's six-page spread. While most of the men featured in the bachelor-of-the-year edition of the magazine looked like they'd been posing for high school senior portraits or college fraternity "party pix," even with the professional photographers giving direction at the photo shoots, Forbes looked like a professional model in all his shots. Her favorite was halfway through the feature. In dark jeans, a bulky gray sweater, and barefoot, Forbes sat on a red sofa—she remembered it from the lobby of the magazine's offices—laughing. She hadn't seen that side of him often but wanted to.

She glanced down at the article below the photo. The interviewer had asked Forbes who his hero was.

"My parents," Guidry responds without a moment's hesitation. "They proved that one can be successful in career and family, building Boudreaux-Guidry Enterprises into what it is today while also raising seven children, making sure we had plenty of love and plenty of discipline. They can do no wrong, in my book."

Alaine flung the magazine back into the recycle bin, not caring that three subscription cards went flying to different corners of the converted-bedroom office.

Uncertainty tore at her heart—the heart with which she'd believed she trusted him; the heart he could so easily break if she let him.

But not if she didn't give him the chance. She pushed the chair back to the desk and sat—on the folder—and opened her e-mail program. There they were—the e-mails from Shon Murphy this morning. When she'd responded to the first one that she couldn't meet someone tonight, he'd almost immediately sent back the alternate time of nine thirty Saturday morning. She hadn't responded.

She pulled it up and hit REPLY. Hopefully it wasn't too late already.

Saturday, 9:30, Beignets on Spring Street is fine. Tell him I'll be wearing a black-and-white polka-dot shirt and black capris.

She sent it and closed down the computer, ignoring the several new e-mails at the top of the list. Fatigued from the day's emotional turmoil, she went to bed, silencing her cell phone when it started ringing just after ten o'clock. If it was an emergency, family and work had her landline number. She stared at the cordless phone on the nightstand, waiting to hear it ring, but it didn't.

She rolled over and closed her eyes.

Sleep didn't come.

At midnight, more exhausted than she remembered being in a very long time, she got up and took some p.m. painkiller for her headache and to, hopefully, help her fall asleep.

An hour later, she still lay on her back, staring at the ceiling.

If she prayed, would it do more than bounce off the ceiling? She took a deep breath and let it out slowly. "Okay, Lord. Obviously, I don't know what's going on here, but it seems like You're going way out of Your way to make sure there's nothing I *can* do but try to step out on faith and trust You in this."

Her rash decision to jump up on stage to defend Forbes flickered through her mind. She rolled onto her side, pulled her knees up, and wrapped her arms around her legs. "Why'd You let me make such a fool of myself? Please don't let Mother and Daddy be too angry with me."

She lay there for quite a while, trying to find peace within, silently praying for sleep to come. When it didn't, she stretched out on her back again, staring at the patch of moonlight on the ceiling.

"Please show me how to trust You; show me what You want me to do. And help me to leave this situation in Your hands and not try to run out ahead of You and do things on my own. Because I can't handle it on my own. I can't figure it out for myself." Her eyes grew heavy, and she yawned. "And I'll never understand Forbes Guidry without Your help."

Sleep came. But when the alarm went off at six o'clock, her head throbbed and she did not look forward to the day to come.

For the first time in more than ten years, she paid as little attention as necessary to her appearance—she'd worry about what her face and hair looked like closer to airtime.

At the office, she went straight to her cubicle, speaking as little as necessary to the co-workers she passed in the hallways, and dug into finishing a few stories for the broadcast.

"Hey, Alaine—whoa, are you feeling okay?" Bekka swung back into Alaine's cubicle.

"I'm just tired." Tired of keeping up appearances. Tired of trying to figure out how to get a promotion. Tired of trying to be the person everyone else thought she should be. Tired of wondering about Forbes. Tired of longing to fall in love and get married. Tired of everything. *God, help me turn it all over to You.*

Bekka, who always showed up for work with little makeup and her hair overflowing the top of a clip at the back of her head, raised her eyebrows in an encouraging gesture. "How'd the meeting go last night?"

Tempted to tell her everything, Alaine had to stop herself. Never knew who might be listening around this place. "We'll have to get together for coffee some time next week, and I'll tell you about it."

"And *him*?"

"Seems like he managed to win just about everyone over. Including my dad." Closing her eyes, she could clearly see her father with his hand on Forbes's shoulder—a sure sign JD Delacroix had accepted Forbes.

"That's a good thing, though, isn't it?" Confusion edged Bekka's soft voice.

"Yeah. That's a good thing."

"You're still not sure how you feel about him, though."

Alaine clicked her pen with increasing rapidity. "I'm still trying to work that out. I trust him—I want to trust him. I want him to be everything he says he is, that he's not just showing us one face and is a totally different person in reality."

Bekka leaned against the edge of Alaine's desktop. "Has he given you any reason to believe he's deceiving you?"

Alaine told her about the magazine article in a whisper. "If he believes his parents can do no wrong, then how could he do what we're asking him to do?"

"But Alaine, you have to think—those interviews were done months ago. Didn't you do yours back in February?" She uncrossed her arms when Alaine nodded. "He didn't know back then that they might be involved in something like this—you said yourself he didn't know until you told him. And not only that, he was talking about them as a child about his parents for a magazine which is all about image. If you'd read that about him without this—thing going on, wouldn't you have found it endearing he'd feel that way about his folks?"

The magazine was all about image. Just like her program. Just like *her*. When had she become such a sellout? Stopped looking for what people were deep down instead of just on the surface? She'd become like all of those people who thought they knew something about art but who looked no further than the initial impression they got by gazing at a piece. They didn't examine the hues, the brush strokes, the textures, the use of shadow and light—they didn't even know how to look for it.

"Yeah, I would have found it charming." Just like Forbes. "Thanks for the reminder."

"See you in twenty for the briefing." Bekka patted Alaine's arm and left.

"See ya." Alaine's computer chimed, and she turned to see what reminder had just popped up. ART GALLERY SHOW OPENING WITH MEREDITH, 7 PM.

In her freshman year of college, she'd read a book by one of her professors about how everything he knew about life and relationships had come from his love of art. She'd taken the lessons to heart, learning to look beyond the "frame" and the "image" to the details of what made something—or someone—a masterpiece. She could blame it on her sorority sisters, who couldn't accept her until they'd remade her in their own image. But culpability for losing herself, for losing the person who'd accepted everyone and not cared at all about someone's social status, or appearance or success, rested squarely on her own shoulders.

She ached to have friends again—the real kind, the kind she'd turned her back on at age nineteen when she decided to become someone she wasn't sure she liked anymore. And tonight, she'd try to rectify that by attending the art gallery opening with Meredith and trying to remember who Alaine Delacroix really was.

CHAPTER 20

$\mathcal{A}$laine opened the conference room door at the insistent knocking. She glowered at the intern who stood on the other side. "We're in a prep meeting for the noon broadcast. What is it?"

"Mr. Milton wants to see you. Says it's urgent."

Dread fizzled through Alaine's veins. "Please let him know that I'll be happy to meet with him after the broadcast, but for the next two hours, I'm tied up."

"I'll tell him." But his expression said he didn't think the boss would go for it.

Alaine returned to her co-workers and the meeting continued—until the knocking started up again several minutes later.

"Yes?" Her heart rattled in her chest.

"He said okay, but you're to go straight to his office as soon as you sign off."

"Thank him for understanding and let him know I'll be there immediately after airing." She closed the door and returned to the small conference table.

"What is that all about?" Pricilla asked.

"No clue. Now, where were we?" Getting her two producers to focus on the program notes was easier than returning her own focus to it. What had she done now to deserve to be called into the boss's office? Whatever it was, she would apologize and show him she was turning over a new leaf. Gone was the full-of-herself diva. She just hoped he'd give her a chance to prove it instead of firing her on the spot. Not that he would. Would he?

The inside corner of her bottom lip was raw by the time she got to the set. She had to stop chewing on it when she was nervous, a bad habit she'd started when she forced herself to stop chewing the ends of her pens.

The program went smoothly—thank goodness Major O'Hara's pretaped cooking segment took up more than a quarter of the show. With a few other taped segments, Alaine only had to focus on a couple of transitions, banter with Bekka and Brent before and after the news headlines and weather forecasts at the top and bottom of the hour, and hold an in-studio interview with one of the curators at the Bonneterre Fine Arts Center about the new exhibition, which opened to the public tomorrow.

As soon as she got the clear signal, Alaine unwired herself, took a deep breath, and headed upstairs to the news director's office. The door stood open, but she still knocked to get his attention.

"Close the door and sit down."

Oh, dear. That couldn't be a good sign. She did as bade, clasping her hands tightly together in her lap. "You asked to see me?"

"Yes. What is this?" He flung a quarter-folded section of newspaper at her.

"Um. . ." Not a good time to be flippant. She closed her mouth and looked down at the portion of the page facing her. It was the news-briefs page—the page with snippets of information either too trivial for an article or learned too late for a full article to be written before press time. She was about to ask him what he wanted her to look at when she saw it:

MOREAUX MILLS RESIDENTS FIGHT BACK

Thursday evening, more than one hundred residents and business owners in Moreaux Mills gathered at the community

*center to protest the planned redevelopment of the area by
Boudreaux-Guidry Enterprises. Moreaux Mills Business
Owners' Association president J. D. Delacroix introduced lawyer
Forbes Guidry as the man who will be "making inquiries"
into the merits of a lawsuit against the local corporation and
a development firm they have brought in. Guidry is the son of
B-G's owners. Also taking the stage was Channel Six reporter
Alaine Delacroix, daughter of the business association president.
Continue reading the* Reserve *for further details.*

She might throw up. Trembling, she set the paper gingerly on
the desk. Of course someone had informed a reporter about the
meeting—whether he was there or someone just gave him the
information. With that many people, even though they'd all been
asked to keep it confidential, word was bound to leak.

"I thought you said you didn't have any involvement in what's
going on in the Mills." Rodney leaned his elbows on the desk and
steepled his fingers.

"I don't—not directly. My parents, as you saw, are involved, as
are my brother and sister-in-law. My only involvement was to find
a lawyer who'd be willing to take a case like this against B-G." She
couldn't get fired over this. He couldn't be that petty.

"Need I remind you that you have a duty to this station that if you
know of something newsworthy you're to bring it to our attention?"

"I couldn't. I was bound by a promise of confidentiality."

"We could have treated you as an unnamed source. No one would
have known you were passing us the information."

"I would have known. I know my duty to the station, but I
also know my duty to my family, as well as to myself and my own
conscience. I could not break my word." The DVD sitting on her
desk at home with the finished piece about B-G and the Guidrys
weighed on her mind.

"Well, now the news has been broken, your promise of confidence is
null and void. I want you to be the primary on this story. It doesn't mean

a promotion yet, but if you do as good a job with this—and I want some heavy-duty investigative reporting—as you've been telling me you'd do if I moved you to main news, I'll consider moving you over."

Funny, yesterday she would have given everything for this chance. "No."

"You'll start with something for the six o'clock news today—excuse me?"

"No, I won't report this story. I'm too closely involved in it to be objective. Not only that, but you already have an investigative reporter who's been working on the story and who'll do a much better job with it than I would." And her parents would hold to their promise of dropping out of the lawsuit if she took the assignment.

He rocked back in his chair as if avoiding something she'd thrown at him. "You can't be serious."

"I'm completely serious." She leaned forward. "Listen, Rodney. I need to apologize to you. I know I haven't been the most cooperative employee for the past few years—that I've been the thorn in your side with my mania to get promoted, to do hard news. But I've come to a decision." She swallowed hard. "I want to stay with *Inside Bonneterre* for as long as you'll let me. I have some ideas I'm working on for how I can make it even better, get more involved in the community. If I'm going to start implementing those changes, I'll need all my focus there, not on trying to do the program and investigate what could be one of the biggest stories Bonneterre's ever seen. So while I appreciate your vote of confidence in me, my answer is no."

Rodney's jaw hung slack.

She laughed. "I know. *Invasion of the Body Snatchers*, right? But trust me on this. You want a better reporter than me to handle this story. And I'd like my name to be kept out of it as much as possible. I know I've already put myself into the middle of it by being there last night, but my family has asked me to keep a low profile, to not add my name and image to the media circus that it might become. They don't want me tainted by association if things go badly, I think."

Recovering his wits, Rodney ran his hands over his face. "Well, since

B-G is one of the biggest sponsors of your show, I suppose it's better to keep you away from the story as much as we can. I'd—I know you have creative control over your program, but I'd be interested in seeing your ideas for the new segments you have. We need more community involvement, so I'd like to see if we can take your ideas and create some station-wide initiatives stemming from what you do on your show."

"I'd love to talk to you about it." But not yet. "I'll send you an e-mail with the details once I get them fleshed out a little better. I'll go now so you can get someone else in here and brief them on the Mills story." She dismissed herself and stood to leave.

"Yes. Oh, send my secretary in here on your way past her desk."

"Will do." Though she'd never dreamed it possible, Alaine walked out of Rodney Milton's office with no promotion and feeling better than she had in—in longer than she could remember.

Back at her desk, she checked messages on her work phone and her cell phone. Meredith Guidry. . .O'Hara—Alaine grinned when Meredith had to quickly remember to tack on her new last name—had left a message for Alaine to call her to confirm plans for tonight. And she had a text message from Shon Murphy: U R ON AT 930 SATURDAY.

Not getting her date's name until he showed up at the agreed-upon time and location worried her a bit. She couldn't help but wish it was Forbes and not a complete stranger. But what would people think if her name became romantically linked with Forbes's now? It was no longer just a case of the bachelor and bachelorette of the year becoming a couple. If this became a lawsuit, a relationship between her and Forbes could become a problem for others involved in the case—always wondering if her parents were getting more attention, better representation, than they were because the lawyer was dating their daughter.

Professional distance was what she needed. If she was to be seen out and about on dates with others, it would help put an end to any rumors that might hinder or damage the case.

"So I see you're not packing up your desk." Bekka leaned against the edge of the wall at the opening into Alaine's cubicle. "Pricilla told me why you vanished so quickly after the program."

"Right. Well, he offered me a promotion."

Bekka's brown eyes widened. "Really? Why? I mean, you know how much I respect your journalistic skills, but he's not your biggest fan."

"I know. But I'm mentioned in the newspaper as having been at the meeting in Moreaux Mills last night. He wanted me to cover the story—in addition to continuing with *Inside*."

"And you said yes, of course."

"I said no."

Bekka must have put more of her weight onto the divider than before, because it wobbled, throwing her off balance. She grabbed it to right herself. "You said. . .no?"

Alaine explained her reasons to Bekka—not just about the issue of her integrity in keeping her word to her parents, but about the underlying cause. "I need to find that person I used to be, the one I used to like. I wasn't raised to be a diva. I wasn't raised to smart mouth my boss. I was raised to work hard for what I want, but to be able to stop and recognize when I've been blessed with what I need, even if it's not what I thought I wanted. If I'm going to keep faith with my parents' expectations of me—and God's—I have to do it in all aspects of my career, not just keeping the promise to not get involved in the story. Does that make any sense?"

Pushing her chestnut hair over her shoulder, Bekka gave her a smile like the one Alaine's mother had worn for weeks after Alaine landed the job as sole host and creative director of *Inside Bonneterre* six years ago.

A vast sense of accomplishment welled up in Alaine. She'd prayed about everything else in her life last night. Figured God would answer the prayer she *didn't* pray.

"I know this'll sound patronizing, but I'm proud of you."

"Thanks. I hope to make everyone feel that way about me from now on."

Bekka stayed only a few minutes to chat, then left Alaine so they could both get their work done—Alaine so she would have time to get ready for the black-tie event, and Bekka so she could prepare for the five o'clock newscast.

Alaine dialed Meredith's office number.

"Boudreaux-Guidry Enterprises, Facilities and Events, this is Corie," Meredith's assistant answered.

"Hi, this is Alaine Delacroix. I'd hoped to speak with our Mrs. O'Hara."

Corie laughed. "Mrs. O'Hara has gone upstairs to speak with Mr. O'Hara. Shall I put you through to her cell phone?"

"Oh, no. Just have her call me when she returns to her office—on my cell." Alaine gave the assistant the number, even though she knew Meredith had it.

Half an hour later, her cell phone buzzed. *Forbes Guidry* scrolled across the caller-ID window. She hit the silencer button and returned to the e-mail she was writing for Rodney to explain the ideas she had for incorporating more community outreach elements to her show. She couldn't talk to Forbes right now. He'd get under her defenses and probably get her to admit her true feelings for him.

The phone buzzed again. Meredith this time. She flipped it open and tucked it between ear and shoulder. "Hey, girl."

"Hey, yourself. I haven't heard from you in ages—since we first arranged this. I was starting to wonder if we were still on or not."

"We are most definitely still on. Art, fine food—at least I'm assuming it is since your husband's preparing it—and a fund-raising auction. Who else would I possibly want to go with but the person who's an expert in these types of gala events?"

"You float through those social waters pretty well yourself. I've seen you in action."

"Yes, but tonight, I'll have no camera, no notepad, no pen."

"And I'll have no clipboard, no earpiece, no wondering if every-one's having a good time."

"Just you and me and the art."

"And a hundred or so other people."

"Right." Alaine mentally kicked herself for depriving herself of Meredith's open, honest, and warm friendship for the past month. "Shall we meet on the steps by the Fontainebleau sculpture at seven thirty?"

"Sounds good. Hey, are you wearing floor-length or knee-length?"

"I'd planned on knee-length. The invite said black tie, but it also mentioned cocktails."

"Oh, okay. You're right. Knee-length, then. I brought both with me, just in case."

"You took two dresses to work with you? Why not just change when you go home?"

Meredith let out a wry laugh. "Dear heart, you've yet to realize that I rarely leave here before six on nights when I don't have anything going on in my department—and when I do. . . I may not be working this event, but my catering division is, which means I need to be here just in case some last-minute crisis pops up so that Major doesn't have to take time away from what he needs to get done to handle it."

"Well, at least you get to see your husband when you stay late like that. But I can imagine he's been telling you to go home, that he can handle everything."

A pause on the other end spoke louder than a yes. "We've been having that argument for years; but now he feels like since he's my husband, I'll automatically do what he says instead of doing what I've always done." She sighed. "In some ways, even though I'll hardly ever see him, it'll be a good thing once we break ground on the restaurant. It'll keep him out of my hair here."

Ah, yes. The restaurant Major was opening with Meredith's parents as his investment partners. Not an official B-G business venture but still tied with the development they wanted to do in the Mills—

New leaf. No more negative thoughts about the elder Guidrys. "I can't wait to hear all about it tonight. But if I'm going to make it home to change clothes—since I didn't have the foresight to bring mine to work with me—I've got to get some work done."

"See you tonight."

"Looking forward to it." And she was.

She got the rest of her work wrapped up and the e-mail sent off to Rodney, wished everyone a good weekend, and left work, appreciating the place far more than she had when she had walked in eight hours ago.

Stomach growling when she walked in the house, she fixed a bowl of cereal and ate it sitting on the counter at the kitchen island, bare feet swinging like a kid's. She'd be hungry again before she got to the gallery, but all the better for truly enjoying Major O'Hara's excellent food.

Oh, that reminded her. . .she slipped off the counter, dropped the empty bowl into the sink with a clank, and jogged upstairs to the guest bedroom. On the floor of the closet, in the back, her wedding gift for Meredith and Major leaned against the wall. She wrapped it and carried it downstairs and set it on the kitchen counter, under her keys, so she wouldn't forget to take it with her.

Humming, she went back upstairs to get ready. With the off-and-on drizzle outside, trying to straighten her hair would be pointless; so she plugged in the curling irons and got out the box of bobby pins. After a quick shower to rinse away the day's gunk and wash her face so she could start afresh with her makeup, Alaine wrapped herself in her favorite Turkish bathrobe—the one she'd actually gotten in Turkey.

At six forty-five, her hair in a cascade of curls at the crown of her head, looking pretty good if she did say so herself, in the knee-length, sleeveless black satin dress with the faux-wrap top and the wide, V-neck shawl collar that showed the definition of her collarbones, Alaine grabbed the gift and her keys and headed out the door. Then went back inside and upstairs to her office for the admission passes.

As Alaine had assumed, Meredith waited for her by the chickenlike modern art sculpture in front of the museum, even though Alaine was almost ten minutes early. She handed her keys to the valet and tucked the ticket into her little black purse.

Meredith looked like a 1940s-era movie star, dressed in a chocolate-brown silk sheath dress with a matching three-quarter sleeve bolero jacket and round-toed heels that completed the retro-vibe. What kept her from looking like she wore a costume though, was the modern, smooth, french twist her hair swept up to in the back, with the front side parted and swept behind her ears.

Alaine must look like a child playing dress-up beside Meredith's stately elegance.

To her surprise, Meredith drew her into a hug in greeting. "It's so good to see you. It's been far too long."

"I know. I'm sorry about that. I've been. . .going through some things that made me keep to myself there for a while." Alaine stepped back and tried to make herself taller. But Meredith had at least four inches on her.

"Believe me, I understand. I hope everything worked out okay."

"Not yet, but it's getting there." She motioned toward the front doors, and Meredith fell in step with her. "Before we leave, remind me to give you your wedding present. It's in my car."

"Thank you so much. You didn't have to do that."

"I know I didn't. I hope you like it."

"I'm sure we will."

The atrium-style lobby of the art museum reverberated with voices and music. Alaine handed the admission passes to the concierge. Both Alaine and Meredith were instantly recognized by other attendees and exchanged apologetic looks before being drawn into separate conversations.

At eight o'clock, someone announced that the exhibit was now open for viewing. Alaine broke away from several older ladies and found Meredith, who'd managed to make her way over to the food tables.

Alaine grabbed a canapé and paused for a moment to let the tangy creaminess of the cheese and the herby sweetness of marinated artichoke mingle and dance across her tongue.

Meredith handed her a crystal flute. "Fruit tea."

"Thanks." She grabbed a napkin to wipe away the crumbs from her fingers and mouth.

"Alaine, good to see you. I feel like you've been avoiding me the last few times I've been down to the studio to do my voiceovers." Major O'Hara, dapper in a black chef's jacket edged with silver piping, shook Alaine's hand, then put his arm around Meredith's waist and kissed her temple.

"Chef O'Hara." Alaine grinned at him. "You know how it goes— busy, busy, busy."

"Yeah, especially when your boss is a task-mistress who micro-manages everything you do." He scooted away from Meredith's elbow to his side.

In the company of other acquaintances, Alaine would have been extremely jealous over the display of affection between the couple. With Major and Meredith, she basked in the radiance of their happiness. "Congratulations on getting married. Of course, I'm crushed that you eloped. I was planning on coming out with a full crew to cover it for the show."

"Why do you think we did it?" Meredith winked at her.

"Because Forbes was trying to make you do it his way?" She cringed as soon as the words left her mouth.

But Meredith burst into laughter. "Obviously you know my brother better than either of you have let on." She exchanged a quick glance with Major, who just shook his head. She shrugged and hooked her arm through Alaine's. "Come on. Let's go look at some art."

Most of the other guests had left the atrium. Alaine picked up one of the souvenir booklets explaining the purpose of the Art Without Limits Exhibit and the fund-raiser for the Beausoleil Artists with Disabilities Foundation. Out of the corner of her eye, she caught the bright light of a live, remote camera. Yep. There was the cub reporter who'd been assigned to cover the event for the ten o'clock broadcast. Nope. Not even a twinge of envy. She smiled to herself.

She and Meredith discussed the pieces in soft voices as they moved through the gallery—discovering they both had similar tastes and noticed much of the same aspects of the workmanship.

They rounded a corner, and Alaine released a small gasp. The large, framed painting portrayed a dancing couple who looked quite a bit like Fred Astaire and Ginger Rogers. The artist had obviously studied Monet's techniques because it looked like something that could have been done by the great impressionist.

Beside her, Meredith exclaimed over the excellence of the work, but Alaine was lost for words. She wanted it. The painting represented the two things she enjoyed most in life: art and ballroom dance.

She glanced down at the card under it which gave the artist's name and the name of the piece. A red dot had been affixed to the corner. This piece would be part of the fund-raising auction. She flipped open her little purse—and then remembered she hadn't put a pen in it. Instead, she opened the booklet and located the page the piece was on, which she dog-eared. Surely it wouldn't go for more than what she could afford to pay, would it?

"Excuse me, I want to go make a bid on this one."

"I'll go with you. I saw one I want to bid on, too."

They found the table where the sheets for the silent auction were laid out. Not too many people buzzed around them—but the night was still young. Alaine found the sheet for her painting. . .and groaned in disappointment. Someone had already placed an opening bid of one thousand dollars—far too expensive for Alaine's meager art budget.

Oh, well. It wasn't meant to be.

The camera light caught her attention again, and she turned toward it, only to find it practically in her face. But the person standing to the side of the cameraman wasn't the cub reporter from Channel Six.

"Teri Jones." Alaine gave the woman who was her direct competitor a tight smile.

"Alaine Delacroix. I'm surprised you're not working tonight.

What, did they decide this story was too important for the social-scene reporter?"

"That's rich, coming from you." Before she could wave her off, Meredith joined her.

"And Meredith Guidry." Teri's eyes narrowed as she looked between them. "That's right, B-G is one of your show's biggest sponsors. Should have guessed."

"Well, you guessed wrong. Meredith and I are friends."

"And it's Meredith *O'Hara* now, thank you." The chill in Meredith's voice surprised Alaine, but she didn't want to break eye contact with the vulture for a moment, not sure when the attack would come.

Teri snapped at her cameraman, and he started filming. Alaine adjusted her expression to try to ensure she looked pleasant and happy to be interviewed by the woman who made Jerry Springer look like a social worker—the woman who'd tried to ruin Bekka Blakeley's career so many years ago.

Teri raised her microphone and turned to face the camera. "I'm here with Alaine Delacroix, of Channel Six news, and Meredith Guidry O'Hara, of Boudreaux-Guidry Enterprises. Mrs. O'Hara"—she turned and thrust the microphone in Meredith's face—"what do you think of the exhibit?"

Meredith began to give a glowing review of what they'd seen so far. Teri cut her off midstream.

"Ms. Delacroix, I find it very interesting you're here with an executive director of Boudreaux-Guidry Enterprises tonight. After all, weren't you one of the main organizers of the meeting in Moreaux Mills last night protesting B-G's development plans?"

She'd guessed as much. "I am not involved in the situation. I was there merely as an observer, out of care and concern for my family, who live and work in the Mills."

"It's my understanding you gave a very. . .*passionate* introduction of the lawyer who came out to speak to them—Forbes Guidry, if I'm not mistaken."

Alaine's stomach twisted around that canapé she'd eaten. "Are you going somewhere with this? If so, I'd appreciate you getting to your point so that I can go back to enjoying my evening."

"Touchy." Teri's smile became predatory. "My sources tell me that Mr. Guidry has taken on this case pro bono."

Alaine shrugged. "As I'm aware of no case being filed, I can neither confirm nor deny that statement."

"It's common knowledge that you have a personal relationship with Mr. Guidry—after all, it was on your own, um, show that you aired tape of the two of you taking dancing lessons together."

Alaine raised her eyebrows and shifted her weight in annoyance.

"It stands to reason, then, that if he isn't getting paid for his legal services by the people in Moreaux Mills, he's being remunerated in a completely nonmonetary manner. After all, what wouldn't a girl do to make sure Mommy and Daddy got the best lawyer money—or whatever—can buy?"

All Alaine could do was gape at her. The nasty insinuation hung in the air between them; but before Alaine could recover, Meredith stepped between them.

"If you air that—or any other filth like it—on your show, you will be sued. And I can't imagine your bosses will be happy with you for generating yet *another* slander suit from my family against you and the station."

Teri smirked. "Come on," she nudged the cameraman. "I've got what I need out of these two."

"Meredith, I'm sorry. You shouldn't have involved yourself in that."

Meredith pulled her aside to a quiet corner. "What was she talking about? What case?"

The last thing she wanted was for that to come between them. "I can't talk about it. I've given my word."

"Okay. I won't ask any more about it."

Alaine's stomach hurt. "And I don't want you thinking that I've behaved improperly toward your brother, either. We've spent some time together, and he agreed to do a favor for me—for my family and their neighbors. But there is nothing between us beyond that."

Kindness beamed from Meredith's light-brown eyes. "I never suspected there was." She hooked her arm through Alaine's again and led her back toward the gallery. "But I'm still holding out hope."

CHAPTER 21

*F*at-free, sugar-free, mocha latte." Forbes handed over his Coffee Club card for his twenty-five-cent discount.

"I guess it's not even worth asking you if you want an order of beignets to go with that, Mr. Guidry?" The perky cashier batted her eyes at him.

"As always, the answer is no thank you, Kristi." And as always, he refrained from reminding her that he was almost old enough to be her father. "Just coffee." He paid her for it, then scoped out the large café.

He didn't like this no-name, no-picture deal of Shon's. Petite brunette wearing black-and-white wasn't that much to go on. But right now, no one fitting that description sat by herself at a table or in the armchairs over by the greenery-filled fireplace or out on the deck overlooking the river.

Instead of committing himself to a table before his date arrived, Forbes stood at the coffee bar, feeling very much like a cowboy in one of those old westerns Meredith and Major liked watching so much.

The front door swung open. Forbes straightened. Though backlit, the silhouette entering was definitely female—a petite female. She paused, probably letting her eyes adjust to the dim interior. He checked his watch—9:21. Not just punctual, but early. Nice.

She moved toward the cashier. Forbes's knees went weak. Alaine

Delacroix pushed her sunglasses up on top of her head and placed her order.

Alaine? Could Shon have possibly—but if he had, why hadn't he said anything? Forbes pulled out the copy of the e-mail with the description Shon had sent. Petite. Check. Brunette. Well, Forbes would have called her hair black, but it could work as a description. Wearing a black-and-white top. He glanced back up at Alaine, making sure to keep himself partially hidden behind the coffee-making station. She was wearing a black-and-white polka-dot jacket. Three strikes—er, three hits—okay, so the baseball metaphor didn't work.

He waited for her to make her way down the long counter to the corner where she'd pick up her coffee, and from whence she'd be able to see him.

Their eyes met. Hers widened, and her full lips formed a small *O*. "What. . .what are you doing here?"

"Good morning to you, too." He saluted her with his coffee. "Are you meeting someone here?"

"I. . .uh. . .yes, I'm supposed to be meeting someone here."

"Devastatingly handsome and wearing blue?"

Her face went from ghostly pale to flushed in a split second. "Tall, dark hair, and wearing. . .red." She frowned and pulled a folded piece of paper from her purse. "It definitely says red, not blue. Wait—are you here for. . .are you meeting someone here from Let's Do Coffee?"

His face went hot. "I am. Petite, brunette, wearing a black-and-white top. If that isn't you. . ." He scanned the room again, just to make sure he hadn't missed someone else fitting the description.

"Extra large café au lait," the barista called.

Alaine stepped over to grab the tall, ceramic mug. She poured what looked like half the sugar shaker into it, tasted, and added a bit more sugar. He shuddered. It had to be sludgelike by now.

"So if I'm not meeting you," she said, returning to stand at the bar beside him, "and you're not meeting me, maybe we shouldn't be standing here talking to each other when they do come in, or else they might not realize we're the ones."

"Are you trying to avoid me?" He sipped his latte, enjoying how the strong flavor of the espresso picked up the subtle hint of the skim milk and the light sweetness and chocolate of the sugar-free mocha flavoring, trying not to let himself be disappointed that Alaine wasn't here for him.

"Avoid you?"

"You haven't returned my phone calls."

She traced her finger around the handle of her mug. "I wasn't sure what to say to you."

Setting his cup down, he leaned forward. "I only wanted to thank you. To try to tell you how much what you did meant to me. And to say that I hope your folks didn't give you a hard time for it."

Her gaze dropped to his mouth, but then just as quickly, she closed her eyes and turned her head away. Heat coursed through his body. He'd been wanting to kiss her since the first moment they met—actually a long time before that. Unless his eyes deceived him, she'd just told him she'd thought about it, too.

He took a step back for safety. "I saw your name made the newspaper blurb. That didn't make things worse, did it?"

"My parents understood why I did what I did. My boss offered me a promotion to cover the story." She turned her profile to him and leaned back against the edge of the bar's top, cradling her mug in both hands.

"Congratulations."

"I didn't take it. I have a wonderful job—better than most midmarket TV journalists can boast—and I'd be an idiot to give it up to work longer, harder hours under someone else's direction instead of having the virtual autonomy I have on my show." She took a sip of coffee, and finally looked at him again, her dark eyes sparkling like onyx. "Besides, that kind of journalism demands objectivity, and there's no way I could stay objective about this story."

This time, her eyes stayed locked on his, but he found himself once again leaning toward her, toward those enticing, full lips.

They both startled when the bell on the front door jangled. A tall man—a very tall man—with hair almost as dark as Alaine's and wearing a bright red University of Louisiana–Bonneterre T-shirt entered the café and stood inside the door, scanning the interior.

Alaine looked like she might tuck tail and run. Forbes might aid her, if it came to that.

The man's gaze came to rest on Alaine. Forbes's guard rose immediately at the smile that split the guy's face. He approached them. Alaine grew more stiff, and Forbes couldn't help but be impressed by the guy's height. He had to be at least six foot eight, if not taller.

"I think I'm here to meet you. Petite, black hair, black-and-white polka-dot top and black capris."

Alaine nodded, a silent, forced smile on her face, her shoulders practically flat on the bar from leaning back to look up at her date.

"Alaine Delacroix," the man breathed. "They told me I might recognize you once I saw you, but I had no idea I'd be this lucky. I'm Riley."

Forbes was surprised he couldn't hear Alaine's teeth rattle with the force of Riley's handshake.

"Can I get you something—but you already have something." The lumbering giant at long last noticed Forbes. "You two know each other?"

"Riley, this is a business acquaintance of mine, Forbes Guidry."

Forbes's own teeth knocked together when he shook Riley's hand. "Nice to meet you." No. No it wasn't. He should grab Alaine by the arm and sweep her out of here. Wait—a *business acquaintance?* He turned to stare at her.

"I'll go place my order. Don't go anywhere now, Alaine Delacroix."

As soon as Too-Tall was out of earshot, Forbes confronted her. "A *business acquaintance?* I thought we were well beyond that—friends, at least."

Alaine looked over her shoulder, then pushed him back a few

steps, her hand burning like a branding iron on his chest. "What was I supposed to say?" she whispered. "I'm here in good faith to have coffee with this guy. He's paid for the privilege of being set up on a blind date with someone—who just happens to be *Alaine Delacroix.*" She imitated the way Riley drawled her name. "I need to afford him the same courtesy I would expect to receive if he'd already been here talking to a woman he knows and spends a lot of time with."

Yeah, except Forbes wanted to stake his claim, to let the behemoth know Alaine was spoken for, whether she knew it or not.

The front door chimed again. Forbes didn't want to look, but he did. And instantly regretted it. In walked a woman who could only be classified as *on the prowl.* And she was wearing a black-and-white top—a skin-tight, zebra-striped halter top to be exact.

Alaine's eyes danced with barely suppressed amusement when she looked up at him. "I believe your petite brunette in a black-and-white top just walked in." She picked up her mug from the bar. "Have fun."

⚜

"So glad you find this funny." Forbes narrowed his eyes at her.

Alaine laughed. The only thing that could have made the woman any less suitable for him would be if she were wearing leather motorcycle chaps instead of shorts so short they were almost indecent. Alaine had been a little worried when she realized Forbes was here for a date—and not with her—that he might meet someone he'd like more than her. Though Alaine hated passing judgment based on a first appearance, she was pretty good at figuring people out by how they dressed.

This woman defined *cougar*—an older woman out to snag a good-looking, younger man. Alaine hadn't thought Shon would handle that type; but she supposed as long as the money was green enough, he'd take on just about any client.

Alaine's date, Mr. I-Don't-Know-How-to-Dress-for-a-Coffee-Date, returned to them. With a sigh, Forbes excused himself and went over to speak to Ms. Zebra Stripe.

"Shall we get a table?" Alaine swept her arm to the side to indicate the half-full dining room.

"Yeah. You get a table, Alaine Delacroix, and I'll join you as soon as I get my stuff."

Only with extreme effort did she stop herself from telling him not to call her by her full name. The next half hour would be the longest of her life.

By design, more likely than by chance, Forbes chose a table not too far away and sat so he faced Alaine. As Riley went on about himself, Alaine watched Forbes and his date out of the corner of her eye.

At first, the woman leaned forward, touching her face, her chest, her throat. All signs she found Forbes quite attractive. As time progressed, her hands became more occupied with her coffee cup, then dropped to her lap.

Alaine stifled a grin when the woman crossed her arms, sitting as far back in her chair as she could. Whatever she and Forbes were discussing, the woman didn't like it.

Yep. There she went. Forbes stood and shook her hand, then watched the woman walk out. But instead of leave, he went over and grabbed a newspaper off the rack and returned to his table to read it.

Alaine tried to focus on Riley. But now he was talking about the college baseball game he planned to attend today. And if he said *Alaine Delacroix* one more time—

"You know, Riley," she interrupted, "I really don't follow baseball. Do you like art? I went to the opening of a wonderful exhibit down at the Bonneterre Fine Arts Center last night."

Confusion filled Riley's mossy-green eyes. "Art?"

"Yes. I'm a painter, too. Well, I don't get to do it very often anymore. But I started out as an art major in college." She talked about some of her favorite artists for a few minutes until Riley completely glazed over. Yeah, turnabout's not always fair play. He'd want to leave soon.

"Do you like ballet?" Now she'd make sure he didn't ask for

another date with *Alaine Delacroix*. "The new season of the Bonneterre Ballet Company starts in a few weeks, and I'm thinking about getting season tickets." Not that she would—she couldn't afford the expense. But he didn't need to know that.

"B–ballet?" He glanced over his shoulder toward the door.

"Yes. Oh, and the new opera season starts soon as well." Of course, she hated opera.

"Wow. We really don't have anything in common." He glanced at his watch. "Look at that. If I'm going to make it to the ballpark before the first pitch, I'd better go."

"Oh, really? So soon?"

"Yeah—yes. It was great to meet you." He held out his hand.

"You, too." Alaine didn't want to have her brains scrambled again. She barely touched her fingertips to his. *Don't let the door hit you in the fanny on the way out.*

He hurried away. She thought about calling him back to nag him about putting his coffee mug in the dish tray beside the trash can, but that would probably be overkill. With a laugh, she disposed of his cup, then took hers to the counter for a refill.

While waiting, she turned around to see what Forbes was up to. He still sat reading the newspaper and sipping his coffee—at her table. Typical. Yet extremely gratifying.

With her coffee fortified with sugar, she returned to the table, sat, and pulled the "Style" section out of the stack of newspaper he wasn't currently reading. She pretended to read it for a few moments.

Finally, Forbes lowered the *A* section. "So?"

"So, what?"

"How did you like dear Riley?"

"Oh, he's a lovely man—I'm sure Shon will find the right woman for him soon."

"But. . . ?" Forbes couldn't hide the hint of vulnerability in his eyes.

She thought about stringing him along, but what would be the point? He already knew the answer. "But it isn't me."

He snapped the paper upright and disappeared behind it. "I could have told you that."

"And what about Ms. Zebra Stripe?" Alaine didn't look up from her section.

"Not for me."

"Looked like things didn't go so well." She flexed her jaw to straighten her expression, just in case he dropped the paper again. "Looked like she got kind of mad at you."

The paper rustled, then crumpled when he dropped his hands to the table. "If you must know, I mentioned her age, that I wasn't really looking to date someone significantly older than me."

Alaine cringed. "Oh, that poor woman. That was a horrible thing to say."

"No kidding. Especially since she then told me that we graduated from high school together—and she had skipped a grade a few years before."

"So she's a year *younger* than you?"

He grimaced—and even wearing that sour expression was utterly adorable. "Yeah. Talk about foot-in-mouth. She said when she realized who I was that she'd hoped maybe we could attend our reunion together in the fall. Guess it'll just give all the women there something more to use to gossip about me."

"The girls from your high school class like to gossip about you?" Oh to be a fly on the wall at that reunion.

"Yeah—about how horrible a boyfriend I was or how I haven't been able to have a long-term relationship, ever." He smoothed out his section of the paper and refolded it.

Alaine's heart gave a trill like a piccolo. "They don't know what they're missing."

His eyes, almost as dark blue as his shirt, snapped to hers. She couldn't believe she'd said that aloud. She couldn't do this, could she? Yet if she walked away, would she be giving up the only chance she might have for falling in love? She held his gaze, not caring if her indecision showed.

"You know"—Forbes leaned forward and lowered his voice—"falling for your parents' lawyer isn't the worst thing you can do. No matter what that woman from Channel Three said to you last night."

"How did you—"

"Meredith called me last night to ask me what was going on. I didn't tell her much. Just that we're friends, and that I'm doing a favor for your parents. She doesn't need to be dragged into the middle of this."

"I agree. But Forbes, did she tell you how truly vulgar Teri's insinuations were? Other people are bound to wonder the same thing."

"Let them wonder." He reached across the table and took her hand in his.

Her pulse pounded through her head in dizzying waves. "You don't understand. As a representative of the TV station, and especially because of the nature of my show and my primary viewers being stay-at-home moms and senior citizens, I have to protect my reputation as much as I can. If a rumor like that were to sprout legs, it could create a scandal, and the last thing we need is negative public attention on what we're doing."

His thumb made slow, soft circles on her palm. "You worry too much about what other people think. What do you *feel*, Alaine Delacroix?"

All she could feel right now was the way her body tingled in response to his rubbing her palm. "I..."

Before she could think, before she could react, Forbes leaned across the table and kissed her. Soft, gentle, undemanding, and too quickly ended. Her hand spasmed in his.

"Need more time to think?"

She pulled her hand out of his and reached for the section of newspaper in front of her, folded it in half, and started fanning herself with it. Feel? The only time she ever gave herself over to her feelings was when she was drawing or painting. Which she hadn't done regularly since college. Did she still know how to feel? "If you hadn't found out about this whole development thing our parents are involved in right after the banquet, would you have gone out with me?" He took the paper out of her hand and recaptured it.

"Yes, but—"

"And do you think that if we'd gone out on a date, with no family feud looming on the horizon, you might have enjoyed it?"

"I do, but—"

"And if you'd enjoyed that date, would you have gone out with me again?"

"I probably would have, but—"

"And if we'd started seeing each other regularly, don't you think you'd have fallen in love with me as much as you have while you've been trying to avoid me the past month?"

Lawyers. "I've never said I'm in love with you."

He grinned at her. "But you are. Why else would you have flung yourself in front of me to save me from the verbal arrows those people were shooting at me Thursday night? You risked your parents' ire—as well as this reputation of yours that you're now concerned about—without a moment's hesitation. Not to mention the fact that you sat here not twenty minutes ago and ran off our dear friend Riley just so you could spend more time with me. Really now—opera? ballet?"

"Arrrggghhh." She tossed her head back. "Do you always have to get your way?"

Grinning, he leaned over and kissed her again. Her entire skeleton melted into a puddle of wax, and she could barely focus on him when the kiss ended mere seconds—or millennia—later.

He traced her cheek and jaw with his free hand. "Yes, I always get my way."

CHAPTER 22

$\mathcal{M}$eredith leaned into Forbes's one-armed squeeze. "You look like the mouse who found the cheese."

"It's a beautiful day." He should have asked Alaine to come to church with him this morning. Yesterday had clinched it for him: Alaine fit into his life quite nicely. And while he wasn't ready to take any kind of drastic steps, he wanted everyone to know she was his.

"Really?" Meredith glanced out the bank of windows behind her—on the other side of them, a heavy downpour obscured everything beyond about three feet. "This unusually chipper mood doesn't have anything to do with your attending a certain meeting in a certain area of town with a certain TV news reporter, does it?"

"Maybe."

Instead of breaking into a smile, Meredith's frown increased. "Forbes, weren't you listening when I told you what Teri Jones—"

"You know you can't believe a thing that woman says. How many times have Mom and Dad sued her and that station already?"

"That's beside the point. She will spread the rumor that you're taking payment for handling the Moreaux Mills case in form of. . . well, intimate favors from Alaine." Meredith's voice dropped so low, he barely heard the last part of her statement.

He could tell his shrug frustrated his sister further. "Let people

244

think what they want. In the end, the truth always manages to trump the rumors."

Meredith touched his arm. "Mom and Dad were very hurt when they saw the newspaper article. They don't understand how you could even consider taking on clients who want to sue them."

"Not to sue them. To sue their company. There's a huge difference." He smiled and nodded at several acquaintances passing by in the crowded foyer. Everyone waited for the rain to ease before leaving. They might be here for a while.

"Don't try to argue semantics. B-G is us: It's Mom and Dad, and Major and me. It's the people we work closely with every day." Her volume increased with her intensity. She glanced around.

"No one's listening to us, Mere." He looked around, too, just to be sure. "But you haven't talked to the people who're about to lose their businesses, their homes, everything they've worked for their whole lives, just because Mom and Dad—or B-G or however you want to think about it—want to buy up all of their property as cheap as they can so they can tear it all to the ground and rebuild Warehouse Row and Moreaux Mills in their own image."

"They're only buying foreclosures and from people who want to sell. Some of those people will never make as much as they'll get by selling their property to B-G."

"Not at the scandalously low rate the city council's inspectors set the property values at. Most of them, if they sell, won't even be able to cover the full amount of their mortgages and small-business loans."

Meredith pressed her fingertips to the back of her neck and rolled her head as if to ease tight muscles. "I don't want to fight with you about it. Actually, I don't want to know about it." She inhaled and released a deep breath. "I thought you were planning to attend the art exhibit opening Friday night."

"Oh, you know me and art."

"Yeah, I know. Paint-by-numbers or Elvis on black velvet."

He reached toward her, about to put her in a headlock to make her take that back, but stopped. Not only would it bother Meredith, it would look ridiculous. "You forgot anything made with macaroni and glue."

Major joined them. "Looks like it's letting up a little bit. I'll go pull the car up so you don't have to get soaked."

"That's not necess—"

Major pressed his finger to his wife's lips and stared her down.

She took his hand in both of hers and pulled it away. "Thank you, dear. I would greatly appreciate you for doing that."

"I'll see you over at Errol and Maggie's." Forbes unfurled his umbrella so it was ready to open as soon as he walked out the door.

"At Errol and Maggie's?" Meredith shook her head.

"Yeah. . .for lunch. Like every week after church."

"You mean, you're going?" She took a step forward, utter confusion twisting her features.

Her confusion proved to be contagious. "Of course I'm going. I go every week, just like you do."

"But you know Mom and Dad are going to be there."

He nodded. "Just like they are every week—well, except when they fly off to Boston at the last minute."

"They're going to want to talk to you about this case, Forbes."

Ah, so that's what had her worried—controversy over the dinner table. She'd always had a delicate stomach, easily upset by the least bit of conflict. "They're not going to have it out with me at the table in front of the rest of the family. And if I were to skip out, it would look like I'm ashamed of what I've done or afraid of them, and I'm neither." He pulled his sister into a hug. "I'm a big boy. I can handle Mom and Dad's being a little miffed at me."

"But they're not just miffed—"

"Enough, Mere." He took her by the shoulders and held her at arms' length. "I *can* handle this. Everything's going to be okay. Once I've explained everything to them, I think they'll not only realize I have a point but they'll see things from my point of view and help me work to change what's happening."

Meredith still looked skeptical, but someone called to her that

Major had just pulled up. "Come on, we'll drive you over to your car so you don't have to get quite so soaked."

"Thanks, Sis."

But even with his umbrella, his shoes and pants' legs were drenched just from the few feet he had to dash to get from Meredith's SUV to the Jag. Whether it was her intention to keep Major completely out of the controversy or if she'd actually decided to believe Forbes when he said he could handle facing their parents, she hadn't mentioned it again in the brief, shared car ride.

Driving in rain so heavy made claws of anxiety dig into his shoulders—not because of worrying about his own driving ability, but because of everyone else on the road. By the time he arrived at Uncle Errol and Aunt Maggie's house, the muscles across his upper back were tight to the point of snapping. He remained in the car a moment, doing some deep breathing to try to relax before he walked into what could be an adversarial environment. For all he'd told Meredith that Mom and Dad wouldn't make a scene in front of the extended family, if they were angry enough, no telling what they might do.

He joined his thirtysomething siblings and cousins in the florida room at the rear of the house.

"Forbes!"

"Hey, Forbes!"

"You made it!"

Everyone's greetings were bright, cheery—a little *too* bright and cheery. And who was that with Anne? He took another deep breath and slapped on a smile as the tall, curvaceous brunette slinked over to him.

"Evelyn. What a surprise." He took her proffered hands, but did not move in toward her when it looked like she wanted to exchange a kiss on the cheek.

"I was rather surprised when your parents invited me Friday. I guess they realized how homesick I've been the last few weeks. I usually hit a point after about a month where I go through that.

But never before have my clients invited me into the bosom of their family to help me feel better about being so far from my own."

Right. Knowing his parents, they'd invited her for some reason of their own, probably because of his involvement with the Mills case. "I'm sorry to hear you've been down."

A melancholy realization struck Forbes, the same feeling as when he'd been told at age eight that Santa Claus wasn't real. In questioning his parents' motives behind inviting a lonely woman they worked with on a daily basis to come to Sunday dinner, he'd taken a giant leap away from the person he'd been not long ago who believed everything his parents said and never second-guessed any decisions they made. He'd lost the last remaining vestige of childhood idealism.

His younger brothers and male cousins seemed eager to re-capture Evelyn's attention. Forbes excused himself and ducked out of the room as Major and Meredith's entrance drew attention away from him.

He wandered aimlessly down the hall. He didn't want to go into the living room, family room, or kitchen, where the remainder of the family would be. Being honest with himself, his intestines twisted in knots at the prospect of facing his parents—that they might not hold on to the reserve for which everyone in the family admired them. But would they really do it in front of Evelyn?

The clanging of Maggie's handheld bell echoed through the house. In just a few short moments, he'd find out exactly how his parents were going to react. Steeling himself, he headed for the dining room. He ignored Meredith's doleful expression when he took his seat beside her.

During Papere's blessing, Forbes prayed for wisdom—as well as patience—for the confrontation he was sure would be coming, from the assiduous manner in which his mother avoided making eye contact with him.

Once platters and bowls started going around the table, Forbes got an idea of why his parents might have invited Evelyn on this of all Sundays. She became the center of attention—in which she seemed to revel.

Mom glowed like a proud, well, mother. "Evelyn has done so much in the few short weeks she's been here to further the Warehouse Row project. It's amazing how she's managed to clear some roadblocks that have been hanging us up for months and months."

Evelyn preened under his mother's compliments. "Now, Mairee, don't make it sound like more than it was. I'm just doing my job. It's easier to make something seem simple if one has experience in it."

"I'm only telling the truth, dear. We've been wanting to move on this development project for at least six months, and it's your dedication that's made it happen."

Forbes pushed a wad of chicken and rice casserole around on his plate. He should have listened to Meredith. Fast food from a drive-through eaten at home alone would have been much preferable than listening to his mother fawn over the person who was probably more culpable for the inequities even now bearing down on the good people in the Mills than he could currently prove.

"So is there a groundbreaking date yet?" Major asked. "Jennifer and I have teamed up to do some interviews recently, so I'm eager to know when I might be able to start hiring." He cast a grin at his sister-in-law across the table from them. "After all, I can't let Jenn have all the good candidates simply because she can put them to work immediately."

"For Warehouse Row, yes, we should be breaking ground by Labor Day. That is, of course, as long as we know we're going to be able to go ahead with the rest of the Mills development project."

Forbes tightly controlled his expression when he met his mother's glare. The crowded dining room became chillingly silent.

"After all, what we're doing is best for Bonneterre."

Forbes wiped his mouth and dropped his napkin on the table. Meredith grabbed his forearm and squeezed. With gentle but firm pressure, he disengaged from his sister's silent expression of concern without breaking eye contact with his mother.

" 'Best for Bonneterre'? Don't you mean best for Boudreaux-Guidry Enterprises' bottom line? Because from what I've seen and heard from talking to the people who already live in Moreaux Mills, what's happening is definitely not best for them."

"You can't believe what those people say. They're a drain on our city's resources—always applying for hardship loans and trying to talk their way out of paying their taxes, all the while reneging on their financial responsibilities. We're offering them a helping hand by buying them out."

"After using your considerable influence with the city council to get their property values dropped and their property taxes raised." He shook his head and stood. "I would never have believed my own parents would do something so underhanded—would exploit other people just to make more money."

Near the end of the table, his father shot out of his chair so fast it fell backward with a bang on the floor. "You will apologize for making such an accusation."

"No, sir, I will not apologize. Now more than ever, I believe what you are doing is wrong, and I will do whatever it takes to help the people whose homes and businesses you're intent on ruining." He glanced around the room. No one would look at him.

"Lawson, Forbes." Papere stood as well. "Surely this is a discussion best saved for *private*."

"Papere, Mamere," Forbes inclined his head toward his grandparents at either end of the enormous table, "my apologies for disrupting dinner. And you're right, this is a discussion best saved for another time and another place—when *all* parties are present, including their legal counsel."

Meredith gave a little gasp. He touched her shoulder and pushed his chair out of the way. "Until such a time, I will consider myself excused from all family gatherings." With a final half bow, he walked out of the dining room.

No one called his name—no one came after him. Just as well. At least it let him know where the entire family stood on the matter: not with him.

By the time he made it to his car, his lungs hurt from pressure worse than what he'd experienced the first time he'd been scuba diving and had gone too deep.

But he could handle this. He could. He'd handled everything else that had come his way in life. He could handle this. Except no matter what he'd faced in his life before now, he could always count on his family to be there for him.

Not this time.

The pressure increased tenfold. He pointed the car east and drove, not caring where he went so long as he was moving. The conversation he'd had with Major just a few months ago about honoring one's parents replayed with the vividness of surround sound in his head.

Taking a stand had been the right thing to do. Wasn't part of honoring one's parents helping them see when they were doing something that hurt others? Accepting what they were doing without raising a question as to the ethics behind their actions would be dishonoring himself.

He pulled the Jag to a stop—in front of Delacroix Gardens. Though the rain had slackened to a steady drizzle, the cloud-darkened sky made it possible for him to see movement in the lighted, second-floor dormer windows of the building that looked like a cottage out of a fairy tale. He pulled into the small gravel parking lot at the side of the dual-purpose house. Unsure of where the entrance to their home would be, Forbes approached through the pergola that stood over the sidewalk leading to the shop's front door, not bothering with his umbrella.

A sign hung over what looked like a doorbell button. AFTER HOURS DELIVERIES PRESS HERE. He pressed it; a chime like church bells echoed distantly. In the shelter of the porch, he wiped the worst of the rain from his face and waited.

The door swung open. "We're closed on Sund—Forbes." JD looked as shocked to see him as Forbes was himself at being here. "Come in, get in out of the rain."

"Thanks. I'm sorry for dropping in on you like this."

"Not at all. Our door is always open to you." JD ushered him in and closed and locked the door behind him. "Come on upstairs where you can dry off a bit."

A cacophony of scents slammed Forbes in the nose—sweet and earthy and spicy. . .and utterly homey. He followed Alaine's father through the flower shop's back room—weirdly shadowy and sparkly at the same time, lined with shelves filled with glass vases in every color imaginable—to a staircase at the back.

"Watch out for the lift chair." JD skirted around the seat attached to a beam that ran up the right-hand side of the staircase. "You just missed seeing Joe, Nikki, Alaine, and our youngest son, Tony. Solange and I were just settling down for our coffee and newspaper."

Forbes stopped. "I hadn't considered—I really don't want to interrupt your day."

"Of course you can." JD came down until he was two steps above Forbes and laid his hands on Forbes's shoulders. "And I can tell by your demeanor that you're having a rough day. You've obviously come here because something is bothering you. From what Alaine's told us, I imagine it has to do with your parents' reaction to finding out you're helping us. So let us do what we can to make you feel better."

Forbes tried to clear the cement from his throat. "Thank you, Mr. Delacroix. That means a lot to me."

"Please, I've asked you to call me JD. Come on, now. The coffee should be ready, and Solange has some baklava hidden in the kitchen that Voula Pappas sent over from the restaurant for the store yesterday."

The stairs came up into a hallway, and a warm light at the end beckoned them forward. Forbes entered a kitchen that looked like it was straight out of the 1950s—the happiness and innocence of the decor imbuing him with a sliver of optimism that, somehow, everything would be okay.

"Joseph, who—" Mrs. Delacroix came into the kitchen through the attached, very informal dining area. "Forbes, welcome to our home." She narrowed her eyes in an intense study of him. "You go sit in the living room. I will bring you coffee and baklava." She winked at her husband.

"Best do what she says, son." JD grinned and waved Forbes on through the kitchen.

If the kitchen had been 1950s kitsch, the living room was definitely Mediterranean, from the soft, seaside colors to the terracotta floor tiles to the Portuguese decorative touches around the room. The pressure in his chest eased even more from the warm, welcoming embrace the room wrapped him in.

Moments later, Solange entered with an enormous coffee mug and a plate of pastries, both of which she set on the low table in front of Forbes. He opened his mouth to ask for milk—and to see if they had any artificial sweetener—then realized that Solange had already taken the liberty of doctoring his coffee. It probably would be full fat milk and too much sugar. He'd drink enough to be polite.

As soon as the coffee hit his tongue, he wondered that Alaine would be able to drink coffee made by anyone else. The smooth creaminess coated his tongue—so it was half-and-half, not milk—and she'd added just enough sugar for a hint of sweetness, but not too much.

The muscles in his shoulders started to ease.

JD and Solange let him drink coffee and eat the sticky Greek pastries in peace, allowing his mind and thoughts to settle.

Finally, he took one more swallow of the coffee, set it on the table, and leaned forward, resting his elbows on his knees. "I just walked out on my family's Sunday dinner. I accused my parents of being—" What exactly had he said? "I accused them of being underhanded and of exploiting the people in the Mills. In front of our entire extended family."

"And you're feeling like a bad son." JD swayed back and forth slowly in his plush rocking chair. "If I may take a wild guess, as the oldest son, you've always felt it was your responsibility to step up and fill in for your parents whenever they couldn't be there. You're basically the third parent in your immediate family. Am I right?"

Forbes nodded.

"When anything goes wrong, you see it as a challenge that you can and will overcome."

That went without saying. He nodded again.

"When one of your brothers or sisters disobeyed or openly defied your parents, you took it personally and didn't understand why your parents were sometimes lax in enforcing their own rules with your younger siblings."

Consternated but intrigued, Forbes propped his chin in his hand.

JD continued his slow, contemplative rocking. "But you decided not to go to work for your parents when you finished college because. . .why?"

"Because. . ." He thought back twenty years. "Because I was afraid that if I went into the family business, I'd never be my own man. I'd never see if I could make something of myself without constantly taking from my parents."

"And how do you feel about the man you've become?"

Forbes couldn't answer right away. He had a good life—made an enviable salary, lived in a luxurious home in an exclusive community, drove a high-end vehicle, knew all the "right" people. And he lived alone and ate dinner by himself most nights. "There are some things I'd like to change about myself. Some things I'm working on already. Others I probably need to spend more time studying to see how I can improve."

"Do you think you're a better man than your father?"

"No. I'm a different man than my father."

JD's head bobbed slightly in what could have been a nod. "That's a good attitude to have. I wish I'd realized that before my father passed away. Forbes, you are a good man. You have high morals and ethics. And if I'm not mistaken, you're a man of faith as well."

"Yes, sir." He could visualize everything JD mentioned as if they were boxes of different shapes and sizes. Forbes wasn't sure just how they all stacked together.

"Because I know those things about you, I know that your parents are, deep down, good people. They may have just forgotten it as other influences, such as wealth and prestige, have drawn the curtains over the qualities that they found important enough to instill in their son. The best way you can honor them is to help them remember those greater qualities, help them remember that they're good people."

Air rushed into Forbes's lungs, filling every cell in his body with hope. All of JD's boxes made sense, stacked together quite neatly. "Thank you. That's what I needed to hear. Because the next time I see my parents will most likely be across a conference table with their lawyer—the managing partner in my law firm."

"You have to know that we don't want this to go to court if it doesn't have to. We're praying for an amicable negotiation because we don't want you estranged from your parents, from your family. It might make things awkward."

Forbes could understand how not being welcome at his own family's functions could be awkward for him, but. . . "I'm not sure what you mean by awkward."

JD exchanged a look with his wife—a look replete with mysterious smiles. "Because when you marry our daughter, we want your family to be there to celebrate along with us."

Chapter 23

*A*laine tucked the phone receiver between shoulder and ear and continued writing copy. "Alaine Delacroix."

"Good morning." Forbes's smooth, mellow voice oozed out of the phone to wrap Alaine in warmth.

"Good morning to you, too." Caterpillars of excitement crawled up and down her skin at the thought of seeing him this afternoon. "You sound like you're feeling better today than you were last night."

"It's a new day. The sun is shining. And it's a holiday."

"Rub it in, thanks." She sent the finished copy to the printer so she could read through and make any revisions quickly before she went in to film the studio segments of today's broadcast.

"Since I'm off the hook from going to my family's cookout tonight, I'm all yours today." While he hadn't gone into great detail over the phone last night, her heart still ached knowing that she'd caused a rift between Forbes and his close-knit family by involving him in the case.

"I'll be heading out there in about an hour. I've got to roll some tape and edit together a piece before noon so I can run it during my live segment. So you'll probably want to wait until after one o'clock before meeting me."

"I'd rather come and watch you work."

"I'd rather you didn't. No offense, but I have a really tight schedule with this, and I don't need any distractions." Nor the jittery feeling she got whenever he was around.

"I distract you?" The low growl in his voice very nearly pushed her out of her chair and onto the floor in a swoon.

"Incessantly and unforgivably."

"Well, on that note, I won't tell you what else I talked about with your parents yesterday."

Finding out Forbes had been at her parents' house for almost three hours yesterday afternoon had come as quite a surprise; and when he'd told her they'd talked about his confrontation with his own parents, she'd been truly shocked. He didn't even go into all the details with her.

"I'm not taking the bait. I've got to go. I'll see you a little after one at my parents' place. Don't forget to display your parking permit, or you'll have to park in public parking over by the old mill."

"Yes, ma'am."

Alaine turned around at a rustling sound from behind her. Bekka stood in the cubicle's doorway—if only it had a door—tapping her watch.

"I've got to go. I'll see you in a few hours." As soon as she got Forbes to say good-bye and hang up, she grabbed her copy off the printer along with her steno pad and pen. "Sorry. I know, I'm running a few minutes behind."

"We're okay. We still have a few minutes. How was your weekend?"

Self-consciousness flamed in Alaine's face.

Bekka stopped her and pulled her to the side of the wide hallway. "Tell."

Alaine gave her a quick rundown of the incident at the coffee shop Saturday morning. Her heart raced and cheeks ached with the effort to control her expression as she got to the end of the story. "And then he leaned across the table and kissed me."

"He—what?" Bekka's eyes grew big—as did her smile. "He *kissed* you? On the lips?"

Alaine's laugh echoed down the tiled corridor. "Yes," she whispered, "on the *lips*. Twice."

Bekka pulled her into a quick, bone-crushing hug. "I'm so happy for you. It seems like everything is finally working out for you, as I knew it would eventually."

Alaine pulled her along—they needed to be in the studio. "I hope so. We haven't really talked about what it meant, though he did call me last night and we were on the phone for almost four hours."

"If you didn't talk about your relationship, what did you talk about?"

"Everything—nothing. I found out that his favorite author is Charles Dickens. Something about how Dickens wrote several novels that were scathing criticisms of the legal system in Victorian England and he wrote papers about it as an undergrad. Most of it went way over my head. So I paid him back by talking about art for a few minutes. His sister told me that he's not really a fan."

As soon as they stepped into the frigid studio, they separated: Bekka going to the news desk and Alaine going to her comfy arm chair on stage three to record her studio segments for the show. She pulled her jacket—a lightweight broadcloth in navy blue, with three-quarter sleeves ending in a little ruffle detail—on over her sleeveless red-and-white abstract patterned blouse. She thanked the fire marshal for coming in early and explained the process to him.

An hour later, she pulled her little black Mazda into the gravel lot beside Delacroix Gardens and walked the half mile to the community center where the TV station's van was setting up to broadcast. She left her jacket on the front seat of the van, did a quick sound and picture test with Nelson, and then headed into the crowds already starting to form around the dozens of tents lining the streets in all directions—all displaying DELACROIX RENTALS logos on them—containing merchandise and goods from Mills retailers, food of every imaginable ethnicity from every restaurant in the Mills, and carnival style games that filled the air with what Alaine thought of as the sound of Independence Day.

She went to her parents' booth first and chatted with them while Nelson got some footage of the flowers and potted plants they had for sale.

"Seems busier this early than it was last year." Alaine looked around at the visitors milling about.

"It is. And you know what they say—all publicity is good publicity." Her father rearranged the small pots of sweet peas to fill in holes where someone had obviously bought a few. "I know it's not great for Forbes, but I think everyone will be in the black this month due to the increased traffic we'll see today because the news stories have brought the Mills back to Bonneterre's attention. We've already scheduled appointments to meet with two different landscapers to bid some projects for them in the upcoming weeks."

"That's great. I hope it works out. . . ."

Nelson indicated his readiness, and Alaine switched from daughter playing catch-up to reporter getting sound bites for her piece. After getting quotes from both parents, she sought out some of the more eclectic restaurants' and merchants' displays to make sure that she showed off the cultural diversity of the area to its best extent.

Stepping under the canopy at the tent for Abu Dhabi Restaurant, she bumped into a tall, broad-chested man. "I'll beg your—oh, hey, Major."

Major O'Hara turned. "Alaine, good to see you again."

"I should have known you'd be out here examining all the different cuisine." She turned and motioned for Nelson to start rolling. At his thumbs-up, she held the microphone up in front of herself. "Chef Major O'Hara of Boudreaux-Guidry Enterprises." She paused. "Chef O'Hara, what brings you out to the Moreaux Mills Independence Day Street Festival?"

"As anyone in any profession knows, expanding your knowledge of your profession is vital if you want to keep improving your own skills, so I come out here every year to study—and to taste—the best in multicultural cuisines." He'd come a long way since his first couple of segments for her show, now with a smooth yet casual delivery—and no *um*s or *uh*s and steady eye contact with her.

Next year she'd have him do a segment where he went around from booth to booth and featured some of his favorite food finds—if the Mills still existed this time next year. "You worked in New York City for several years. How does the spectrum of ethnic foods represented at the festival compare with what you found there?"

"I don't know that any city would be able to compete with New York for the range of cuisines available, but those that we do have here are amongst the best I've ever had."

She asked him a few more questions, then wrapped it up. "Thanks, Major. Have a great day."

"Meredith is around here somewhere. Looking for stuff for the house."

"I'll look for her." She did a quick interview with the owners of Abu Dhabi, then moved on to try to talk to another dozen or so people as quickly as she could. By the time she got back to the van to try to edit her story together, she had so many good sound bites that she wasn't sure which ones to choose.

Finally, she got it cut together in a piece she was happy with—just in time to slip back into her jacket, even though she really didn't want to. She decided to stand in the middle of the community center's parking lot—since today it was a no-parking lot—where the building, the kids' pony ride, the inflated air-bounce thingy, and the large banner hanging from the side of the center could be seen in frame behind her. She positioned her two live-interview guests to either side of her so that Nelson had only to zoom out slightly and pan to the right or left for each one. She turned the volume on her earpiece up so she could hear the broadcast.

And then she made the mistake of looking past Nelson when she noticed someone walking toward them.

❧

Forbes grimaced, then raised his hand in an apologetic wave at

Alaine. He'd hoped he'd be able to stay unseen, but the guy in the clown getup had to walk right in front of the shady bench Forbes had found where he was close enough to see her, but not necessarily to hear her.

She rolled her eyes and shook her head and looked back at her cameraman, but not before that cute, deep grin stole over her face. He breathed deeply, enjoying the fragrance of the small sprig of lavender he'd picked up from Solange on his way over here. It would look perfect peeking out from the cluster of dark curls at the back of Alaine's head.

He wished he could have found a place where he could hear her. She seemed to put her two guests quite at ease as she talked to them—they visibly relaxed while she held the microphone in front of each one. Of course, he'd be able to watch the recording of it tonight.

Grinning, he crossed his legs and stretched his arms out across the top of the bench's back. Alaine had laughed harder than he'd ever heard from her when he'd admitted last night he'd been recording her show for years. He'd been surprised when she then admitted that she couldn't stand seeing or hearing herself on camera.

She finished up at ten minutes till one and, after helping her cameraman pack up his equipment, she tossed her jacket over her shoulder and sauntered over to the shade of the oak tree and sat down beside him.

"So what did you think of the horse-and-pony show?"

He wrapped his arm around her in a squeeze but let her go quickly as could feel the heat radiating from her. "I'll let you know after I watch the final thing tonight." He pulled the sprig of lavender out of his shirt pocket and carefully stuck it into the clip holding up most of her hair. He let his hand drift down to lift one of the stray tendrils and placed a kiss on her neck where it had lain.

She shivered, as if with a sudden cold chill, and goose bumps pebbled her skin. "Forbes, I—"

"Hey, you two!" The wheels of Joe Delacroix's chair whispered

KAYE DACUS

across the pavement toward them.

"Joe, your timing leaves a bit to be desired."

Forbes couldn't decide if Alaine was cuter when she was frustrated or disgruntled. Right now, disgruntled was winning.

Joe grinned shamelessly at his sister. "Mother sent me to find you two to find out if you wanted to join the family for lunch. We're going to pick something up for them and take it over to their tent."

"What about your tent?" Alaine repositioned the lavender in her hair, stood, and started walking toward her brother—then stopped, turned, and extended her hand to Forbes.

His heart bounced like the kids in the inflatable castle fifty feet away. He twined his fingers through hers and joined her and her brother, not caring where they went, wanting only to know everyone around them understood he'd won her heart—and she'd won his.

Though Alaine tried to convince him to try Ethiopian, Thai, Egyptian, and Mongolian food, he wanted nothing but Greek food—which was to be found in one of the largest pavilions he'd seen so far. From all appearances, he guessed that the entire Pappas clan was there helping out—and every single one of them greeted him by name.

Voula loaded them up with food—and wouldn't let Forbes pay for any of it. Before she let them leave, she whispered something in Alaine's ear, then kissed her on both cheeks.

They each needed both hands—both arms—to carry all the food.

"What was that all about?" Forbes asked once they cleared the Pappases' marquee.

"What?"

"What she whispered in your ear." His stomach rumbled at the rich, meaty, spicy aromas wafting around them from the bags and boxes they carried.

"I have no idea. Whatever she said was in Greek. But I think she was telling me how lucky she thinks you are."

"Lucky?"

Alaine wrinkled her nose at him. "To be with me, of course."

He wanted to kiss her, but the armload of food made it impossible. "She's wrong."

Alaine's eyebrows shot up. "Oh, really?"

"Really. Because it's not luck. God knew I needed you in my life, and I firmly believe He brought us together." Okay, forget the bags. He moved around in front of her and leaned over their respective burdens. His lips almost touched hers—

"Hey, Alaine Delacroix! Forbes Guidry!"

With a groan of frustration, he straightened. Alaine's frustrated look wasn't quite as cute as the disgruntled one.

He turned to see someone he'd never met before in his life coming toward them, followed by. . .he groaned and moved back to Alaine's side. He'd managed to avoid both Major and Meredith earlier, and he'd hoped to avoid any attention from reporters who might recognize him and want to ask him about Mom and Dad and the case. Obviously, he'd hoped in vain.

"Forbes Guidry, what can you tell us about the Moreaux Mills case?"

"I have nothing to tell you about it." The box tucked under his left arm started dripping something down his elbow.

"Is it true that you're going to be suing your parents' company for the residents of Moreaux Mills against the wishes of your own law firm?"

Ah, so he hadn't been wrong in figuring the reason he'd received three phone calls from Sandra Landreneau this morning—which he hadn't answered—had something to do with this case. "I still have no comment."

"Has your involvement with this case created any tension between you and your parents?"

Now the sauce dripping down Forbes's elbow was the least troublesome thing happening at the moment. "No comment."

Fortunately, the reporter soon grew frustrated with his "no comment" answers; and when Alaine was no more forthcoming with information, he gave up and went away.

"What took y'all so long?" Joe asked when they made it back to the Delacroix Gardens tent.

Forbes glanced at Alaine. She skirted around her brother to the large plastic folding table behind the wood-and-glass display tables and cases and set her bags and boxes down. "We ran into a reporter who questioned us about the case and didn't want to take 'no comment' for an answer."

"Ah, Forbes, let me—" Solange took his cargo and held his arm away from his body in her strong, calloused hand. She led him over to the ice chest at the back of the tent, dunked a paper towel into the pool formed by the melting ice, and wiped the sticky brown liquid off his arm. The frigid cloth against his skin was a welcome relief from the heat of the sun and of the food he'd been toting.

He leaned over and kissed her cheek. "*Muito obrigado.*"

"*De nada.*" She blushed and waved him away. "You go sit, eat."

Nikki and Tony returned with a large bucket of boiled crawfish, a big brown grocery bag from the Ethiopian restaurant, and something that smelled like pickles and beer in a brown bag inside of a white plastic bag.

"No kimchi?" JD poked through all the bags and boxes on the table.

"We figured since you're the only one who can stand it," Nikki said, sliding a bag onto the table under her father-in-law's arm, "that you could go over to the Lees' tent and enjoy it over there. But we did bring this." She opened the double bagged offering.

He stuck his head practically inside the bag. "Bratwurst and sauerkraut!"

Out of respect for the Delacroixes and their neighbors, Forbes tried some of almost everything on the table—most of which he'd never even heard of before, and all of which he enjoyed. He thought about what his family would be eating tonight to celebrate the anniversary of the country's independence: grilled hamburgers and hot dogs, chips, lemonade and sodas, and cake and ice cream made by Aunt Maggie. What he'd always thought of as an all-American meal.

Looking around at the half-dozen or so cultures represented on the table—which didn't include this family's Portuguese heritage—he thanked God for giving him a glimpse of what constituted a real all-American meal.

"You're quiet all of a sudden." Alaine looped her arm over his shoulder and leaned in close, her whisper tickling his ear.

He craned his neck and kissed her cheek. "Just counting my blessings."

"Yeah, well, if you're done counting," Tony laughed, "could you pass the Pad Thai? Blessings aren't making my stomach stop growling." He ducked the flurry of napkins Nikki flung at him.

Melancholy lodged like a chicken bone in Forbes's throat at the immediate and unavoidable comparison of his own siblings to Alaine's. They, too, enjoyed teasing another sibling's or cousin's new beau—and pretended to disapprove of each other for doing it.

Alaine squeezed his arm and glopped a spoonful of something on his Styrofoam plate. Sorrowful understanding filled her dark eyes, and she mouthed, *I'm sorry.*

He closed his eyes and leaned over to touch his forehead to hers in silent gratitude.

Joe commented on a possible new contract from someone who'd stopped by his booth earlier, and the focus of conversation changed, allowing Forbes a few minutes to compose himself and rejoin the lighthearted banter around the table.

Soon, Joe and Nikki decided they'd been away from their display tent long enough. Tony volunteered to man Solange and JD's tent so they could go have some fun. And Alaine took Forbes by the hand and led him back out into the afternoon sun, away from the fans that had been keeping the nearly unbearable heat at bay inside the tent.

"Come on. I want you to see everything."

Alaine seemed to know everyone and introduced Forbes to the owners of each business. He remembered some of them from the meeting and did his best to recall their names—which the signs on each tent helped, since most of the businesses bore their surnames.

A couple of times, she ducked into a tent with no warning. The second time she did it, he caught a glimpse of a reporter trailed by a cameraman coming toward them.

By the time they'd visited every single booth, tent, trailer, or table under a tree where people sold their wares, cooked, or exhibited displays describing the services they provided, Forbes couldn't hold back his awe.

"How could I have never known any of this existed down here?"

Alaine half-smiled, head cocked to the side. "Because you were raised to believe that 'down here' was a place filled with poor people who're a drain on Bonneterre's resources."

He blanched at hearing her say almost verbatim what his mother had said at lunch yesterday. "You're right. We grew up thinking that anyone from the Mills was from the wrong side of the tracks." He gave her a sardonic grin. "If the railroad tracks around here didn't run north and south along the river."

She gave him a wrinkled-up-nose grin. "Wrong side of the highway, then. One of my suitemates at the sorority admitted to me a few years ago that she voted against me during rush week because I was from the Mills and she didn't think I'd be the right kind of person." She sighed. "Now I wonder if she was right."

"What do you mean?" He let go of her hand and put his arm around her shoulders to pull her in close, then kissed the top of her head. "Of course you're the right kind of person. You're the perfect kind of person."

"But I wasn't when I met them. Forbes, what you see now is a persona I've carefully cultivated over the last decade. Before I got into that sorority and those girls decided to give me a complete makeover, I didn't care about clothes or shoes or handbags or makeup or anything like that. All I cared about was dancing and my art."

He didn't say anything for a moment, letting the sound of the crowd, the distant carnival games, and the '40s-style big band currently playing in the community center and being broadcast through the PA system wash over him.

Finally, he moved to stand in front of her, put her left hand on his shoulder, took her right hand in his, and placed his other hand around her back, and as if he'd been born doing it, Forbes started waltzing with Alaine. Staring down into her chocolate brown eyes, he didn't have to think about the rhythm; it pulsed through him like a second heartbeat, until it was the only thing in the world besides him and Alaine.

"I don't see a persona—I don't see *Alaine Delacroix*." He returned her amused smile at his imitation of Riley's intonation of her name. "All I see is the woman who fills the emptiness in me I didn't even know was there until I met you. All I see is you. And that's all I'll ever want to see."

The song ended. The rosy glow of the setting sun reflected in the unshed tears welling in Alaine's eyes. He placed her other hand on his shoulder and wrapped his arms around her waist, pulling her close. "Promise me you'll always be you, that you'll never hold back and pretend to be or feel something that isn't totally, 100 percent you."

She nodded, her throat working visibly when she swallowed. "I promise," she whispered.

He kissed her tenderly. . .and ever so thoroughly.

CHAPTER 24

$\mathcal{F}$orbes looked up at the knock on his office door. "Samantha, good. I've been wondering where you were. I need you to clear some time on my schedule over the next few weeks. I have a group of claimants in a new case I'm taking on. I'll need a couple of associates, as well, to assist with research and depositions. Make sure they know it's pro bono."

His secretary didn't stir. He glanced up again. Concern blossomed at the fear on Samantha's face. "What's wrong?"

"I was just in Mrs. Landreneau's office. She. . .she asked me about the files I copied for you from the partners' file room."

His mouth went dry. "What did she ask?" The calls he'd avoided from Sandra Landreneau yesterday—obviously she'd decided to try another tactic. But the terms of his partnership gave him the right to take on "cases of conscience."

"She just asked me why I'd been copying B-G files—asked too if you'd told me why you wanted them. I told her what you told me: You were looking for precedent for a case you're researching."

"And what did she say to that?" He stood and put his suit coat back on.

"That I'm not to copy any more B-G files for you." Samantha entered the office and leaned on the back of one of the guest chairs, gripping the back tightly. "What's going on? I heard a couple girls in the restroom whispering that you're going to be suing B-G for a group of business owners in Moreaux Mills."

"Only if I can build a case. I'm still fact-finding." The phone rang. Forbes straightened his tie. He didn't need to look at the caller-ID window to know who it was. "Tell her I'm on my way up." He walked past his assistant, then paused and turned. "I'm sorry you got dragged into this."

Wide-eyed, Samantha nodded and returned to her desk to answer the phone.

Forbes didn't make eye contact with anyone in the halls or stairs. So they were all gossiping about him, were they? Ah, well. That was the least of his troubles.

Mary glared at him over the rim of her glasses. He gave her a tight smile but didn't stop.

For the first time in a very long time, Sandra Landreneau didn't smile at him when he entered her office. "Close the door, please."

Forbes reminded himself of his position of partner, of his name on the masthead. Yet the sensation wouldn't go away of being eight years old and about to be punished by his mother for cutting off all of five-year-old Meredith's hair. The fact that Meredith had handed him the scissors with which to do it hadn't carried any weight with Mom.

He unbuttoned his coat and sat in one of the guest chairs, giving the best performance of being at ease that he could muster.

"I assume I don't need to show you the newspaper articles? Nor point out that while I was trying to get in touch with you yesterday, you were out gallivanting with Alaine Delacroix in Moreaux Mills." Sandra tossed the "Style" section from today's paper across the desk. A large color photo of Forbes and Alaine dancing together under the fireworks was featured above the fold on the "Seen About Town" page.

He stopped himself from grinning and made a mental note to contact the paper to see if he could get a digital copy of that photo. "No, ma'am. I am aware of it."

Sandra pulled off her reading glasses, letting them hang by the beaded chain around her neck. "As a partner, you are not required to have your clients or your cases vetted by the rest of us."

"No."

"*Unless* such a client or case would be directly contrary to the good name of the firm."

"I have not done anything that endangers the reputation of the firm. On the contrary, what better light can be shed on FLM&G than the publicity that can come from taking on the plight of a dozen or so Bonneterrans who are about to lose their homes and businesses to suburban sprawl and retail development?"

"Pretty speech. Save it for a jury." The lines around Sandra's mouth deepened. Must be time for another collagen injection. "Aside from the fact it would have been nice to have some forewarning before phone calls from all the media outlets in town started coming in looking for an official statement, before you agreed to meet with anyone in this matter—publicly or privately—you should have given some thought to the fact that Boudreaux-Guidry Enterprises is our most important client. Taking a case against them is against the best interest of the firm."

He waited for her to make a point, but she sat there, looking expectant. He raised his eyebrows. "And?"

"And—it should be obvious. The partnership agreement of this firm—which you signed when you became an equity, name partner—clearly states that no partner is to take on a case that is in direct conflict to the current work or clients of the law firm. I caucused the other partners, and we are all in agreement: Drop the Moreaux Mills case."

He couldn't let her see the panic that chewed through his nerves. "I respectfully submit that this case falls under the 'case of conscience' clause in the agreement. I will not drop it."

"Forbes, you're not thinking this through. If you insist on taking this case, it could be grounds for demotion to nonequity partner—if not termination. Take tonight to think about it, and give us your answer tomorrow."

Everything he'd worked for since he'd decided at seventeen years old that he wanted to become a lawyer teetered on the edge of this decision. In the fourteen years since he'd finished law school, he'd been on the fast-track: from the prestigious law firm in New Orleans where he'd worked right out of law school to coming home in triumph as the youngest senior associate ever to work at Folse, Landreneau & Maier law firm at age twenty-eight, only to become the youngest name partner of equity status at age thirty-one.

If he took the Moreaux Mills case, he could lose all of it. The prestige of having his name joined with some of the most respected legal minds in the state. The weight his name carried on legal documents because of his position here.

If he didn't take the case, he would be betraying JD and Solange, Joe and Nikki...and Alaine. He would be smothering his own ethics. And worst of all, he would be refusing to follow through on the feeling deep within that God had led him to this case, that God was calling him to take a stand here and now.

"I don't need to think about it overnight. My answer will be the same. If there has been wrongdoing by Boudreaux-Guidry Enterprises—or any entity they're doing business with or have influence over—it is my duty to help those who have been wronged seek justice." He stood. "If that's all? I have some depositions to schedule and motions to certify class to file."

"Not in these offices and not making use of any employees or associates of FLM&G. This case is not sanctioned; and if you insist on taking it, you will not utilize company resources in the handling of it until the partners vote on whether or not your taking it violates the partnership agreement."

Forbes nodded. "Just let me know when that meeting will be, and in the meantime, I'll get back to work. Is that all?"

She nodded back. "For now. You'll want to get your book of business ready for evaluation, based on the outcome of the vote."

"I understand. Enjoy what's left of the morning." That the other partners would be upset by his decision to take this case, he'd expected. But that they'd try to say it violated the partnership agreement floored him. Could they truly be so frightened of how Mom and Dad would react that they'd force Forbes out just to avoid that scenario? Or could it be that the other partners were privy to certain information that proved Boudreaux-Guidry Enterprises had acted in harmful ways that circumvented or broke the law?

And how would he ever be able to handle a full-blown, class-action lawsuit by himself without the assistance of associates and paralegals?

By the time he'd made it back down to his office, he'd started formulating a plan. "Samantha, clear as much of my schedule as you can. If you can get me a couple of hours this afternoon, I'm going to see if Russ LeBlanc can fit in a meeting with me."

"I assume you're talking about the Moreaux Mills case and not the Pichon case?"

"Yeah."

"She just called me and told me I'm not to help you in any way for that case, that you're not allowed to use anyone here to help you with it." Samantha reached around to the credenza behind her desk and pulled several sheets of paper off her printer. "So I took the liberty of printing you a list of some part-time people you can use for help, if you're willing to pay them yourself."

"Samantha, I think I love you."

"Yeah, well. . ." She held up her left hand, displaying a sparkling engagement ring. "I'm already taken."

"And you waited this long to tell me?"

"It's not like I've actually seen you before now." She canted her gaze toward the ceiling and back down with an arched brow. "When was I supposed to tell you, with both of us being called into the principal's office this morning? Besides, hearing you say, 'I told you so' is one of my least favorite parts of this job." She grinned at him.

"But I did tell you so." He took the printout from her. "Speaking of the Pichon case, I need you to type up the response to the latest motion from the plaintiff—it has to be submitted today."

"Will do, boss."

Forbes kept the smile on his face until his office door clicked shut. He made it to his desk before doubling over in almost physical pain. He dropped into his chair, arms wrapped around his stomach.

"God, I'm confident I did what I was supposed to do—what You've been telling me to do—with this case. I believe in it. I believe it's right. So why do I feel so wrong about it?"

Alaine typically didn't have to drive home in rush-hour traffic, but working late today had been worth it for the glorious afternoon and evening she'd had yesterday. Her heart pounded again at the memory of Forbes's arms around her, of his kisses under the star-strewn sky, of dancing together to the big-band music under the Mills' own small fireworks display.

She laughed aloud. Forbes had obviously been practicing his dance steps. And even though he wanted to waltz to every song, she had to hand it to him—she'd never seen him so light on his feet.

With a sigh of relief, she turned off Spring Street into the condo complex. Several cars blocked the mailboxes; she'd walk over later—maybe even see if Forbes might want to meet her and go for a walk around the neighborhood with her.

She drove around to the Cheapside portion of the neighborhood... and slowed before she reached her driveway. With the westward angle of the sun casting long shadows over the fronts of the row of town houses, she couldn't be sure—

She stopped. Someone was sitting on her front steps. Taking her foot off the brake, she figured she could ease past and just keep going if the person looked like he might mean to harm her.

Two driveways from her own, she relaxed—and then smiled. Forbes, in a loose T-shirt, knit shorts, and trainers, sat with his forehead cupped in one hand, twirling a leaf by its stem with the other. He startled and looked up when the garage door started to open.

Alaine tried to calm her riotous insides at the sight of him. She'd never seen him dressed so casually—even yesterday, his red T-shirt had been a silk blend and his navy shorts, chinos with a crease down the front.

He entered the garage before she could get her work bag out of the trunk of the small sports car. "I'd kiss you, but I'm all sweaty."

Her pulse exploded like a racehorse out of the gate at the Kentucky Derby. "I don't mind."

His blue gray eyes twinkled—and yet seemed to hold a measure of sadness—and he leaned closer and gave her a perfunctory peck on the lips. "Hi."

"Hi, yourself. What brings you over this evening—and in such a state?"

"I was out jogging and figured you had to be home soon, so I decided I'd wait for you to see if you might care to take a walk with me." His expression sobered, and the hint of sadness she thought she'd seen turned into a palpable aura of disconsolation.

Her throat tightened with the desire to say something that would ease his burden—and the knowledge that she probably couldn't. "Come inside and get some water while I change clothes."

She left him in her kitchen and jogged upstairs to her room. Not caring that half the contents of her bag spilled out onto the bed where she tossed it, she stepped into her closet and stripped out of her suit—carefully separating the pieces that were hers and the pieces that needed to go back to the store that sent clothing over that she had to wear because of the agreement the station's sales staff had worked out. The yellow boucle tweed jacket had looked horrible on her in the mirror—she could only imagine what it did to her under the floodlights in the studio.

Biting her bottom lip, she allowed a tinge of amusement to crack through her concern for Forbes. Maybe she'd suggest they stop at his place so she could watch his recording of today's program just to see how bad the jacket looked.

She slipped into a pair of gray yoga capris and a pale pink tank top, and carried her pink and gray athletic shoes out into her bedroom. She sat on her hope chest to pull her socks on.

Just from the short time she'd known Forbes, she'd learned that he didn't show any emotion he didn't want people to see. For his control to have cracked so hard she'd been able to see his pain, he must have heard something bad at work today.

Forbes. Oh, Forbes. The idea that had been plaguing her for the past several days came back with a cold reality: Forbes had sacrificed his time, his dignity, and his family for this case.

She stopped in the motion of tying her right shoe and rested her forehead against her up-bent knee. "Lord, thank You so much for bringing Forbes to us—to me. I don't deserve him. None of us deserves the sacrifices he's making for us. Help me—help me and Forbes—to figure out some solution to bring justice to the people of the Mills without Forbes having to make more sacrifices. I don't want him to lose his family, God. Show me what I can do to help."

Downstairs, she found Forbes on a bar chair in very much the same position he'd been in on the front steps, despondency oozing out of him. She took a few moments to stretch, her concern growing.

"Ready?" She tried to sound chipper.

"Yep. Got you a bottle of water, too." He handed it to her.

She took the bottle and grabbed the extra garage-door opener and mailbox key out of the kitchen junk drawer. She clipped the remote to her waistband and slipped the key ring onto her left pinkie finger. "Let's go."

They walked in silence the first several minutes—and at no leisurely strolling pace, either. By the time they'd made it up the gentle hill leading into the heart of the community—toward Forbes's more exclusive section—Alaine almost had to jog to keep up with his long, quick strides. And since she hadn't walked regularly since the beginning of summer—which meant sometime around the end of April—every muscle in her legs and every air sac in her lungs protested painfully.

After fifteen minutes of this, she stopped and leaned down, bracing her hands on her knees, to catch her breath—hard to do when the evening air clung to her like a sweaty gym sock in a steam room. "Forbes—if you want to run some more, why don't you take a few laps and then come back and get me when you're ready to slow it down."

He stopped and looked around as if surprised to discover she no longer bobbed along beside him. The fierceness in his eyes vanished when he saw her. "I'm sorry. I guess I still have more frustration to work off. I thought I'd worn myself out before you got home." He walked back to rejoin her.

Holding her water bottle between her knees, Alaine straightened and pulled her hair band out, combed the escaped curls back up off her forehead, face, and neck into a ponytail near the top of her head, and wrapped it up with the band again, keeping it all folded up together instead of letting it swing free. She then took a huge swig of the water.

Forbes reached over and touched a curl she'd missed behind her ear. "The managing partner at the firm threatened to terminate me if I don't drop the case."

Alaine staggered back, the uncertainty in her knees in direct proportion to the blow to her soul. "That settles it. You have to drop the case. We'll find another lawyer—your friend, Russ LeBlanc. Surely he'd be willing to take on the case. I've already made you lose your family; I couldn't bear it if you lost your job, too."

He actually smiled at her. "Hold on, now. I've reviewed the partnership agreement we all signed, and they have no grounds on which to terminate me. But. . ." He reached for her hand and started back up the hill, much slower this time.

Alaine matched his pace. "But?"

"You know I've spent a lot of time in prayer about this case, about what taking it might do to me and to every relationship in my life."

"Yes. I've been praying, too."

"I am certain God is telling me to continue on with the case, that He'll take care of everything else—my family, the law firm, everything."

Alaine glanced up at his stoic profile. His dark hair curled around his temples, forehead, and neck where he was sweaty. And even though perspiration rolled down his face—as it was about to do on hers—she didn't find his very masculine, very sporty aroma the least offensive.

Shaking her head, she looked away from him so she could concentrate on the subject at hand, not on all his attractions. "It's good you have that confidence. I just wish we could see where this is all headed—if it's going to go to trial or if your parents will see the light and decide to change their plans and help the people in the Mills instead of trying to run them out."

"See, here's the thing. I met with Russ LeBlanc this afternoon. Because my partners are going to be pains about the case and not let me use any resources at the firm, I needed to find some help. And the more I talked to Russ, the more I realized just how much I envy him."

"What do you mean, envy him?" Alaine tripped over a rough spot in the pavement, but with her hand firmly held in Forbes's, she didn't lose balance and recovered before he could react.

"I mean he's so happy, so fulfilled with what he does at the community legal aid center. He hardly makes any money—I have no idea how he is going to make ends meet with four brand-new babies."

Alaine gasped. "He had quads?"

"His wife did, yes. Three girls and a boy. And Carrie's going to have to go back to work as a social worker in less than five weeks because Russ barely scrapes a living from that center. But I've never met two happier, more contented people than the LeBlancs. And I can't help comparing my own sorry excuse for a life with his. He's done something, made his mark on the community. He may not have material possessions, but he has something more. He has dignity and honor and the title of 'neighbor' as Jesus defined it in the parable of the good Samaritan. And you want to know the sad thing?" He pulled her into a grassy area under an enormous oak tree.

"What?" Her throat ached in sympathy for the pain and longing in Forbes's voice.

"Even with as much as I envy what Russ has and wish I could be that kind of lawyer, the idea of giving up my share of the law firm's profits, of losing my extremely high hourly billing rate, of foregoing the incentives and bonuses we dole out to ourselves every year, of not being able to afford the luxurious life to which I'm accustomed—the idea of losing all of those things, those material things and more, terrifies me."

Alaine rested her hands on the sides of his waist. *Let Your words flow through me, God, because I don't know what to say to him.* She breathed in and opened her mouth. "I don't think it's giving up the material things that is what you're really afraid of."

He raised his eyebrows.

"I think it's the sense of control that having all those material possessions gives you the illusion of. With your money and power and prestige, you can fix any problem, keep any situation from getting out of control. And if you can't personally do it, someone in your Rolodex can." Shocked at herself, Alaine tried to stop the harsh sounding words. "But if you think about it, your friend Russ is the one who's really in control. He's in control because he's given up control—to God. He isn't controlled by the need for money or luxury or power or prestige. Sure, he doesn't control who his clients are and how much they can pay him, but he controls his own happiness. You'll never know what it is to have true control of your life until you realize you have to let it go and let God have control of every aspect of your life—including where your next paycheck is coming from."

Forbes stared at her. Alaine started to apologize several times for what she'd said, but the words wouldn't come. After a long time, his expression eased and a smile slowly overtook his eyes and lips.

"So are you saying that you wouldn't care if I went to work with Russ LeBlanc and didn't have a steady income and couldn't afford things like Jaguars and the most expensive town house in Bonneterre?"

She swallowed hard and thought about what her sorority sisters would say—which was exactly the opposite of what was right. "I wouldn't mind. Because I didn't fall in love with your income or your car or your house. I fell in love with who you are, what you stand for."

His eyes flickered in the reddening sunlight as they darted back and forth, searching hers. "Say that again," he whispered.

"I love you, Forbes Guidry. I don't care if you have to sell the town house and buy a cheaper car. What I care about is that you're happy and that you do what God is calling you to do so that you can be proud of your work every day."

He cupped her face with his large, soft hands and kissed her until her eyes—and toes—crossed. "I don't deserve you, Alaine." He pressed his forehead to hers with a mischievous smile. "But you don't have to worry about me losing the town house and the Jag. They're paid off."

CHAPTER 25

*T*he next weeks passed in a blur for Forbes. He hadn't worked such long hours since his first few years as an associate at the firm in New Orleans. Though he'd convinced the other three partners that they couldn't terminate him—his argument for its being a case of conscience worked—they still refused to allow him to use company resources for it. And with the threat of a review of his book of business pending—the record of all of his clients and the money he was bringing in with each one—he not only had to keep up with all of his current clients but still work on bringing in new business.

The flurry from the media over the case died down after his initial filings for injunctions to keep all of the claimants in the suit from being foreclosed upon, but it flared up again the second week in August when Forbes officially filed the class-action lawsuit.

His one attempt to try to reconcile with his parents and see if they could resolve this without the legal action—by dropping by their home on a Sunday evening and being unceremoniously turned away—had resulted in his receiving a phone call from Sandra Landreneau, legal counsel for Boudreaux-Guidry Enterprises, telling him to cease and desist from trying to contact her clients directly.

To try to make things easier for the rest of the family, especially Meredith and Major, he stopped going to all family functions, including the Thursday night cousins-and-siblings dinner. But at least in that, he had some consolation: Thursday night became his regular date night with Alaine—a welcome relief in what had become a routine of sixteen- to eighteen-hour days, at least six days a week.

Russ LeBlanc had made a small room in his converted-house law office available for Forbes to use for working on the Mills case, but most of the time, Forbes worked on it at home. He'd filled the formerly vacant large guest suite on the fourth floor of his town house with long folding tables and plenty of boxes to hold the sheaves of paperwork the case generated—on both sides. But he had Sandra Landreneau address everything to him at Russ's address.

Before Russ had left the courtroom one afternoon, he informed Forbes a package had been dropped off for him at the legal aid center from FLM—Forbes had long since stopped thinking of his initial as part of the firm's name in this case—no doubt yet another round of motions to dismiss to which Forbes would have to spend all night writing responses.

Mr. Pichon pumped his hand again. "Thanks, Forbes. I really appreciate your work on all of this. I don't even care that we have to share the court costs with them. I'm just glad we won."

"You're welcome. I'll be in touch about when and how to make that payment early next week." Instead of euphoria over winning the case, all he could think about was how much that neighborhood would change now that Mr. Pichon could sell his lot to anyone willing to pay the price he'd ask. He dawdled in the hallway until his client disappeared into an elevator rather than share one with him.

The halls of the courthouse echoed with emptiness. Forbes checked his watch—and drew in his breath between clenched teeth. With an elevator all to himself, he called Alaine.

She picked up on the second ring. "Hey. I'll be ready in about fifteen minutes."

"Hey to you, too. And don't rush. I hate to do this to you again, but I'm going to have to push our date back about an hour. And would you mind if we didn't go see that movie? I've got to go by Russ's and pick up some paperwork on my way home—motions and briefs I'll need to read through tonight." He exited the elevator and waved at the security guards who buzzed the main doors so he could get out.

"Do you. . .do you want to just cancel tonight?" Alaine's voice went reedy.

Guilt—tinged with resentment—pierced him. If it weren't for having met Alaine, this case wouldn't be taking up most of his life. But if it weren't for this case, he might never have fallen in love with her. "No, I still want to see you tonight."

"Oh, okay." Her voice returned to a more mellow, happier tone. "Because if you need to cancel and spend all evening working, I'd understand."

"I'll pick you up at seven thirty. Are you still thinking favorable thoughts toward Italian food?"

"So long as it's at Palermo's, yes."

"That's what I thought. I'll call and see if they can move our reservation back."

She let out a dry laugh. "They will."

"How do you know?" He climbed into the Jag.

"Because everyone always does what you ask them to."

He snorted, thinking about the paperwork facing him tonight. "Not anymore."

"Okay, everyone outside of your family and the law firm."

A drop of rain with the volume of a fire bucket doused the windshield when Forbes pulled out of the parking garage. "I'd better get off the phone. It's starting to rain, and there's still a lot of traffic in downtown. I wouldn't want to have to cancel permanently."

"See you in a little while."

"Bye." He dropped the phone into a cup holder and pointed the car south, toward Moreaux Mills and Russ's legal aid center. As Alaine had predicted, the hostess who answered the phone at Palermo's Italian Grill was only too happy to change their reservation to seven forty-five.

Lights still blazed through most of the windows of the center when Forbes pulled up. Even with his large umbrella and a short few feet to the door, his back and legs got a pretty good soaking from the diagonal rain. The front door was locked and he'd left the key in his briefcase in the car, so he rang the bell.

The glow of the interior backlit Russ when he opened the door. "I was wondering where you were."

Forbes shook off the umbrella before crossing the threshold. "Did the paralegal I hired come by with something for me, too?"

"Yeah, while we were in court, apparently. My secretary put both of them in your office."

Forbes smirked at him. Both of them had gotten quite comfortable with the idea of Forbes having his own office space here. But all things considered, having watched what Russ did on a daily basis, Forbes had to admit he wasn't cut out to provide community legal aid. He much preferred paying clients. He just wasn't sure he'd be able to go back to FLM&G after this. If he didn't need his income from his partnership there to finance the Mills case, he'd have already separated from them and hung out his own shingle—over that vacant Victorian row house office building on Town Square, right next door to Anne's wedding planning business—and a ten-minute walk from his home.

He greeted Russ's assistant and paralegal—hard at work in the kitchen with paperwork spread out all over the lunch table—and went down the hall to the small former bedroom serving as his office. Atop the thrift-store desk sat two thick, yellow envelopes. He scooped them up, gave the shabby room one more look, and turned off the light.

At Russ's office door—which had been the house's master bedroom—Forbes stopped and leaned against the jamb. "How's Carrie holding up?"

"Fourth day back at work. Called me at least a dozen times before noon in tears wanting to quit her job and stay home with them." Russ sighed and rubbed the back of his neck. "I can't help thinking that if I'd gone your way—if I'd taken that job with Folse, Landreneau & Maier as a senior associate when you were promoted to partner—she'd be able to stay home with the babies and we wouldn't have to worry about how we're going to balance paying all the bills with making sure the kids have more than just the crucial essentials for survival."

"And if you had taken that job, you would have had money, yes, but your soul would have died. You would have hated being on that side of the courtroom, defending the big business owners and trying to squash the little people. I'm finding it harder and harder to stomach these days." Forbes's head felt suddenly heavy, and he leaned it against the door facing.

Russ gave Forbes a sympathetic look, even though Russ had been the lawyer for the losing side in the Pichon case. "Yeah, can't wait to see what the papers have to say about that tomorrow—that you stuck it to one community while trying to stick up for another."

Forbes groaned. "Oh, that's poetic. Why don't you call the editor and give them that line?"

"Sarcasm doesn't suit you, Forbes." Russ wagged his index finger at him in an admonitory gesture. "Besides, their prose is purple enough without my help. They should be paying you a bonus for all of the news you've generated for them this year."

"Yeah, well, between the society pages and the front page, I can't tell if they love me or hate me. They love showing pictures of Alaine and me at any public event we attend—which is just about every event she covers and drags me along to. And they love digging up every last sordid detail of how this case has created a wedge between me and my family, how I'm the black sheep."

"Or the white sheep, depending on who's writing the article." Russ's desk phone rang, and he glanced down at it. "It's a client. I've got to answer."

"I'll see you tomorrow."

Russ waved and picked up the receiver.

As if Forbes weren't already stressed enough, the pounding rain and limited visibility wound the cords of his muscles even tighter. He smiled. Maybe he could convince Alaine to give him another one of her miraculous shoulder massages before they went to dinner. He glanced down at the clock. A quarter to seven. Maybe not. He'd be cutting it close just to get home and change clothes before time to pick her up.

When he turned into the cul-de-sac, the Jag's headlights flashed on a dark object in his driveway—a car he didn't recognize. Waiting for the garage door to open, he glanced up at the front door. A shadowy figure stood at the top of the steps. He pulled the Jag into the garage.

Before he could get around to the end of his car, the mysterious person hurried into the shelter the garage provided.

Evelyn Mackenzie lowered her blazer, which she'd been using as an umbrella with no effect. Her dark hair lay plastered to her head. He averted his eyes from the way her now-transparent white blouse clung to her torso.

"What are you doing here?" He hadn't meant to sound that gruff.

"I need to talk to you." Evelyn stepped forward, her feet making squishing noises in her spike-heeled sandals.

"Without your counsel present, that's not a good idea." He turned to retrieve the packages and his overstuffed briefcase from the car.

"This is off the record—just between you and me." She grabbed his arm. "Please, Forbes, it's important."

"I have to leave here at seven thirty, so it had better be quick." He risked another glance at her, and her trembling and bedraggled appearance gave him a little twinge. "Come inside and dry off and get warm."

"Thanks."

He led her up one flight to the main level. He was about to point out the powder room near the kitchen, but that wouldn't do. He only had hand towels in there. "Come on upstairs."

The guest bathroom on the third floor opened directly off the landing—the door adjacent to his bedroom door. The proximity couldn't be helped. He reached in and turned on the light.

"Towels are there"—he pointed to the plush green ones hanging on the bar beside the tub—"and there's a hair dryer in the linen closet. And if you'll hold on just a second, I'll loan you a dry shirt." Because if they were going to talk, he was going to have to look at her.

In his closet, he grabbed the first T-shirt off the top of the stack he usually wore when running—the one he'd gotten for participating in the charity 10K run last weekend for the Warner Foundation to raise money for the cardiac care unit at University Hospital. Though his parents had helped start the foundation and were the biggest supporters and donors, he'd signed up to participate way back in the spring. And he never broke his promises.

He waved at Evelyn in the bathroom mirror. She turned off the hair dryer.

"Here." He thrust the shirt at her. "It's never been worn."

"Thanks."

He nodded and escaped back to his room. Closing the door of the closet behind him, he quickly changed out of his damp suit into dark-wash, slightly distressed jeans and a light blue, silk T-shirt, then grabbed his olive brown sport coat. The hair dryer stopped. He carried his shoes and socks out into his bedroom, just as Evelyn knocked on the open door.

"Forbes?" Her gaze swept his room, and she took a few steps across the dark hardwood to the area rug, putting her within five feet of him. She'd knotted the T-shirt in the back in such a way that what should have been a very unprovocative tent on her slender frame now had an almost indecently snug fit.

His insides foamed. "Let's go downstairs to my study." He checked his watch. "I can give you about ten minutes.

"Okay." She preceded him down the stairs, her blouse and jacket bundled under her arm, her sandals dangling by the heel straps from her fingers. At the bottom of the stairs, she halted, and he took over the lead, turning immediately left into the study that occupied the front corner of the main floor.

"Wow. This is some room." Evelyn trailed her fingers over the back of one of the leather club chairs as her eyes scraped across the spines of all the books lining the built-in cherry cabinets.

Forbes draped his jacket across the back of his Queen Anne–style armchair and sat to put his socks and shoes on. "What did you want to talk to me about?"

"Hmm?"

He glanced up and almost bolted out of his chair to slap her hand away from Dickens. She ran her fingertips across the leather binding and gold lettering on the spines of the treasured volumes.

Gritting his teeth, he returned his attention to getting his feet encased in the dark brown socks and leather dress shoes. "Why are you here, Evelyn?"

"What—oh, yes." She finished her slow circuit of the room and came back around to perch on the edge of the club chair nearest him. "It's about your parents, Forbes."

His heart and lungs froze solid. "What about my parents? Are they okay?"

She reached over and laid her hand on his knee. "Physically, yes, they're fine. I'm talking about their emotional state. They miss their son—they miss *you*. They're trying very hard to understand why you felt like you needed to take this stand against them, but they're ready for you to come back home, to make a gesture of reconciliation."

Forbes finished tying his shoe, then dropped his foot back to the floor, dislodging Evelyn's hand from his knee. He leaned against the high back of the chair, rested his elbows on the armrests, and clasped his hands in front of him. "They have a funny way of showing it. Last time I tried to contact them, tried to see if we could reconcile this, they had their lawyer call me back and demand I cease trying to contact them."

"About the case, yes. But they're still your parents, Forbes. If you went to them as their son, not as the lawyer for the other side, things would be different." Evelyn crossed her legs, and her skirt, too short to begin with, rode up even higher.

Forbes cleared his throat and ignored the way the surface of his skin tingled at the flash of thigh he caught before he averted his gaze.

"I find it interesting that you, who has what could be described at best an adversarial relationship with your father, are here advising me in parental matters."

"It's because I have such a bad relationship with my father that I'm here, Forbes. I don't want to see happen to you what's happened to me—I don't want to see this case come between you and your parents. I'll admit it straight out: I'm insanely jealous of the relationship that you—and your sister—have with your parents. It amazes me that Meredith can work so closely with them every single day and still have a close enough relationship with them that the three of them have lunch together, alone, at least once a week."

Forbes let out a small huff. Those lunches had been his idea—a time for Meredith to be able to share her concerns and problems with her parental bosses instead of bottling it all up inside and putting up with their running roughshod over her and her department. "Things are not always as they appear."

"No, but that's true in your situation as well. They're not mad at you, Forbes. They understand you felt like your conscience was telling you to take this case. I think they respect that about you. Now they want to reestablish their relationship with their son." She leaned forward, clasping her hands around her knee. Had she intentionally pressed her upper arms close into her sides?

He surged out of the chair and paced the perimeter of the room, coming to a stop at the window that overlooked the cul-de-sac in front of the house. "If they're so eager to reestablish our relationship, why haven't they contacted me? They know how to get in touch with me. They know where I live—obviously, because they told you how to get here."

"Actually, that was Meredith." Frustration laced Evelyn's voice. "They haven't contacted you directly because they aren't sure if you would accept a direct line of contact from them. Why do you think I'm here?"

He turned, crossed his arms, and leaned his hip against the windowsill. "You want me to believe that my parents sent you here as their emissary? You—an outsider? Someone who knows next to nothing about our family, about how we relate with each other?"

"Who better than a neutral party?"

Answering a question with a question. His guard rose even higher. "Did my parents send you?"

"Forbes, why else would I be here?" She pushed herself out of the chair and stalked toward him.

He stopped her with the look he usually reserved for hostile—or otherwise uncooperative—witnesses "Yes or no. Did my parents ask you to come to my house and talk to me about a reconciliation?"

The sweet seductiveness left Evelyn's expression. "Not exactly, no." She closed the space between them until she stood almost toe-to-toe with him. She ran her index finger down his sternum. "I came because I'm worried about you, Forbes, because in the time we spent together earlier this summer, I came to. . .care for you."

Forbes tried to take a step back, but he'd made the mistake of allowing her to trap him in the corner. "Don't do this."

She ran her hands up his arms to his shoulders and leaned forward until her body pressed up against his. "We all want you to come back. Your family needs you. And you need them."

He took hold of her upper arms to try to push her away as gently as he could. Last thing he needed was for Evelyn to bring an assault charge against him.

Stronger than she appeared, she hooked one hand behind his head. With neck and shoulder muscles already sore, he found it hard to resist the pressure of her hand.

Suddenly, her lips crushed against his.

He pushed harder against her upper arms and finally broke the kiss.

The rasp of a throat clearing blasted across the quiet room. Evelyn jumped back; Forbes wiped his mouth on the back of his hand.

Alaine stood in the doorway, her expression inscrutable. "The garage door was open, so I let myself in."

CHAPTER 26

*A*laine willed her knees to stay solid beneath her. When Forbes hadn't shown up by seven thirty, she'd figured she'd save him the hassle of picking her up by meeting him here. But at least now she knew the truth behind why he'd wanted to push their date back an hour.

Past experience with boyfriends who'd cheated on her screamed for her to leave the house—slamming every door behind her as she went—and never speak to Forbes again. But she stood her ground. When she first walked in, Forbes and Evelyn—*Evelyn Mackenzie* of all people—appeared to be entwined in a passionate embrace. But when Evelyn showed herself to be the aggressor and kissed Forbes, the reasonable part of Alaine's brain kicked in and told her not to believe what she thought she saw.

Alaine raised her eyebrows and looked at Forbes, trying to keep every trace of accusation out of her expression. "Don't we have dinner reservations?"

Forbes's posture went limp for a split second; then he composed himself. "Yes. Seven forty-five, which means we'd better go or we're going to be late." He walked past Evelyn and joined Alaine at the door. His blue gray eyes decidedly worried, he leaned over and kissed her cheek. "This wasn't what it looked like." His breath tickled her ear.

"You can explain over crawfish-stuffed fried ravioli."

"I guess I should be going then." Evelyn grabbed a bundle of clothes and a pair of hideous stiletto sandals from the floor beside the chair Alaine usually occupied in this room—that would change as of now.

Alaine gave her a tight-lipped smile. "Yes, that would be a good idea." *And never come back!* she wanted to scream. With pressure from her shoulder, Alaine positioned Forbes so she was between him and the hussy when Evelyn passed them to exit. "Be careful driving in the rain."

Evelyn stopped by the stairs. "Oh, Forbes, your shirt." She reached behind her back and started undoing the wad of fabric, as if she was going to take it off right then and there in front of God and everybody.

He closed his eyes and held up a hand. "Keep it. I was never going to wear it."

Alaine trailed the woman and stood at the top of the half flight of stairs leading down to the front door. Evelyn turned around and looked before opening the door. Alaine smiled and waved. "Nice to see you again. B'bye."

Okay, so maybe catty wasn't the most Christian way to go. But she couldn't help herself. She'd barely started to turn around when Forbes pulled her into an overwhelming hug.

"Thank you so much for showing up when you did." His voice sounded muffled in her hair.

"Yeah, well, I'm hungry, and I was tired of waiting. So"—after a few seconds' struggle, she succeeded in pulling away—"let's go. I had to park behind you because the other side of the driveway was occupied, so I'll drive." She softened slightly at his hangdog expression. "Anyway, I know how much you hate driving in the rain."

She made a mad dash to the Mazda while Forbes, with his giant umbrella, closed the garage door using the security keypad outside. As always, once he got into the car, he fought with stowing the oversized umbrella without sprinkling them both with water.

Alaine pulled out of the driveway. "So. . .Evelyn Mackenzie paid you a visit tonight."

Forbes rubbed the right side of his neck. She softened a little bit more—but no, he had a ways to go to get out of this doghouse. "She was standing at the front door when I got home from Russ's. Said she needed to talk to me. I told her I only had a few minutes."

"And the T-shirt?" Alaine rolled to a stop at the light leading out of the complex and cast him a sidelong glance.

"It was either give her something to change into or try not to look at her sitting there in a soaked white silk blouse. You'd think she'd have learned to carry an umbrella with her by now."

The light turned green. "Uh-huh. So what was it she wanted to talk to you about?"

"My parents."

"Your—" She stole a look at him, alarmed. "Are they okay?"

He nodded, and she turned her attention back to the road.

"That was my first reaction as well. She came under the pretense of telling me that my parents miss me and they want to reconcile with me. That she's worried about them and what this estrangement is doing to them."

"That's ironic, coming from her—at least what you've told me about her." Alaine checked her mirrors, then looked over her shoulder before changing lanes.

"I said that to her, too. That's when she tried the. . .*other* tactic."

"The old 'if you can't beat 'em, seduce 'em' tactic? The hussy." If Alaine didn't think spitting were disgusting, she'd spit. "Coming on to my man like that."

He squeezed her shoulder. "So. . .you believe me, then? That it was all her? That I didn't want to have anything to do with it?"

"Forbes, one thing I've learned in almost two months of dating you is that if you wanted to kiss her, she wouldn't have had to practically strangle you to make it happen." She pulled into the parking lot at Palermo's. "Ooh, look, someone saved us the best parking space." She whipped into the space just a few feet from the covered walkway leading to the restaurant's front door.

Though utterly silly, she sat in the car and waited until Forbes came around and opened the door for her. Sometimes, she enjoyed his old-fashioned ways. Other times, they made her feel ridiculous. But that was something she could deal with for now.

He didn't let go of her hand once she exited the car, but kissed it several times over. "Have I told you recently how crazy I am about you?"

"Or just plain crazy." She laughed, but deep down, the fact that, after all this time, he still hadn't used the *L*-word bothered her. They were going to the same church; he had Sunday dinner with her family every week; he even called her his girlfriend in front of other people. So why couldn't he bring himself to declare his love?

"Well, well, well. If it isn't the supercouple of Bonneterre."

Alaine and Forbes both turned at the familiar voice. "Hey, Shon." Alaine hugged Forbes's neighbor and client. "What brings you out tonight? Don't tell me you have a date!" She winked at him.

He glowered back at her. "No, as a matter of fact I'm working. Let's Do Coffee is hosting a mixer tonight—it's something new I'm trying. I've invited a select group of clients to come in for an informal meet and greet. Afterward, each one will fill out comment cards, and I'll match them up for coffee dates from there." He moved past them and opened the door. "I'd ask y'all to join us, but since you're both off the market, it would defeat the purpose. Although. . ." He eyed them. "I could bring you in as an LDC success story."

Forbes let out a barking laugh. "Yes, but would that be truth in advertising? I mean, seeing as how you set us up with Riley and Zebra Woman, not with each other."

Shon's dark eyes glittered, reflecting the multiple bulbs in the chandelier above them. "*Au contraire*, monsieur. I may have sent other people to the coffee shop at the same time you were there and implied those were the people I wanted you to meet, but I knew they weren't right for you." He pulled them aside so other customers entering could get to the hostess stand unimpeded. "Forbes, why do you think I gave you a free, three-month membership?"

Forbes glanced at Alaine. She shrugged, and both looked back at Shon.

He sighed. "Because Alaine had just signed up for a membership. And I knew from the first time I met her that even if you hadn't had an eighth-grade-level crush on her for a couple of years, she was the right woman for you. But when I took her registration money, I was committed to setting her up with someone I felt was a good fit for her."

"Thanks for refunding that money, by the way." Alaine squeezed Shon's wrist.

Shon ducked his head. "Well. . .after your 'dates,' even though it did get the two of you together as I'd hoped, I felt guilty about how I'd set you up." He turned on his heel and marched over to the hostess stand.

"Yes, Mr. Murphy, we have you set up in the Milan Room in the back." The hostess called someone over her headset, then looked up questioningly at Forbes.

"We'll be with you momentarily," he told the girl, then pulled Shon away with what looked like a painful grip on the upper arm. "What do you mean, how you set us up?"

Shon cleared his throat and glanced around as if to make sure no one could hear him. "Riley and Zebra Lady aren't actually LDC clients. They. . .well, Zebra Lady, as you call her, is one of our coordinators—her name is Laura. And I play basketball with Riley twice a week down at the YMCA. Oh, and Forbes—Laura told me about the whole age thing."

Now it was Forbes's turn to duck his head in embarrassment. "Yeah, tell her again how sorry I am."

"She got a huge laugh out of it. We threw a surprise party at work last week for her fiftieth birthday."

❦

Forbes didn't have the energy to look at the caller ID on the phone when it rang. A few seconds later, the intercom buzzed. "Forbes, she wants you upstairs."

Suppressing the desire to sleep for a week, he hit the button.

"Thanks, Sam." Feeling like one of the living dead, he trudged to the elevator.

While he'd enjoyed the two hours he'd lingered over dinner with Alaine last night, it had meant staying up until two o'clock in the morning, reading all the new motions and briefs. Then he'd woken up at five o'clock with stabbing pain in his shoulder and neck. Since none of the over-the-counter pain relievers he had at home seemed to be doing any good, he got up, got dressed, and came into the office to get some work for his other clients out of the way so he could get out of here early this afternoon and try to get in to see his doctor.

Straightening his tie and jacket—but he couldn't do anything about the dark circles under his eyes—he stalked past Mary's vacant desk and into Sandra's office.

He drew up short just inside the door. At the conference table under the bank of windows, sat managing partner Sandra Landreneau, partner emeritus—and city councilwoman—Tess Folse, and partner Hayden Maier. Mary watched him owlishly from the opposite end of the long table, a stenographer's notebook in front of her. His bowels twisted into a knot.

"Come in and shut the door, Forbes."

He was getting really sick of hearing Sandra say that. He took the seat directly across from her—beside Hayden—and took a slow, deep breath.

"Mary, please start taking notes," Sandra directed. "This is an emergency meeting of the partners of Folse, Landreneau, Maier, and Guidry, Attorneys at Law, LLC. It has become increasingly apparent that an amendment to the partnership agreement is needed." She handed a piece of paper to each of them to read. "In short, the amendment states that no partner shall take a case against an existing client of the firm; to knowingly do so will be grounds for demotion or separation. This amendment is retroactive."

Forbes's skin went clammy. Amendments to the agreement only needed a majority, not a unanimous, vote. Stepping outside of his own situation, he could see the merit of the amendment in protecting the partners and the firm from accusations of conflict of interest.

"The floor is open for discussion."

"It seems very well laid out to me," Tess looked over her reading glasses. "No questions or comments. Hayden?"

The youngest of the three women—only seven years older than Forbes—looked up from her copy. "It's in the best interest of the firm. Forbes?"

God, why is this happening to me, now? Hearing that the other three were in favor of the change—probably discussed and drafted between the three of them without his input—what would be the point in arguing? "No comments or questions."

They all gaped at him for a long moment. Sandra shook herself out of it first. "Very well, then. All in favor of amending the partnership agreement thusly, raise your right hand."

Sandra, Tess, and Hayden all raised their hands. Big surprise there.

"Opposed, by same sign."

Forbes raised his right hand.

"Amendment is approved and goes into effect immediately." Sandra reached for another folder, which she opened, then turned and laid in front of Forbes. "Pursuant to Amendment 16, paragraph (c), as you are the signatory counsel for the case of *Moreaux Mills v. Boudreaux-Guidry Enterprises*, this is your one-week notice. You have seven days from today to decide between leaving the firm or resigning from the Mills case. If you decide to leave the firm, you will have fourteen days from the date of your decision to contact your book of business to inform them you're leaving. If you resign from the Mills case, no further action will be taken against you nor will this situation reflect negatively on you.

"Your answer must be made to the other three partners in writing by"—she looked at her watch—"nine o'clock next Friday morning." She pulled the folder to her and wrote the date and time in the appropriate blanks, then slid it back toward him. "Please sign and date at the bottom indicating that you understand the reason you've been given this letter and that you will abide by it."

He did so—surprised that blue ink instead of blood flowed out of his pen.

"Do you have any questions?" Sandra's reading glasses swung on their beaded chain as she retrieved the folder.

"No, ma'am." He pushed his chair back a little. "Now, if that's all, I have a very busy day today."

"Mary will make a copy of this for you." Sandra held up the file. The gray-haired secretary scuttled over and snatched the folder.

Forbes stood and gave a little half bow. "Good morning, ladies." He followed Mary from the office but hung back when she went to the photocopier. No sense in getting too near the bear in her den.

"Here." She thrust the copies at him, then craned her neck to look around him toward Sandra's door. "And off the record"—she lowered her voice—"I think it's horrible that they're doing this to you. I think it's a right noble thing you're doing for the people down in the Mills. I grew up down there, you know. My daddy was a foreman in the lumberyard before the paper mill shut down."

Forbes could have sat down in the middle of the floor and laughed—or cried. He settled for kissing the irascible woman's cheek instead. "Thanks, Mary. And your secret is safe with me."

The crisis—the panic—didn't set in until Forbes made it back down to his office. "Hold all calls please, Samantha." He blew by her desk, not even looking at her because if she had the least sympathy or concern in her eyes, he might lose it.

After closing the door, he couldn't get his coat and tie off fast enough—pulling off one of the buttons in the process, which skittered across the wood floor. He flung the coat and tie onto the small conference table, not caring about the paperwork they scattered.

"Why now, God? I had everything under control. I was handling everything."

Well, maybe the situation with the family wasn't controlled or handled as much as compartmentalized and not thought about. And attending a different church to avoid the uncomfortable encounters with his family wasn't controlling or handling the situation, but running away. And while he was handling working eighteen-hour days, six days a week, he'd long since lost the feeling that his life was in any way, shape, or form under his control.

Excruciating pain shot down the side of his neck and across the top of his right shoulder. He stabbed his finger on the intercom button on the phone. "Samantha, cancel the rest of my day. I'm going to the doctor, and then I'm going home."

"Y–yes, boss."

He looked around his office. Typically, he'd take most of the paperwork now scattered across the table and floor home with him to work on over the weekend. But not today. He retrieved his coat and tie—and the button that had rolled behind the ficus tree—grabbed his nearly empty briefcase, and walked out, locking the door behind him.

Snarled traffic and pain every time he moved his head didn't improve Forbes's mood. "What do you want from me, God? All my life, You've put me in situations where I've had to take control. I don't understand what I'm supposed to do."

When no audible answer came, Forbes turned the radio on and switched it from the news station to the next preset. He'd caught it just as a new song started. The twangy guitars and old-fashioned organ music sounded familiar. Yep—this was one he'd listened to with the guys as a possibility for the quartet. He sang the opening line along with the Southern gospel group on the radio.

" 'All to Jesus I surrender, all to Him I freely give.' " His throat nearly closed at the impact of the words.

Control or surrender?

He pulled into the parking garage at the medical center and turned off the engine. Silence filled the car—but a silence different than any he'd ever experienced. He tried to bow his head, but pain stopped him. He closed his eyes and found a comfortable position.

"Lord, I don't know how to surrender. I only know how to control. But I feel like You're telling me it's time to let go and let You handle everything. I can't promise I'll never try to control anything again.

All I can do is promise to try to surrender my will to You and ask for Your help in learning to do it."

He sat a little while longer, enjoying the moments filled with nothing to control, then got out of the car feeling, for the first time in weeks, that things might work out okay, after all.

Following a three-hour wait and a diagnosis of stress-triggered muscle spasms, Forbes picked up the prescription muscle relaxers and painkillers on his way home. Deciding he deserved an indulgence, he stopped at Maxi's Diner in midtown and ordered a deluxe cheeseburger with onion rings *and* french fries to take home for lunch.

He changed into running shorts and a TV-station-logoed T-shirt he'd gotten at one of Alaine's live remote events, then carried his food and a bottle of sparkling water upstairs to the fourth-floor media room to watch the recording of Alaine's program on the big-screen plasma television, which he usually didn't use unless he had people over to watch movies. He fast-forwarded through the first ten minutes of headlines and weather—even though he really liked Bekka Blakeley the few times he and Alaine had gone out with the newscaster and her veterinarian husband. He wasn't watching this for news.

As soon as Alaine's face appeared, larger than life, the pain in his shoulder eased—though it had been almost half an hour since he'd taken those pills. He devoured the junk food while watching the love of his life on TV doing her thing.

Soon, though, he slowed, then stopped eating altogether. Keeping his eyes open seemed to be his most important task at the moment. Giving in to the fatigue, he stretched out on the sofa—on his left side—and promptly fell asleep.

An incessant buzzing sound woke him. He caught the phone just as it vibrated itself off the coffee table. "Hello?" His voice sounded like he'd eaten lava rocks for lunch instead of a burger.

"Forbes?"

He cleared his throat. "Yeah, Mere, it's me."

"Oh—you aren't sick are you?" The concern in her voice warmed his heart.

"No. Just taking a nap."

"Taking a—you aren't *sick* are you?"

He laughed—and it felt good. "I have muscle spasms in my shoulder and neck. The drugs the doc gave me knocked me out." He blinked the bleariness out of his eyes and squinted to focus on the small clock on a shelf of the built-ins. Almost five o'clock. That had been a long nap. "What's up?"

"Major and I were wondering if you and Alaine would be interested in meeting us at Magdalena's for supper tonight. He did that guest segment with the head chef from there that aired today, and they invited us to come to the restaurant for dinner tonight at six—and told us to bring guests. So I thought of you and Alaine, since we haven't seen you in several weeks."

"Please tell me that Evelyn Mackenzie isn't going to be there."

"No. Why?"

He launched into the story as he gathered up the remnants of his lunch, now soggy and unappetizing to look at, and carried the detritus all the way down to the garage to put straight into the trash bin.

"And she told you that I gave her your address?" Meredith sounded not just appalled but outraged.

"That's what she said." He rolled his head, then his shoulder, testing the muscles. Still painful, but nowhere near as bad as before.

"The liar. I'm so glad she left today."

Forbes tripped on the stairs going back up to the main floor. "What?"

"She didn't tell you last night that she was going back to Boston today?"

He sank onto the steps and rubbed his stubbed toe. "No. Why'd she leave? And when is she coming back so I'll know when to start worrying about her showing up at my house again?"

"She's not coming back. Mom came in and told me this morning that they'd come to a mutual agreement that Evelyn had done everything she needed to do here and until. . .until the case is settled, there isn't anything else Mackenzie and Son can do for us."

The doorbell echoed from upstairs. "Hey, Sis, someone's here. I'll call Alaine and get back to you about dinner tonight. You said six o'clock, right?" He jogged up the remainder of the stairs to the front hall.

"Yeah. But if y'all need extra time, we'll wait for you."

He finished the conversation with his sister and tucked the phone in his pocket before opening the door.

Alaine stood on the other side of it, her fine brows pinched together. "Are you okay?"

He stepped back so she could enter. "Yeah, I'm fine. Why?"

"I called your office before I left work, and your secretary told me you'd left this morning and said you were going to the doctor and then coming home. What's wrong?" She planted her fists on her hips.

Laughing, he pulled her into a hug. When her arms went around his waist and tightened, he almost forgot his pain. He told her about the doctor visit and the diagnosis.

She tilted her head back, mischief twinkling in her dark eyes. "So it's official? You really are a pain in the neck?"

He leaned down to kiss her, ignoring the way his neck twinged at that angle. He ended the kiss quickly, for his own safety, and tucked her back into his arms, resting his cheek on the top of her head. "I was on the phone with my sister Meredith when you arrived."

"Really?"

"Yeah. She called to see if we'd like to meet her and Major for supper at that Spanish restaurant—Magdaline's?"

"Magdalena's. Oh, they've got great food. But"—she pushed against his chest, and he allowed her to move back a little—"how do you feel about meeting them for dinner? I know you've been trying to limit your contact with them to try to protect them."

"No, I've been avoiding them to try to protect myself." The words came out of his mouth before he'd even thought them through. "But that's over. I'd really like to go if you want to."

"I'd like to. I've missed Meredith."

"You don't talk to her anymore?"

"I figured you knew that, seeing as how we never talk about her."

"No. I thought you probably just weren't telling me when you'd talked to her or seen her."

"Out of respect for you, I've also been limiting my contact with her and Major, though it's slightly harder with him since he does come into the studio at least one day every week for a voice-over session."

He kissed her forehead. "Thank you for that. But I don't want you giving up your friends just because of me."

She smiled and shook her head.

"So, how fancy is this restaurant?" He looped his arm around her neck and escorted her up to the main floor.

"Shirt and tie, chinos or khakis. Not overly fancy. What time are we supposed to meet them?"

Instead of turning right at the landing and going into the living room, he turned left and led her into the study—but then, as soon as his eyes swept over the corner, he looked down at her, regretting his decision.

But Alaine was already moving away from him. She walked over to sit in the club chair nearer the fireplace instead of the one she usually sat in—the one where Evelyn had perched last night.

"Forbes?"

"Huh? Oh, we're supposed to meet them there at six."

Alaine looked at the antique clock on the mantel, then checked the time on her cell phone. "Forty-five minutes." She bounced back out of the chair again. "I'll run home and change clothes and pick you up at five thirty."

"Pick me up?"

"You told me you've taken prescription painkillers and muscle relaxers and slept at least three hours this afternoon. I'd rather not have you fall asleep behind the wheel, even though we aren't going far." She raised up on tiptoe and kissed his cheek. "I'll see you in a little bit."

He grabbed her hand before she got past him and pulled her back for a real kiss. "Have I told you recently how much I love you?" He'd meant to save it for a special occasion, but now was as special a time as he needed.

Alaine's face paled, but her eyes glowed. "No, as a matter of fact you haven't."

"How remiss of me." He cupped her face in his hands. "I love you"—he kissed her forehead—"very"—the bridge of her nose—"very"—the tip of her nose—"very"—her left cheek—"very"—her right cheek—"very much." He pressed his lips to hers and lost himself in the wonder and joy that came from finding the one thing in life he could easily surrender to: love.

CHAPTER 27

$\mathcal{A}$laine still hadn't stopped tingling by the time she pulled into the restaurant parking lot. He'd said it. He'd actually said it.

She cut the engine and popped out of the car—only to come face-to-face with a disappointed-looking Forbes.

"Oh, fine." She unlocked the car and climbed back in just so he could open the door and assist her out. "You're so weird."

"Nah, he's just a control freak." Meredith and Major joined them. Alaine stood back while Forbes and Meredith hugged, holding on to each other for a long time, seeming to try to catch up on two months' worth of missed communication in hushed tones.

Alaine chatted with Major, who had some ideas for upcoming segments to feature executive chefs at other restaurants in town, which Alaine was all in favor of, especially when he mentioned several restaurants in the Mills.

Finally, Meredith and Forbes finished their whispered conversation. Meredith hugged Alaine in greeting, and the foursome entered the restaurant. The hostess showed them to a table in the back of the restaurant—a table for six. Forbes balked, and Alaine had to stop with him, since he had hold of her hand.

"Who else is coming?"

"What?" Meredith looked at the table. "Oh, we asked Anne and George to come as well, but they had a wedding rehearsal tonight so couldn't." She looked at Major, who gave a slight nod. "We thought about asking Mom and Dad to come but didn't want to cause any trouble."

Major rubbed his hand in a circle on his wife's back. "And I wanted Meredith to be able to actually eat and enjoy the food tonight."

The executive chef came out; and as soon as he saw Alaine, he turned incoherent—in English or in Spanish. She even tried Portuguese, which only sent him further into raptures. Listening carefully, she managed to get the gist of what he was saying—that just since the show aired that afternoon, their phone had been ringing constantly for bookings.

Within minutes of their arrivals, plates of tapas appeared on the table. Each dish held a measure of familiarity for Alaine, being from the same part of the world as her own ethnic cuisine, which Mother made so well and so often. And yet the chef's signature shone through in each presentation. She'd have to bring Mother and Daddy here—maybe get Joe and Tony to pitch in and bring them for their anniversary or something.

After tapas came six or seven main courses, which were set in the middle of the table so they could try some of each. Forbes reached for the dish closest to him but put it down and reached for his Blackberry.

His expression clouded as he read whatever message he'd received that was urgent enough to look at during dinner. But he clipped the device back to his belt and squeezed her hand before going back to serving himself.

"So, anyway," Alaine said, returning to her conversation with Meredith and Major, "I played softball on the girls' team at church during the summer a few years. I hated it. But it was either that or soccer, and I disliked soccer more. Too much running around. In softball, they stuck me in the outfield, and at eight or nine years old, most girls aren't going to hit it past the bases. And those who were serious about playing the game—you know, who wanted to go on to play in high school or college—played in the city league anyway."

"But what about watching it?" Meredith asked. "We're usually out there on Friday nights playing, but the citywide interchurch pastors' conference is this weekend, and since so many of the teams have their pastors on their teams, they gave us a bye weekend. You ought to come out next Friday to watch us play. As a matter of fact, I think my team might be playing the ladies' team from your church."

"Are the stands air-conditioned?"

Meredith and Major both laughed. "You're right, Forbes, she is perfect for you."

Forbes sat silent, contemplating the food on the plate in front of him, not reacting in the slightest to his sister's comment. Alaine exchanged a concerned look with Meredith, then turned and touched Forbes's shoulder.

He startled and snapped his attention away from his untouched main courses. "I'm sorry. What was the question?"

"It wasn't a question, we were just worried because we lost you there for a minute." She rubbed her hand lightly along his shoulder. "Is it bothering you again?"

"No, it's not that." His jaw took on a hard set. "It's nothing. Let's just enjoy dinner."

"We can't enjoy it if you aren't." Meredith put her fork down. Alaine and Major followed suit.

"Was it the message you received a few minutes ago?" Alaine nodded toward the phone.

"Partially." He sighed, wiped his mouth, and tossed the napkin on the table beside his plate. "Something happened at work today. I—the other partners called a meeting to vote on an amendment to the partnership agreement. . .which is basically the contract we all signed when we became equity partners in the firm that states how profits are to be divided, how we're to conduct business, and what, if any, actions can lead to separation—getting fired."

Alaine's heart sank. "So they finally did it?"

His lips pressed together in a grim line. "I have one week to decide if I'm going to leave the firm or if I'm going to resign as lead counsel for the plaintiffs in the Mills case."

More like *only* counsel than *lead* counsel, but she wasn't going to quibble.

"Then, a few minutes ago, I got an e-mail from B-G's lawyer—who is the managing partner of the firm that's just given me an ultimatum—saying that B-G wants to meet with counsel for the class, me, to discuss another offer."

Alaine frowned. "But we're—they're not asking for a monetary settlement. What are they talking about?"

"What it means is that they're going to change the amount they're offering to buy everyone out. They just don't *get it*." Forbes's hands, which had been braced flat against the table now balled into fists. "Why can't they see what they're doing is wrong? Haven't I staked everything on that assertion?"

Alaine laid her hand atop the closest fist. "You just have to have faith that God is going to show you how to get through to them. You have to let go of the idea that if you just work hard enough or sacrifice enough, they'll see the light and change over to your perspective. It was never going to be as easy as asking for a different dessert than the other sixty people at the banquet receive." She ducked her chin and gazed up at him.

He dislodged his hand from hers and bumped it gently under her chin before leaning over to kiss the tip of her nose. "You're correct, of course. But that still leaves the decision about the job. I believe in the merits and principles of this case so much so that I have already staked my career on it just by taking it. But I have to be sure I'm not making the decision to choose the case over the firm for reasons that are less than. . .objective."

Alaine interpreted his significant look at her. "You're afraid that our relationship might cloud your judgment because my family is involved. Would it make any difference if I told you that I'd still love you no matter what you choose? Because that's the truth. I want you to be happy, Forbes. I don't want you to ruin your career on a case you don't believe in just because we're dating. Nor would I want you to ruin your soul by staying in a job that's become increasingly unsatisfactory for you in the past couple of months. I mean, come on, think about how often I've heard you complain about the Pichon case. About how if you had your choice, you'd have been sitting in Russ's position in that argument."

Forbes didn't say anything for a long time but put his napkin back down on his lap and started eating again, for which Alaine was grateful. The tapas had been tasty, but not filling. She could almost hear Forbes praying about his decision, and she interceded on his behalf the entire time.

After several minutes, Meredith returned to the innocuous topic of softball. Alaine kept half her attention on Forbes, though.

A few minutes later, a "eureka, I've found it" smile overtook Forbes's handsome face.

"What?" Alaine asked.

"Tomorrow, I'm going to find out who's the real-estate agent for that vacant office space next door to Anne's on Town Square." He shoveled a huge spoonful of paella into his mouth.

A chunk of beef from Alaine's *cocido Madrileño* slipped off her spoon and plopped back into the bowl. "You mean. . .you're going to start. . ."

"My own law firm. I have several clients who'll follow me over if I hang out a shingle, and there are a lot of good people out there who need more help than what a community legal aid center can provide— but can't afford a billable rate of five hundred dollars per hour or more. I can run things the way I want to, take on only the clients I want to."

Alaine could hardly stay in her seat from wanting to dance around the table in joy. "Sounds like a plan."

"Of course, it's going to take a while to get it up and going, and even longer before I start to see a steady income." He raised his eyebrows and cocked his head.

"Good thing you already own your town house and car outright." She winked at him. "I'm sure you have savings you can live on for a few months. Some things are worth working and waiting for."

❧

The office space had seemed much larger than this when Forbes had done the final walk-through last week before signing the closing papers. The large, open room that comprised the first floor of the converted Victorian row house smelled of fresh paint and sawdust from the newly laid wood floors. The furniture he'd rented—from Joe Delacroix—to suffice until he could afford to buy all new stuff hadn't filled the space by any means, but now, with the dozen claimants included in the class action for the lawsuit seated in every available chair—including the four he'd borrowed from Anne next door—the room felt tight and overcrowded.

His nerves fought to get the better of him. This would be his first official action as the sole lawyer at the Forbes Guidry, Attorney at Law, law firm, without the prestige of being a name partner in the most successful law firm in town.

JD and Joe Delacroix, bless them, had worn themselves out helping Forbes get everything set up so that they could meet with Sandra Landreneau and Forbes's parents here instead of in the more intimidating executive conference room at Folse, Landreneau & Maier.

Alaine finished her phone conversation with someone from her work and came to stand in front of him. She made a fuss over the position of his tie's knot, then smoothed her hands down his lapels. "I'll be praying for you the whole time."

"Thanks. I'll need it." He kissed her cheek. As Mom and Dad and Sandra had not yet arrived, Forbes needed to use this time wisely. He went to the middle of the room and asked for quiet.

"I'm not certain exactly what they're going to come in here and offer." He looked around and tried to make eye contact with everyone. "But no matter what they say, don't react—positively or negatively. This is like haggling at a bazaar. If you show the least sign of vulnerability or emotion, the other side has you where they want you.

"What's most likely to happen is that they're going to come in, make their offer, and then give us time to discuss it so we can decide if we want to respond immediately or take longer. No matter what they offer, I intend to ask for at least a week to respond; that way we can come up with a counterproposal."

Rustling sounds behind him quickened his pulse. "Does everyone agree?" Nods and murmured agreement surrounded him. "Good."

The front door swung open, and Sandra Landreneau processed in like a queen—with Evelyn Mackenzie following her like a spoiled princess, and Mom and Dad like supplicants waiting to perform their lieges' bidding. Forbes's heart sank. Evelyn's reappearance spelled doom for a reasonable settlement offer.

"I'll go now." Alaine touched Forbes's arm. "Don't forget, I'm praying."

He caressed her cheek. "I love you."

"Love you, too." She wrinkled her nose at him and went outside, past the large front window toward Anne's office.

"Ms. Landreneau, are you ready to proceed?" Forbes asked, motioning for them to sit at the long table, where JD and the other business association board members sat waiting.

"We are."

Forbes took his seat, then signaled for Sandra to begin. He took copious notes during her twenty-minute opening statement—none of which represented much more than her legal double-talk that basically said that her clients had done no wrong and therefore the residents of Moreaux Mills represented in this case should consider it an honor to receive an increased settlement offer from the defendants.

Through continuous covert glances, Forbes tried to gauge what his parents were thinking during all of this. His father looked grim, his face set in that infuriatingly unreadable expression he'd developed for hiding his emotions. Mom's mouth grew thinner and thinner the longer Sandra talked. Evelyn smiled slightly but looked only at Sandra.

"...and it is therefore the privilege of the plaintiff to receive—"

"Ms. Landreneau," Forbes interrupted with a sigh, "it's almost three thirty. Most of these people have taken time away from their jobs—time for which, unlike you, they are not getting paid. Can we dispense with the posturing and get on to the settlement offer? Some of us would like to get out of here sooner rather than later."

Outrage flashing in her eyes, Sandra inclined her head. "If you insist."

Forbes flipped to a clean page of his legal pad, steeling himself to show no outward reaction no matter what he heard.

Sandra finished rustling through her notes. "The defendant, Boudreaux-Guidry Enterprises, under advisement from myself and their partner firm, Mackenzie and Son, have agreed to offer an additional 20 percent of the value of each property represented in the class; and if the terms are accepted, the plaintiffs represented in the class cannot solicit bids or buyers for—"

A hand slammed down, open palmed, on the table. Forbes—and everyone else in the room—jumped.

"That is *not* what we agreed to." Mom stood, one hand on her hip, the other pointing at Evelyn and Sandra. "I want to go back to the original settlement offer. Original—"

"Don't say anything else!" Sandra jumped to her feet. Forbes wouldn't have been surprised if the lawyer had clapped her hand over Mom's mouth to keep her from saying anything else.

He kept his startled amusement under lock and key. "Do you need a few minutes to sort this out with your clients?"

"No—"

"Yes, we do," Mom answered.

"Fine." Forbes stood as well and looked around at all of his clients. "I would imagine y'all want a break as much as I do. There's a coffee shop just a few doors down that has a public restroom if you need it. Let's give Ms. Landreneau and her clients fifteen minutes, shall we?"

Forbes caught JD by the arm to have a private word with him at the back of the group crowding out through the front door, and by the time Forbes made it out onto the wide, shady sidewalk, he had only one goal in mind.

Everyone crowded around him once the front door shut behind him, wanting to know what just happened and how it would affect the case. He tried to set their minds at ease, while edging toward Anne's office. Finally appeased, everyone moved down the covered sidewalk toward the Beignets S'il Vous Plait coffee shop.

His hand barely touched the doorknob on Anne's front door when Alaine came out, holding her cell phone toward him. "Mother wants to talk to you."

He pressed the small phone to his ear and listened in complete silence to what Solange had to say, thanked her when she finished, then handed the phone back to Alaine.

"What was that all about?"

"I'll tell you later." He placed her hand in the crook of his elbow and led her to the bench against the wall between his and Anne's offices. He waited for Alaine to sit first, then sat beside her and took her hand in both of his. "Do you realize, if I lose this case, or don't get a favorable settlement or ruling for the people in the Mills, it could ruin my little fledgling law firm?"

"Even with other clients, this case is that big a deal?"

He cocked his head and tapped her forehead with his finger. "Uh. . .it's why I was forced out of my previous law firm."

"But I mean, big enough to be something that if you lose, you'll never work in this town again kind of thing?" She waved his hand away and leaned into his side, resting her head on his shoulder.

"Potentially."

"I've already told you I love you no matter what happens. And I know that God has your future in His hands, and He's not going to lead you down a dead-end street."

"I know. I just wish. . . ." He leaned his cheek against her soft hair.

"You just wish you had God's omniscience so you could see

everything that was coming so you could control it."

"No. I just wish the future wasn't quite so uncertain."

"But without uncertainty, there'd be no need for faith."

"There are some things about the future we can control, you know." He turned her hand over and made lazy circles on the palm with his thumb.

A shudder wracked Alaine's body; he smiled. He liked knowing he had such an effect on her. "Like what?" Her voice came out strained.

"Oh, like making wise decisions—decisions based on godly principles, not worldly advice. Living each day with our eyes open for the opportunities God is putting in front of us. And most importantly, realizing when waiting for a more opportune moment to do something is stupid." Keeping hold of her left hand, Forbes turned and went from bench to one knee on the sidewalk in a flash.

Alaine jumped and let out a little gasp—as did several people around them who'd returned from the coffee shop. JD stood out of his daughter's line of sight, a big grin splitting his face.

Forbes kissed Alaine's hand. "I was planning to wait until tonight while we were out dancing, because I wanted this to be connected with one of your favorite things in the world. But I find myself unable to wait any longer." He pulled the small velvet pouch out of the inside pocket of his suit coat and shook its contents into his other hand.

Though wracked with nervousness just half an hour ago waiting to find out what would happen with his parents, nothing in the world had ever felt more right, more comfortable, than this moment in time as he slipped the platinum band with the large marquis diamond onto Alaine's finger.

He clasped her hand in both of his. "I love you more than anything in the world, and I cannot live without you in my life. Will you marry me?"

Two huge tears rolled down her cheeks, but he'd never seen her smile grow so wide or beam so brightly. "Yes, yes, yes, yes, yes, yes, yes, yes!" She flung her arms around his neck.

With a whoop, Forbes jumped up, hoisting Alaine in his arms, jubilating in her response and the cheers of the crowd around them.

He lowered her feet to the ground and leaned down and kissed her right and proper, drawing more cheers and wolf whistles from the crowd.

JD came over to hug his daughter. Anne's office door swung open, and she and George joined them. Forbes could hardly wait until JD and Anne finished hugging Alaine to pull her back into his arms again.

The door of his office burst open.

"No!" Mom's voice echoed under the canopy covering the sidewalk. "I don't care what Mackenzie and Son recommends—they're the ones who got us into this mess in the first place. I want to know what *my son* recommends." Forbes's mother halted abruptly—Dad had to swerve to keep from running into her from behind. The small crowd parted for them.

Forbes wouldn't let Alaine step away from him. He wanted his parents to be able to figure out what had just happened here.

"I am warning you, Mairee, Lawson, if you fire me and cancel the Mackenzie contract, you're taking your business down the road to ruin."

Forbes had never seen Sandra Landreneau so red in the face. And from Evelyn's narrowed eyes, he could tell she instantly recognized the tableau outside for what it was.

Sandra seemed to be the only one oblivious to what she'd walked into. "This is not a case about sentimentality or hometown values or whatever the other nonsense was you were talking about in there. This is a case about profits—about what's profitable for us and for the city."

A beatific smile transformed Mairee Guidry's face from that of a tired, middle-aged woman to a woman in her prime. She turned on her former sorority sister. "You're wrong, Sandra, which is why we're firing you. This is not a case about money. This is a case about *love*. And if Lawson and I hadn't been so blinded by the pursuit of money, we would have recognized it all along. But that's a mistake we still have time to rectify."

"Sentimental dreamer. You always were, Mairee." Sandra wagged an accusatory finger in Mom's face. "You mark my words, though. One of these days, it'll come back to bite you."

Mom shook her head. "Never in a million years. We could lose Boudreaux-Guidry Enterprises tomorrow, and you know what? I think I'd consider it a blessing. It's because we were more focused on business that we almost lost our dignity and our integrity. But even worse than that, we almost let ourselves lose our son, whose good opinion of us is not, I hope, forever lost, and whose forgiveness I pray we can one day deserve." With those words, she turned to face Forbes. "Because I would really like to be invited to the wedding."

Disentangling himself from Alaine, Forbes met his mother halfway and hugged her, then his father. "I love you both. You know that. And forgiveness is needed on both sides for things that have been said—or unsaid—over the past several months. But we have all the time in the world for that."

"And we would like to sit down with you and everyone here," Lawson made a sweeping gesture of the couple dozen people crowded around, "to discuss our new plans for revitalizing Moreaux Mills and assisting the current homeowners and business owners there in any way we can to save the Mills."

A chant of "Save the Mills" went through the little crowd.

Alaine joined Forbes and was instantly pulled into a jubilant hug by Mom and was then sandwiched when Dad encircled both of them in a hug. She emerged laughing.

"Anne," Mom called over Alaine's head, "we'll need to call Meredith—and Alaine's mother—and get on both of your calendars to start discussing the wedding plans. I'm thinking spring, in the gardens at Lafitte's Landing."

"Mom!" Forbes covered Alaine's ears with his hands. "Don't say things like that to her. I'm thinking we might pull a page out of Meredith's book and elope."

Alaine pulled his hands away and turned around to stand between his mom and Anne. "Not on your life. We're going to have the biggest most elaborate wedding Anne can give us—and I'm going to cover it for my program." She poked her finger into his chest. "And the only answer you're allowed to give about anything is 'yes, dear.' Because if there is one thing that is definitely *not* under your control, my love, it's me when it comes to the wedding I've been dreaming of since I was eleven years old."

Mairee laughed and pulled her into another swaying hug. "Oh, I'm going to like having you for a daughter-in-law. And we have a couple of months' lost time to make up for."

"But not today." Forbes caught Alaine's hands and drew her close again. "Tonight, I'm taking my fiancée dancing because it's what she loves to do."

"You—dancing?" Dad hooted.

"Oh, Mr. Guidry, he's a wonderful dancer."

"Yeah, Dad, I am. But it's because I have a wonderful dance partner."

"Okay, okay, it's getting a little thick out here." Mom laughed, then kissed them both on the cheek. "We'll expect you at our house for dinner Saturday night. And Forbes, we'll call your office tomorrow to set up the first Save the Mills meeting."

The Mills crowd followed his parents down the sidewalk, clamoring to have their ideas heard for how to revitalize the area.

JD kissed his daughter's cheeks and shook Forbes's hand. "Will we see you Sunday for dinner? Or maybe this week you should go to your family, since you haven't seen them for so long."

Forbes reached out and clasped his future father-in-law's shoulder. "You are my family, and we'll be there for dinner Sunday."

JD snuffled and dashed the back of his hand across his eyes. "Alaine, you'd best call your mother soon. I'll be home in about twenty minutes, and you know how she'll react if she hears all the details from me."

Alaine looked at her father, then at Forbes, then back at her father. "Wait a minute. Did you—Forbes, did you tell him. . . ? Was that why Mother wanted to talk to you?" She laughed. "I'm not just marrying a control freak, but a gentleman control freak."

They said good-bye to her father, and Forbes pulled Alaine back into his quiet, empty office. After a long kiss, Forbes went around to sit behind his desk—or at least the one he was using until he hired a secretary who'd need it, and until he got the air-conditioning vents upstairs working.

"Hey, I've thought of a slogan for your Web site." Alaine perched on the edge of his desk.

Forbes still couldn't get over the fact that he'd asked Alaine Delacroix to marry him, Forbes Guidry, the perpetual bachelor of the year. He wondered how many anniversaries they'd have to celebrate before he truly realized how blessed he truly was. "Oh, yeah? What's that? The most devastatingly handsome lawyer in Bonneterre?"

She leaned over and kissed his forehead. "No. Forbes Guidry, the lawyer who made a case for love."

Kaye Dacus holds a Master of Arts in Writing Popular Fiction from Seton Hill University and is a former Vice President and long-time member of American Christian Fiction Writers. A Louisiana native, she now calls Nashville, Tennessee, home. To learn more about Kaye, visit her online at kayedacus.com.

If you enjoyed

A Case for

then read

Stand-In

and

Menu for
Romance